POSTCARDS
FROM THE
VOID

POSTCARDS
FROM THE
VOID

TWENTY-FIVE TALES
OF HORROR AND DARK FANTASY

Guy N. Smith ♦ R. Perez de Pereda ♦ Sarah Cannavo
Peter Oliver Wonder ♦ Douglas Fairbanks ♦ Lucian Clark
Joshua Bartolome ♦ Steven M. Fonts ♦ Nicholas Paschall
Antonio Simon, Jr. ♦ Apara Moreiya ♦ Stephanie Kelley
Thomas Vaughn ♦ Jill Hand ♦ Richard Beauchamp ♦ Adam Millard
Daphne Strasert ♦ Richard Ayre ♦ Robb T. White ♦ David Clark
David Owain Hughes ♦ Johanna Vandredi ♦ Nick Vossen
Michael Warriner ♦ A.P. Hawkins

Postcards From The Void
Published by Darkwater Media Group, Inc.
8004 NW 154 Street #623
Miami Lakes, FL 33016

www.DarkwaterMediaGroup.com

ISBN: 978-1-954619-37-1

Premium Paperback Edition

STORY COPYRIGHTS

IMAGE CREDITS
IN ORDER OF APPEARANCE

Haun, Max. *Little girl at Coral Castle – Homestead, Florida*. 1963. Black & white photoprint. State Archives of Florida, Florida Memory

Gunter, Herman, 1885-1972. *Ruins of New Smyrna Sugar Mills – New Smyrna, Florida*. 1929. Black & white photonegative. State Archives of Florida, Florida Memory

Ed Leedskalnin sitting in a chair at his Rock Gate Park in Florida City, Florida. Between 1923 and 1936. Black & white photoprint. State Archives of Florida, Florida Memory

View inside the Coral Castle attraction in Homestead, Florida. Not before 1969. Color slide. State Archives of Florida, Florida Memory

Pexels.com. *Stonehenge under nimbostratus clouds*

Sisal factory. 191-. Black & white photonegative. State Archives of Florida, Florida Memory

Sugar Mill – "Pensuco" in Dade County. Between 1906 and 1926. Black & white photoprint. State Archives of Florida, Florida Memory

View of Yulee Sugar Mill Ruins Historic State Park – Homosassa, Florida. 1969. Black & white photoprint. State Archives of Florida, Florida Memory

Pexels.com. *Brown carriage wheel*

Pexels.com. *Adventure alpine background black and white*

Pexels.com. *Cabin covered by snow*

On the Circle – Sebring, Florida. Sl sn, 19--. Black & white postcard. State Archives of Florida, Florida Memory

Pexels.com. *Street tree nature wallpaper*

Pexels.com. *Church with outdoor fountain*

Pexels.com. *Architectural photography of brown brick building*

Pexels.com. *Apartment architecture building business*

Aerial view of Turkey Point Nuclear Power Plant – Dade County, Florida. 1972. Black & white photoprint. State Archives of Florida, Florida Memory

Turkey Point Nuclear Power Plant – a Dade County, Florida. 1972. Black & white photoprint. State Archives of Florida, Florida Memory

Pexels.com. *Close-up of built structure*

Pexels.com. *Abandoned ancient antique arch*

Pexels.com. *Brown brick road*

View of the amusement park at night – Daytona Beach, Florida. 1970. Black & white photoprint. State Archives of Florida, Florida Memory

Charles H. and Emmaline A. Powers homestead. 1886 or 1887. Black & white photonegative. State Archives of Florida, Florida Memory

Pexels.com. *Brown and gray concrete 3-storey house*

Pexels.com. *Abandoned ancient architecture black and white*

Pexels.com. *Abandoned architecture Auschwitz concentration camp*

Morrow, Stanley J. *Silver Spring Hotel from across the spring.* Between 1882 and 1887. Black & white photoprint. State Archives of Florida, Florida Memory

Hunt, F. W. *Postcard of the Koreshan Unity's pioneer log house in Estero, Florida.* Not after 1925. Black & white postcard. State Archives of Florida, Florida Memory

Amusement park attraction – Panama City, Florida. 1967. Black & white photoprint. State Archives of Florida, Florida Memory

Nighttime scene at the Miracle Strip Amusement Park attraction in Panama City Beach, Florida. 1988. Color slide. State Archives of Florida, Florida Memory

Pexels.com. *Green printed door building*

Pexels.com. *Scenic view of the castle*

Pexels.com. *Alley architecture building city*

Pexels.com. *Abandoned house*

Pexels.com. *Straight road surrounded with grass*

Pexels.com. *No person landscape travel desert*

Pexels.com. *White concrete building on desert*

James Fannin home, at the bluff. 1925. Black & white photonegative. State Archives of Florida, Florida Memory

Residence: Jacksonville, Florida. 19--. Black & white photograph. State Archives of Florida, Florida Memory

Stone, Robert L., 1944-. *House on Redland Rd. called "Coral Castle" — Homestead, Florida.* 1999. Color slide. State Archives of Florida, Florida Memory

Pexels.com. *Adventure cold daylight fog*

Pexels.com. *Brown and black concrete building*

Pexels.com. *White dragon statue*

Bok Tower on Iron Mountain at Lake Wales. 1930. Black & white photonegative. State Archives of Florida, Florida Memory

The Circle in downtown area — Sebring, Florida. Sl sn,19--?. Black & white postcard. State Archives of Florida, Florida Memory

Pexels.com. *Grayscale photo of chair inside the establishment*

Pexels.com. *Sun rays through the tree leaves and mist*

TABLE OF CONTENTS

A Note From
The Publishers[1]

This book was published to celebrate our tenth year in business. It contains some of the best original horror and dark fantasy you'll ever read. In addition, it represents one of the most ambitious projects we've ever undertaken. Our best efforts in craftsmanship and book design went into its creation.

To put it short: this was a labor of love, and it is our gift to you.

Thank you for a fantastic first decade, and here's to the next.

Your friends at Darkwater Syndicate,

Antonio Simon, Jr.   R. Perez de Pereda

Apara Moreiya   Douglas Fairbanks

---

[1] **Publisher's Note**: Darkwater Syndicate, this book's original publisher, operated from 2008 to 2020.

INTRODUCTION

Ever notice how, if you're told not to do something, there's a reason you shouldn't; but if you're told not to go someplace, there's a story instead?

Don't eat sugar. Why? Because it'll rot your teeth.

Don't go into the woods. Why? Ever hear of the big bad wolf?

Oftentimes, the places we try to keep people out of are real, while the stories are make-believe. This book turns that premise on its head—neither the stories nor the places are real, but the photographs are. Before you start picking apart the incongruities of how a photo can exist while its subject might never have, I posit to you this: never having seen a big bad wolf, can you picture one in your mind?

If you've ever read a fairy tale, I'm certain you can. And the fact that you and I, and just about everyone alive has some notion of what a big bad wolf is, that means it must exist on some level.

It must, and indeed, it does. Deep within the reptilian portions of our brains that understand only wants and fears, it is here the murderous wolf of old stalks with fangs bared. But he is not alone, for in this place where our worst nightmares are conceived is where there arise the stories that keep us from straying too far from the security of home.

These stories are made of the same stuff that drove hesitant mariners to scribble "There be monsters here" at the fringes of ancient maps.

To all who visit these blighted places: safe journeys, and beware.

CIRCLE OF EVIL, BLACKHILL, SHROPSHIRE

BY: GUY N. SMITH

An uneasy silence was evident to Peter Brownlow as he and his wife, Judith, and seven-year-old son, Jamie, ate their evening meal. Something was troubling Judith, Peter was well aware. She had been her usual lively self earlier in the day. That was before she had set off to visit their nearest neighbours, Dick and Mary Roberts, at their farm on the far side of the adjoining common land. Either something had occurred whilst she was there or on the trek across.

He was also aware that Tia, their ageing black and white springer spaniel, was uneasy, lying beneath the table and not eager for any tit-bits which might be offered to her. Jamie, too, was unusually silent. It was certainly odd, to say the least.

Something was definitely wrong but he was reluctant to broach the subject in front of the youngster. Later, he decided, after their son had gone up to his room.

Peter was now a full-time novelist, having recently resigned from his employment in banking over in the Midlands. His second novel in the horror genre had sold extremely well, enabling him to branch out on his own and move with his family to this remote dwelling on the English/Welsh border. For them, a new era had begun.

"Off you go and play then," Judith's voice trembled slightly as Jamie pushed his empty plate away. "Bed in an hour even if there's no school tomorrow. I'll be up to say goodnight later."

Tia whined softly and Peter was aware of her trembling as she pushed herself up against his feet.

He leaned down to stroke the spaniel. "What's troubling you?" he asked his wife.

Judith carried the empty plates to the sink in the corner of the room, ran the taps, stood with her back towards him. There was no mistaking her anxiety, she was trembling visibly.

"I... I don't really know," came her whispered reply.

"What d'you mean you don't know? Something's scared Tia and Jamie as well as you. Come on, let's hear about it."

"Something... strange is going on up there on the common," she answered, her back still towards him. "It happened on the way back and sort of confirms what old Dick Roberts said, although he clammed up and was reluctant to go into detail. It's that old stone circle at the far end, Pete."

"What about it? It's an old druid circle, been there for a couple of thousand years. When Dick Roberts bought the land, the National Trust put an embargo on it so that he wasn't allowed to demolish it. Nothing wrong with that, is there?"

"No, except that it's still a *druid* circle. God only knows what went on up there once. Dick refuses to go near it. Even when he's grazing his sheep on the common."

"For what reason?"

"He wouldn't give one. Said it was a bad, bad place, then just clammed up. He said don't go near it after dark. Told me to hurry up and get back home as it was already dusk."

"And...?"

"The sheep keep well clear of it. They were bunched up down at the bottom end, bleating, like they were scared, too."

Tia whined beneath the table.

"A mix of legend and vivid imagination, I'd say." Peter lit a cigarette. "Rumours that have grown out of all proportion so that folks actually believe them. Sheer nonsense."

"As I skirted the stone circle, Tia bolted homewards. I didn't catch up with her until I reached the gate just up from here. She was waiting there for me, trembling, tail between her legs. And not just that..." Judith hesitated, she was shaking so much that the cutlery in her hand rattled.

"I take it something frightened you as well?"

"I... can't really explain what I saw. Up there, on the highest point of the circle, silhouetted against the dying light of the evening

3

sky was… a cloaked and hooded figure, standing there… watching me!"

Peter exhaled a cloud of cigarette smoke. "It was probably one of the youths from the village, dressed up deliberately to scare folks. You know what a nuisance some of them are, trespassing all over the place." His attempt at an explanation sounded weak. Tia was shaking at his feet as though she recalled that apparition or whatever it might have been.

"It was terrifying, Pete," said Judith. "I ran like hell and I'll never go up on the common again. I'm sure it was a druid but I can't explain further. Old Dick is scared of the place and now I am… and so is Tia. Animals sense things beyond our ken."

"I think you've let your imagination run riot."

"Well, I'm only telling you what I saw."

"I think you should forget about it."

"I'll never forget it, which is why I need a break from this place. When we moved here it seemed idyllic, now… I'm going to go and stay with mum and dad for a week, try to get it out of my system if only for a short time. I'll take Jamie with me; it's half term so he won't miss school. I don't want him to know anything about this. Maybe we should consider selling, perhaps move into the village."

"No way. We've only just settled in here. I'm in the middle of my next novel and I can't afford the distraction. Go and have a break with your folks and in the meantime I'll try and get to the bottom of this nonsense."

"How?"

He hesitated. "Well, for a start I'll go and have a look around the stone circle, see if I can find any clues pointing to youths playing pranks. Tomorrow I'll drive you into Shrewsbury to catch a train to Birmingham."

"All right." She sounded relieved. "But, Pete, promise me that you won't go up there after dark."

4

"I'll go in the daylight," he snapped. After an initial exploration of the circle, his next move depended upon what he found, if anything. Right now he was convinced that it was some sort of prank. Or maybe just figments of folks' imagination, Judith's included.

Beneath the table, Tia whined again. That in itself was somewhat disconcerting.

The drought was now in its fourth week, the grass beginning to brown, losing its late spring lush texture. Farmers and gardeners were praying for rain, and water authorities had now banned the use of hosepipes.

Peter locked the front door of their cottage, surveyed the panoramic view of the distant hills and the common up ahead. He had left Tia indoors; she had not shown any inclination to accompany him. Her nervousness since that evening when she had returned with Judith had not diminished. She was even reluctant to go outside in the garden, all of which was completely out of character for this lively and curious canine.

"I'm going to damned well find out what's going on up there," he told himself as he set off up to the parched thirty acres of grass which had formerly been common land prior to its purchase by Dick Roberts. The rumours and speculation which abounded in the area had doubtless fuelled fear. Country folks were well known for their superstitions.

It was a steep climb up to where the ground leveled out. He took his time, stood and surveyed the distant stone circle situated on the sky line. At his approach, a flock of crows took to the wing, cawing angrily at being disturbed. Beyond, a raven glided, and high above, a buzzard circled plaintively.

"There's something up there that interests them," Peter spoke aloud. He became a little uneasy, told himself not to be stupid. These border hills abounded with corvids and birds of prey which often attacked and killed young lambs. Maybe one of Dick's flock had fallen victim to their predations. He would soon find out. There had to be a logical explanation to all the rumours irrespective of the locals' whispered fears.

The stone circle was directly ahead of him now, huge boulders surrounding an upright one overshadowed by a twisted oak tree draped in mistletoe. He paused and a hint of a shiver ran up his spine. Even in the morning sunlight this place was eerie.

He wondered how those druids of old had transported giant stones weighing many tons up here, for there would have been none lying around in close proximity. That was another mystery. Something else puzzled him. Dick Roberts ran a flock of around forty ewes on the common, and throughout the length of his trek, their droppings were in abundance. But now, fifty yards or so from the circle, there were none in evidence. *Like even the sheep feared to graze in close proximity to the stone circle*, he thought.

His mouth was dry. That tingling up and down his back began again. With trembling fingers he lit a cigarette, inhaled deeply. So far everything about this ancient place was creepy.

He moved forward, and that was when he became aware that the rough grass intermingled with the stones that were lying flat, like it had been well trodden, and fairly recently too.

"Tourists, ramblers, no doubt," again he voiced what he hoped was an explanation for this. "They like visiting historic sites." It sounded feeble.

He rounded an obstructing hawthorn bush, and that was when he came in full view of the towering altar, a grim, upright rough stone some eight feet high with lichen growing from top to bottom. Beneath it was a flat rock about six feet in length.

"Oh, my God!" Peter let out a cry of sheer horror at the sight which greeted him.

Lying sprawled on this rock was the naked body of a young girl. A hand was splayed across her features as though she had been attempting to hide her eyes from something terrifying. Her legs dangled over each side of the rectangular stone and her mouth was still wide from her final scream as death had claimed her. But, there were neither marks nor traces of blood on her tender flesh.

Peter thought that he was going to faint. Bent double, he threw up, turned his head away from the awful scene.

He had to get away from here as quickly as possible. He glanced around him, fearful that whoever was responsible for this horrific deed might be lurking amidst the surrounding stones, and that he would be the next victim to lie stretched on that altar.

There was nobody nearby, at least nobody that he could see. He turned away, almost fell, his legs weak and threatening to throw him to the ground. Staggering and stumbling, he made it away from this circle of death.

First, he must notify the police. He had not brought his mobile with him, for mostly it was impossible to obtain a signal in this remote area. His landline was the only alternative.

It seemed an eternity before he reached the cottage. His hands were shaking so much he had difficulty inserting his key in the front door.

Tia remained beneath the kitchen table, still exhibiting signs of extreme anxiety. It was as though she knew what had happened up there on the stone circle.

He made it to the phone and gave a garbled message to the police, having to repeat himself several times. They promised to dispatch officers immediately and ordered him to remain at home as they would be taking a statement.

God, maybe they thought that he was the murderer! His latest fear had him sprawled in an armchair, awaiting the arrival of the law.

Two detectives showed up at Cwm Cottage later that afternoon. Polite and relaxed as they were, Peter had no doubt that he was under suspicion. They had to explore every avenue, and he was the starting point.

Routine questions concerning his background and the whereabouts of his family were followed by the anticipated, "Why did you visit the stone circle this morning?"

He gave them an account of his wife's fears a couple of evenings ago. As if in support of his account, the dog whined under the table.

"We shall not know the cause of the girl's death until the autopsy has been completed, which is being carried out today. At this stage we will not be releasing the girl's name but her parents have been informed. We gather that she was obsessed with the occult, had a virtual library of books and related matter. It would seem that she set out to investigate the stone circle. We have also established that she travelled by train to Craven Arms. How she arrived up here is yet to be discerned, but she may have accepted a lift. Do you mind if we check your car over?"

Peter nodded, despite the sinking feeling in his stomach. At the moment, they were regarding him as their number one suspect. He remained indoors whilst the officers went outside to his Subaru Impreza. They most certainly would not find anything there relating to the girl, but, all the same, it was an unpleasant experience. Doubtless they would conduct a DNA check.

"Thank you, Mister Brownlow," said the taller of the detectives as he came back indoors. "We will be back in touch shortly. In the meantime we shall speak to Mister Roberts, the owner of the land. Thank you for your assistance. Good day to you."

Now all alone, Peter wondered how he was going to get through the coming night. He decided not to phone Judith; she would find out in due course. It would most certainly be reported in the newspapers in the next day or two.

He locked the door, feeling incredibly uneasy. It seemed that there was indeed some basis for the rumours about the stone circle. Who had trodden the undergrowth flat? Tia had sensed something, and still did. Presumably the girl had gone there because of her interest in the occult. But how had she died? If it was from natural causes, then surely her corpse would have been lying on the ground and not splayed on that sacrificial stone. Perhaps she was trying to re-enact some pagan ritual. Were there "things" up there, evil manifestations? During the period of his brief visit he had felt that he was not alone.

Tomorrow, he would visit old Dick Roberts. The latter had always been reticent about his refusal to go anywhere near the stone circle and likewise his sheep clearly avoided the place.

I'll damned well find out what's going on up there, he vowed, and felt somewhat easier for that decision.

The following morning, just as he was preparing to set out, the phone rang. The caller was Detective Inspector Lewis of the CID.

"The autopsy has revealed that the victim died from natural causes. Her name is Jessica Walters and she is aged eighteen. She was a shop assistant in Shrewsbury, lived by herself in a flat. Apparently her doctor was treating her for a condition which could have proved fatal at any time. And did. We won't be troubling you again, Mister Brownlow."

Peter exhaled with sheer relief. "Come on, Tia, old girl, you're coming with me. And we'll give that stone circle a wide berth!" he added as they left for the Roberts farm.

Dick Roberts was in his early eighties, a stooped and weather-beaten figure wearing a smock tied around the waist with a length of baling twine. He was forking muck out of a shed when Peter entered the muddy farmyard.

"Good mornin' to you, Mister Peter." He propped his fork up against the wall. "Terrible business this. The cops were here yesterday, danged if they weren't thinkin' that I might've killed that poor lass! Anyhow, they phoned this mornin' to tell me that she'd died sommat natural. Or so they think!"

"Yes, it's a curious business." Peter followed him into the stone-flagged kitchen where Mrs. Roberts, wearing her usual pink and white apron, was already putting the kettle on to boil.

"I think you know more than you're telling about the circle." Peter wasted no time in coming to the purpose of his visit. He related Judith's experience, her fears and those of Tia. "Come on, Dick, the sooner you put your cards on the table, the better. I want to get to the bottom of this for all our sakes."

The farmer pursed his lips. He glanced at his wife and was silent for a few moments.

"I didn't tell the cops much, they wouldn't've believed me, anyway. But, between us, there's... things livin' up there that certainly ain't human. Like your dog, mine won't go near the place, nor the sheep. I see'd 'em a time or two, silhouettes up on the circle, robed and hooded, watchin' me. Them's the old druids, come back to claim what was once theirs. I shouldn't've bought it 'cause they think I stole it from 'em. I know'd only too well that somebody would get killed — sacrificed — one day and I thank God it wasn't me or my missus. That poor girl's death was a warning and, mark my words, there'll be others. But what can I do? How can I give it 'em back to satisfy 'em?"

Peter nodded. He had half suspected what the old farmer was telling him.

"What can we do, Mister Peter? I'm due for retirement, maybe if I sell and move away I'll find peace. It will go on, though; whoever buys the farm from me is likely to end up on that sacrificial altar. They sacrificed that girl, make no mistake about that, but they're clever enough not to leave any evidence."

"I'm going to sort it!" Peter thumped the table. "I have to, for all our sakes."

"How?"

Right now he did not know, but there had to be a way, and he would damned well find it.

"You watch what you're doin'!" Dick raised his voice. "Last year I did some heather burning as close to the circle as I dared get. Had to stop with the burning as it was getting dusk, daren't leave it. It was then I saw 'em, standing atop, looking down. Furious they were, they didn't like it one bit, like they were afraid the flames would spread up there."

"Afraid of fire, eh?"

"Seems that way. Me, I was scared to hell. One of 'em came to the edge of the circle, but wouldn't step outside it, thank the Lord. That was when I got a glimpse of his face... in the glow from the flames." The farmer shuddered at the memory. "Never seen anythin' like it and hope I never do again." He paused, fell silent.

"Go on, Dick, tell me."

"It… it was a skeleton face. No flesh on it, if he had eyes then they were sunk deep in their sockets. And the mouth… broken teeth, wide in a snarl of anger. Like he was cursing me but no sound came. I didn't hang about, I ran like hell for home, afraid that whatever they were they would follow and catch me. But they didn't. Seems like they're prisoners inside the circle, can't escape from it. Thank God!"

"So, by some weird supernatural force they've claimed back what they consider is rightfully theirs. Well, at least they're confined there, or we can only hope so. Outside the stone circle we can assume that folks are safe. That poor girl ventured inside and died. Probably from shock." Peter rubbed his brow and sighed deeply. "Yet she was laid out on that sacrificial stone like they were offering her to their ancient gods."

"The sooner me and the missus are away from here, the better." There was no mistaking the old farmer's terror. "Trouble is, all the locals live in fear of the circle and no incomers will buy this place if they get wind of what's gone on up there."

"I'll think of something." Peter drained his mug and stood up.

"Don't know what. The way I see it, those druids, or whatever they are, are here to stay. Get interfering with 'em and you could well end up stretched out on that sacrificial stone."

Peter was thoughtful as he set out on the trek back to Cwm cottage. He paused at the bottom of the hillock, stood looking up at the ring of jagged stones. Nothing moved. A raven was perched atop the twisted oak on the summit. The huge, black-feathered bird, watched him intently, sheer evil in its very posture. A slaughterer of newly born lambs, plunderer of the eggs of ground nesting birds. A scavenger by nature.

Its huge beak opened, uttered a double *cronk*.

A warning directed at him? Subconsciously Peter backed away, unable to take his eyes off this feathered foe of the hills. Another couple of *cronks*—they sounded almost human, a warning—"Keep away, keep away."

Crazy, but unnerving. He recalled that which the old farmer had told him. The stone circle had belonged to the ancient druids and somehow they had returned to reclaim it.

Tia paced impatiently beside him as he stumbled on his way, resisting the temptation to break into a run. It was absurd, that corvid of the uplands issuing its own warning to him as though it sensed his intention to somehow destroy that place of ancient worship.

Like it was its guardian.

Before he reached home, an idea had germinated amongst his confused thoughts. He recalled how Dick had related the time when he had been heather burning on the common and the flames had spread close to the circle, those cloaked and hooded figures silently screaming their hatred and... fear. Fear of fire? Maybe... maybe they could be burned, spirits from the past consumed and destroyed by an inferno.

That evening he formulated a plan, crazy as it seemed, but he could not think of an alternative. Heath fires were common in the countryside during long spells without rain, when the grass and undergrowth was tinder dry. Some were the work of arsonists, others ignited by the scorching rays of the sun through a fragment of discarded broken glass.

A blaze on the common would not arouse undue suspicion, and it would be difficult for the fire brigade to attend to it swiftly. By the time they arrived, there would be a blazing inferno.

He knew what he had to do, and it was a formidable prospect.

The following morning he drove several miles out of town. It was too risky to use the local garage. Police were sure to make enquiries about the fire, and anyone filling two five-gallon containers with petrol was sure to arouse suspicion. His hands trembled as he lifted the heavy containers into the trunk of the car.

It was a crazy, daring scheme, he thought on the journey back home. It seemed that those dreaded occupants of the stone circle were only seen after darkness had fallen. Whether or not they lurked there, invisible to human eyes during the daylight hours, it was impossible even to guess. It was a frightening prospect, up there alone, a human arsonist versus unknown evil.

It was as he unloaded his purchases that he further developed his plan, one which might afford him protection from unspeakable evil. If he went up to the perimeter of the circle in full daylight and poured petrol around the outside, then all that would be necessary was a swift visit at deep dusk to ignite it at intervals. The blaze would quickly form a complete circle, trapping the sinister occupants within, sweeping inwards and destroying everything in its path. He would still have enough time to hastily retreat if the fire spread outwards onto the common.

The prospect was terrifying but, he decided, it was the only way. So, early that afternoon, he set out, again leaving Tia in the cottage, weighed down by his heavy double load. His progress was slow, pausing for breath every hundred yards or so, sweating, regarding his distant destination with no small amount of trepidation.

He was within a hundred yards of the stone circle when he heard the frantic barking of a dog some distance behind him. Turning around he saw to his amazement that it was Tia. She had stopped, refusing to approach closer, just standing there.

Maybe he had neglected to shut the cottage door after his departure? In any case, she had escaped and followed in his footsteps, but was now refusing to join him. Her message was only too clear, a frantic warning to him. *Come back before it's too late!*

"Stay there, then!" He raised an arm to reinforce his command. "I'll be back in a few minutes."

She sat down but continued to bark. There was no disputing that she was aware of the danger ahead.

It was a slow and laborious task, moving yard by yard around the outer perimeter of those gigantic stones, pouring petrol at intervals. There was an eerie stillness everywhere, not so much as a breath of wind. He had half expected to find that raven perched atop the twisted oak but there was no sign of it. The silence was uncanny.

His task completed, he set off back downhill. Tia was still sitting, waiting patiently for his return. She was clearly disturbed but wagging her tail as she fell in at his heels.

"So far, so good." He leaned down and stroked her. "Now I must wait for nightfall!"

At the onset of dusk Peter left the cottage, a couple of boxes of matches rattling in his coat pocket. This time he ensured that the outer door was firmly closed and locked. Tia had retired behind the sofa, trembling but apparently resigned to the situation. She seemed to guess in her own inexplicable canine way where he was going, and this time had no intention of following him. She had previously delivered her warning about visiting that dreadful place and had deemed it futile in attempting it a second time.

Dusk was already creeping in over the hills and with it a mist which would thicken in the nocturnal hours. Peter began to hurry. His mouth was dry and he did not relish the prospect of the task ahead of him.

It shouldn't take long, just a few minutes, he attempted to allay his fears; a speedy completion of the circle, dropping a lighted match every ten yards or so would do the deed. The dry undergrowth would ignite quickly and then he would be homeward bound, leaving whatever inhabited that awful place to be consumed by the blaze.

I'm an arsonist; a worrying thought, even if my act is justified. Doubtless somebody in the village below would see the blaze and summon the fire brigade but by then he would be safely home. If questioned by the police then he would deny all knowledge of the fire. "Didn't even see it blazing up there, officer. I drew the curtains early and worked at my desk for a couple of hours."

All the same, guilt blended with his mounting terror.

At last he arrived on the outskirts of his destination, glancing about him, afraid of what he might see, but there were only the rapidly darkening silhouettes of those mighty stones and that gnarled oak tree in their midst. At least that bloody raven wasn't perched in the branches!

Movements in the air above had him looking up. Bats. They were jinking to and fro, catching insects for their nightly feed. *Nothing to worry about*, he consoled himself. There were always bats around his home, anyway.

He flicked his torch on, held it whilst he extracted a match from the box, spilling a couple to the ground. No matter, he had plenty. He struck one, it broke in half without igniting. *Fuck it!* He selected another. It lit and he applied it to a clump of grass. Damn it, he should have marked those on which he had poured petrol, stuck an upright stick by each one. Now it was all guesswork and this slowed his progress.

A dried clump burst into flame, and it was on to the next a few yards further on. Success again. As he moved along he heard the crackling of fire in his wake. Two more. The blaze was starting to spread. More spilled matches. He fumbled the second box from his pocket.

As dancing flames lit up the night sky, he started to panic. A rush of flames scorched him with their intense heat, had him stumbling back inside the stone circle, tripping and falling.

And that was when he realised that he was trapped within the spreading, roaring wall of fire. He stumbled upright, fell once more.

The fire had spread much faster than he had planned, jumping from one petrol soaked clump to another with unbelievable speed. Thick smoke gushed, swirled, had him coughing. His eyes were smarting.

He tried to run ahead of the mounting inferno but it outdistanced his efforts, the sheer heat driving him back into the circle.

Oh God, he thought. He was trapped! There was no escape; the entire perimeter was ablaze! Smoke was filling his lungs. He bent double, coughing and choking.

In sheer desperation he stumbled on, eyes streaming. Perhaps somewhere there was a gap in the fire surrounding the circle which would enable him to rush through and escape to safety. He staggered one way, then another. There was no break in the wall of flames!

His foot caught in a tuft of grass and he fell headlong. His body hit something rough and solid during the fall, spinning him halfway round and dropping him sprawled onto his back. His heart lurched when he recognized it for what it was—the sacrificial altar beneath its towering headstone. Directly above him, hidden by the smoke clouds, that raven was calling again, incessantly now, like it was mocking him.

You're going to die!

He struggled to rise, but slumped back. It was almost impossible to breathe now, his chest heaving, his throat rasping. His flesh was being toasted. Any second, his heat-shriveled clothing would burst into flames.

And then he saw the figures watching him, three of them; there may have been more in the background. Their long, flowing cloaks somehow resisted the encroaching blaze. Hoods hid their features until they threw them back to reveal faces that had no right to exist in a human world.

Fleshless, deep sunken eyes which glinted evilly in the glow from the fire; cheekbones and mouths agape displaying broken and blackened teeth; nostrils wide, impervious to the smoke which swirled around them—evil incarnate.

The heinous figures encircled him, bending over him. They were waiting for him to die, a victim of a dreadful sacrifice. Terrified, he mouthed a plea for help. No answer came, but somewhere that raven was still croaking.

A hand touched him, fleshless fingers that were icy cold in spite of the searing heat. They closed around his throat, choking him. Those terrifying features came close to his own and the stench of their breath was putrescence akin to that of rotted flesh, stronger even than that of the inferno which blazed all around.

19

He felt his senses slipping from him, knew that he was going to die. His captors were somehow impervious to the searing heat, the leaping flames. Only in his final seconds of life did realisation filter through his tortured brain. His plan had been futile, nothing could destroy the evil that lurked within the circle.

Hell itself had risen from the bowels of the earth, together with those condemned to eternal damnation. He would become one of them, destined to eternal purgatory, a slave to the Dark One within the Circle of Evil.

About The Author
Guy N. Smith

Guy N. Smith is a best-selling author with over 100 books to his name. Genres include: horror, mystery, fiction, westerns, children's fiction and a number of non-fiction titles. He has also penned many short stories for anthologies and the legendary *London Mystery Selection*.

In between his writing he has had a varied and interesting career. He worked in banking, was a private detective and had his own shotgun cartridge loading business before becoming the Gun Editor of *The Countryman's Weekly*.

For nearly four decades he has lived with his wife Jean in a remote area of the Shropshire/Welsh border hills. Guy has his own shooting, deer stalking, and organic small holding. They have four grown-up children and two grandchildren who live in various parts of the UK.

CARCER,
PENNSYLVANIA

By: R. Perez de Pereda

Fuck you, I'm not telling you where Carcer is, so don't bother asking. You wanna know what happened there? Go to the library and ask to look at the microfiche. Everything I told the newspapers is in the archives.

Ah, but you've already checked the archives, haven't you? I figured. How else would you have found me?

You're sharp, I'll give you that much. Carcer happened sixty years ago, so your looking me up must have taken some legwork. There aren't too many old timers still around who knew the place back when it was a steel mining town.

Chances are you already have the "official" story. You know: that the town was unknowingly built atop a pocket of radon gas, and that the gas started filtering up through the ground and suffocating people in their homes.

That's bullshit.

The newspapers will tell you only six people died before the National Guard was called in to evacuate the place.

Also bullshit.

More like several hundred people died in Carcer, many of them kids not a year old. None lived long enough for the parish priest to baptize them. And as for the others who perished in Carcer, a good third of them were the guardsmen sent to clear out the place.

I'm sure you also know about the fire that burnt down the steel mill. Don't you find it a tad suspect that the guardsmen did nothing to stop the blaze? It's funny, too, how nobody found it odd that the mill caught fire during the evacuation. Nobody in town would have thought to cause such mischief—that mill was the town's livelihood, and Carcer couldn't exist without it. And certainly no one would have had the nerve to cause trouble during the evacuation. Only a few hundred people lived there, and you'd expect folk to be on their best behavior when two companies of guardsmen roll up.

That's five hundred men, with their rifles and artillery.

Yes, I said artillery—what else did you think it'd take to demolish the mill? The place ran for acres. There's no way some flunkies with a gas can and some oily rags could have set fire to the whole place. And before you jump to any conclusions, radon is an inert gas. It doesn't combust. You couldn't ignite it if your life depended on it.

Something evil lives in Carcer. It's still there, in the ground, and it's best not spoken about. But since you're not one to be deterred easily, let me offer you a chair and tell you what really happened.

The name's Phil Heckert. Back in the day, I was a corporal with the National Guard. We'd been called in to put down a riot by labor union demonstrators. That's what I recall our original deployment papers saying. Slick political whitewashing after the fact turned our mission into an environmental crisis evacuation to cover up the truth.

Under my command were four men who made up our fire team: Hank Sutton and John Paul Allen, riflemen; Lou Thomas, machine gunner; and Charlie Jefferson, radio operator.

We were part of the first company that rolled into town in the winter of '58. The second company, in charge of hauling in our big guns, got sidetracked by treacherous snowfalls. As they wouldn't arrive until hours later, it fell to us to pacify the area.

Except that, when we got to town, there wasn't anything to pacify. The place looked abandoned.

On the outskirts of Carcer was a welcome sign, an eight-foot-tall billboard hand drawn in cursive. It was white, with red lettering: "Carcer. Industry. Service. Progress." Beneath that was a section boasting the town's current population that looked like it hadn't been updated in ages, and this likely because the town wasn't keen on admitting that their numbers hadn't increased in years.

Beyond the sign was the main drag. It had the look of your typical Small Town, USA. First up was a general store made up of Chicago bricks. Judging by its construction, it had likely pre-dated the community. Tattered green awnings hung over each of its windows and lent ragged shade to its front porch. Past that was a tiny schoolhouse with wood cladding on its sides and flaking white paint. Then came your civic buildings—a meeting hall, a small church, a library the size of today's walk-in closets.

Further in, a side street intersected the main road. Down this way were the town's businesses—a druggist's, butcher's, haberdasher's—all of them closed, their windows dark.

The buildings looked serviceable enough, but in awful need of maintenance. While there wasn't a broken window or kicked-in door to be found, none of the structures had seen a coat of paint since they were erected. Everything in town was being consumed in gray-green mold that reached up from the paved sidewalks as much as from the sooty black deposits that settled onto their roofs. Thinking about that soot made me take pause. It was tar-black and oily, like greasepaint. The soot had overtaken the buildings, latched onto them with what looked like a mass of shadowy black hands stretching arthritic fingers to clutch at the town's throat. Looking into that perfect blackness was like peering into a bottomless well. It called to mind that saying by Nietzsche: "If you stare long into the abyss, it also stares into you."

This all was enough to make me shudder, but what unnerved me even more was that our transport truck was headed for the source of those deposits, the steel mill on the outskirts of town.

Gray skies and a cold, insipid drizzle greeted us as we pulled up to the mill's wrought iron gate. The building loomed in the near distance like a decrepit Bavarian castle at the end of a treacherous mountain path. Had this been a folk tale set in bygone years, it'd be the perfect place for a vampire to haunt. The complex was a massive rectangular shoebox of stone and iron. Slatted skylight windows jutted from its ceiling at sharp angles. Wherever there weren't skylights there were smokestacks. Easily over fifty feet tall apiece, they stood like massive middle-fingers. The stacks were the only proof Carcer was still populated — those furnaces were working at full tilt, feeding bilious plumes into the swirling black vortex of industrial exhaust above the mill.

Our caravan halted at the gate long enough for our captain to shout his demand for entry through a bullhorn. When that got him no response, the lead truck in our convoy backed up, then charged the gate. It took several tries, but the truck got through, not looking any worse for the wear.

We rolled up to the mill's front entrance, and it was here that we got the order to get out. I slung my rifle onto my shoulder and hopped out the back of the transport. My boots crunched into fresh snow that wasn't quite white, and when it melted, left behind a residue that was oily, sticky, and foul-smelling. Even the weather in Carcer was off.

We weren't on the ground to the count of five when all the windows in the place blew out and the air went thick with bullets. The townspeople were holed up inside, and armed to the teeth with shotguns and rifles. A sniper's bullet caught our captain right in the neck as he stood alongside his convoy. He clapped a hand to his gushing artery as he dropped to his knees, vainly trying to staunch the bleeding. He had no chance—the man was paler than the snow as soon as his body hit the ground.

I ducked behind my convoy truck and took pot shots at the windows. I was blind-firing—I couldn't see the men shooting at us from within the darkness of the mill.

The men in my command were scattered. We were down a rifle—Hank had taken one in the chest as he scrambled out the back of the truck and went face first into the light dusting of powder that covered the driveway. His body lay still, the corona of blood fanning out from his chest overtaking his head, looking like a halo on a medieval religious icon.

John, Lou, and Charlie were huddled behind the front fender of the truck next to mine. Lou sat on the ground, wrestling an ammo belt into the machinegun between his outstretched legs.

"John! Charlie!" I shouted at them, and when they looked in my direction, I yelled, "Grenades out!"

We each had two apiece, and we let them fly, hurling them into the windows. Some other men around me did the same, and the inside of that mill was lit up as if by firecrackers.

Lieutenant Willis, now our company's acting captain, got on the bullhorn and ordered a charge. I grabbed my rifle and joined the rest of the men sprinting for the mill's front door. Meanwhile, Lou and the other machine gunners sprayed the windows with cover fire.

The opposition had put up a flimsy barricade. We breached the entry and flooded into the building, but had to stop when the men at the front refused to advance. Something at the depth of the mill had rattled the men so badly that some even turned around and ran back into the rush of guardsmen headed inside. I pushed to the fore and understood when I laid eyes on what they had witnessed.

The entry level to the mill was a sort of mezzanine with a metal catwalk that hugged the perimeter walls. It was viciously hot and dark inside, the only light coming from the blazing orange glow of the slag pit one level beneath where we stood. Cranes were built into a sort of ceiling-mounted conveyor system that moved along guide rails a hundred feet above the pit of molten metal. On the hooks were what looked like square cages, about three feet to a side.

At first, I couldn't tell what was inside the cages. Everything in that place was set out in dark silhouettes against the burning glare from the pit. Then the bottom of a cage swung open once it was above the center of the slag vat, and bodies spilled from the cage like dice cast from the hand of a careless giant.

They were people—living people. Even with the deafening roar of the furnaces, I could still hear their screams as they tumbled through the smog-choked air and landed, with tiny splashes, in the pool that swallowed them up. Tiny blazes sparked on the surface of the pit where they vaporized as the bubbling metal pulled what remained of their bodies under.

There was a nervous energy about the place, as though whoever had set the machinery in motion was pushing harder than ever to make a tight deadline. Cage after cage, packed to the brim, emptied into the pit. There was little wonder why the town looked empty when we rolled through; the people had all been rounded up and brought here.

The victims were mere silhouettes against the hellish blazes, falling like rain. Big silhouettes—adults—small ones—children—some no bigger than newborns, and there wasn't a damn thing any of us could do. Maybe it was my nerves, or I don't know what, but for some reason, I heard the babies crying louder than anything else. In they went, faster and faster, until the surface of the pit was popping and bubbling like a boiling kettle.

I dropped to my knees, crying, both hands cupped over my eyes like a stone angel at a gravesite. It was just too much, too horrible. The guardsman beside me doubled over and threw up, his spew falling all over yet another who had fainted outright and lay on the floor, pallid as a mackerel. We were packed tightly on that catwalk, but no matter where you stood, you got a front row seat to the horror.

Suddenly, the plant shook to its foundation. The only thought on my mind was to escape, because I figured the artillery had come and they had begun shelling the place. I glanced out the window and froze. Sure enough, I could see our howitzers some ways away, but their barrels were down. They couldn't have fired; they were only just getting set up. If that blast wasn't the big guns, then whatever it was, it had come from nearby.

The building shook again, shaking concrete dust from the walls. The gantries that spanned the length of the pit snapped free of their moorings and sank into the pit of molten metal. Guardsmen around me were in full retreat, except for a handful who stayed behind to cover their withdrawal.

Then—sure as I'm alive and breathing—I saw a large shape rise from the pit. A dome rose from the glowing metal, looking like the curved bottom of a cereal bowl turned upside-down, but huge—massive. The more it rose, the more it tapered away at the bottom, and it took me a moment to realize I had set eyes upon a giant human face made of glowing, molten iron.

I screamed and dropped my rifle, backing away from the horrid face on tottering legs. The body drew itself up from the pit until its shoulders cleared the edge, then reached for the guardsmen in the catwalk with a burning orange hand. They were packed too tightly to get out in time—a dozen men got swept into the monstrous palm, the hand sputtering and fizzling as people burned alive in its skin of jellied metal.

I ran for the exit—head down, legs pumping for all they were worth. I wasn't quite out of the mill when I heard a terrible noise. I'd never heard anything like it before or since. It was like the roar of the wind when a train charges past, and within that sound was the crash of a three-car pileup and the shrillness of a circular saw grinding a copper pipe.

The metal man had spoken.

What it said, I can't begin to guess. It was a language I did not understand, spoken much too loud for my ears to discern. The force of its breath slammed my back like a pneumatic hammer. Its breath carried me and several others the rest of the way through the mill's doors, dropping us in a bruised heap some ten feet from where we'd stood. Then came the heat and smell of its breath—dear Lord, there isn't enough sulfur in all of hell to make anything stink so bad. Its breath reeked of rotten eggs, and char, and death.

Charlie, our radio man, was standing by a group of MG's posted beside our trucks. He nearly fainted when he saw us swept airborne and thrown to the turf.

In terms that were neither uncertain nor terribly pleasant, I told him to get his thumbs out of his ass and get everyone into the trucks. Charlie, me, and a bunch of guardsmen piled into a convoy as I jumped in behind the wheel and gunned it out of there. We had scarcely rolled through the mill's front gate when, off in the distance, the big guns let up a salvo to level a city block. Several, in fact—I don't know how the acting captain justified the price tag of our munitions to the top brass in his after-action report, but I can tell you this much: they fired those guns until they went dry. Panic seemed to grip the artillerymen with each successive volley. The cadence of their firing devolved into a disorganized free-for-all. The gunners loaded anything on hand—armor piercing, high explosive, flares, white phosphorus—and shot it as fast as they could. Our radio men still at the mill were screaming: "Danger close! Danger close!" Their cries blared through our speakers until they suddenly cut to static, then silence.

Sight unseen, the artillery boys must have known something bad was in that mill, and they wanted it dead. What we didn't know was that we, the first company, had been sent on a suicide mission. Not that anyone told us, but it dawned on me that our job was to hold the mill while the field guns blew the place, and us, all to hell.

No one spoke as I sped down the treacherous, snowy roads. Then there was a bright flash in my rear-view mirror. I cut my eyes to look, but the light overtook our truck, blinding me for a heartbeat. When next I could see, the sky was ablaze. A mushroom cloud of atomic fire erupted above the seething crater that was once the Carcer steel mill. From that pit there came a massive groan—

metallic, like an orchestra brass section, and yet strangely human in its pain.

I floored the accelerator and didn't look back.

Still serious about going to Carcer? The fastest way to get there is to die. Take my word for it—if there's such a place as hell, then it's Carcer.

Assuming you did know where it was, if you were to visit the site of the Carcer mill today, you'd probably only find a lake. That atomic shell left a massive crater where it struck ground, and decades of annual snowmelts since then have likely filled it.

But don't be fooled, the evil is still there.

Nothing that evil ever dies.

ABOUT THE AUTHOR
R. PEREZ DE PEREDA

Born in Cuba in 1941, Ramiro Perez de Pereda has seen it all. Growing up in a time when then-democratic Cuba was experiencing unprecedented foreign investment, he was exposed to the U.S. pop culture items of the day. Among them: pulp fiction magazines, which young Ramiro avidly read and collected. Far and away, his favorites were the *Conan the Barbarian* stories by Robert E. Howard.

Ramiro, now retired from the corporate life, is a grandfather of five. He devotes himself to his family, his writing, and the occasional pen-and-ink sketch. He is Darkwater Media Group's Head Acquisitions Editor — that is to say, he heads the department, he does not collect heads, which is a point he has grown quite fond of making. Indeed, it's one reason he likes his job so much. He writes poetry and fiction under the name R. Perez de Pereda, often signing his work with a single, enigmatic "R."

Within Darkwater Media Group, he is known as "the captain." Others refer to him as their adoptive Cuban uncle. Still others call him "he who flips desks" despite it only happening that one time — well, that one time that he will admit to, at least.

FELICITY'S WELL, NEW JERSEY

By: Sarah Cannavo

Most stories like this start out with some dumbass teenager explaining that they and their dumbass teenager friends went to X or did Y because it seemed like a good idea at the time, something fun to do on Friday night, at least until things started going as bad as anyone with a brain and basic knowledge of horror movies could've told them they would. It's all fun and games until someone gets butchered.

I'll admit, I had my doubts about taking a trip to Felicity's Well, but we all went anyway, for something to do and to finally find out what all the fuss was about. After all, there *is* something undeniably intriguing about a whole town rotting to ruins in the heart of the woods, especially when you've grown up getting warned away from the place for reasons no one seemed to really know. So if someone's wondering why we went, I guess that's the best reason I can give: we wanted to find out once and for all why it'd been abandoned.

And we did.

God help us, we did.

There were four of us on the road: my boyfriend, Grady Rochester, driving because it was his truck; Wade Faulkner, Grady's childhood best friend and the tall, dimpled, good-looking "Genuine Nice Guy" no group of dumbass teenagers can truly be complete without; Jill O'Malley, Wade's girlfriend; and me, Danny Ferraro, cursed with the name Daniella by my mother and known better around town as "That Girl," as in "That Girl's sure got a mouth on her, don't she?" and "That Girl's gonna come to a bad end, you mark my words." I've considered it, but I'm gonna do my damnedest not to, just to prove everyone wrong; I'm stubborn that way. Grady says it's one of the things he loves about me, one of the few things fit to print. To him I'm not "That Girl"; he says "My Girl," and I like that a whole lot better.

A fifth passenger of sorts rode gripped between my legs in the passenger seat: my trusty baseball bat, a slugger I'd pounded nails through until it was good and spiked. I wasn't about to walk into the Pine Barrens without some form of protection against whatever we might find, be it woods weirdos, the Jersey Devil himself, or, after the summer we'd just had, huge-ass greenhead flies, the true Jersey state bird. I always feel safer with my bat slung on my shoulder; it's the reason I don't have to sleep with my bedroom door locked and my stepfather can't use his right hand too well anymore. So I brought it along that day, and nobody said word one about it.

"You sure you know where you're going, Grady?" Jill asked, leaning forward between the front seats, pale brow furrowed.

Jill was pretty enough, but also too intelligent and on the whole too nice to be a cheerleader, with a warm smile and a long ponytail of loose light golden-brown curls; seventeen, like we all were. She worked at the local fabric store, brought meals to elderly shut-ins after school, and had been crowned Miss Junior Cranberry Queen 2016, last year. I could smell strawberry shampoo as her hair tumbled over her shoulder, her eyes turned half-worried on Grady. "Isn't this place hard to find?"

"Yeah," Grady said, "but we're on the right track, I think. Mike at the garage said he and his buddies went when they were younger, but there was too much brush and they turned back. He told me where to start, though." He nodded towards the crumpled piece of paper, marked in pen, he'd taped to the truck's battered dash. "It'll be a hell of a walk, but I think we can make it."

"'Course we can," Wade chimed in genially, flicking his dark brown hair out of his hazel eyes as he wrapped Jill in his arms, tugging her back. "Don't worry about it, babe."

Jill squirmed, squealing, as he covered her with playful kisses, then began kissing him back, giggling. I didn't know whether to smile or gag.

It was a bit of both. Disgusting as their puppy love was—as all PDA is except your own—it was nice to see things were working out for them, considering it was their second at-bat. Grady'd told me how devastated Wade had been when he'd shown up at Grady's house, three months before, at 2:00 a.m., having just stumbled across Jill hooking up with Matt Borin, Wade's hockey teammate, at another teammate's party.

"I have no idea how he drove to my place without wrecking," Grady'd put it, and I could believe it, knowing how much Wade loved Jill. The biggest hearts break the worst.

But two weeks before our trip they'd gotten back together, and when I'd asked Wade why he'd answered in true Wade Faulkner fashion: "Because I love her, Danny."

"She cheated," I pointed out.

"Well, yeah. But I know she didn't mean to hurt me, so why shouldn't I give her a second chance?"

I don't know if I'd have been so forgiving if Grady screwed me over like that, so willing to put my heart back in the hands that'd shredded it. I didn't want to imagine pain like that, much less risk it twice. That was Wade: too nice for his own good sometimes.

But things were going well, making the drive a lot better than it might've been. It was an October Friday, after a half-day of school. The windows were down and a warm breeze sent my brown hair whipping around my face, making Grady laugh. He let me blast

A7X as we followed Mike the mechanic's directions deeper into the Pine Barrens.

Sunlight streamed into the truck and melted golden on Grady's strong, smooth jaw, in his short brown hair and in his light eyes. A few times he caught me looking at him and shot me that smile of his, the one that got him into and out of trouble equally well. Along the way he leaned in and kissed me and I kissed back every time, fire spiking in my veins vivid as the autumn foliage blurring by outside the truck. We were seventeen, headed off to do something stupid, and at the time, that was freedom.

What you have to understand is that the Barrens are full of ghost towns like Felicity's Well; places with names like Ong's Hat and Mary Ann Furnace and Hog Wallow, early settlements abandoned when people discovered how acidic the soil was (which made it useless for farming); or towns built up around mills, iron furnaces, and glass factories that shuttered when the local industry went under. The people who stayed behind became the Pineys that people in "civilized" society tell stories about.

Growing up in the area, as we all had, you hear that crap *ad nauseam*, along with how, though the soil isn't good for growing jack-shit, the wetlands are perfect for cultivating blueberries and cranberries. Half our parents worked at the nearby Ocean Spray plant in Bordentown—a good chunk of our class probably would one day, too—and every year we heard the same facts spewed at us during field trips.

Most of those field trips were to a recreation of Felicity's Well, where they told us it'd been a cranberry-harvesting town. Named for Felicity Ahearn, wife of the town founder, it'd been abandoned some time during the late 1600's. What they didn't tell us was *why* it'd been left to the Barrens, because nobody knew. Local historians blamed the usual suspects (disease, violent natives); rumors flew of witchcraft, Jersey Devil attacks, pirates... Pick your theory. Until somebody went in to find out, each was as likely as the others.

And nobody really *had* gone in, because nature had reclaimed the surrounding area so thoroughly, that reaching, let alone exploring, the place was difficult enough to deter the usual thrill-seeker.

We reached the trailhead and started walking. Eventually, the brush we'd battled our way through began to clear, the sandy soil becoming more of a path, though evidently not one walked for ages.

"Hey, guys, I think we're almost there," Grady said, grinning as droplets of sweat glistened on his skin. He'd taken his red hoodie off, carried it over his shoulder the way I hefted my bat, and his T-shirt clung to him in a way I admired despite the burn in my muscles and the new rips in the knees of my tight black jeans, joining the ones I'd slit intentionally.

"Thank God," I said, standing with him. I'd knotted my black leather jacket around my waist, as Wade had his, which made me feel marginally less sticky and disgusting, but it also meant the sunlight filtering through the trees edging the rough trail struck every bit of skin my red halter top left bare. My black leather boots were scuffed, and as a bonus, stained orange in places from the soil and streams tinted by iron ore and cedar.

Buck up or fuck off, Danny, I told myself and turned, yelling back at Wade and Jill, who were holding hands and trailing us, "Hurry up, or we're leaving your sorry asses for Mama Leeds's little boy!"

Grady laughed, slinging an arm around me. Catlike I pressed back against him, catching my breath as Wade and Jill took their sweet time catching up. We watched as she plucked a leaf from his gleaming hair and tucked it in the pocket of her yellow dress, laughing, as Wade lifted her up and spun her several times, always careful with her, a lanky gentle giant.

"Hey." Grady caught and squeezed my hand while we waited. "I ever tell you I love you, Danny?"

I bumped him with my hip. "I must love you, too, or else I wouldn't be traipsing around out here getting devoured by insects."

39

I expected Grady to laugh, but he frowned instead, looking thoughtful.

"Hey, baby, what's up?" I asked.

"I haven't been bitten once this whole time," he said, looking startled now. "A day like this, we should've all been swarmed, but I haven't even seen any bugs around, have you?"

I hadn't. I realized then; my joke had been out of habit, expectation. At the realization something hummed in my head, as if someone had tapped my skull with a tuning fork, and something gripped me momentarily—a warning, maybe, or just plain worry.

"That *is* weird." I shrugged. "But why look a gift horse in the mouth, right?"

"Right." Grady seemed to relax, and for the moment I forgot about it.

A few minutes later, we all crested a small rise, and there it was.

Felicity's Well.

"Jesus, this is creepy," Jill said, rubbing her bare arms briskly, as if gripped by a sudden chill. Wade, for once, didn't say something to comfort her. He was staring, as we all were, at the ghost-town sprawling below us amid the dense groupings of pine and oak trees. Standing there, seeing it, not as the sanitized, quaint reproduction we'd been dragged to since we were kids but as it really was — decimated, desolated — was a shock to the system. I'm not too proud to admit my hands tightened on the neck of my bat reflexively, the way they would had a branch suddenly snapped behind us in the stillness.

Because it *was* still; still and utterly silent. No bugs buzzed in the heated afternoon air, no birds sang in the blazing branches around us; their absence made the air feel heavier somehow, made my ears thrum with an empty echo. And adding to the unease crawling up and down my spine was that from my vantage point I couldn't see signs of any wildlife anywhere among the overgrown outbuildings or half-collapsed homes: no squirrel scurrying about, no bear or deer prints in the soil.

But I told myself it was the angle I was looking from that kept me from seeing any, that no animals were hanging around because the sound of humans crashing through the brush, rare for the area, had scared them off.

Had to be.

Still, none of us moved until Wade clapped Grady on the back, grinning cheerfully. "What're we waiting for? Isn't this what we came to see? C'mon, guys, let's go."

Beaming broadly despite a scratch on his left cheek from a branch he'd hit on the way in, Wade went first down the rise, helping Jill down after him.

Grady glanced at me. "Ready, Danny?"

I shouldered my bat again, its weight reassuring. "You bet your perfect ass I am," I said, and together we skidded down into the empty, waiting town.

It reminded me of shells scattered on the beach, the hollow buildings strewn haphazardly now that time and nature had rotted some away and destroyed the order they'd once had. Some of the houses, half-collapsed, had overgrown grass bursting through gaps in their wooden walls and out their glassless windows. Out of the hulk of what might have been a general store, or something similar, a whole pine tree had grown, roots reaching out like tentacles from under the ruptured entrance and branches spread shuddering over the shattered roof.

In some places, nothing stood. The only reason we knew anything had been there was because we could spot the outline of foundations choked in overgrowth.

"Hey, take a picture!" I called, posing in one with my bat, and Grady obliged, laughing while snapping the shot.

"Maybe we should get a place here after graduation, Danny, whaddya think?" Grady asked. "Seems like a nice, quiet little town."

"Good school, too," I said, gesturing towards the little schoolhouse, a shack of weather-stained boards across the street from us that couldn't have held half our class. Its front door was gone, and through the open entryway I could see a few splintered chairs and a lump that might've been a desk overturned on the dirt floor.

"Perfect." Grady wrapped his arms around my waist from behind and kissed and nipped my neck, knowing it always made me laugh.

"I'll start picking out curtains!" I snorted.

"Hey, guys, check out what we found!" Wade called, popping into sight a few yards distant. When we joined him and Jill, she was standing by a cylindrical object cobbled together with uneven gray stones. A rope hung on one side, disappearing into its wide, dark mouth.

"Is that...?" I started.

42

Jill nodded excitedly. "Felicity Ahearn's actual well!" she bubbled. "It's still here!"

We circled around it, peering inside. The stone was surprisingly cool and oddly slick beneath my hand, and the well went deeper than we could see. Grady dropped a small rock down it and when the splash finally came, it was distance-muffled and followed by the soft lapping of water at the well's walls. Gazing down into the blackness after that, I imagined myself tipping forward, falling, and felt a rush of vertigo, the earth shifting beneath my feet. *Shit*, I thought, stepping back.

Nobody noticed my brief break of composure, though, because that was when Jill screamed.

"*Ohgodewgrossgetitoffme!*" she shrieked, grinding her hands together, dress flaring like a sunbeam as she spun away from the well.

So somebody finally saw a bug, I thought, and I remember feeling an odd sense of relief at that.

But Jill hadn't; part of the well was furred with moss and her hand had landed square on some, and as she hopped around trying to brush it off I caught sight of something small carved on a well-stone, exposed when a chunk of moss dislodged.

"What's that?" I asked, pointing, and we all clustered around, Jill calming down and rejoining us. "Looks like initials—no, a symbol?" I looked at Grady. "Got your penknife on you, baby?"

He pulled it from his red hoodie and handed it to me. "You're not the only one who brought protection."

I used the flat of the blade to pry more moss free, exposing the small etching. It *was* a symbol, though not one I'd ever seen before: swirling dark lines or tentacles weaving around each other and spilling from some dark center mass. A quick glance and you would've thought it a simple spider web of cracks in the stone.

"What is that?" Wade's hair fell over his forehead as he leaned in to look.

"I have no f—Grady?" I looked over, realizing he'd stepped back.

The startled look was back on his face. He pointed at the symbol. "I don't know what it means," he said, "but Mom has some family records dating back to colonial times, and that mark's on an old family tree. We have no clue why—hell, we figured somebody spilled some ink or something. But that's it."

"What the fuck," I muttered. My fingertips lingered above the mark, but I didn't touch it—somehow, the idea made my skin crawl.

Jill chewed her bottom lip, working cherry gloss away. "Well, your family's from around here, isn't it, Grady? All ours are. Maybe the mark means your ancestors came from Felicity's Well."

"Maybe." Grady didn't look relieved, though, and I couldn't say I felt much better myself.

Wade, of course, tried to make the best of things. "All right, Grady. Look who's got some weird-ass family history."

Grady grinned, ducking as Wade tried to ruffle his hair. "Mine's weird? Your grandma was a bearded lady, wasn't she?"

Wade laughed and flung a clump of pine needles at Grady. "Not true. That was my great-aunt." He took off, jogging towards a small stone house with half its thatched roof stove in. "So are we gonna keep exploring or what?"

"Don't trip and fall on your ass," Grady called after him. "It'd suck to get brain damage out here."

Jill and I shared a look, eyes rolling fondly, and followed the boys.

I'd guess we were exploring for about an hour before we found the barrel house, but I can't be sure. Absorbed as we were, nobody checked the time, and anyway, time itself seemed suspended in that town as we went through trying to figure out just what had happened there, partly due to the time-warp effect of stumbling over relics from the 1600's but mostly because the more we explored, the more it began seeming something very, very bad had happened to the vanished townspeople.

Many buildings, stone and wood, bore scorch marks; in places there were just bare patches of earth where not even the smallest stalk of scrub grass poked through. And yeah, you could argue lightning strikes had done that damage; maybe they even had done some.

But no lightning strike had pocked the church walls with shotgun blasts, or smashed the colonists' furniture to splinters, or stained knives, farm tools, even broken chunks of pottery with blood. As we wandered through the town, we found these things and more scattered all around, in buildings, outside, the blood dried by now to resemble rust but not enough that we didn't know what we were seeing.

"Je-sus," Wade said, looking sick when we found a hatchet stuck into the outer wall of a house at head level, a dark stain sprayed around the buried blade. "Jesus Christ."

"What the hell happened here?" Grady said, looking around as if expecting any moment to be ambushed, the dead town to come alive with madmen or monsters leaping shrieking from the trees towering around us.

Jill didn't try to guess; she was bent over gagging into a bush. I flexed my hands on my bat, swinging it back and forth in front of me. "Maybe the Eagles lost a game and the townspeople rioted," I suggested, but not as steadily as I'd've liked. I can handle a lot, but even I was freaked the fuck out. *Whatever did happen, Danny, whoever did it is long past dead and gone,* I told myself, but neither that nor humming the Ramones under my breath helped calm me much.

But we didn't leave. Disgusted, unnerved as we were, we stayed, because we were intrigued, too. Maybe morbidly so, but it wasn't like we could help any of those poor bastards anyway, just hope one of these horror scenes held a clue as to what'd happened.

45

We found it in the barrel house, one of the largest structures and the most intact one still standing. In the off-season, the cranberry harvesters worked making barrels to store the berries in, I remembered from a field-trip speech as we made our way gingerly up the wooden-planked steps. The structure we were in had to be where they'd stored those barrels; some racks crammed with them still stood, and other barrels lay smashed and split like overripe fruit throughout the place amid patches of moss and mold. A sharp, bitter tang filled the air and stung my nose; Jill looked ready to hurl again.

"Maybe you should grab that hatchet and bust a few of these open, Wade," Grady said, nudging a nearby barrel with the toe of his boot. "Could be some of the townspeople are in here."

"You're sick, baby," I murmured with a smile, leaning into him.

But Wade didn't seem to hear; he was halfway across the room already, kicking aside a broken barrel and squatting to peer at something on the floor. "Hey, guys, that weird symbol on the well? It's here, too."

And it was, branded small and dark on a floor plank. We all crouched around it, and a few seconds later I frowned. I put my hand over one of the floor's uneven seams. "Hey, guys, do you feel that? It's—"

"—cool air?" Grady finished, hand next to mine.

"A draft?" Jill's brow knit.

Wade's eyes gleamed. "There's something under here."

I reached out, felt around, and after a minute my fingertips caught in an uneven part of the seam. My heart quickened. I tugged, and with an ear-cleaving creak and puffs of dust, a section of planks swung up, revealing a shaft descending beneath the floor.

"Holy shit." Grady leaned forward, shining his phone light down the shaft. I snagged his T-shirt to keep him from pitching forward, then we all looked down with him.

The shaft wasn't as deep as the well. We could see the packed-earth bottom, and there were rungs in the wall heading all the way down, coated in what in Grady's phone light looked reassuringly like rust. There was some kind of chamber beyond, but we couldn't make out much.

I looked at the others, and it was obvious we were all thinking the same thing.

"Who first?" I asked.

"What the hell." Grady swung down into the shaft, muscles flexing, and his feet found a rung. "For all we know my great-great-however-many-great grandfather dug this hole with his own two hands, right?" He handed me his phone to light the way.

"I've seen this movie before," Jill said. "It doesn't end well."

But she followed Wade down. I went last, Grady taking my bat and the light for me, and when I hopped down from the last rung, boots thumping on the floor, I wiped my hands on my jeans and fished for my own phone. Beams of light from four phones bounced off the chamber's walls, illuminating patches of rough rock. It was just enough light for us to grasp the larger picture.

The symbol from the well was here, too, but much larger, writhing across almost a whole wall—and it wasn't alone, either. Other symbols were carved all around the room, various sizes and shapes, not the half-assed graffiti sprayed in neon paint by people whose only knowledge of the occult came from heavy-metal albums and Harry Potter movies, not by a long shot.

These images were old and detailed, the obvious work of someone—or a gang of someones—who'd taken their time and known what they were doing, painstakingly carving the designs into the dark rock—*a labor of love*, I thought, and shuddered, the winding arms of the master symbol seeming ready to peel from the rock and reach right for me.

"Yeah, I've definitely seen this movie before," Jill said, sounding shaken. Wade wrapped an arm protectively around her.

"I think I found… There's a lantern over here. Lemme see…" Grady didn't smoke but he always carried a lighter, and after a minute he'd managed to light the lamp, painting us all with flames and shadow as he held it up, hung it on a hook driven into the wall.

"Somehow seeing it all doesn't make it better," I said. "But hey, at least there's no corpse pile."

"That's my girl." Grady grinned. "Bundle of sunshine."

"Are we going to talk about this?" Jill said, voice strained. "Because this is getting weirder than I thought it would."

"Means we have a better story to tell when we get back," I said, snapping photos of the carved walls with my phone — trying to, anyway. Maybe because of the low light, none of the symbols showed up as more than black blurs on-screen. *Fuck it. Save the battery.* I shoved the phone in my pocket, shrugged my leather jacket back on. It was cool in the chamber, and I heard a faint but distinct drip somewhere nearby.

"I'm serious, Danny!" Jill exploded, and we all looked at her, for a moment startled more by her than our surroundings. We'd never heard her raise her voice before; hell, I hadn't really thought she could. If I was "That Girl" to our town, she was "That Nice O'Malley Girl," the kind my gran would've called a "dollbaby." But here she was yelling, hands balled white-knuckled at her sides, stomping a high-topped foot with a face paled by anger and fear. The kid had some balls after all. I felt a surge of admiration beneath my shock.

Wade touched her shoulders gently; she shrugged him away.

"Don't you *feel* it?" she demanded, eyes shining in the lantern light. "Don't any of you feel—there's something *wrong* here, this room, this whole creepy village! And you can call me a pussy, but I can't shake the feeling that if we hang around here any longer something bad's gonna happen to us. We can call somebody when we get outta here and they can get, I don't know, a team together to check this place out, but not us, okay?" She broke off, burying her face in her hands.

"Hey," Wade murmured, startled still. "Hey, Jill, you want to leave, that's okay, we can go. There's nothing to worry about." He kissed the top of her head. She buried her face in his chest, whimpering.

Grady agreed, and as he did I noticed he was holding something wrapped in his hoodie. I pointed with my bat. "What's that?"

"A bunch of papers, it looks like," he said, and I heard the rustle of delicate pages. "I found 'em wrapped up near the lantern, but I can't really make out what's on 'em; maybe when we get back up I'll be able to."

I snorted. "Lemme guess, this is the part where we find out it's some kind of journal telling us exactly what shit went down out here."

"Oh, you've got to be fucking kidding me."

I stared down at the pages we'd spread on the ground in the center of town, sunlight slanting further now across the aged paper. Delicate and rough-edged, some sheets were just fragments now, while on other pages the words had worn away, random ones here and there, whole lines and half-paragraphs.

"I was *joking*," I protested, but these pages weren't. Not a journal, but a kind of open letter. The writer claimed to be the daughter of Mattias and Felicity Ahearn—a married daughter, evidently, because she gave the name Prudence Rochester, turning Grady pale—and it began: "If anyone should find this..."

In it, my boyfriend's great-great-however-many-great grandmother explained, from what we could make out on the stained, faded pages, that from the time of the town's founding there'd been a secret group within it—a cult, which practiced "Other Artes than the Church approved of" and was led by none other than Felicity herself.

"Even colonial housewives needed hobbies, I guess," Grady said. He sounded unsteady, and I could sympathize. The world seemed to sway beneath my boots. My head spun, and I rested my hand on Grady's shoulder for support.

"It gets weirder," Wade said, looking ahead to the next decipherable segment.

"How could it?" Jill asked.

But it did.

According to Prudence, the cult had trapped the dark being Or'oth, whose sigil the group had adopted as their mark. Or'oth was a wrathful, insidious horror who, "like the Demon Belial in the Old Testament, gluts himself upon the blood men spill, his sole purpose that of destruction and hostile intent." They had managed to distill his essence somehow, kept it hidden away in their secret meeting place.

According to Prudence, things were going great until the cult members were accused of witchcraft—the charge unrelated to their practices dedicated to Or'oth. What exactly they had done was lost to a water stain. The group was summarily tried and executed by hanging; among them, Prudence's mother. Her grieving father was found dead mere days later, having shot himself in his room with his musket.

In the witch-hunt that swept the town, the cult headquarters was discovered and ransacked. Most of their arcana were destroyed—including the trapped essence, which escaped into the cranberry bog just west of town, its very lifeblood.

According to Prudence, Or'oth's essence must have lingered in the fruit during the growing season, because when the harvest came—a bountiful one, one the town celebrated after "the blight of the Wytchcraft trials"—so too did the settlement's end. During the height of the harvest celebration, those who'd eaten the berries... changed.

"They became as men and women Possessed, filled with such hatred, such rage, that they hardly seemed Human any longer. Not half an hour elapsed between their eating the cranberries and the beginning of their violence. Such brutality I had not seen before, and I fervently pray I shall never see such again. Brother attacked Brother, Mothers their children, neighbor slaughtered neighbor as every buried resentment churned to the surface, no matter how old or petty. Under the influence of this corrupted fruit, the smallest slights became cause for the greatest violence."

We read in horror how the townspeople slaughtered each other, how Prudence and the few other settlers who hadn't eaten from the harvest hid away as their families and friends murdered everyone in an orgy of destruction, homes burning, blood soaking the streets. By morning most of the affected villagers had killed each other off,

51

and Prudence and the other unaffected townsfolk killed the remainder and burned the dead before abandoning the settlement.

"Let the wretched Barrens, and damned Or'oth, have these ruins; let God and Nature reclaim them, if they can. We leave this place in hopes of finding peace elsewhere—so that the child I carry may grow and spend its life far from the horror that claimed the rest of its kin—but knowing we will always be haunted by the evil that destroyed our homes and the souls of our loved ones. I leave this message here for whoever may stumble upon this cursed place and wonder what happened, the final testament of Felicity's Well, written by the hand of Prudence Rochester, in the year of Our Lord 1649. GOD SAVE US."

We were silent. Then I spoke.

"Demon *berries*. Only in New Jersey."

"You don't believe it?" Jill was hugging herself, bone white.

"No friggin' way." Grady shook his head. "It *can't* be true. Oh, the townspeople butchered each other, sure, but Or'oth's essence? It was probably a bad crop, people got fucked up, and the survivors just blamed demons—they blamed demons for everything then."

Jill persisted. "What rot or whatever can make people slaughter each other like that, Grady?"

"How the hell should I know?" he shot back. "Do I look like a damn fruitologist, Jill?"

Our voices could've struck sparks as they clashed. Before we got too into it, though, Wade stepped in, ever the peacemaker.

"We can settle this right now. Prudence said the bog was west of here, right?" He set off.

Jill yelped: "Wade!" and we followed, his long legs carrying him quickly through the town as we rushed to keep up.

It wasn't that far from town to the bog, and the path was clearer, relatively speaking. I was startled to notice how low the light was slanting now, shadows gathering in closer clusters; we were surrounded. It was growing cooler, too, and even as I told myself

52

the idea of some Lovecraftian horror infecting a cranberry bog was superstitious bullshit, out in that eerie isolation it was easy to see how somebody could believe it.

We broke through the last bit of brush and there it was, the bog. October is the peak for cranberry harvesting, and as the sun's last rays spilled down, the glistening ruby-skinned berries made it seem the water they bobbed in had turned to blood, so thickly they covered the surface. I swallowed hard and fought the thought away.

"Wade, man, are you gonna…?" Grady said.

Wade strode to the water's edge, boots squelching, and bent, plucking a plump cranberry and rolling it between his fingers. "Why not?" He shrugged, smiling. "I'll eat it, prove it's fine, and we can all head back to town, no more arguing."

He popped the cranberry into his mouth, chewed thoughtfully. The three of us stood back, watching, the only other sound being the chill breeze stirring the water.

"Doesn't taste any more evil than a regular cranberry," he said, shrugging again as he swallowed.

A minute passed in silence, and another, Jill fidgeting all the while. "Well?" she burst out eventually. "Do you feel any different, Wade?"

"Nope. I still feel like me," he said, looking himself over as if waiting for some mark to appear heralding the raising of some latent homicidal impulses. Jill pushed past me and Grady and rushed to Wade, wrapping her arms around him.

"I'm me," he said, a kiss punctuating the assurance. "Still me, Jill, I promise."

I let out a breath I hadn't consciously held. "Well, alrighty then," I said, shouldering my bat. "Since Wade's apparently not about to go *Crazies* on our asses, I say we get back to the truck and head home. I don't wanna be stuck out in the Pine Barrens with the likes of you all night. I've got a reputation to think of."

Laughing, talking, we left the bog behind, lighting our way back to town with our phones. Its emptiness was even more unnerving in the growing dark, especially now that we knew the reason for it, draped in old-world explanation as it was, and I was both glad we'd come and glad to be leaving.

Sorry 'bout the berries, folks, I thought as we passed the hatchet in the wall.

Grady carried Prudence's papers in one arm, his other arm around me. "Reconsidering that house here?"

"A little." I grinned. "Neighbors don't seem like the friendliest folk in the world."

"Duh, Danny," Grady said. "It's Jersey."

It hadn't been long, twenty minutes, maybe, and there was no obvious shift, no warning whatsoever. We were slowly making our way through the overgrowth when Grady and I turned to make sure the others were keeping up, just in time to see Wade pull from under his jacket the hatchet from town and swing it before Jill could scream, burying it deep in her skull.

"I've wanted to do that all day," he said with a blood-splattered, satisfied smile.

Grady and I stood there stunned, paralyzed. All the air had left my lungs, all thought my mind, trying to process the sight of Wade, who had all the savagery of a golden retriever puppy, grinning over his girlfriend's crumpled corpse sprayed with her blood and brains.

"Wade..." I whispered, the word worming its way out of the narrow tunnel of my closing throat. "Wade...?"

He laughed. "You should see your faces." Bending, he yanked the hatchet from Jill's head; it came free with a sound I'll never forget, and my stomach heaved hotly. "You look so *surprised*. That makes this even better."

Grady looked like a wax statue, cast in the mold of someone in the throes of catatonia. My mind screamed to run, grab Grady, go, but the panicked signals weren't reaching my feet. "Why?" I whispered to buy time.

"Why?" Wade's disturbingly dimpled grin disappeared. Somehow the darkness in his eyes shone, glimmering like a knife-edge, offering glimpses of what burned in his brain, festering until his inhibitions disappeared.

"Damn it, Danny, maybe you're not even as dumb as they give you credit for."

He put a boot on Jill, pushed; her corpse rolled doll-like, lemon-colored dress darkened with blood and dirt.

"She says she loves me, then one night I walk in on her with my buddy's dick in her mouth. I'm supposed to, what, just let that go? Nice guys have feelings too, you know."

I couldn't feel my fingers as I choked up on my bat, tensing, struggling to keep from falling into the yawning maw of horror that threatened to swallow my mind, a soft warm blackness that'd get me killed. "You forgave her!" I screamed.

The sound jolted Grady, who stepped back, leaving me a clearer swing.

Wade smiled. "Did I?"

Part of him had—the good part, the loving part that would forgive any hurt caused him by someone he cared about, especially Jill, who he'd lived and breathed for; that would forget his own pain for the sake of others—the dominant part.

But some other part—hurt, bitter—had brooded over Jill's betrayal, growing blacker, angrier; seething unacknowledged in Wade's heart. I doubt even at his lowest he planned to kill her, but that hurt part of him had wanted retribution, for Jill to suffer some way for what she'd done to him, and once his human decency was overridden, suppressed—what had Prudence said? "The smallest slights became cause for the greatest violence," and that was no small slight.

"Or'oth," Grady said, voice cracking.

55

Wade flipped the hatchet from hand to hand. "No." He grinned. "Still me."

Buck up or fuck off, Danny. Pushing past the shock, the fear, I swung my bat and by some miracle connected, catching Wade's left arm with an echoing crack and an enraged snarl from him. His sleeve was torn and blood sprayed beneath it; one of the nails had caught his skin.

"Danny, run!" Grady grabbed my arm as Wade ripped free and lunged for us, the two witnesses.

We ran.

In daylight the trail had been treacherous enough. In darkness, blindly crashing through brush trying to trace our frantic way back to the truck without getting separated or caught by ravening Wade, I was sure we were going to die. Grady and I skidded and tumbled, patches of moonlight the only illumination we had; my lungs burned and my heart filled my throat, sweat streaking my scratched skin.

"*Da-nny. Gra-dy.*" Wade's singsong ripped through the trees somewhere to our left. Feverishly I cast a glance that way but couldn't pick him out from the mass of shadows.

"Danny, the truck…" Grady panted, eyes wide.

"I know." My bat was a leaden weight straining my arm, but I wasn't letting go. "We have to—"

"No, I mean…" Grady swallowed, breath catching. "Wade knows where the truck is, too."

Branches snapped nearby. We looked at each other and took off again.

But we must've taken the wrong way somewhere, because the surroundings we were pounding through turned even less familiar, and it wasn't a trick of the dark.

"Shit," I spat, throat stinging as we skidded to a stop. "Grady, we'll never find the truck like this."

"I know, but we can't exactly wait around here, either."

Dirt streaked his face from a fall he'd taken. Shadows rippled through the branches of the night-black pines, but more than that I could feel the miasma of malevolence awakened in Felicity's Well surging like dark arterial blood around us, hot and furious, no product of fear or paranoia but as real as the bat in my hands.

"We have to keep going," Grady continued. "It's our only shot—maybe we'll find a road. Any road."

"Or wander into a bog, or find a bear—"

And then Wade was on us, with a guttural cry leaping onto Grady, hatchet-head gleaming in the moonlight. They fell, tangled, and I couldn't tell who was who, no clear shot, and then the blood-spattered hatchet flashed and Grady screamed, a sound that ripped so roughly through me I was dimly surprised I didn't start bleeding.

They rolled and I saw Wade was on top. "Get the fuck off him!" I screamed, slamming my bat down hard; Grady kicked from beneath and Wade crumpled to the dirt, down but not out.

"Grady—!" I rushed to him, reached out and found his left side wet and sticky with blood. Wade's hatchet had caught him in the ribs; I had no way of knowing how bad the wound was. "*Ohgodohgodohgod...*"

"Danny..." Grady gritted his teeth. "We have to go before he..."

Already Wade was stirring.

"Come on, baby." I slung Grady's arm around my shoulder and we stood, Grady stumbling and nearly dragging us right back down. "It's okay, we're okay," I said, but I could feel his blood soaking through my shirt to stain my skin as we hobbled forward.

"Danny," he panted, "I can't—"

"Shut the fuck up and walk," I said through gritted teeth. "I'm not leaving you."

"Appreciate it." He chuckled weakly.

Sweat and tears blurred my eyes; fear blurred my mind. Even now I can't remember much about how we made it through, adrenaline driving Grady and me onward until finally we found a trail and clung to it, Grady's blood staining our tracks, until the trees thinned and let us out blessedly on the side of a road. Which, we had no idea; we didn't care. I laughed hoarsely, half-hysterically, and set Grady down carefully in the coarse grass. His breath was quick, shallow, blood pumping from the ragged gash in his side.

"I'll go flag down help." I squeezed his wet, red hand. He didn't answer; his Adam's apple and eyelids fluttered. I squeezed his hand harder. "Grady!"

He squeezed back, weak as his laugh had been. "Yeah. Go, Danny. I'll be okay."

Whatever miracle decreed we'd find the road lingered a little longer; a minute after I started looking headlights appeared down the long black curve. In disbelief I whooped and started waving my arms, shouting for help as the driver—a woman—slowed.

I can only imagine what we looked like to her—beaten, covered in dirt and blood; Grady half-collapsed behind me in the grass—but she rolled down her window.

"Oh, thank God," I started, but then Grady yelled, "Danny!" and I whirled in time to see Wade lurch out of the trees nearby, teeth bared and bloody hatchet raised, but too late to tell my heavy arms to swing, swing just one more time, crack his fucking skull open—

—but Grady moved, sticking his leg out, and Wade went sprawling. The hatchet flew from his hand, landing harmlessly a few feet away. Wade, however, landed hard, his head striking the ground, and lay still. Grady half-crawled to his best friend's side and felt for a pulse, streaking Wade's neck with his blood as he did.

"Is he...?" I asked.

Grady shook his head. "No. He's alive."

Exhausted, every inch of me trembling, I leaned against the car, gradually becoming aware that our would-be rescuer was screaming. "What the hell? What the fuck's going on here?"

"You wouldn't believe us if we told you," I said wearily, and went to help Grady up.

You probably saw it on the news. "Horror in the Barrens," the headlines blared, and with the same morbid curiosity that'd kept us exploring Felicity's Well, people devoured the story. A small-town golden boy like Wade Faulkner having a psychotic break in the middle of the woods, killing his girlfriend and trying to butcher his best friends, who were raving about some unholy being named Or'oth—oh, yeah, they ate it up, all right, and I hoped they'd all choke on it. I'd thought they whispered about me before; after that night, the whispers grew deafening, lodging under my skin, an itch I couldn't scratch, and I got a few rides home from the cops after cracking windshields I wished were bones with my bat, not that it helped all that much.

I screamed, cursed, tried to explain, but didn't cry until the hospital doctors treated Grady, until they finally let me see him and his eyes fluttered open and found me.

"My girl," he murmured, smiling.

I wept then, climbed into that narrow bed with him crying like a baby, harder than I ever had, and I knew he understood.

After they discharged Grady, we went to see Wade in the psychiatric hospital they'd locked him away in. Physically, he'd recovered from every break and scrape, but otherwise, he hasn't and probably never will.

He's not kill-crazed anymore; he's nothing anymore. Certainly not Wade. A shell of himself, he didn't stir from his state even when we walked into the room. Grady tried to talk to him and I sat there biting my lip, trying not to throw up or burst into tears again. An effect of his psychotic break, the doctors said. We knew it was deeper than that; part of Wade's mental decimation was due to having an ancient evil rooted there, furrowing blackly into his brain, but more than that it was Wade's own horror and guilt over what he'd done to Jill—what he'd *chosen* to do, once he was ripped down to his rawest, most primal part; he could never recover from that knowledge.

Nobody believed in Or'oth, of course, although I read in one article a brief quote from some researcher who said the name was mentioned in one or two esoteric texts. The name described a being of great darkness who thrived on human hostility. As you can imagine, that never made any front page.

Felicity's Well is still standing, as far as I know, empty and enveloped in the Pine Barrens, the mark of Or'oth brooding throughout it and on the backs of my eyelids whenever I try to sleep now.

"Curiosity killed the cat; satisfaction brought him back," they say, but it can't bring back Jill, buried on a rainy Monday beneath a heart-shaped marker of dark pink granite; and it can't bring back the Wade we knew, who loved her; and it can't bring back the peace of mind we had before we went exploring that hellhole. I know now, way too late, that sometimes ignorance *is* bliss.

There was talk of arranging some scientific expedition to the bog, to see if there's some contaminant that could've caused the killings, Wade's and the settlers', all those centuries ago. Nobody's gone yet, though, and I hope they don't, that they leave that place as undisturbed as we should've until it's completely swallowed by nature, until even the goddamn legend is lost to memory.

And if they *do* go, I hope to God nobody eats the berries.

ABOUT THE AUTHOR
SARAH CANNAVO

Sarah Cannavo is a writer of prose and poetry living in southern New Jersey, a short trip from the Pine Barrens. Her poems have appeared in anthologies such as *Where the Mind Dwells*, *Carrying On*, and *Untimely Frost*, and will be included in the upcoming collection, *Darkling's Beasts and Brews*.

She's currently trying to finish writing a novel and has told herself that she's really going to do it this time, and has recently finished putting together her first collection of poetry.

DIABLO PASS, CALIFORNIA

BY: PETER OLIVER WONDER

"Reno, here we come!" Darren shouted as their small sedan made its way up the winding mountain road. His girlfriend, Wendy, sat in the passenger seat while Kate and I sat in the rear.

"Roll up the window and turn the heater on," Kate requested. She pulled the faux fur lined hood of the jacket she wore over her head.

I nudged her arm with the bottle of spiced rum pulled fresh from the backpack I had resting between my feet. "Here, a little bit of 'The Captain' will help us all get a little bit warmer, huh?"

Cheers erupted from the two in front while Kate rolled her eyes. "You guys are so immature," she said, a smile creeping across her lips as she took the bottle. She unscrewed the cap and poured some of the brown liquid down her gullet before contorting her face, coughing, and gagging.

Everyone in the car laughed at her.

"Oh, come on! That stuff tastes like candy!" Darren teased from the driver's seat.

Wendy grabbed the bottle out of Kate's hand and took a drink. She, too, choked on the harsh taste of the rum.

"You girls are hilarious," Darren said, grabbing the bottle and taking three big swigs. "God dammit, that's good!" he exclaimed, liquor dribbling down his stubbly chin.

"Okay, okay, that's enough of that while you're driving," Kate said, taking the bottle from him.

"Yeah, I agree with that one, dude," I added. "Tomorrow is my eighteenth birthday. I want to go gamble and not just wind up as a stretch of bloodstained road in the middle of nowhere, if you don't mind."

I took the bottle from my girlfriend's gloved hand and downed some of it myself. I cringed, doing my best to avoid making a face of disgust. When next I bobbed my head up, I saw something through the windshield that immediately caught my attention.

"Whoa, what's that up ahead?" I asked, pointing.

There was a clearing in the trees to our right. Beyond it, smoke was billowing up above the snow-covered earth.

"Oh, babe, we have to go look," Wendy said to Darren. "It might be an accident; someone might have gotten hurt."

"Yeah, all right," Darren replied. "How do we even get over there?"

He continued to drive along the highway until we saw a brown sign which read "Diablo Pass."

"That's got to be it," Kate said, her face practically in my lap as she watched the smoke continue to rise, now not far to the right of our vehicle.

Just ahead in the road was a turn-off that was usually blocked off by a large steel arm with a chain around it. As the vehicle crawled up to the blockade, Darren could see that the thick links had been cut, and the road ahead was now open to traffic.

"No trespassing. Extreme hazard warning," Darren read the sign on the bar. "What do you say, guys? Push on and see what this is, or back to the road trip?"

Wendy pulled out her phone. "I don't have any signal. If someone is trapped out here—broken down or worse—there's a pretty good chance they won't have any cell service either. They'll be stranded without help until someone else stops."

"Your birthday, your call, Charlie," said Darren.

"Yeah, I'm with Wendy on this one," I replied. "It's like twenty-seven degrees outside right now. If someone is stuck out here, that could be a death sentence. We can go gambling any old day, but how often do you get the chance to rescue someone? Now, that's a birthday story that could be told for ages! I say we check it out."

"Then it's settled. Onward, ho!" Darren decreed.

"What about that warning sign, guys?" Kate asked sheepishly. "No one else thought that was a little... I don't know, cryptic or something bad like that?"

"What do you mean?" Wendy asked.

"Well, it doesn't even say what the extreme danger is. It could be a landslide area or cougars or... It could be anything!"

"Be that as it may, this weather is an extreme danger to anyone who gets stuck in it. Especially with no cell service," I said. "There's nothing to worry about. Darren is going to take it nice and slow up this road."

Ahead, the patches of black asphalt beneath the thin snowfall were replaced by an unpaved dirt road. To the left side of the road was a sheer drop-off that ended in snowy treetops rising up from below. A strong gust of wind knocked snow from some of the higher boughs and rocked the car.

"Not to mention it's called 'Diablo Pass'," Kate continued. "Does that not mean anything to anyone? That's Spanish for Devil

Pass. It was probably named that so the name alone would be warning enough to keep people from coming here. And it clearly wasn't enough, so they put up that sign, that blockade, and chained it shut. It's a scary name and a narrow, scary, blocked-off road with smoke coming from an unknown, nearby source. Are we positive we want to continue down this path?"

The couple in front laughed at her obvious fear.

I did my best to suppress my own laughter and offered her the bottle again. "Here, babe. This will help take the edge off."

She looked away from the window and wrapped her fingers around the bottle with a cringe. "Talk about a bad choice of words. Pass me the bag, would ya?"

I picked up the bag and set it on the seat between us. Kate unzipped the main compartment and withdrew a small bottle of soda.

"This will help take the bite out of this stuff," she said, unscrewing the cap to chug one quarter of the sugary contents. She filled the new space in the bottle with the rum and passed the liquor bottle back to me.

"Thank you," she said.

"You're welcome, sweets."

"You guys smell that?" Wendy asked. She rolled her window down and stuck her head out. "It smells like barbeque."

"Smells like burnt hair to me," said Darren.

The column of smoke was ahead of us. The road was dark as it started to peel away from the highway and slope steeply downward. Darren flipped on the high beams to more thoroughly make out the line where the road dropped off into nothingness.

"Slow down," Kate said, fear in her voice.

"I'm only going fifteen miles per hour, settle down."

In the center of the darkness in front of us, an orange glow began to spread. There was a gentle curve in the road where the driver must have lost traction and careened off into the trees.

"Jesus Christ," Wendy said. "It's a damn good thing they didn't go off in the other direction. How far do you think it is until you'd hit the bottom over there?" She leaned over Darren to peer over the side of the cliff, bumping his arm and causing the car to sway.

"Hey, quit screwing around up there," Kate said, digging her fingers into my arm, terrified.

Daren and Wendy couldn't help but delight in seeing how freaked out she was.

"It's not funny!" Kate shouted. "You said you'd be careful! This is a hazardous area in poor weather conditions. Take this seriously, please."

"Yeah," I spoke up. "Let's try to act like real grown-ups for just a little bit, okay guys? We'll go back to fun times once we get back on the way to Reno. Quit messing with Kate before she gets all grumpy."

"I'm pulling over now, anyway," Darren said. "No more driving danger. Are you happy now?"

"I'll be happy when we're checked into the hotel and done driving for the weekend." Kate crossed her arms in front of her chest and looked out the window.

Darren rolled to a stop and turned on his hazard lights. "I think we'll be fine here. Looks like this road doesn't see too much traffic. How about you girls wait here while Charlie and I go and check things out? Hopefully, whoever was driving was already picked up and we can just call this mystery solved." He stepped out of the car and shut the door behind him.

"Don't worry, okay babe?" I said. "I'll be right back. You stay here and keep warm." I blew her a kiss and her grumpy expression allowed a brief smile to sneak through.

The cold hit me like a brick wall when I swung the door open. A gust of wind caught it, slamming it shut, narrowly missing my fingers in the process.

Darren was already at the crashed vehicle, which had been flipped onto its side—the roof had struck a tree and the car folded partway around it. I jogged through the inch-deep snow to catch up as he made his way around the hood to see what was inside the car.

"Oh, shit! Chuck, get up here and help me out!"

I ran the rest of the way to him to see what kind of situation we were dealing with.

The windshield was smashed away. Someone was still strapped inside the passenger seat. It looked as though he had tried to escape through the hole left where the windshield used to be, but received several cuts in the attempt and never freed himself in time. His skin continued to crackle as it charred in the fire. The tree around which the car was wrapped was also beginning to catch fire, adding a natural smell to that of burning human and diesel.

"Holy fuck, what do we do, dude?" I asked.

"I don't know, dude, what *do* we do?"

"Where's the driver?" I stepped back from the car and looked around for a trail leading away from the wreckage. "Oh, fuck. Do you see this? Is this blood?"

It looked as though the victim had dragged himself up the path, though it could also have been someone else who carried the driver from the wreck.

"He sure as shit didn't get up and walk away," Darren noted, still looking at the car. "That's a lot of blood on the seat and all around here. Do you think a bear got him or something?"

"I don't know. I'm going to tell the girls to not get out of the car, in case it is wild animals or something," I told him. "You follow this trail and see if you find him passed out. He couldn't have gotten too far on his own."

I ran back to our car, unsure of what exactly I was going to say to the girls. Opening up the driver's side door, I said, "Uh, things aren't looking so good out here."

Kate and Wendy glanced at each other before Kate took a long sip from her bottle.

Wendy asked, "Is someone dead?"

"Yeah, don't go over there. It's not something you want to see. At least one person is dead and it looks like one is… missing."

"What the hell do you mean they're missing?" Wendy demanded.

"I'm not sure exactly. Maybe they got out and went to look for help. They wouldn't have gotten far, though. There's a lot of blood."

Darren yelled in the background, causing me to spin around just in time to see him running in our direction, then stop suddenly — though he didn't simply stop. It was as if he were frozen in time for a moment. I watched as the… the *something* lifted its head over his shoulder and closed its jaw around on his neck. The girls both screamed as blood gushed out and fell to the white ground.

"Oh, fuck, fuck, fuck!" I said, sitting down behind the wheel and slamming the door shut. "What do I do? What do I do?"

I watched as Darren collapsed in a heap. The thing that had attacked him was neither human nor animal, but appeared to be some of combination of the two. It wore no clothing, and its arms, legs, and torso looked like they had been stretched and thinned out. Its ribs protruded through the skin, which appeared to be a purplish-gray. The thing climbed on top of my best friend and dug its long, spindly fingers into his chest before tearing it open and sticking its face inside.

"Drive! Just drive!" Wendy shrieked.

I grabbed the gear selector and slammed it into drive and mashed my foot on the accelerator. The tires spun without traction.

"Why isn't it going anywhere?" Wendy cried beside me.

"It's the snow! You have to ease into the accelerator," Kate said from the backseat, sticking her face between headrests. "You're supposed to keep calm!" she shrieked into my ear.

I eased my foot off the pedal until the tires finally bit into the snow and the car began to move.

"Where the hell are you going?" Wendy demanded.

"I don't fucking know! Away from that thing!" I shouted back.

"But the highway is the other w—"

"Do you want me to stop and try to turn around when there could be more of those things out there?"

From the overhang above, a large clump of snow fell onto the windshield, blinding me. A gust of wind pushed the front of the car toward the sheer rock wall beside us. I flicked on the windshield wipers to clear the snow, but too late for me to correct our course— our car slammed into the mountain, hurling me from my seat and onto the center armrest.

What came next happened so fast.

I didn't notice my knee bumping into the gear selector when I was flung out of my seat. I had hit my head against the roof of the car and both girls were now crying—Kate was begging me to get the car started and Wendy kept saying "Darren" over and over again. I clambered back into my seat and slammed onto the accelerator again. The engine whined, but nothing else happened.

Blood trickled from the top of my head and got into my right eye. The windshield wipers had cleared off the glass and I could see we weren't moving. Before I could put it back into gear, the rear door was pulled open, causing Kate to scream as she was snatched from her seat.

"No! Kate!" I screamed after her.

I forced my door open and tumbled out onto the hard, red dirt road. Blood from my forehead splattered against the snow like paint on a blank canvas. It didn't look like Kate's blood had been spilled, but when I looked up, she was nowhere in sight.

"Kate!" I shouted out into the darkness.

Though I was dizzy, I made it to my feet. I could barely make out the sound of Wendy shouting, "Wait for me," as she climbed over the center armrest and out the driver's side door, nearly stepping on my right hand as I pushed myself up from the ground.

"Kate!" her shouts echoed from all around as I made my way to the edge of the road.

I was afraid she might have gone over the cliffside, but I saw there was a gradual slope in that direction that one could safely negotiate on foot. There was a path made by something with large feet and long legs, judging by the gaps in prints.

"Over this way," I told Wendy before I sat down and started to slide down the hill on my ass.

"You're fucking crazy if you think I'm going down there!" she shouted as I started my descent.

"That's fine," I replied without looking back. "Stay with the car. Lock it up and keep it ready to move!"

The slope grew steeper and I began to pick up speed. Before I was too sure of what was going on, I was sliding out of control. I managed to grab onto the trunk of a sapling that was just barely within my reach, and this halted my forward progress. I looked up to see if Wendy was following me. She was nowhere in sight.

Looking to my left, I saw the footprints and veered off, heading deeper into the forest. Down here, the snow was much deeper and softer. I managed to dig my heels in and keep going.

"Kate, I'm coming for you," I shouted.

It was deafeningly quiet up ahead. It made me feel all the more vulnerable out there in the wilderness. I'd never felt so out of my element before in my life.

Before long I picked up the trail the creature and Kate had left. Alongside the trail was a fallen bough. I hefted it in both arms and continued down the path.

The farther into the woods I got, the more I expected to see what it was that I was chasing. I expected to hear Kate's cries. I expected to find something that told me I was on the right path. Instead, I found a small lean-to structure erected against a tree. It was just a few branches tied together with a few different kinds of rope and a bed made up of fresh boughs of spruce needles. The thought struck me like a mallet—whatever this creature was, this was where it bedded down.

The sound of a breaking branch seemed to echo from all around as I stood near the small shelter. I stood perfectly still, trying to hear where the creature was coming from.

My heart nearly jumped out of my chest when I finally heard Kate cry out my name. "Charlie!"

Reacting on instinct alone, my legs drove me toward the sound of her voice. I lifted the thick bough over my shoulder, gripping it at the base with both hands.

"Kate! Where are you?" I barked out into the dark, snowy forest. The only response came in the form of her muffled cries, and I was thankful for them—at the time.

I raced off past the creature's den as fast as I could manage in the thickening carpet of snow. It was up to six inches here, and I no longer saw any trace of the thing's tracks—it could have gone anywhere. Then I heard the sound of a breaking branch overhead. The tree limbs shook violently.

"Get down here, you piece of shit!" I yelled at the beast.

There was no way of anticipating the sudden drop off just ahead of me as I ran almost blind in the darkness. This defile was much steeper than the one by the side of the road earlier. The snow concealed all the terrible, jagged rocks below its blanketed surface. As I tumbled down the mountain, my legs and back took the brunt of the damage. My right ankle completely shattered and the ACL in my right knee tore apart, snapping like a rubber band. My limp and battered body cartwheeled down the hillside. By the time I hit bottom, my flesh was torn ragged, my nose broken, and my liver bruised, but I was alive and conscious.

And I was absolutely terrified.

At the base of the cliff, I saw another of the lean-to structures. This one had a trail leading out into the forest. I felt completely pathetic. At that moment, I was nothing more than a meal for some unknown predator. I had even been delivered to its front door after being recently tenderized. I spat out blood and snot as I sobbed and waited to either bleed to death or get torn to shreds like Darren had been.

I hadn't any strength to lift my chin from my chest when I heard the *crunch, crunch, crunch* of footsteps coming in from my right. It was all I could do to hold my sobs back and keep my freezing body still so I might pass for dead.

My eyelids were clenched shut as whatever it was poked at me. I rocked back and forth, but gave off no sound, despite the intense pain that rippled throughout my entire body. Another poke came, and I couldn't resist the tremor that came automatically as I choked on my tears.

There was no third poke. Instead, it grabbed onto my coat and began to drag me through the snow. At this point, I could no longer hold my cries back. I screamed out in agony as my wounds were dragged against the freezing ground. My eyes snapped open and I saw what looked like a man in a fur coat dragging me behind him. A rifle was slung across his back.

"Oh God, thank you!" I said, crying even harder at my unexpected change in luck. "Kate," I tried to explain.

I gave up as I watched the huge cliff beside me. It stretched up for what looked like forever from way down here. I was in awe that I had managed to survive the fall. I wondered if it would have been better if I had just died instead of living on in this condition. As it turns out, the worst part of the whole ordeal is living with the memories of the part that I have yet to tell.

I think I passed out as I was dragged from the mountainside. The next thing I remember was the agony in my ribs as he tried to hoist me up the steps to a cabin. Blood welled up in my mouth as he squeezed me, and I yelped out in pain. My body felt like a thin plastic bag filled with tiny shards of glass. The only thing that kept me from giving up and yelling for him to stop was the warmth I could feel coming from the fire inside. Before that moment, I hadn't realized how violently my body was shivering. I did everything I could to help as I pushed with my mangled legs.

There were only five steps, but I felt as though I had climbed back up the cliff I had just fallen down by the time I got to the floor of the cabin. The door slammed behind us and I felt I could relax at last. As I looked around, I noticed that my right eye had swollen completely shut.

"Th-thank you," I said, truly grateful someone had risked their life to save mine. "Wh-who are you?"

"My name is Keelut. It is my sacred duty to protect those who stumble through these woods."

"M-my friends… are they…?"

He was putting on some sort of backpack device. I couldn't tell what it was, only that it had a hose that ran from his pack to a device in his hands. "If your friends are still here, they're dead already, I'm afraid."

More sobs hurt my ribs. "What the hell was that thing?"

"Wendigo. They're all over the place, here. The presence of you and your friends and the vehicle will draw more of them out. They'll take us by surprise if I don't act fast. I'll return when I can."

And then he was off once more, letting in a chilly gust as he charged outside, and slamming the door shut behind him. An orange glow came in through the windows, accompanied by a horrendous shriek as I faded out of consciousness once more.

The door flew open and a roaring gust of wind came rushing in with it, waking me from my slumber. Keelut backpedaled into the cabin as he sprayed a stream of fire out the door. Once he was in the clear, he slammed the door shut behind him. He turned to give his back to the door and collapsed to the ground before it, panting heavily. His face was a bloody mess.

"I think that was the last of them," he said between breaths. "Just give me a minute and we'll get you out to the sled."

My head was spinning. I rolled my head to the side and saw the floor beneath me was wet with my blood. I had assumed my wounds had stopped bleeding, thanks mainly to my low body temperature and restricted blood vessels. Keelut, however, was quite warm from all his effort. His body let up steam from the cold. He pulled the hood from his face, revealing three deep claw marks across his eyes and nose.

The wind was howling ferociously outside.

He pushed himself off the door and dropped the flamethrower from his back—it rang out with a *clang!* as the empty canisters struck the deck. "You need to prepare yourself quickly," he told me. "It's time to move."

He bent at the knees beside me before grabbing my shoulder and thigh and lifting me on top of his shoulders.

"Ow, God!" I yelped. It felt like a broken rib had pierced through my skin, and I hoped one hadn't punctured a lung as well.

"I'll get you out of here. Just hold on," he said before opening the door.

The moment we were outside, it felt as though my core temperature dropped ten degrees. The trembling in my body became even more dramatic as Keelut took off in a run. Every part of me shook as Keelut's shoulders ground into my ribs and his arm bent my legs around his head, my right leg dangling limply at the knee. I opened my eyes and saw through the flurry of snow that there was a yellow snowmobile with a green, wooden sled tied to the back of it with a blue rope. It was only about ten paces away, but every step felt like it was about to kill me as I tried my best not to scream into Keelut's ear.

"You'll be safe in here. Trust me," he said as he dropped me onto the sled.

I was no longer able to hold back my screams as I fell onto my back. I was sobbing like a toddler as he covered me up with a blue tarp.

The snowmobile's engine roared to life and I nearly slid right off the sled when he hit the gas and we took off. I couldn't see anything, but there was something I could hear above the howl of the wind. It was like we were being stalked by a pride of lions—the roars sounded like they were coming from all directions.

Keelut made a sudden left turn and I nearly went over the edge of the sled. It felt like we were now going up an incline as we

76

accelerated. A load of snow fell onto the part of the tarp covering my face, almost smothering me before I could manage to shake free.

The roars got louder. Somehow, they continued to close in on our position. Keelut sped up even more and the tarp flew from my feet and started flapping above my head. I had to hold on to keep myself from flying off. The tread from the snowmobile kicked up white powder that rained down all over me.

In the distance, I could hear the horn of a train not too far off. Keelut took another sharp turn, sending my sled tumbling completely over. I was fortunate to have landed right side up after just barely managing to hang on. My driver gave a quick glance over his shoulder to ensure his cargo had remained in place—or maybe it was to see if anything was following us.

I strained to turn my head and see what was there in the dark woods behind us, but was unable to look past my shoulder. My forearms were burning from holding onto the sides of the sled. After so much abuse, the sled began to creak under my weight and I wondered if it would simply give out beneath me.

There was a subtle left turn followed by Keelut maxing out the accelerator. Not more than five seconds later, we were both airborne; the wooden sled—its tarp flapping like a cape—trailing the snowmobile with Keelut flying it like a jet in the storm. A slight twist of the sled allowed me to see what was directly beneath us. It was what he had called a "wendigo" and it was so much more horrible from such close proximity.

Its open mouth housed long, narrow and sharp teeth. It let out an ear-piercing scream as it reached toward me with its unnaturally long arm. Its eyeballs were as white as snow as it stared at me with an angry scowl.

The wind caught the sled at just the right time to turn me over and land me safely on the other side of the dried-up creek bed. My heart was racing and I felt like I might lose consciousness again, but the adrenaline kept me going. Again, I heard the train horn blare, this time sounding much closer than it had previously.

I wasn't sure what I was watching as Keelut moved his hands about wildly. I was all the more confused as I watched him turn around to straddle his seat backwards and draw his rifle, plucked fresh from his shoulder.

He moved fast on our tiny snow-rocket and I wasn't sure what it was all for until he fired. That part happened in slow motion in my mind. Smoke and light exploded from the barrel that was only several inches above — and almost directly over — my face. The end of the rifle rose as the projectile exploded from the tube. The next thing I knew, I was showered with blood and chunks of skull.

Suddenly we were airborne again. Another blast from the train horn caused my ears to ring painfully. It was loud enough to vibrate the roots of my teeth. This jump was a quick one, but without guidance, and it did not land well. Keelut flew backwards as if he were snatched up by some invisible, monstrous force.

The sound of steel grinding against steel made the horn blast seem like nothing in comparison. My frozen body writhed as it flew through the air. Keelut smashed his back into a tree with such force that his body folded backward around its trunk, his head shattering against the bark. I continued on until I cleared the tree line and slammed into soft snow before the sled came crashing down on top of me. The tarp whipped wildly in the wind.

The scream of steel continued on for some time as I sat beneath the wooden sled. At the time, I honestly didn't know whether I had died or not. I think I gave up on life and even wanted to be dead, but something inside of me decided it wasn't time for that yet.

Eventually, the whine of metal on metal came to an end. It took a while, but I heard rushing footsteps headed in my direction. I remained face down in the snow. I lacked the strength to move.

A man approached; I could barely make out his features with my one good eye. It didn't take him long to find me, thanks to that tarp flapping the way it was. He flipped the sled over and gasped when he saw my face, mangled and more closely resembling a spaghetti omelet than anything you'd find in human's anatomy.

He was careful with me as he put me back onto the sled. "Don't worry, we're going to get you to a hospital as soon as we can, okay buddy?" he said.

I don't think I ever found out the name of the man who saved me.

When I told the police what had happened, they told me they were never able to find Keelut, my friends, the car, or even the sign saying there was a place called Diablo Pass. If it wasn't for these scars and horrible disfigurement, I'd question my sanity. But I'll never forget the events of that day no matter what anyone says.

ABOUT THE AUTHOR
PETER OLIVER WONDER

Hidden in a remote location in California lives a man who responds to the name Peter Oliver Wonder. Though little is known about him, several written works that may or may not be fictional have been found featuring a character of the same name.

Devilishly handsome, quick-witted, and as charming as an asshole can be, Peter has come a long way since his time in the United States Marine Corps. Making friends wherever he goes, there is never a shortage of adventure when he is around.

The works that have been penned under this name are full of horror, romance, adventure, and comedy, just as every life should be. It is assumed that these works are an attempt at a drug-fueled autobiography of sorts. Through these texts, we can learn much about this incredible man.

CORN HAND
ILLINOIS

BY: DOUGLAS FAIRBANKS

No-no-no please — please! No more! For the love of Jesus, don't!
No more!

Oh... Oh Christ...

Please...

Don't let them hurt me anymore.

I've already told you everything I know.

I don't work for any government.

I'm not a spy, I'm an American citizen — I have rights!

My name is Allan Landis. I'm an accountant, and... and... a ufologist — *amateur* ufologist. It's a hobby. I've got a blog and a podcast. One of my listeners called in during my program a few months back and told me about Corn Hand, saying how it's become a hub for unidentified flying objects. You know: lights in the sky, things like that. It's the last place I remember being before waking up here.

Wherever here is.

Look, first off, I didn't mean any trouble. I came out to Illinois to watch the skies, maybe gather a little info for a book I'm writing on my UFO adventures, that's all.

I rolled into Corn Hand the Friday before Labor Day, figuring I'd take advantage of the long weekend to check the place out. It's practically deserted. So few people live there that it's not even on census maps, but the Internet is a great place for finding that friend of a friend who brags on public forums about having been places that shouldn't exist.

They've got a main street with a line of businesses, most of them shuttered up. Old style prairie houses stand around the town's central hub, the majority of them sporting broken windows and aged paint that flakes away whenever the wind blows. The place weathered the Great Depression and the dust bowl era of the 1930's, but never grew to be much more than a small gathering of about eight families. Even less people live there now, mostly old-timers, descendants of the town's founders.

Eisenhower's federal superhighway program was what sunk the town. Once the highway bypass was built in the early sixties, the two-lane road that led to Corn Hand was obsolete. No one drove that road anymore, and so the world just forgot the town existed. Hell, the place doesn't even have a post office anymore. The old postal building was a narrow wooden structure, looking almost like a doghouse, and only wide enough for its sole employee to sit at the service counter built into its front door. It's the town's police station now — at least, that's what the mayor told me, who also happens to be the town's only police constable. Michael Donnegan is his name.

The evening I arrived, Mayor Donnegan and I shared a meal at the diner. It was a greasy spoon sort of place, where everything is chicken-fried and comes with gravy. Donnegan himself is an affable man of Irish stock, in his seventies, smartly dressed in slacks and an Oxford with the sleeves cuffed at the elbows, a wide-brimmed hat and a tin badge on his chest. His mirrored aviator sunglasses dangle by a leg from his shirt pocket when they aren't balanced atop a nose ablaze with gin blossoms. His father was mayor before him, and when his dad passed on, the town elected him to fill his father's shoes. He's done such a good job that no one has thought to run against him, and so he wins the office by default, or so he told me. Seeing as the town hadn't had any visitors in quite some time, he treated me to dinner.

He wasn't halfway through his cheeseburger and fries when I told him my purpose for coming. The color drained from his normally flushed cheeks, and he asked me to repeat what I'd just said as he set his cheeseburger back down onto his plate. He glanced up from his food to make eye contact, then nonchalantly turned his eyes away when he'd noticed he'd been staring. With an almost imperceptible stutter, he asked if I'd be staying long, adding that there was no place in town that offered overnight accommodations.

I paused before answering, reading his expression. His demeanor shifted from country-folk hospitality to curt, no-nonsense command tone. I reassured him I would only be staying a few hours, and planned to leave by nightfall. It was a half-truth, but one he was willing to accept. He drew his cloth napkin off his lap and patted the sweat off his brow, then placed the napkin onto the table. With both hands on the tabletop, he rose, excusing himself by saying that he had some pressing town matter to tend to.

I nodded and returned his smile, knowing I was being fed a lie. In a town as small as Corn Hand, unless the place was on fire, there was no business so urgent that it needed seeing to so late in the evening. I thanked him for his hospitality and wished him a good night, watching him as he left our booth. I rose a short while later, but discretely kept an eye on him. Instead of leaving the diner,

Donnegan rounded the lunch counter and entered the service area, headed for the rotary telephone mounted in the wall in the corner. He dialed a number and waited, shooting furtive glances about the eatery. The person on the other end must have answered, because he cupped his mouth with his free hand, then shifted to give his back to the dining floor.

I had no idea who he called or what they might have discussed, but I got the distinct impression I had worn out my welcome.

After dinner, I drove out to the hills at the town's outskirts. The high ground made for an excellent vantage point. I could see clear across the town as its residents closed up shop for the evening. It was dusk by 6:00 p.m., and the town was dark by nightfall a half hour later—not a single light on in any of the businesses or homes. That served my purposes well enough, because Corn Hand offered one of the clearest skies I'd ever seen, short of what you might find in a nature preserve. No car headlights and no street lamps meant a night sky devoid of light pollution.

I clicked on my battery-operated lantern and rounded my van to the rear hatch to pull out my equipment. First to come out were a chair and a folding table, on top of which I set up my laptop. I had a motorized tripod telescope with infrared and electromagnetic field sensors built in. A digital feed ran from the telescope to my laptop, so whatever it was pointed at was piped onto the screen along with data on ambient radiation and fluctuations in EMF's. All this ran off the pull-start Honda generator I'd bolted onto the interior of the van's rear hatch. The generator was wired into the van's electrical circuitry as a fail-safe, so if ever I ran out of gas or the generator cut out while I was in the field, I could run my equipment off the van's battery for a couple minutes.

My chronometer read 7:04 p.m. when I commenced observation. I spent the next two hours scanning the skies, getting a bunch of really nice shots of the heavens but nothing else. I was about to doze off when my laptop screeched, startling me awake. In the lower right hand corner of the screen was a digital gauge that looked like a VU meter in an old stereo. All night long, that needle had kept to the green at the far left, twitching occasionally with the ambient EMF's. Now the needle was flicking from left to right in even pulses, going from zero to max once a second.

My first instinct was to look straight up and around me, but that turned up nothing. Whatever was causing the EM flux could not be seen with my eyes alone. I shifted my gaze back to the laptop and maximized the screen picking up the feed from the telescope's sensors.

At exactly 9:22 p.m., my equipment captured an image of some unidentified object in the sky above Corn Hand. I am certain it could not have been a planet, comet, or even an airplane—none of those could have moved the way I saw this thing move. The object seemed to judder, darting about quickly but only short distances, keeping mostly to the same location in the sky. It was a bright, roughly circular object with soft edges, looking like a baseball diamond made up entirely of light. It expanded, doubling its size in the span of about two seconds, and then cast off three more shapes just like itself that flew in a holding pattern around the original shape. The three smaller shapes circled the first object and then darted away beyond my field of vision. Shortly afterward, the original object spun in place and slingshotted away, heading west.

I checked my chronometer again as I opened my journal app to note what I had witnessed. The experience had lasted all of four minutes, nineteen seconds.

Now, at this point, I figured I'd gotten everything I would out of that night. It would have been a fine time to hit the hay—I'd driven nonstop for six hours just to get here, and I was beat.

Still, tired as I was, I was too excited to sleep. Instead, I clambered back into my van and pulled out my broadcasting equipment. I hauled out the portable satellite dish and erected it on the van's roof, then ran cables to my laptop for an impromptu video podcast. The dish and its electronics array had cost me a pretty penny — some twenty grand about a year ago — but the capability to broadcast to the Internet from anywhere in the world was absolutely invaluable. No one in Corn Hand had broadband Internet, not even Wi-Fi. If you wanted to go online, you'd have to resort to dial-up.

I set the dish to auto-seek as I opened my webcam application. After a minute of searching, the dish found an uplink. The satellite supplying my Internet signal would be overhead for the next fifteen minutes, meaning I had to act fast.

I set my webcam app to record my face and simultaneously mirror what was on my desktop screen. Then, I scrolled to the 9:22 timestamp and played back the data my instruments had recorded during the encounter. That way, I could provide a voice-over to the events exactly as I had seen them unfold during those fateful four minutes.

My laptop screeched; I paid it no mind as I continued speaking into the camera. I should have, though, as it was the first sign that something was wrong.

At first, I was unaware something was amiss. My PC's EMF alarm had screeched just like that throughout the four minutes of the encounter. But what clued me in to something being terribly wrong was that my impromptu broadcast was currently at the seven minute mark. Since the recording from earlier that evening had played back in real time, it would have ended at four minutes. The EMF alarm in the recording should have stopped blaring.

I minimized the webcam app but kept it running in the background. With that window out of the way, the live feed from my telescope and instruments filled my desktop space.

The EMF meter was pegged to the far right so hard it didn't so much as twitch. The readings it was picking up were off the charts. Strangely, though, the telescope picked up no visuals in any of the spectra it was set up to detect. Nothing on UV, infrared, or natural light. It was as though a black woolen blanket had been thrown onto the telescope's lens.

I looked up at the sky out of sheer nervous reflex, and nearly leaped from my chair. Where before there had been a cloudless sky of brilliant stars there was now an oppressive, low-hanging cloud that was impossible to see through.

The fluorescent lantern I'd set at the corner of my folding table flickered, and then grew brighter, its bulb glowing intensely white until it burst with a pop and the acrid tang of burnt-out electronics.

Lights began to flash all around me—it was hard to tell where they all were coming from. My van's taillights blinked on and off, the headlights and cabin lights too, all of them growing in intensity as they blinked faster and faster until they exploded like a string of firecrackers. The taillights blew out so forcefully that they took the rear lenses clean off. Inside the van, white-hot sparks rained down from the live wires where the cabin lights had been, setting the cloth seats ablaze.

The Honda generator sputtered, then went into a harsh, loping idle before dying with a sharp backfire. Smoke rose from its top where the spark plug that powered its internal combustion had shot skyward from its coupling like a rocket.

Plumes of smoke let up from my laptop, smelling of charred silicon. Black bands swept across the display like an old television powering on, this giving way to the Microsoft "blue screen of death" error message, until finally the display went black as holes the size of pennies opened up on its surface and boiling jellied LCD ooze poured onto the keyboard. I pushed myself away from the table and spilled to the ground onto my face in the nick of time as my laptop exploded, the monitor cartwheeling into the air as the keys flew off the keyboard like popcorn kernels in a microwave.

I got to my feet and swept my gaze across the destruction that was playing out before me. The fire in the van was gaining ground and would soon engulf its rear. When that happened, the gas tank would turn the vehicle into a bomb.

At a loss for what to do, I ran as far as I could from the burning wreck until I was utterly spent. The van was well out of sight by this time, hidden behind the rolling hills, the light from its fire peeking out over the crests like a faint aurora borealis. A minute later, the van went up in a thundering blast, leaving behind a mushroom cloud of fire that streamed burning slag from the heavens in every direction.

I figured the worst was over by then, but was I ever wrong. Suddenly, a beam of light pierced the heavy cloud cover. It was a fluorescent spotlight, and extremely powerful. I glanced up at its source but had to shield my eyes. It hurt to look at it.

I felt as though something had forced me to the ground. The next thing I knew, I was lying face down on the grass, and then, inexplicably, I couldn't feel the grass anymore. Actually, I couldn't feel anything anymore, as though I had been hoisted aloft into the air. I got the impression I was being drawn upward, toward the source of the light. The closer I got to it, the more all-encompassing it became, until I was so inundated with dazzling white light that I could see nothing.

My eyes snapped open and I could see again, although my vision was blurry, like looking through glasses smeared with clear grease. I was somewhere else — precisely where, I can't hazard a guess; I only knew that moments ago I was lying face down on the grass, and now I was face up on an examination cot.

I could not move — it was as though I was conscious but my body was paralyzed.

A shape leaned over me from behind my right shoulder, and when I saw it, my breath caught in my throat. While I couldn't pick up on any fine details, I could tell a few things. It was human-like, though not at all human. Its head was disproportionately large compared to the rest of its body, especially at the crown, looking almost like an inverted pear shape. It had fish slits for nostrils and massive black eyes — they looked like those river stones people use to line their ponds and fish tanks. Its body was a pallid, sallow gray, with a sickly thin physique.

Another creature appeared shortly after the first, this one showing up beside my knees. Like its companion, it leaned over the cot where I lay, studying me in the manner a doctor observes a patient on a medical gurney.

The two looked at each other briefly. They said something that came off to me as gibberish but they appeared to understand each other. They were harsh, guttural noises and wheezing sounds. Then they shifted their attention back to me. The first creature put out its hand — a tiny, four-digit thing with gangly fingers — and covered my eyes with it, and then there was a swathe of light, and I knew no more after that.

The first thing I recall when I woke up the following day was Mayor Donnegan helping me to my feet. My head ached as though from the fiercest hangover I'd ever suffered through. I meant to speak, but my throat was sandpaper dry. I could hardly manage a croak. I put an arm across his shoulders for support, and together we limped to his police car, where he helped me into the backseat.

We chatted as he drove. He said that he'd heard an explosion the night before and drove out to the town limits only to find my van going up in flames, but no trace of me anywhere. As it was already dark and he didn't have the resources to assemble a search party, he waited until daylight to seek me out. Sure enough, he found me several yards from the burnt-out husk of the van, lying naked under the sun, more dead than alive.

He was animated as we spoke, back to his old, welcoming self, with no trace of that cold suspicion from our awkward time in the diner.

And yet, something felt off. He seemed too chipper to suit the circumstances. He didn't bother to ask what I was doing out in the field, naked, or why my van had caught fire. Were I a police officer in his shoes, I would have suspected someone like me of being an arsonist or high on some powerful drugs. My behavior should have merited a few questions, at least.

I glanced up into the car's rearview mirror and saw Corn Hand fading into the horizon behind us. I called out to Donnegan, leaning forward into the spot between the two front seats of his police cruiser. Without warning, he mashed the brake and yoked the wheel hard, pitching the cruiser into the dirt at the roadway's shoulder. The car bucked upward when it came to a halt, the momentum hurling me into the backseat. Before I was too sure of what was going on, Donnegan was outside the vehicle, opening the rear door and shouting at me to get out.

He extended a hand to help me exit. I clasped his hand, and he tugged me toward him, and in the same motion he stabbed his stun gun into the crook of my armpit.

There was a split second of pain, and then my body fell into the cruiser's backseat.

When next I awoke, I was here.

I don't know what sort of operation you're running, but I can guess you're all government spooks. The lab coats, the "men in black" business suits, the secret service earpieces, the assault rifles — I can take a hint. If this isn't Area 51, it's something like it, am I right?

I don't expect you to answer that, but I'm pretty certain I'm right.

That's my story. I haven't held anything back. You can ask me to tell it again and that'll be some four or five times I'd have told it, but you won't trip me up in a lie. It's the truth.

Hey wait a minute, get back here — where are you going?

Look, I swear to God I won't tell anyone, just please, let me go. I didn't do anything wrong. Hey, come back!

I have rights!

Don't shut the door — don't...!

ABOUT THE AUTHOR
DOUGLAS FAIRBANKS

Douglas Fairbanks (no, not *the* Douglas Fairbanks, it should be noted) is an enigmatic individual. If there are two things he enjoys above all, they are being different and telling a good story. Perhaps he gets it from having been conceived on an oil platform off the coast of South America to a Belizean mother and an American expatriate father, a claim that serves these purposes splendidly, despite his unwillingness to corroborate it.

Regardless, he is an unnervingly talented individual, in the sense that he is at his best when he is getting things done for others, so long as they don't ask how he does what he does. That would "spoil the magic," as he is wont to say, and might also lead to indictments, which he is often quick to add.

Ever cool and collected—sometimes to disturbing levels— Douglas serves Darkwater Syndicate as an associate editor working closely with Ramiro Perez de Pereda.

He writes horror and bizarro fiction.

BEDBURG,
NEW JERSEY

BY: LUCIAN CLARK

Four years ago, during my freshman year of high school, I first heard the story of little Bobbie. It was an urban legend about a grade-schooler who took a dare for five dollars to head to an abandoned town called Bedburg, out in the Pine Barrens.

The story goes, he never made it back. In fact, according to the police, he didn't even make it to the town. Getting there would have been a tough hike on an adult, let alone a small child. When they sent his remains to the autopsy lab, the police concluded he'd fallen prey to wild animals, likely a cougar. There was also talk of wolves or feral dogs having been the culprits, except that there are no wolves in the Jersey Pine Barrens since trappers killed them forever ago.

My story starts while we were out drinking one night at the edge of the Pine Barrens. It was a cold October night, and the threat of winter on the wind made us shiver. Despite the miserable weather, we were having a good time, except for Kyle. He was uncharacteristically paranoid, and kept insisting we turn back. No one paid him any mind though, figuring that he'd settle down after he'd put a couple more drinks in him. But as the night went on, he got progressively antsy to the point where he was becoming a buzzkill.

It might have had to do with where we were camped out. We were not far from Bedburg, and could reach the abandoned settlement after a determined trek through the woods. The urban legends had probably gotten to him. After all, the place had been the topic of our discussions for much of the night.

In its prime, Bedburg was a bog ore mining town. The settlement dried up seemingly overnight with the collapse of demand in bog iron in favor of coal. No more industry meant no more people; they packed up and left town in search of employment elsewhere. Since Bedburg had never developed into anything significant, few, if any records of the migration were kept.

"I'm telling you, I saw something," Kyle said. "Out there, in the trees," he added, pointing to the woods beyond the reach of our fire. "I'll bet you a hundred bucks I saw something—no, better yet, I know I saw something. I'll bet you a hundred dollars if you spend the night in Bedburg."

He took a swig of beer to steel himself. Speaking of Bedburg, with all the rumors surrounding it and while in such close proximity to the settlement, was almost a dare in itself.

"Yeah," Kyle went on, his tone a little bolder. "Whatever it was I saw out there had to have come from Bedburg, and I'll bet you a hundred bucks if you can prove me wrong."

"Easy money," I said. I wasn't even one beer in and I shook hands on the bet. One night out in the woods? No sweat. I'd done that plenty of times.

To sweeten the pot, we agreed that I would spend Halloween night in Bedburg. What better night was there to go into a haunted old town than the night when the spirit world intersected with the world of the living?

The day before I set out, I consulted old maps and hiking paths. Bedburg lay in the Barrens about twelve miles from the nearest paved road. That road led into the Barrens only about two miles, which meant that the remaining ten would make for a tough hike through the thickest, darkest part of the forest.

It was nothing I felt I couldn't handle. I had spent half my life out in those woods, so I knew how to get around pretty well. Even so, I made sure to pack appropriately—this would be my first time going to Bedburg. Haunted or no, the last thing I wanted was to be caught unprepared in a town in the middle of nowhere.

When Halloween finally came, Kyle drove me to the edge of the Barrens. He sent me off with a kick in the ass and a wave. Even though he wasn't the one going into Bedburg, he seemed more nervous than me. In fact, he was eager to see me off and leave, as if he knew what was out there. I wasn't even five minutes down the path before I heard the tires of Kyle's Jeep screeching away.

What the maps had called a "road" turned out to be an uneven and narrow stretch of cracked asphalt that led into the forest. I wasn't far along the path when the trees behind me seemed to block the way back. The trees seemed to respond to my presence like something out of that horror film, *The Evil Dead*.

You can enter, but you can never leave, I heard the trees whisper as their boughs closed in around me.

I shook these thoughts from my head. I'd just started on the path, and I was too committed to making good on the bet to psyche myself out now. Besides, I'd be a hundred dollars richer by this time tomorrow.

Eventually, the paved road turned away from my heading. I stopped here to consult my map and compass by the light of a flashlight I'd packed. It was still daytime, but the tree canopy grew ever thicker the further I ventured into the Barrens. Where I stood, it was a dusky green twilight—still light enough to see, though not bright enough to pick up on finer details. Once I was sure of where my destination lay, I turned off the paved road and pushed into the overgrowth.

The foliage here was thicker than I had anticipated. A forest hike was one thing, but traversing this section of the Barrens called to mind a jungle explorer hacking at vines with a machete. The tree canopy above was nearly solid, admitting only pinholes of light by which to see. I could hardly see the trees before me; all I saw were their outlines. It wasn't much better down at the ground level either. I could not advance a step without either ducking under a bough or pushing aside a branch. Even a bulldozer would have as much trouble getting through.

I wondered how far Bobbie had made it through this stretch of the wilds. As much trouble as the hike was for me, it'd be impossible for a ten-year-old.

And then another thought hit me: what lived here?

I'd seen squirrels and rabbits, even a deer along the paved road through the Barrens; but since entering this patch of the woods, I'd not seen any form of animal life. I stopped and listened for birdsong and heard none. It was deathly quiet, with only the creaking of distant branches high above my head as they swayed with the breeze.

Every square inch of this place was taken up by plant life, to such an extent that no animals could live here. This begged the question: what killed Bobbie?

I checked my watch and shook my head. My plan was to set out for Bedburg early enough so that I could arrive just before dusk. I'd scope the place out and find a good spot to set up a tent and campfire, and then settle in for the night. I had not counted on taking so long just getting there. At this rate, it'd be past nightfall by the time I arrived, assuming I could find the place in the dark.

My stomach rumbled. Now was as good a time as any for a meal, and with the encroaching cold of nightfall, I'd need the extra calories to press on. I set my pack down and leaned against a tree to eat. I scanned the woods as I tucked into my meal, watching for any signs of movement. Between the darkness and the tightly-packed trees, I could see nothing beyond five feet. It was peaceful, and quiet, but unnervingly so.

A sound like a branch snapping perked my ears. It could have been a branch, but then again it could also have been the sound of an old bough starting to give under its own weight. That happened sometimes in the thickest parts of forests, where the trees grew so big they could no longer support themselves and their limbs sloughed off by gravity alone.

My thoughts turned back to little Bobbie. Could that noise have been a cougar stalking me like the one that had preyed on Bobbie? I looked up from my meal and scanned ahead, turning up nothing. If there was indeed a cougar out there, I figured I'd see it before too long. They had excellent night vision, which meant their eyes were highly reflective to observers even in low light. I'd see the flash of its eyes soon enough, not that this bothered me any. Cougars rarely attacked people, and when they did, their victims were either small children or people who didn't know how to handle them. An adult human could give a cougar a run for its money in a fight. Oftentimes, you could scare them off with loud noises or threatening movements.

I thought back to the police investigation photos taken when Bobbie's case was still fresh. Kyle's neighbor's girlfriend was friends with the son of the police detective assigned to Bobbie's homicide. He had snatched the police photos while his dad was passed out drunk on the couch, made copies, and brought them to school. Solely to appease my morbid curiosity, I asked to see them. I wish I hadn't—I hadn't gotten through half of them when my stomach threatened to empty its contents onto the cafeteria floor.

The police photos were nothing like the pictures the newspapers and television broadcasts ran. Whatever had gotten Bobbie had torn him to pieces. His face was half gnawed off, exposing his skull. Birds had plucked out his eyes. His upper body lay a few feet from where his legs and lower torso were found. His intestines were pulled out of his gut; several of his internal organs were missing entirely.

For as much of a mess as the scene of his death was, something just didn't add up for me. The killing looked too... intentional. It's hard to describe. I mean to say: given the shape his body was in, only certain organs were missing, as though these were what his killer was after. His body looked like it was torn apart in afterthought. You would expect a wild animal to strike only while its prey is still resisting; it would have no need to tear the body in half if a quick shot to the neck is enough to bring the prey down. And was a cougar even capable of ripping a human body to pieces? Also, who ever heard of a cougar that ate only the internal organs and forewent so much more edible flesh?

I pushed these thoughts aside. The forest was getting to me. That was twice already that the urban legends about Bedburg had stolen into my mind. I could not allow the stories to psyche me out when there were still many miles left to go. Another glance at my watch revealed it was 3:33 p.m. The weatherman had predicted the sun was due to set around six. I had a little under three hours to get to Bedburg, and no time to waste.

Shouldering my bag again, I resumed my hike, this time aided by my flashlight. I moved carefully, scanning the ground ahead for good footing. One wrong move and I might twist my ankle on a tree root, and that would be the end of my trip. Thankfully, I'd told people back home where I was headed and when I expected to be back, so if I went missing, they'd know where to search for me. Even so, I might not be found for hours.

Every now and then, little Bobbie and the Bedburg legends crept back into my thoughts. To keep this from happening, I occupied my mind by identifying what plants and trees I came across in my hike. I also kept an eye out for evidence of predators, but found none, which I found strange. Since turning off the paved road, I hadn't seen scat from bears or cougars, nor claw marks on the trunks of trees, or even bones.

I came upon Bedburg almost by accident. While hiking through the brush, I pushed through some low-hanging branches and found myself in a clearing. Before me stood a huddle of wood and stone buildings. Their roofs had long-since caved in, leaving only their walls standing. Several had already collapsed into rubble.

A few paces in from the edge of the forest, I found a patch of ground that looked like it had once been a cobblestone road. The stones were covered in moss and had settled unevenly into the roadbed, but taking the road was a welcome change compared to the treacherous woodland terrain. I walked past the ruined structures, shining my light into their windows, and wondering what life must have been like when Bedburg was populated.

The houses along the road were tiny compared to modern homes. From what I could tell from their remains, these homes consisted of two or three rooms at most. Following a bend in the road led to the shells of what once had been more substantial buildings. While I could only hazard a guess as to what they were, I would say these were businesses. They were better built, and constructed in a row, often sharing a wall.

The road dead-ended at the center of town. The structures here were arrayed in a circle around a plaza in which sat the ruins of an old church. Like the businesses, the church had fared the elements better. It was a narrow building, deeper than it was wide, with a door set between a pair of tall windows that might once have housed stained glass panels. The windows and door were long-gone.

The church's roof and side wall had caved in, revealing the depth of the structure. There was an altar, as was to be expected, with a stone pulpit next to it. Looking upon the church made me recall some of my research into Bedburg's history. This structure was the bedrock on which the community was founded back in the 1600's. Given that the town's founder was a man of the faith, it came as little surprise that extra care went into the church's construction.

According to the scant records on Bedburg, the community was founded by Reverend Michael Stubbe, a German immigrant. He was described as pious to the point of zealotry; and yet, for all his devotion to the faith, he was also known to have certain eccentricities that were not looked upon kindly by the rest of the town. Among them was his unusual fixation on a wolf's paw belt he was always seen wearing. This raised eyebrows because the belt was not part of a reverend's outfit. Indeed, the belt had the look of a magical totem. Much as it would have been unseemly for a reverend to wear such a blasphemous trinket, Stubbe was never seen without it, and rumors arose that he even slept with it on.

Reverend Stubbe was respected, but not liked. It was said that he moved his family to several American cities before founding Bedburg. While one can only speculate why he moved so much before settling in New Jersey, it was believed his overbearing nature and curious idiosyncrasies quickly made him a pariah wherever he went.

And then, from one day to the next, Bedburg just ceased to be, its people having vanished seemingly overnight. There were no records on this exodus, no documentation telling why the people left or where they went. The rest of the world only became aware that the town was gone when debt collectors rolled in to make good on past-due accounts, and found the place abandoned. Strangely, the townspeople had left in a hurry—meals were left uneaten on dinner tables, clothes had been left out to dry on lines.

No one ever found any evidence of foul play—there were no bodies or signs of a struggle. This only served to generate wild rumors: tales that the rapture had occurred and taken only Bedburg. More sinister rumors smeared Reverend Stubbe as a Satanist who moved the community into the Ramapo Mountains, where they would become the renegade group of mutants known as the Jackson Whites.

My brain was abuzz with all the theories I'd uncovered in my research, and a few I think I made up myself. I shoved these aside as I focused on more important matters, such as setting up camp.

As nightfall descended, I huddled close to my campfire for comfort. I was frightened. History has a way of inserting ghosts into old places, and Bedburg was several centuries old—plenty of time in which to harbor ghosts of its own. People had lived and died here, and their bones were buried under the very soil upon which I sat. My skin crawled at the thought.

Much as I tried to dispel these thoughts, they would not leave. There were ghosts here. I could hear them whispering in the leaves whenever the wind blew. I could hear their bones crunching underfoot with each step I took. In the flickering light of my campfire, I could see them against the supernaturally dark shadows among the trees. I saw their movements out of the corner of my eyes. Sometimes, there was even the red flicker of ghost lights in the depths of the woods.

Poltergeist had taught me all about Native American burial grounds and what it meant for those who dared trespass. What would happen to me for daring to sleep on these grounds? And especially on Halloween, when the division between the worlds of the living and the dead was at its thinnest? Would I end up like little Bobbie, dead with my eyes devoured by birds? I regretted taking the hundred-dollar bet.

I bit my tongue to calm down, focusing on the pain instead of ghosts. The metallic taste of blood filled my mouth. The fire popped and hissed with my blood and phlegm as I spat into it. I wasn't going to last the night if I didn't calm myself down.

There was no such thing as ghosts, I reassured myself, and I was alone in this abandoned town. The sense of being alone calmed me—it meant there was nothing here that could do me harm. To help clear my mind, I made a checklist of important tasks that needed to be done. Chief among them was learning my surroundings. I decided to explore the ruins.

Flashlight in hand, I set out into the cobblestone street. Typical of communities of its era, Bedburg had myriad little twisty alleyways one could easily get lost in. I picked up a stone and used it to mark the sides of buildings I passed, so that I could retrace my steps later.

I hadn't gone very far when I decided I should turn back. Despite being the end of October, the dead cold of winter had begun to sneak up in the night. Thankfully, the pine trees insulated the woods, shielding any within from the howling wind. Where I stood, though, the cold was still a threat, even if the wind couldn't get at you directly. That is what got you this time of year—the biting cold that slowly wore you down. I tightened my jacket and set out for my rudimentary camp, already envisioning warming myself beside the campfire I'd left burning, except that when I turned in its direction, there was nothing but darkness—no welcome warmth, no flame to guide me home.

I fought to keep from panicking. Had I made a wrong turn? Had the fire simply gone out?

To my left, a twig snapped. The sound of it breaking filled my ears and it set my heart racing. Panic seeded thoughts in my mind — what had I heard approach? A bear? A cougar, like the one that got Bobbie? Whatever it was sounded large. I had to get away.

My fight-or-flight instinct took hold. My muscles twitched in my legs and acted before my brain knew what was happening. I took off blindly, crashing through the forest at the town's fringe, making a beeline toward where I'd left my tent. I would be safe there — I had to get back.

Then came the sound of another branch snapping under a footfall — not one of mine, I was sure. Whatever was in these woods was stalking me.

Branches slapped at my face while my legs got tangled in the underbrush. Blood trickled from my torn skin. I tripped over a fallen log and was sent skittering in the dead leaves, but was up and running again before I could even register that I had fallen. My flashlight seemed useless, bouncing from shadow to shadow, failing to penetrate into the darkness.

Off in the distance, something red flickered among the shadows, and I ran toward it. Could this be my campfire? Not possible. For it to have burned down so low, I would have had to have been gone for hours.

A stitch in my side caused me to stop and lean against a tree to catch my breath. The light of the dying embers was further away than I at first had thought. And yet, as hard as I had run, how could I not be at my campsite? In a moment of clarity, I remembered my watch had a compass on it. The dial spun dizzily, unable to find true north. The time was stuck at 3:33 a.m. with the second hand twitching at the thirty-three second mark.

My knees trembled. I was lost. In a haunted forest. At night. My mind reeled as I tried to figure out what to do and where to go. Shakily, I swept my flashlight across my surroundings. All I saw was darkness and trees. Everything looked the same. Off in the distance, I caught another glimpse of flickering embers. There was only one way to go, and it was towards the warm comfort of the campfire. This would be my north star.

I ran until my legs nearly gave out, then slowed to a walk. Above me, an owl screeched. I spun on my heels, my flashlight seeking out the source of the noise before I realized what I had heard. I sighed softly, wiping my brow, exasperated at my own jumpiness. Then, when I felt ready to start off again, I spied another set of embers glowing in the night—except these had lit up in the opposite direction I had been traveling.

I raised my flashlight for a better look. The beam caught two red embers hovering in the air. I turned in place, the beam following my movements, so I could get a better grasp of my surroundings. Several other embers seemed to spark up in the forest around me as the flashlight beam crossed their paths, each of them lighting up in glowing red pairs.

I rubbed my eyes with my shirtsleeve—I could not believe what I was seeing. The lights seemed to peek at me from around the trees, twinkling like a constellation of red stars.

I was sure I was hallucinating—exposure and exhaustion can do that to a body. I took a breath to steady myself, then drew my hand back and slapped myself hard across the face to get my mind to focus. When my eyes reopened, the red lights were still there.

Fear gripped my heart. I couldn't breathe. My guts turned to ice when I realized that what I thought were the embers of a dying fire were in fact eyes—many pairs of eyes—watching me from the trees.

I was surrounded by them—whatever they were.

These weren't cougars, bears, or even wild dogs; none of those had red eyes.

The crunch of something advancing through the undergrowth cut through the dead air like a knife. My legs tensed, and my fingernails dug into the flashlight. A low rumble underscored the rustle in the trees—a growl. I spun to face the source of this new sound, and screamed.

The thing—whatever it was—crouched on its haunches, its giant clawed hands nearly dragging on the ground. At the end of its forepaws were talons the size of daggers. Dark, matted fur, looking almost like moss, covered its body from its twitching black nose to the tip of its canine tail. And its eyes—its eyes gleamed in the light like the eyes of a predator, except they glowed bright red like the very fires of hell.

As if it could sense my fear, the creature stood up on its hind legs to its full height and threw its head back. A howl tore from its canine throat, piercing the night air. Warmth trickled down my leg as I pissed myself.

I fell backward and scrambled away, propelling myself with my hands and feet against the forest floor until at last I caught good footing. A rough hand closed around my upper arm and I thrashed against it, wriggling free but not before its claws gashed deeply into my flesh. The pain came on in searing waves, but I plowed through it, my mind too panicked to register the extent of my injury. All that mattered now was to run to safety.

They were all around me now—I could feel their eyes on me, anticipating my movements. Their hot, stinking breath was like vapor on the back of my neck as I pumped my legs ever harder.

Something like a steel bear trap clamped around my leg and gave a twist, sending me to the forest floor. Without looking back I stamped against it with the heel of my other foot until it let up with a pained whimper. Its jaws had cut hot red rails into my calf muscle. I dragged myself to my feet and fiery pain exploded in my leg when I put pressure on it.

I took two hobbling steps, then looked back. The pack leader had stopped giving chase and just stood on its hind legs, watching me with hateful red eyes. All around it, red embers — the eyes of its pack — watched from the shadows between the trees.

The leader threw its head back and let up an ear-splitting howl. The rest of its pack joined in the raucous chorus. I watched for a split-second longer, then turned and ran for all I was worth on that bad leg.

To this day, I don't know why they stopped. Maybe they hunt for sport, and when they saw I was injured they considered me unworthy prey. Maybe, if I believed in magic, I might say something supernatural kept them bound to the site of old Bedburg. I don't know, and I don't think I ever will.

I limped through the Pine Barrens for the better part of the night. It was still dark when I came across an old home just outside the forest. I remember banging on the front door. A light came on inside, and there was shouting, although I can't say I made any sense of it. Blood loss from my injuries had dulled my senses almost to nil. The last thing I recall is passing out in one of the porch chairs.

Then I awoke here, at Lady of Lourdes Hospital, in your care.

From the look on your face, I can tell you don't believe me. I wouldn't believe me either if someone came into the ER and startled rambling about werewolves.

Fine. I don't care either way, but I know what I saw. That bite on my leg is proof enough. It doesn't match anything a bear, wildcat or feral dog can do. And if you like, you can put in your report that I overheard the police officer at the door talking to the doctor about how that bite looks just like the ones on little Bobbie when he went missing.

You probably won't. I'm just saying.

I have a theory for what happened at Bedburg. Being laid up has given me time to think. I've spent days searching the Internet for information on the Stubbe family. Buried under pages and pages of search results, I came across the website of an amateur folklorist. It was in German, which my browser horribly translated into English, but I got the gist of what it said.

It turns out, there was a rash of mysterious serial murders in the German heartland during the late sixteenth century. Contemporary reports held that the killer's victims were found torn apart, their bodies slashed open and their guts strewn about. A man with a knife could not have cut the victims so badly, and, by appearances, so violently; nor were the deaths the result of animal attacks.

Just before the terrified populace took matters into their own hands, constables caught the murder suspect, a man by the name of Peter Stumpp. He was ultimately charged with "werewolfery, witchcraft, and cannibalism," for which he was sentenced to death by being tied to a wheel and having his limbs broken with the blunt side of an axe head.

Following the execution, the Stumpp family was stigmatized because they were related to the killer. One of Peter's descendants, Michael Stubbe, left Germany for the American colonies in an attempt to flee this persecution. Michael, also known as Reverend Stubbe, would eventually found the community of Bedburg.

Here is where things get extremely strange. The similarities between the murders in the folk tale and the *modus operandi* of little Bobbie's killer are too strong to be ignored. And, given what I saw in the Barrens, I'm certain Bobbie could not have been their only victim.

Am I sure of what I saw and what my research has turned up? Absolutely.

Do I expect you to believe me?

Of course not.

For that, I suppose you'll want hard evidence. I guarantee, you'll find it in Bedburg, only, you'll have to look for it yourself. I'm never going back to that Godforsaken place—not on your life!—and certainly not for just a hundred dollars.

ABOUT THE AUTHOR
LUCIAN CLARK

Lucian Clark is a Southern New Jersey born and raised author. They have had both fiction and non-fiction works published on websites such as *The Advocate* and in the anthology *Werewolves VS*.

Their love of horror started at a young age when they first watched *Hellraiser*, and since then has dominated their tastes in film, writing, and gaming. While a fan of horror's many genres, monsters and the paranormal have always been king.

When not writing or reading, Lucian spends their time on social media and playing video games.

BARKER, ALBERTA

BY: JOSHUA BARTOLOME

It wasn't supposed to happen.

The OB-GYN told us that Annie would give birth in December, but without any reason whatsoever, she started having labor pains in the final week of October, while we were on a trip to her parents' home in Calgary.

Our family doctor reassured us that my wife was perfectly healthy. Exam after exam showed that nothing was wrong with our unborn son, and so we went on our trip with high spirits, expecting nothing but a quiet drive.

This is why I refuse to believe that it was merely a matter of bad luck that her water broke as we traveled down a desolate highway at 6:00 p.m. on a Sunday evening.

Something wanted us to be there.

Annie's cries of pain were heartrending.

It sounded as though she were being stabbed in the abdomen with a kitchen knife. I had never heard anyone scream like that, ever.

While trying to control my trembling hands, I gripped the steering wheel tightly and kept an eye out for any passing cars. I was going twenty kilometers above the limit, and I didn't want to be pulled over by a roving traffic cop.

Strangely, Highway 63 had been empty ever since we left our home in Fort McMurray an hour ago. I kept my foot on the gas pedal, sending the Lincoln that I had inherited from my grandfather blasting down the road.

We were at least an hour away from the nearest town. I knew that no matter how fast I drove, we would never reach a hospital in time. I had to call for help.

Using my free hand, I activated my Bluetooth earpiece and called 9-1-1. All I got was static. I slammed my fist against the wheel, cursing the horrible cellphone reception.

Annie's plaintive wailing brought me back to my senses, however, and I calmed myself down enough to attempt another call.

"9-1-1, what's your emergency?" a female operator answered my call after a single ring.

"My wife's giving birth," I said. "Please help us."

"Are you driving to a hospital right now, sir?"

"Yeah, but we're pretty far. We just left Fort Mac, and I'm not sure we'll make it."

"Did your wife's water just break?"

"She's bleeding."

"I'll need you to stay on the line. I'm tracking your signal and it looks like you're driving close to a clinic."

"Where?"

"It's in the town of Barker. You'll have to keep going another three kilometers."

I squinted, trying to peer into the horizon for any sign of a town. "Lady, there aren't any other towns here between Fort Mac and Breynat. Are you sure about this?"

"Sir, I know that you're worried, but I need you to trust me. If you follow my instructions, I can guarantee that your wife will have all the medical assistance she'll require for a safe and successful delivery."

I wanted to reply, but the tone of that nameless woman's voice, so cold and self-assured, made me catch my words before speaking.

As far as I could remember, there were no settlements along this isolated stretch of asphalt and the thick barren woods that flanked it.

"You'd better be right," I said after a moment's pause.

The sour smell of blood began to fill the interior of the Lincoln, leaving a taste of copper in my mouth. Annie was bleeding at an alarming rate. A brackish red puddle had formed on the floor mats beneath her feet.

I kept on driving.

Still, I couldn't see any town in sight.

"Am I close?" I barked into the Bluetooth earpiece.

"Five minutes away," the operator replied.

Then, as if on cue, I saw a green, pockmarked metal board posted on the side of the highway. Beside it was a gravel road cutting through a field. The sign's faded, white letters read:

BARKER, ALBERTA
POPULATION: 50

I couldn't believe it, but directly ahead were the silhouettes of houses and businesses looming in the distance.

For a moment, I remembered a joke that my grandfather used to say about a homeless man who saw a giraffe in the zoo for the very first time, and then declared that, "There ain't no such animal," while staring at the long-necked quadruped eating grass in its cage.

There ain't no such town, I thought. *Not around here.*

As we drove through the village of Barker's main avenue, I noticed that the lights in the shops and houses were turned off. Aside from the faint, orange glow of street lamps on every corner, there were no other sources of light along the roadways.

Annie's screams had faded into weak, almost inaudible whimpers. Blood loss had already taken its toll on her body. Judging from the agonized expression on my wife's face, I could tell that Annie was still in pain, but she no longer had the energy to struggle.

And yet, in spite of the dire circumstances, I couldn't help but think something was very wrong with our surroundings. Our car passed by two warehouses, a hardware store, a thrift shop, a grocery, and a quaint little family diner—all of them dark and empty, with no townsfolk in sight.

"Where is everyone?" I whispered.

I saw no cars driving down the road, no people strolling along the sidewalks. It was only 6:15 in the evening; it was still early. Even in rural Alberta, the small backwater towns usually weren't as deserted as this.

"Sir, you need to focus," the female operator spoke up. "We have to reach the hospital as soon as possible. Do you see a stone rotunda just ahead?"

"Yeah."

"Keep going north. You'll see the clinic on the right."

I toed the gas pedal, catapulting our Buick down the quiet roads. I saw the rotunda ahead and our car fishtailed along its edge. For a second, I caught a glimpse of an intricately sculpted brass mastiff standing atop a stone pedestal at the rotunda's center, its fangs bared in an eternal, frozen snarl, while the stylized fur on its back bristled.

The statue didn't bother me at the time because I was more concerned with the survival of Annie and our son. Things are different now. In hindsight, and the more I think about that statue, the more I feel as if its eyes had been watching as our car drove past, observing us, following us, like a wolf stalking a pair of rabbits.

Soon enough, to my relief, I saw a bright red neon emergency sign flashing like a lighthouse beacon in the midst of a storm. The sign's crimson glare bled across the parking lot which housed only a pair of ambulances that looked as though they came straight from the 1970's.

"Baby, we're here," I whispered to Annie while parking the car outside of Barker Community Hospital. She barely responded to my words, merely nodding, eyes half-closed.

Unbuckling my seatbelt, I told my wife that I was going to leave her, just for a second, to call for help. She didn't answer. Her head lolled to the side as she slipped into unconsciousness. Silently, desperately, I prayed to God and whoever was watching in heaven that we weren't too late.

"Help!" I screamed as I exited the car and ran to the hospital's front entrance. "Someone, please! Help us!"

"You have to go inside," the operator said in my earpiece. "There should be a duty nurse at the front desk."

I kicked through the front doors, charging into the hospital without breaking stride, only digging my heels in to stop once I was in the center of the lobby.

All the lights were on, and the clipboards and pens and charts lay in neatly-ordered rows across the reception desk, but I couldn't find any doctors or paramedics or medical staff anywhere.

The place was empty.

"Hello?" I shouted, and my voice echoed across the empty concourse. "My wife's dying, for God's sake!"

No one answered. Only the rhythmic thrum of ventilators could be heard throughout the emergency ward.

"Sir?" the operator's voice buzzed in my earpiece. "What's going on?"

"There's no one here!"

"Calm down. Maybe it's a slow night. There should be two nurses in the E.R. department."

"What do you think I am, blind or stupid? I'm telling you, lady, there aren't any people in this fucking place!"

I wanted to give up right then. Feelings of fear and desperation came in nauseating waves that made me want to throw up. My heart pounded, my head filled with noise as I felt my resolve crumbling away.

"Don't lose your head, Martin," the operator said.

"What?" I said in a breathless whisper. "What did you just call me?"

"Your name," she replied. "I heard your wife saying it. Take a deep breath and calm down, because you won't be of any help to anyone if you start panicking."

I closed my eyes and tried to control my breathing.

"I'm sending over an ambulance," she continued in the same monotone drone. "They'll be driving all the way from Fort Mac, but they should arrive in about an hour."

"Are you shitting me?"

"Martin, your wife is losing a lot of blood, and we're both gonna do what we can. But we won't get anywhere if we don't work together. You have to do your part, all right?"

I bit my lip hard enough to draw blood. "Tell me what to do."

"Find a wheelchair. We need to get her inside the ward so we can staunch the bleeding."

When I returned to the parking lot with a wheelchair in tow, I discovered that Annie was barely breathing.

"No, no, no," I muttered. "Please, don't do this."

Her skin was paler than it had any right to be. She drew in short gasps of breath through her half-opened mouth like a fish dying on dry land.

"Stay with me, baby, c'mon," I said as I lifted her into the wheelchair. Blood dripped from between my wife's legs and left a glistening trail on the ground as I wheeled her into the emergency ward.

Before we came to Barker, I had never known what real hopelessness felt like. It's hard to accept that there are some things a man can't do for his family. I wouldn't wish that kind of despair on anyone, even my worst enemies.

"Martin, save our boy," Annie said weakly. "Please."

"I'll save you both," I replied as I rushed her through the hospital's corridors.

Annie just gave me this tired, sorrowful gaze, which I tried hard to ignore as I pushed the wheelchair into the nearest operating area I could find.

The surgical lights in the operating room had been left on as though someone were expecting us. I'd noticed this detail, but hardly had time to reflect upon it in the heat of the moment.

"Promise me," she said in just above a whisper.

How could I say no when she looked at me with those eyes?

"I will," I replied to put her at ease. "I promise."

Operating tools sat in rows on nearby medical overbed tables; the scalpels and forceps and other sharp implements twinkled with a vicious gleam beneath the sterile glow of fluorescent bulbs.

Just then, the operator spoke to me.

"Martin? Are you there?"

"I'm right here."

"I need you to help your wife lie down on the bed."

"She won't stop bleeding."

"We'll try to stop it. Hurry."

Annie had fallen unconscious. I gently tapped Annie's face to rouse her a bit.

"Baby?" I said. "I'm gonna lift you up, okay?"

She didn't answer.

"Annie?"

Trembling, I placed my index finger beneath her nose; I couldn't feel any air being exhaled. My hands next went to the side of her neck. I couldn't feel a pulse.

"Oh God," I said, starting to panic again. "Oh, Jesus, Annie! Wake up!"

"Martin, talk to me," the operator said in a firm tone. "What's happening? Is your wife all right?"

"She isn't breathing. I can't feel a pulse."

"Try again. Blood loss slows down a person's heartbeat. It can be hard to feel."

This time, I touched her wrist. Like before, I couldn't feel even a single, subtle tremor, no matter how hard I pressed down on the vein. Sobbing, I tried shaking Annie, vigorously, but she wouldn't respond, not even when I slapped her repeatedly on the cheek.

"Baby, don't do this, don't leave me," I said, crying. There was no use denying reality as it unfurled before my very eyes: Annie was dead, and there was nothing I could have done to save her. In that second, I could feel my grief intermingling with something darker, something akin to rage, but much, much blacker and more insidious.

"She's dead," I whispered into the Bluetooth earpiece.

Whoever that bitch was—the one sitting behind that phone, nameless, faceless, and beyond my reach—I wanted to strangle her, to butcher her, to hack her body into pieces.

"I'm sorry," the operator said. There seemed to be remorse in her words, but that didn't matter.

I was beyond consoling.

"Fuck you, bitch," I shouted. "*You're* sorry? If you hadn't sent us here, my wife would still be alive!"

119

I slumped down to the floor, weeping. I wanted to die right then and there, and I begged God and the devil to end my life, because I couldn't bear the pain any longer.

Better oblivion than this.

"Look, I know you're upset, but if you don't hurry up, your son will die," the operator replied matter-of-factly as if it were no big deal. "It takes ten minutes before the baby suffocates due to lack of oxygen and blood."

"What the hell are you talking about?"

"Do you want your child to live, Martin?"

At first, I didn't understand what she was trying to say, until my gaze crossed the surgical tools.

"No," I said, shaking my head. "No fucking way!"

"You have nine minutes and thirty seconds left."

"I am not cutting my wife!"

"She begged you. You promised."

"Jesus Christ, do you even understand what you're asking of me? I'm not a surgeon! I can't!"

"That's why I'm here. I'll guide you through the steps. You have the right tools lying around somewhere, correct?"

I didn't want to admit it, but she was right. I had already failed my wife. I didn't want to fail her again.

"Follow my instructions, and your son will live," the operator continued. "Don't, and you'll lose him, too. Time's running out, Martin. You have eight minutes left."

I closed my eyes for a second.

"All right," I said, breathing a sigh. "What should I do?"

"Are you ready?" the operator asked. "Let's start."

I gritted my teeth and began the long, bloody process of carving my son, my own flesh and blood, out of his mother's womb. First, I set my wife gently onto the sterile operating table, her blood spilling all over my arms, my clothes, and my chest.

Afterwards, I used a pair of surgical scissors to cut away Annie's blouse, exposing her swollen belly. For a second, I saw her flesh rise as our baby reacted to the stimulus and kicked hard. Seeing this almost made me weep in relief. He was still alive. Our son was alive.

Grabbing a scalpel from one of the trays, I gathered the last vestiges of willpower left in my soul.

I will not, and I cannot describe what happened during those eight minutes. The sounds, the sights, and the smells of that room will never leave me until the day I die.

Like a clumsy, maniacal butcher, I followed the operator's instructions and desecrated the helpless body of the one person that I loved most in the entire world.

I don't know how I managed to perform a C-section on my wife without breaking down or throwing up. There are moments in a man's life where he is forced to do the unthinkable, to do what is necessary, no matter how degrading it is, or violent. Some men fold and crumble. Others soldier on. A man can never know what kind of person he is, and what he's capable of, until he's compelled to do terrible things against his will.

To get myself through this horrendous task, I imagined that Annie's soul was standing right beside me, stroking my shoulder, telling me that "It's okay, it's okay." That this is what she would have wanted. Only our son mattered, and everything could be forgiven if I managed to save his life. Annie was dead. Our baby wasn't.

When at last I managed to pull our newborn son out of my wife's womb, a monstrous sort of joy filled my heart. Yes, Annie was dead, and yes, I had done the unimaginable, but at least, at the very least, my son survived the ordeal. He bawled, and screamed, and cried furiously as if he were outraged by the violence I had perpetrated.

I continued to follow the operator's instructions, snipping off the umbilical cord and then swaddling my son in a blanket before placing him in a nearby incubator.

"You did well," the operator said.

I didn't have any strength left to answer. Instead, I sat down on the floor, bone-weary and tired beyond words.

"The ambulance will be coming soon," the operator went on. "You should get some rest. You've certainly earned it."

"What do I tell them?"

Annie's blood had soaked my clothes. How could I explain to anyone what I had done? If the paramedics saw Annie, they would think I had murdered her.

"They'll understand," the operator consoled me. "You did what you had to do, Martin. You saved your child's life. Now, it's my turn to help. Leave everything to me."

"I can't sleep. Not here."

"Shhh. Close your eyes. We'll take care of your son."

Although I wanted to stay awake, a dreadful sense of fatigue overcame my body. Leaning back against the wall, I found my eyes fluttering as I drifted toward unconsciousness. Before succumbing to a deep, dreamless sleep, I glanced at the incubator where my son lay, still crying, wailing, begging for his mother's gentle hands.

"Michael," I whispered. "His name is Michael."

I don't know how long I had been sleeping, but when I finally opened my eyes, the operating room was dark. Only the dull glow of red emergency lights filtered into the area. Looking at my watch, I thought at first that it was still 6:15 p.m., but after tapping its glass surface, I soon realized that it had stopped.

What had happened while I was asleep?

Where was my son?

Panic hit my veins, feeling like battery acid in my bloodstream. I glanced around the dimly-lit operating room, searching for the incubator that housed my frail, vulnerable little boy. It wasn't there. I couldn't hear his plaintive screeching anywhere. I tried to calm myself down by thinking that, perhaps, the paramedics had taken him.

But if that were indeed the case, then why did they leave me here? They should've woken me up, questioned me about Annie and the horrible things I had to do just to save Michael from drowning in the amniotic fluid of his mother's womb. The operator had promised me she would take care of everything—what was going on?

When my eyes crossed the bloodstained operating bed, I saw that my wife's lifeless body had also been taken away. I got the notion that something was terribly amiss, but then again, nothing had gone right ever since we arrived here.

"Michael?" I called out while hobbling out of the operating room, a pounding headache jackhammering my skull. I didn't know what else to do except call my newborn son's name, although such an act was, ultimately, useless. Michael was barely an hour old, and he would never recognize my voice even if I shouted myself hoarse.

But I had to do something to keep myself from sliding into a lunacy induced by pure, overwhelming despair, and saying Michael's name, over and over again, in the darkness of that accursed hospital felt like intoning a prayer against the shapeless things that slithered in the shadows.

"Michael, where are you?" I called out again, futilely, in a sobbing scream. *Please*, I thought, *you've already taken too much from me. Give me my son back.*

Then, as if reading my mind, a familiar voice blared through the overhead speakers. During that moment, I knew, beyond certainty, that we had been led to the town of Barker for a purpose.

They wanted my child. They wanted Michael.

"He's safe," the operator's soothing voice said. "We would never harm your son. He is precious to us. It has been so long since we have welcomed a new member of our family."

Hearing those words sent a searing current of terror through every nerve and fiber of my being. I wanted to run screaming like a madman out of that place. My legs trembled with each step, and yet I kept on walking, pressing forward, exploring the corridors, searching for a sign that could show me where they had taken Michael.

"I'll do anything," I cried out. "Just give him back."

"What exactly can you offer us, Martin?" the operator replied with a cruel, inhuman laugh. "There is nothing good and pure left in you, nothing that we can use."

I spotted a trail of blood leading into another hospital wing. The blood slithered past a closed set of double doors with two red emergency lights shining above them.

"Leave, now, or die," the operator warned. "Do not return to this town, or we shall flay your soul and show you sights that will make the sun grow black with horror."

"He's my son! You have no right!"

"Do not scorn our mercy, little human, little piece of flesh." The operator's tone suddenly transformed, becoming a chorus of voices that belonged to thousands of people, men and women, young and old, all talking simultaneously.

"We chose to spare your life because you brought this child to us," the operator said. "Our patience grows thin."

"Fuck your mercy," I replied with false bravado.

Growing up in a farming community in rural Alberta, I was hardened by daily fistfights with the local Mennonite boys. Life around these parts was a constant battle. I wasn't the kind of guy who would shirk away from a scrap, even the ones that I knew I would lose. This fight wasn't any different. I risked losing everything. My life. My own soul.

But this was a risk I was willing to take. For Michael. I would do anything and everything for him.

I had already proven that.

I pushed the doors open and walked into the shadows.

I didn't know that I was walking into a morgue.

Scores of black body bags lay on steel gurneys within that blood-spattered room. Some of these containers squirmed. I didn't have the curiosity or the madness to unzip these things and look inside.

My senses had gone numb by then.

Not even the bizarre squelching noises coming from the closed room at the end of the hall were enough to dissuade me from approaching. What were they doing inside? The closer I came, the more sounds seemed to emanate from behind the next set of double doors. White light filtered through two semi-transparent glass windows. Through them, I could see shadowy, indistinct figures darting about.

A buzzing filled my head, sounding like insect wings vibrating at a high frequency. The shrill noise was enough to bring me to my knees, so deafening that I thought the blood vessels inside my ears would burst.

When the unnatural din subsided, I rose to my feet and stumbled onward to the morgue where I thought that Michael was being held captive. I was wrong. He wasn't there. But I did see things in that room, indescribable things, faceless things that looked like naked, sexless human beings with the wings of cicadas. They had no eyes, or ears, only mouths lined with blackened, rotting teeth.

In the center of the room, lying on an autopsy table, was the body of my wife, the only woman I had ever loved.

And they were eating her.

I ran.

Like a coward.

My mind splintered into a dozen jagged pieces after seeing what those creatures did to Annie. There is only so much horror that the human consciousness can process before its flame dies, snuffed by the cold, bony fingers of fear.

Callous, mocking laughter followed me as I ran out of the ward and jumped into the Lincoln. I sobbed and screamed hysterically when I started the car and drove away.

I kept on going—past the rotunda with its statue of the snarling dog, past the abandoned shops, houses, and buildings that flanked the road into Barker—and I did not stop until I made it to the township of Breynat.

What happened in the days that followed cannot compare to the horrors which I had witnessed, but it would not be an overstatement to say that my life was ruined, forever.

I will not go into detail about the legal proceedings that have hounded me ever since I escaped with my sanity barely intact. But I have to make it known that I didn't abandon my son. I tried to go back. I even brought a constable from the Boyle RCMP detachment to accompany me, since I didn't dare return to Barker, not without a gun.

When we arrived at the spot where Barker's signpost once stood, the bewildered police officer found nothing but trees and a field of uncut grass flanked by rows of thick woodland on both sides. I insisted that this town actually existed, that I had honestly driven along its streets and smelled the petrichor rising from the rain-kissed asphalt, but he wouldn't believe me.

We drove along that empty stretch of highway until we ended up in the outskirts of Fort McMurray. Then we turned around and traveled to Breynat again, and during those two trips, we saw no houses, no buildings, no shops, not even a dirt road that might lead to Barker. It had vanished, completely, into thin air.

In the end, I was handcuffed, thrown in jail, and indicted for the murder of my wife and son. The blood on my shirt, which tested positive for Annie's DNA, was used as evidence of the horrendous crime I was charged with. Nonetheless, even during the lengthy trial that attracted the attention of both local and foreign media, I didn't change my story — that a town called Barker took my family away in the most brutal and horrifying manner.

The female lawyer who handled my case, in a brilliant but utterly dishonest move, claimed insanity as a legal defense, something which I vehemently opposed. Why should I lie to save myself from jail? I have already gone through hell, I have seen what it looks like, and there is nothing that any courts of human justice can do that would be worse than seeing my dead wife being devoured by demons.

Through some stroke of devilish misfortune, the jury accepted this defense. They declared me innocent by insanity.

After five years inside a psychiatric institution in Edmonton, I was set free due to good behavior. Annie's grieving family protested my release, which broke my heart even more. But by this point, the damage was already irreversible, and I didn't have the time to dwell on the mistakes of the past or on broken relationships.

I had a job to do.

Ever since my release, I've been traveling all across North America and Europe, searching for information about mysterious towns that have appeared and vanished without explanation.

This has led me to the hidden corners of the world, seeking forbidden answers and finding very few. But I keep on searching anyway, and I believe that my journey is almost finished. I wasn't the first person to have experienced this sort of bizarre phenomenon. Far from it.

Throughout human history, men, women and children have strayed into towns like Barker. The earliest reports of such places can be found in the *Unaussprechlichen Kulten* written by Friedrich von Junst in 1839. In it, he described malignant creatures known as the "Feldgeister," the field spirits, or faeries in English and Irish mythology.

These things are not the tiny, friendly beings often seen in Disney movies. They are a malevolent, uncanny, and ancient people who have lived for centuries in the hollow, forgotten places of the earth, where old blood was spilled on old soil. They cannot reproduce like other creatures, and the only way they can continue their lineage is by kidnapping and transforming infants and young children.

Children like my son.

I believe that the thing that led us there, the female 9-1-1 operator, was actually a faerie of the sort that von Junst called "Die Roggenmutter," the Rye Mother, the oldest and most dangerous of their kind. I don't know what sorts of monstrous things they've done to Michael, but I swear that I will, somehow, find a way to undo the Rye Mother's dark magic.

And so, now, armed with my hard-won knowledge and a sawed-off shotgun loaded with blessed silver buckshot, I travel down the lonely roads of America, searching for a place that exists beyond space and time. I've traded my grandfather's Lincoln for a black V-8 Interceptor, something that can go fast and hard and has the roar of an enraged beast chasing after its helpless, frightened prey.

I'm no longer the coward that ran away like a little child. The Feldgeister have taken all hope, and joy, and goodness from my soul and left nothing but a seething fury.

I will bring fire and death and violence to the town of Barker. I will burn down its buildings until nothing remains but a smoldering field of ash and cinders. When that time comes, I will take back from those sons of bitches the dignity and the love they stole from me.

And then I will see my little boy again.

Wait for me, Michael. I'm coming for you.

ABOUT THE AUTHOR
JOSHUA BARTOLOME

Joshua Bartolome is a Filipino-Canadian writer living in Calgary, Alberta. His prose poem, *The Cadaver*, was shortlisted for the Montreal Poetry Prize, while in 2017, his screenplay, *The Red Death*, won the Silver Screamfest award for best horror script. *Aswang*, a tale of poverty, misery and violence, was published in the anthology, *Tales of Blood and Squalor*. Another short story, *The Last Confession of Dottore*, will be published in the upcoming *We Shall be Monsters* anthology.

ENERGY BEACH, FLORIDA

BY: STEVEN M. FONTS

Search in every map ever made of this country, and you'll likely never find Energy Beach, Florida. Which is not to say there isn't any such place—I have been there. And having found it, I wish I never had, because of what happened there.

Energy Beach is where I killed a man.

There were three of us: Claudio, Raul, and me. We were into urban exploration before that term even existed. Back in our day, it was called trespassing without getting caught.

All of us were college buddies. I was in my twenties; Claudio was the old man of our group, well into his thirties. Raul had scarcely hit the drinking age and hung out with us more for the beer than for the adventure.

After we'd learned about Energy Beach's existence, it was my job to find it. I was working part-time in the county records bureau then, which was a huge help toward locating obscure places that might pique an explorer's interest. Remember, this was 1982, and we didn't have the conveniences of the Internet or GPS yet.

As it turned out, everything about Energy Beach is one big clusterfuck. It's not a beach, nor is it on any power grid. The closest it comes to living up to its name is that the land was deeded as an easement to a power company back in the 1940's. But unlike most legal rights-of-way, this easement encompasses the breadth of the community's land area—about two square miles. That didn't stop overzealous developers from attempting to sell the land, notwithstanding that they neither owned it nor acted with the power company's consent. The fiasco came to a head when the parties sued in court. The power company ultimately won, but it was a hollow victory—they declared bankruptcy a year later and left Florida with nothing to show for their efforts. Determining who owns Energy Beach today is a thorny legal question, but one thing is for certain: regardless of who owns it, the state police are keen on deterring trespassers.

Once I was fairly sure of where our destination lay, we put Raul in charge of getting us there. It was an open secret that his dad was one of the biggest cocaine dealers in Miami. His family was absurdly wealthy and had all the toys to show for it. He scored us the use of his dad's Mercury triple-outboard and two ATV's.

Claudio's family owned a deli restaurant, so that meant he was tasked with getting us provisions. The morning we set out, he showed up with a chest cooler full of sandwiches and another stocked with beer. But that wasn't all he brought. Claudio lived out west, in the county's backwoods, so he felt he knew better than any of us what we'd need for a journey to the middle of nowhere. Forget bug spray and sunscreen. Strapped crosswise on his back were two padded gun cases, one for his rifle and the other for his double-barrel shotgun.

Once the boat was loaded, Raul took the helm and I set a course. We traveled at a fast clip, arriving within an hour at the southeastern-most point of Biscayne Bay.

Even without the benefit of signposts or maps, we knew we had arrived when we set eyes upon the place. It looked nothing like its name suggested, which meant we were in the right spot.

There was no white sand beach. Instead, there was a flat expanse of ankle-high scrub grass beginning at the water's edge that ran to the horizon in every direction. But here's the odd thing—the land had been carved into an alternating pattern of turf and canals. The canals were as wide as the strips of land flanking them, and each was about thirty feet across. Seen from a distance, the layout might resemble the grille on a space heater.

Raul steered the boat to within fifty feet of the shoreline before the bay got too shallow to navigate. We rolled our ATV's out the back of his boat into the calf-high water, strapped our gear to them, and drove them to dry land. Once there, we unpacked and helped ourselves to an early lunch.

It was eerily quiet. The place was devoid of life. There were no birds, no fish, no turtles or snakes. There weren't even mosquitoes, which I found strange, given that we were sitting in marshland. The place ought to have been swarming with them.

We had each finished a round of beers when Claudio stood up and slung a leather rifle case over his shoulder. He took an ATV and forded the canal directly ahead of us. The water was waist-high, but neither that nor the canal's mucky bottom were any match for the machine's knobby tires.

He dropped it into neutral and revved the throttle twice.

"Let's race," he said.

I got astride our other ATV. Raul grabbed the second rifle case and joined me. He took the bitch seat—that is to say, he got on behind me and hung on.

It was hardly a fair contest, with my ATV bearing the weight of two riders, but none of us cared. We were here to explore, not to win a pissing contest over whose machine was fastest. Claudio and I gunned our quads simultaneously, catapulting us along the strips of turf. Our machines topped out at thirty miles per hour, and the land just kept giving us room to run. There was no way to tell how far we went along that path; all I know is I had the throttle wide open the whole way through.

Claudio eased off the gas so I could pull up alongside him, and then signaled to stop. He killed his engine and sat up straight, his hands cupping his eyes as he swept the horizon with his gaze.

"Jesus Christ," he said.

"Say again?" I replied. My ears were ringing from the engine's drone. With all the things we'd brought with us, we'd neglected to bring helmets.

He armed the sweat off his forehead. "This place just goes on forever. Is this all there is, or is there anything out here worth a visit?"

"This is it, as far as I know."

His shoulders drooped. "Well, okay," he said, trying not to sound too disappointed.

Raul stepped down from the ATV and gave a full-body stretch, but stopped partway into the motion. "Hey, you hear that?"

"I can't hear shit," I said, my pinky jammed into my ear to unclog it.

He clasped my shoulder and turned me in the direction he was pointing.

It was a white single-prop airplane, the type people used to call doctor-killers. It approached from the west, flying so low that its call sign numbers looked like a highway billboard. Then it banked left, in the direction we were facing, and dipped lower. Something fell out of the back of the plane and hit the ground off in the distance. The plane then climbed sharply and veered out toward the ocean.

"What the hell did we just see?" asked Claudio.

"It's a drop," Raul said out of reflex, and then regretted it.

"One of your dad's business partners?" Claudio ribbed him with a smirk.

"Shut the fuck up about that." Then, getting back on the ATV, Raul said, "Let's get out of here."

Claudio started his engine. "I say we have us a look."

"No!" Raul shot back.

"Why not?" asked Claudio, crossing his arms. "Don't you want to see how your dad makes his money? That's the first interesting thing we've seen since coming here."

"He's right, you know," I told Raul as I gave the ignition key a twist.

"What're you doing?" Raul stammered.

"I'm going with him. If you don't want to go, you can stay here." I straightened up in the saddle and looked around. "Wherever here is."

His bottom lip quivered. "All right, fine. But then we're getting right back on the boat and going home."

We drove for a long time. It had to have been at around noon when we arrived where the drop had been made; our shadows were directly underneath us. Up ahead, lying half-immersed in the canal next to Claudio, was a duffel bag.

Claudio was the first to get there. He hopped off his machine and went to take a look. Raul and I arrived a moment later.

"Hoo-hoo!" said Claudio, laughing, as he reached into the duffel and pulled out two tightly-packed bricks of uncut cocaine wrapped in cellophane. He held them aloft, one in each hand, beaming an ear to ear grin. "Look what I've got here. I've hit pay dirt, fellas!"

"Put that shit back right now!" Raul yelled.

Claudio paid him no mind as he reached for the folding knife on his belt and cut a package open. Fine white powder sprinkled out from within. He dabbed some to his tongue.

"Holy fuck, it's the real deal!" he said, letting up a big belly laugh.

"I have a bad feeling about this," Raul muttered, then looked out toward the bay to our right. In the distance, a yacht plowed through the waves. "Hey, guys?" he said, not taking his worried eyes off the yacht. "We've got company."

The pleasure boat coasted to a stop a couple hundred feet offshore. I cupped my eyes and squinted, and could just barely see people moving to the boat's rear. They were unloading jet skis into the water.

"This isn't cool, guys," Raul said, his voice wavering. "We should put the stuff back and make like we weren't here."

Claudio batted a palm at him. "Cool it, kiddo. It's just some rich family out for a day at the beach, that's all." He hefted a brick in his fist to judge its weight. "How much do you think one of these will fetch?"

"Fuck if I know, man," I said. "A couple grand?"

"You want?"

I shook my head.

He offered Raul some.

Raul put out both hands and waved his arms in crisscrossing arcs, leaving no question about his desires.

"Hey guys," Raul spoke up, "they're coming to pick up the drop." He looked out toward the water again.

The twin jet skis raced parallel to the shore but did not seem to be coming any closer to where we stood.

"They've seen us," said Raul, "they're scoping us out. Once they find out we don't belong here, they'll give us all Peruvian neckties."

He stuck his tongue out for emphasis as he made slashing motions around his neck.

Claudio stuck his tongue out too, and with one hand made as if he were jacking off. "Calm the fuck down, kiddo. Your nerves are getting the better of you."

"No! I know what they're capable of—we're leaving, now!"

Raul's hands flew to the rifle case slung across his back. In a heartbeat, he'd unzipped it and had gotten the Winchester into his hands, its barrel trained on Claudio. He held it awkwardly, stiff-armed and level to his gut, as though it were some odious thing he wanted nothing to do with.

"Easy with that," Claudio said, his tone low and even. Palms out and arms at shoulder height, he advanced. "That thing's loaded. You don't want to hurt anybody."

Claudio's hand slunk toward the gun case strewn across his back.

"Don't!" Raul threatened, his voice shrill with fear, raising the gun to peer down the sights. "Toss me your gun!"

Claudio lobbed his rifle case to our side of the canal. It landed with a thud at my feet.

"Pick it up," Raul told me. "Put it on, and get us moving!"

He cut his eyes to the pleasure boat out in the bay. As if our thoughts were synchronized, Claudio and I did too.

The yacht was anchored in the bay with no one aboard. Meanwhile, the jet skis were circling back around. They cut a sharp turn and went full-throttle in our direction.

Raul huffed a frightened breath. "They're coming!"

Claudio screamed, sending our heads whipping one hundred eighty degrees around. He fell forward onto his face and broke the fall with his palms, his fingers digging shallow runnels into the peaty soil as something in the canal behind him dragged him into the water. He screamed again, and there was a massive splash as he flopped over backwards in the air, hitting the water with his back.

He sprang out of the canal, paddling overarm towards dry land when his head went under again.

Something massive and black, looking like a huge triangular sail, burst from the canal and slapped its surface hard, casting water into the air in a broad spray. The black thing vanished, and what surfaced next looked like a stark white length of wooden board that turned over and was gone under the water just as quickly.

Claudio floated up to the surface and beat an exhausted arm against the water, eventually hauling his languid body up the canal's embankment. He was face down and breathing shallowly as if succumbing to shock, his back rising and falling in quick spurts.

A raspy yelp tore from his lips, as though he didn't have enough breath in his lungs for anything stronger, and then, after two more breaths, he caught his wind and howled with pain.

His left leg was gone, severed above the knee. Ragged bits of bleeding meat flapped at the end of his thigh, where the pointy stump of his shattered femur jutted out of the garish red mess like the business end of a javelin.

And then, with a guttural roar, a beast of an alligator surged out of the canal like a cruise missile fired out of the top of a nuclear submarine. Its jaws were open wide, exposing the pink and white meat of its gullet. Its mouth clapped shut onto Claudio's other leg, its fangs digging into the flesh above and below his knee. The monstrous reptile thrashed its head sideways and Claudio went up into the air like a tattered flag in a stiff breeze, his limbs flailing about his torso.

I tugged at the zipper of my rifle case. The case tumbled out of my hands as the zipper pulled apart, spilling the sawed-off shotgun it contained to the grass.

I looked up from the ground at my feet to the monster eating Claudio alive.

"Shoot it!" I screamed, remembering Raul still held his rifle.

I regretted having said that immediately, realizing I'd expected too much of my friend. The shot would have been challenging even for a marksman, and Raul was just a scared kid who knew nothing of guns except which end the bullets came out of. What happened next was what I expected would happen, and what I most feared.

In an unthinking panic, Raul raised the sights of his gun to his face and pulled the trigger. It went off with a crack that echoed across the desolate swamplands, and more recoil than Raul had expected. He tumbled backward, falling onto his ass with the gun coming to rest beside him.

The alligator was in mid-swing with Claudio in its jaws. Claudio's head whipped forward from the beast's colossal thrashing, his chin pinned against his collarbone. Suddenly, his head swept up and away from his chest as though yoked backward by an unseen force. The shot had pegged Claudio squarely in the forehead, cratering the spot between his eyes with a blazing red pit. The crown of his head popped off and flew up and away from the back of his skull, taking with it a chunk of scalp the size of a drink coaster that soared three channels over and landed with a splash in the canal beyond.

Claudio's body went limp, the inertia of that fatal bullet sending him head over heels backward down the canal's slope. The alligator let go momentarily, and then bit down onto his torso and spun sideways down the defile, disappearing with him into the brackish water in a flurry of violent splashes. The swamp was quiet once again, the only sound being those last droplets of water that rained down onto the brown surface of the canal.

"Oh my god," Raul murmured through trembling lips. It all had happened so quickly that he hadn't had time to take it all in. "He's… he's dead… I… k-killed…"

Then, likely remembering that there were Peruvian drug lords on jet skis looking to kill us both, his gaze went flying toward the bay. The boat was still there, but the jet skis were long gone. In retrospect, they very well could have been just a family out for a day on the water and not the hardened criminals we had made them out to be.

Raul hardly had time to turn back in my direction when I shoved the muzzle of my gun into his chest and gave him both barrels. It was loaded with buckshot, and the short barrel gun firing at contact distance resulted in a tremendous blast of force and heat. When the flash cleared, Raul was on his back with a ragged hole blown through his chest. Everything below his left nipple to his hip was gone, and what remained of his right side was held together by a ribbon of tissue no wider than an index finger.

The rest of that day was a blur. Blame that on jangled nerves and dehydration. I walked my ATV several canals over from the spot where we'd found the drugs, all the while keeping an eye out for that murderous alligator. Since I wasn't atop the ATV, it left shallow tracks, merely crushing the grass without turning up any dirt. Shallower tracks wouldn't last as long, I reasoned, and it'd be harder to follow any trail the tires would no doubt leave behind. Once I was a few lanes over, I saddled up and gunned my machine up the channel, driving north until the ATV's fuel tank went dry. Partway into that ride, I ditched the shotgun, flinging it into the canal at my side, which accepted it eagerly into its still, brackish water.

I left the ATV behind and set out on foot, walking a straight line through miles of wilderness. That's where my memory cuts out. The next thing I knew, I was in the back of a rescue helicopter with a needle stuck into my arm. I'd passed out from heat exhaustion. I came to learn later that the family on the yacht had radioed the police when they heard gunshots, and the boys in blue had come running. Had it not been for sheer happenstance, I'd have been a gator's dinner.

That's not all I discovered. It turns out, there's a good reason the police don't want anyone in those lands—those waterways are cooling canals for a nuclear power plant a couple miles up the way from where we parked our boat. The plant pumps in ocean water to cool its reactor core and then dumps the hot water into the canals. As if that weren't reason enough for the cops to keep trespassers away, the local wildlife absolutely loves the warm canal water.

By wildlife, I mean the alligators that breed in those canals in record numbers.

Once the doctors were convinced I was all patched up, the cops had their turn with me. They turned me loose in a matter of days. No one ever found the bodies or the gun, and I kept quiet, so they never could pin my friends' disappearances on me. They fined me a hundred bucks for trespassing and I cut that check gladly, considering the charges could have been far worse.

I'll admit: sometimes, I regret the choices that I made, but there simply weren't two ways about it—Raul had to go. If he had lived, he would never have owned up to killing Claudio, even if it was an accident. It'd have attracted too much heat to his father's business. In all likelihood, he'd have ousted me to the cops, or shot me dead on the spot, or even asked his father to send guys to take me out.

I don't mind telling you all this, and I don't care who you tell. It won't make any difference. Three can keep a secret if two of them are dead, and with all the alligators that call Energy Beach home, it's not like any of them are talking.

ABOUT THE AUTHOR
STEVEN M. FONTS

Estêvão Magalhães Fonts, better known as Steven, was born in Minas Gerais, Brazil, in 1977. He emigrated to the United States to study journalism and now works as a freelance photographer. He lives in Deerfield Beach, Florida, with his wife, two sons, and a Great Dane named Abílio.

Grizzly Peak, Colorado

By: Nicholas Paschall

It all started about twelve years ago, when Yuki and I were climbing in the Colorado mountains, near the Grizzly Peaks. It was summer, and the snow was melting in a slow but determined fashion, creating a warm, if not misty, view of the valleys below us. The mists billowed down around us as we scaled the near sheer cliffs in our ever-present need to see where we could reach in the heights of the local wilderness. We'd been dating for maybe two years at that point, and had been engaged for a little over three months, and I'm not ashamed to say that Yuki had promised me some "adult" fun once we reached the summit of the next vista. With her lean figure and trim muscles, she was a compelling package that I could rarely keep my hands off of. She always said the same of me, especially when I allowed my hair to grow out into a ponytail, which I often did.

We were in our early twenties, both going to a local college to become personal trainers. We'd met while learning about advanced nutrition from an older woman who was still in fit condition and insisted on teaching the class in workout clothes, as she would often have us run laps to get us to work up an appetite to eat some of the healthier snacks she'd make us prepare.

"How can you expect to promote it if you haven't tried it?" she'd said as I'd gagged on a seaweed milkshake, much to Yuki's amusement. I'd been just as amused when she'd sampled the jalapeno chips, so I didn't feel too bad about the embarrassment I'd had that day.

We'd taken to each other like fire to wood, and of late had taken an interest in outdoor sports. This would have been our thirty-second time scaling the mountains, taking a new path each time so that we could enjoy the challenge.

Up on the mountain, we'd been steadily climbing since dawn the previous day, using pitons, rope, and harnesses to keep us safe while we used climbing picks to establish footholds. I'd had a cramp in my right leg for at least three hundred feet, but hadn't said anything out of fear that Yuki would make fun of me. Suddenly, I heard her gasp from above me.

Looking up, my eyes widened as I saw her pulling her arm back from a hole she'd caved in through a thin sheet of shale. She looked down at me, her short black hair done up in a ponytail with her eyes wide.

"What?" I asked, curious. "Do we need to find a path around?"

She shook her head and cleared her throat, a sudden gust of wind tugging at us to pull us from the cliff face like beetles from a tree. When it passed, she just peered down at me with a growing smile.

"I think I found something," she said, excited at the prospect.

"Like what?" I asked. It wasn't uncommon to find old mines or hidden alcoves where natives had rested only to die from exposure while on a climb. Despite the summer weather we'd both been wearing long sleeves and tight, heat-trapping leggings.

"I think I found a passage," she cried out as the wind passed, taking her pick and swinging with one hand, shattering the shale covering. Sharpened slivers fell past me and down into the mists below. I remember how it clattered noisily on the way down. Looking up, my eyes widened as I took in the sight of something I had never seen before while on a climb.

A door–well, a set of double doors, to be precise — made from some old wood that'd weathered the cold well enough. The solidly built doors hung on iron hinges and had handles that formed a V when they came together. A letter G had been drawn in flowing script on the surface of the doors, although it was hard to see as the paint was old and flaking.

Yuki climbed up into the tunnel, which ran about four feet before stopping at the doors. I followed after her, pulling myself over the lip onto flooring that had been laid with small flagstones.

"What do you suppose it means?" Yuki asked, walking up to the door to run a hand over the G, wiping away the top-most layer of dust from it. She turned and looked at me, eyes sparkling with inner light. "It looks like nobody has disturbed it, like, ever!"

"I've never heard of anything like this being out here in the mountains," I said, shaking my head. I rubbed the back of my neck and reached into a side pouch to pull out my smartphone. Looking at it, I wasn't surprised at the lack of cellular service. I flicked on its light and camera before pointing it at Yuki.

"So, Ms. Onodera, what do you think of your most recent find?" I asked in a mock-serious tone, causing her to spin around to stare at me.

She gave me a saucy wink and cocked her hip to the side. "Well, if I had to make a guess, I'd say that this is the work of aliens!"

"Really? Aliens?" I laughed loud and hard. "You watch that show way too much babe…"

"What? You know it can't be any natives, they didn't build with metal. And look," she exclaimed, pointing at the iron hinges covered in dust and built-up grime, "metal! And this is on a sheer cliff! Who else would build into a sheer cliff?"

"Not arguing that it's strange," I said, shaking my head. "Just saying that jumping to aliens seems silly, as this could have easily been done by people. Lot of people inhabited America for the past few hundred years, who knows who did this?"

"I say we crack it open and look!" Yuki said, pulling her smartphone out as she reached for the handles.

"Wait!" I said, putting my hand on hers to stop her. "Are you sure that's wise? It was pretty well hidden; what if it has some, I don't know, *historical* value or something? Maybe we should climb down and get some experts up here?"

"C'mon Eric, don't be a pussy!" Yuki exclaimed, throwing my hand off. "We'll just poke around a bit and see what's on the inside. If it's some strange burial chamber, we'll back out and leave it for the experts. I just want to see what we discovered."

"I don't know..." I said, looking out of the tunnel and into the fog surrounding the mountains.

"Oh, show some backbone!" she growled, slapping me on the ass as she pushed the door open. With a long and low creak, the door swung inward, its bottom grinding against the flagstone path set into the wide, squat tunnel.

Inside, our phones provided feeble light against the crushing darkness of the passage. I still remember the smell of old grease and iron that wafted in the stale air, the stench of an old workshop that'd been long forgotten.

The light from our phones was enough to light up most of the tunnel, had we kept them aimed in one direction, but Yuki was too busy running hers along the wall in search of any clue as to what this strange building was. Past the doors, the tunnel walls were made from slabs of cut granite stacked together like Lego blocks. The slabs were set seamlessly into each other, devoid of any mortar. I'd read of societies in Central America making structures from heavy stone by fitting blocks into each other and allowing gravity to hold them together, but I'd never expected to see an example of this in the United States.

"This is amazing!" I said, running a hand along the wall to feel how the seams were so closely pressed together, to the point where one could barely tell there was a difference between one block and the next.

"I know," Yuki replied. She aimed her light to the ceiling, which prompted me to look up.

Great curved pieces of stone, each easily weighing over a ton, sat perched atop the walls. The curved panels converged in the middle of the room, each supporting the other like stones set in an archway.

Hanging from the roof were lengths of old chain that drooped like vines. None of them were the same length—it gave the impression that these chains had once supported something, but

149

whatever it was had caused the chains to snap with the passage of time. I glanced around the chamber, but could not find anything on the floor that might once have been suspended from those chains.

Yuki approached a length of chain and studied it. An old, blackened crust sat at the end of it; the mass crumbled when Yuki prodded it with her phone. The links were stuck together, held in place by the gunk that seemed to be as old as the chain itself.

"What do you suppose that is?" I asked.

Yuki shrugged. "Maybe they used to hold candles, and it's a buildup of wax?"

"Crunchy wax?" I asked, snorting at her suggestion.

"You have a better idea?"

"No," I said after a moment, reaching out to poke at the gunk with a gloved hand. It crumbled like crystallized honey, falling to bits that reflected a deep violet in the light. Looking at flakes, I frowned. "They almost look like gemstones, but they can't be."

"Like amethyst?" Yuki asked.

I nodded, proud that she remembered the work we'd been doing on our *one* required science class. We'd both selected Geology because of how often we went climbing.

I looked her over as I lifted the chain a bit, turning it in the light. "Wonder what it is? And why the chain is embedded in the stone?"

"I think there's more to this than we can tell at the moment. Think about it. The door looked out of place—Old World European, if I had to guess. The architecture in here reminds me of an old church. And hell, I don't know how they shaped the rocks and got them into this tunnel so easily."

I nodded. Granite wasn't easy to cut, or shape, and here we had thousands of blocks placed in perfect symmetry to hold together a tunnel deep into the mountain. Judging by the scent of the catacombs, I guessed that the place was older than anywhere else I'd ever been. It smelled of old earth and dry stone. Not a trace of water could be detected, and the sweat from our bodies and frost dripping from us was the first moisture to have entered the chamber probably since before America was founded.

151

Rubbing my thumb over the crumbling bits of crust at the end of the chain, I frowned as a new scent filled the air. A coppery tang lingered the more I played with the chain, one that to this day reminds me of dark things lurking just beyond one's sight The chain had a build-up of the material that, even to this day, confounds me as to its purpose. Once thing was certain, though—it reeked of blood.

But I'll get to that later.

Moving on from that chamber, we entered another room that looked similar to the first. Yuki led the way, going on and on about how exciting the place was. Me? I was creeped out. The floor was covered with what looked like a bedding of silk that rose up to our knees. The further in we walked, the more I felt as if we were delving into some alien world.

We reached a spiral staircase heading downward. I had my doubts about pressing on, but Yuki insisted. The stairs wound around a stone column covered in spider webs and dust. Even through the grime, I could see some old writing carved into the stone. I brushed away the cobwebs and instantly recoiled as a dozen spiders spilled out of the webs I had disturbed. Their fat brown bodies and spindly legs flooded out of the opening as I jumped back.

"Are you all right?" Yuki asked.

I swatted at my arm with my other hand, brushing the spiders off me. "Yeah," I huffed, "I think so." My eyes settled upon the writing on the column, and I took a surprised breath.

"What is it?" Yuki asked.

Leaning in close to touch the writing on the column, I murmured, "It's in English." Cautiously, I swept away more of the spider webs and read aloud. "We know that we are all children of God, and the whole world is under control of the evil one..." I glanced at Yuki. "Odd. That has to be a Bible verse, huh?"

"Sounds like one," Yuki agreed. "Makes you wonder about this place even more, don't it?"

"Yeah. Let's keep moving. There are spiders everywhere, so keep your eyes open for webs. Don't want you getting bit."

"I'd just let you suck out the venom," she said, turning her head to wink at me.

She giggled when I slapped her ass.

The stairs let out into an open room that I would have mistaken for a cavern had it not been for the finished quality of its interior. The floors were tiled and the walls were polished smooth. Looking at the musty white stone flecked with sparkling bits of gold, I cursed under my breath.

Yuki noticed, and asked me what was wrong.

"The floor is covered in marble tile," I explained. "*Marble*, Yuki. That means it was dug up from somewhere far away and brought here to be laid down. There is no way this could have been done by some rag-tag group of settlers or natives. This was planned, extensively."

The clinking of metal on metal above our heads drew my attention. "And to top it off, the ceiling here is outside of our lights' range, and has chains hanging from it. Have you any idea how difficult it might have been to build this place?"

Yuki nodded her agreement. "Look up there," she said, pointing to a strand of chain that ended in a large hook. A dry-rotted basket hung sideways from it; its other support had broken off long ago.

"Well, that's new," I said, stepping forward to examine it further.

Ahead of us was a new section of the cavern that resembled a workspace. In with us were an anvil, a forge, and a dry-rotted workbench covered in ancient blacksmithing tools. To the right of the table was a pile of ingots, all dusty and mussed with detritus, which reflected a faint golden sheen when our cellphone lights swept over them.

Yuki stopped in her tracks, seemingly unable to speak.

"Baby?" I asked. "You okay?"

"G-G-Gold!" she stammered. "So much of it! Imagine what it's worth!"

"Imagine how hard it would be to get it down from here," I had to remind her. "We're just two people, with canvas backpacks already loaded with survival gear *that we need*. Take some photos of it, and keep it in mind to tell our grandkids one day."

"Surely one bar won't be too much, would it?" Yuki asked, but by then I'd moved on to the forge. Within the furnace was a mixture of slag and refuse that would need to be cleaned out to make the forge serviceable again.

I turned my attention to the table. Atop a tarnished silver plate sat a chunk of meat rotted down to a shriveled husk. Beside the plate was a cup, its contents little more than sediment and murky sludge left behind after the liquid within had dried up.

"Someone left here quickly," I said, looking back to Yuki as she stood up to face me. "And I mean fast. They left their meal here and didn't come back. The forge has a lot of leftover trash metals in it, too — it would have been cleaned out if whoever was here intended to return to work."

In a broken barrel beside the forge was a half-finished sword. "Look at this," I said, pulling it out. The cross-guard was incomplete, leaving a bare handle wrapped in rotten leather. "See? It's ruined. No blacksmith would leave this half-finished."

I jumped when I heard a rattling of chains from above, and pointed my light towards the ceiling. I saw nothing but darkness and swaying metal links. Yuki was busy studying some intricate handles set aside on a workbench and didn't seemed to notice, so I wrote it off as my nerves getting the better of me.

"Come on, let's explore further," I said, tossing the sword to the ground.

The two of us approached an open doorway that showed signs of a struggle. Its hinges had been broken off their supports. Shards of rotted wood littered the floor.

Walking through the narrow passage, we entered a massive hall that held a number of workstations. All around us were forges of various sizes with pipes leading from a vat that had a coal burning stove beneath it. The equipment was in a terrible state of disrepair.

I took a step forward and my foot bumped into something that made me stumble, but Yuki caught me before I could fall. When I looked to see what it was I'd tripped over, my pulse raced.

A human skeleton lay strewn out on the floor. The bones had been broken in several places, and from our vantage point, they almost looked hollow, as though the marrow had been sucked out. Its hand lay a few feet from where we stood. In its clutch was a rusted sword, its blade covered in the black sludge we'd seen earlier.

Yuki gasped and covered her mouth to stifle a scream.

Further into the room were four more skeletons. Like the first, their bones had been hollowed out and pitted. Following the trail of bodies, I stopped in my tracks upon finding a pile of bones as high as my hip.

"Jesus," I said under my breath as I shined my light from one side of the pile to the other. These people had tried to fight back against what killed them. This much I could tell from the assortment of weapons among the bones—ancient weapons: morning star maces, swords, and hammers. It chilled my blood just thinking that they never had a chance. That these bodies were stacked so high in this spot meant whatever killed them did so quickly and efficiently.

Yuki took photos of the remains, the flash of her camera dazzling me for a moment. I turned and told her not to do that just as I heard the clinking of chains wriggling in the air.

"Yuki?" I said, turning to look at her.

She was stock still, frozen in place as eight chains slid out of the darkness above her. Each of the chains ended in jagged barbs. I tried to find my voice, but couldn't, as I stared at the chains slowly easing themselves around her.

"What is it?" she said.

Those were her last words ever.

Suddenly, the chains all lashed themselves around her, the barbs sinking into her flesh. She thrashed against the restraints but it was futile—she looked like a marionette flailing against its strings. The chains ensnared her torso and legs, leaving one arm—the one with the cellphone—to thrash about helplessly.

I stared in shock as she was pulled up into the darkness, the light of her phone revealing a spider web of interconnected chains.

The light flashed over a pockmarked vermillion mass of flesh. It had massive arms but no legs, and its skin was pierced with great iron rings from which the chains hung. I couldn't see its face, or even if it had one, but its giant pair of golden eyes flashed each time Yuki's light crossed them.

I screamed and ran. Blinded by panic, I headed further into the cavern instead of back the way we had come. The light from my cellphone barely illuminated my path. I soon found myself in a room hardly larger than a closet. It was stuffed to overflowing with the bones of those who had made their last stand here. I realized this too late to stop in time and crashed into a wall of bones. The impact put me on my ass and jostled the bones so they spilled out, nearly covering me. I scrabbled away on hands and knees, and once I was on my feet again, I snatched up a sword that had emerged from the pile and made a break for it.

Heading back through the chamber where the beast had taken Yuki, I kept my head down and ran for all I was worth. I could not see the monster or its chains, but I could hear it—it ate noisily, sucking on Yuki's blood in horrible wet slurps as chunks of her meat hit the ground in sodden splatters. I was almost clear of the chamber when a chain lashed out and constricted around my ankle. It yanked my leg backward, sending me into a headfirst dive. I screamed as the barbs cut through tendons, ripping the meat from my bones. Meanwhile, the rustles from the darkness meant other chains were whizzing forward to take me.

I turned over onto my back and swung the blade at the chain. The sword lopped the chain clean off, leaving only the end that was still embedded in my foot. This bought me enough time to get back on my feet and start hobbling away.

I hadn't gotten too far when the mass of chains caught up to me. I choked up on my sword and swung it like a baseball bat, lopping the ends of the chains off in one fell swoop. A roar of pain from deep within the cavern accompanied a shower of scalding oil that

157

doused the exposed parts of my body. I screamed again, covering my face in the crook of my arm to protect my eyes as the chains I'd severed thrashed on the floor like cut lizard's tails, each of them spewing more of that foul, stinging fluid. The creature drew back, buying me a few more precious seconds to get away.

I limped through the long tunnel that led to the entry portico, looking over my shoulder every so often for signs of the monster. While I couldn't see it, I could hear the clinking of its chains following me from just beyond the reach of my light. When finally I could see the exit and the daylight pouring through it, I redoubled my efforts. I was almost home, I told myself.

And then it emerged again—great lengths of chain, like spider legs, surged forward and latched into crevices in the stone to drag the bloated figure along. Its lower torso consisted of ragged, torn flesh, looking like it had been pulled apart in a vicious accident. Its skin was burned and red, scarred beyond recognition, and heavily muscled. Its bald head was tiny in comparison to its torso, and set into it were those blazing yellow eyes, looking like a pair of caution lights.

With a final heave, I flung myself through the door to the outside world and dragged myself arm over arm away from the hatch. The monster recoiled from the daylight, stopping just short of the door. Glowering at me with its inhuman face, it flung something at me that was caked in gore before retreating into the shadows. The object skittered along the ground and came to rest beside my feet. Then, with a frustrated roar, the monster seized the door grips with its chains and shut the door on itself.

It took me hours to get back to civilization. By the time I did, I was weak and near delirious from blood loss. My foot was a mangled mess.

Naturally, the police got involved. They would never believe the truth, and so I told them that Yuki and I had been attacked by a bear in the mountains. I had to tell them something, or else they would suspect I had killed Yuki on our climb. I showed them her cracked and bloodied cellphone as proof — what the monster had flung at me before retreating — and it was enough to convince them not to charge me with murder-one.

But I know the truth of what really happened that day. I know the secret of Grizzly Peaks. I haven't spoken about this in so long, and I doubt I ever will again. Every time I close my eyes, I see those monstrous yellow eyes staring back at me; every time I go to sleep, I hear it tearing Yuki's flesh in gobs to suck the marrow from her bones.

It's too much to bear, and I fear I don't have long for this world. If you have any sense, you'll think twice before you try climbing those mountains, else you'll find the door and the nightmare that lurks behind it.

ABOUT THE AUTHOR
NICHOLAS PASCHALL

Born and raised in Texas, Nicholas Paschall started his career in writing at an early age, jotting down stories on scraps of paper when he could and saving them to read aloud at lunch to all his friends. The teachers, upon learning this, asked him to stop as the stories weren't exactly school-friendly, but this only spurred him on to continue his career as a writer.

After a stint as a journalist and editor, he started his career as a horror author. It was brought on by reading a book he found dull and listless, which, after lending it to a coworker, he was informed it was terrifying. He thought he could do better, and has been publishing ever since.

He's been published in nineteen different printed anthologies and magazines, served two years as a recurring columnist for *Dark Eclipse Magazine*, and is a current columnist for *The London Horror Society*. His work can be found across the web, where he spins new yarns for all to enjoy on a daily basis.

Visit him at www.nickronomicon.com.

STRATOSPHERE HEIGHTS, NEW JERSEY

BY: ANTONIO SIMON, JR.

Stratosphere Heights?

That place shut down before I was born.

No, that's not right.

Wait... ah yes, I remember now. I wrote an article on the place a while back for a book the historical society was putting together.

It was built in 1896 and stood until the mid-sixties, when they tore it down to make room for a freeway on-ramp. They used to call it the eighth wonder of the world. In those days, you could get away with making big claims like that one. Those were different times, before laws against false advertising and the generalized cynicism that has since settled into society like a hardening of the arteries.

It was a fine place. My dad took me there several times when I was a kid. Its steeplechase was taller even than Coney Island's (by inches, so the claim was debatable), though its hot dogs beat Coney's by a mile. Jersey Bombers, they called those dogs, their world-famous one-pound beef franks nestled into buttered buns they toasted on the grills. The park also had its version of the big swing, a bunch of rollercoasters, a tunnel of love, a Ferris wheel — just about everything you'd expect to find in a top-notch amusement park of its day.

Which is exactly what it was.

Just past the ticket-taker's gate was the grand carrousel, the park's centerpiece. It was the biggest one of its kind I've ever seen, even to this day. The platform was so wide that the animals rode four abreast, and it had more than just horses. It had zebras, it had giraffes, but my favorite was the ostrich. There was only one, so my brother and I fought over who got to ride it. I was bigger, so I often beat him to the ostrich, and he'd have to settle for riding the rhino. It was either that or the sleigh, but that was no fun because the sleigh didn't bob like the animals did.

And when the ride operator rang the bell, that was when you knew to reach for the brass ring, because if you snagged one of those you got a free ride. I swear, one time I caught so many rings in a row that my butt was planted in that ostrich's saddle for the better part of an afternoon.

By the time I was in my teens, the place had already started to go into decline. Times were changing, and so was the neighborhood. Admission wasn't free anymore, but for your money you also got a few new rides. They put up a log flume, a glass house, a carnival midway—even a petting zoo.

There was a girl I knew in high school, her name was Daisy Lattoure. Her dad owned the Chevy dealership outside of Newark, which made him practically the richest man in the county. Everybody in my grade had a crush on Daisy, but only I had the gumption to ask her out. Wouldn't you know it, she said yes! That weekend, I took her out to the Heights. I even got fresh with her in the tunnel of love—she was game, and I wasn't one to quit while I was ahead.

Ah, it was such a nice place... I really wish my father would have taken me while it was up and running. I never got the chance to visit when I was a kid, you see. It's a shame what happened to the place, too. They tore it down in '66 to build the interstate, but it had been closed down for a while before then because of an incident that happened there.

Toward the end of the amusement park's life, the neighborhood around it got rough. That part of the city got more than its fair share of muggings and murders, but if there was one person who finally drove the nails that sealed the park's coffin shut, it was the Jersey cannibal.

They never caught the guy, and not for lack of trying. It's not like he was very good at covering his tracks either. It's said the cannibal took at least five victims. The police would find their bodies dumped at the beach, or in a park, or in an alley trash bin. He liked girls. All of them would have bite marks all over their bodies, mostly on the thighs, the buttocks—like he chewed the meat right off them while they were still alive.

Those were scary times. I remember the police coming to my school every week to talk to us about the cannibal. It was mostly neighborhood awareness stuff, like not talking to strangers and what to do if you believe you're being tailed home by someone suspicious.

163

Things really hit home for me when one of my classmates missed a week of school. We didn't know it at the time, and the family was tight-lipped about it, but the cannibal had taken a girl by the name of Daisy Lattoure. It was such a shame—she had a heart of gold, which you wouldn't expect from a girl from a rich family. Her dad used to own Lattoure Chevy, you know. Not Rockefeller money by any stretch, but the Lattoures lived well.

They found her body impaled on the wrought iron fence that surrounded the Heights. She was hanging sideways, her belly run through on a fence spike that entered her abdomen just above the hip, arms down by her drooping head and legs sticking out the other way, looking like a cheerleader frozen in the act of performing a cartwheel. The cheeks on either side of her face had been gnawed away, exposing her full complement of teeth gleaming white through rivulets of blood that streamed off her pink gums. The cannibal must have considered her street food—I bet he thought he'd catch a quick bite and then stick her someplace out of the way, so he could come back and nibble on her some more after she'd been cured in the sun like a ham.

I can joke about it now—hell, enough time has passed since to take the edge off—but back when that all was still fresh, it was horrible.

About twenty years after the murders, the newspaper ran a piece on the cannibal. Short of the bodies, there wasn't much hard information on him, and so the piece focused on the rampant speculation that arose in the killer's wake.

Although the police never corroborated it, it was believed the cannibal holed up in the tunnel of love at the Heights after the place closed for the night. I never believed that—who would? It was too sensational to be true. The park operators flat-out denied that rumor as well, but people started to doubt their credibility when they posted a night watchman to patrol the grounds.

Interestingly enough, when the paper interviewed the security guard years later, he claimed he spent most nights outside the tunnel of love. When asked for his reasons, he said he believed it was the place most trespassers would likely want to hang around in, what with its being dark and inconspicuous. It didn't stop some people from thinking he was the cannibal, but there never was enough evidence to file charges, so the murder cases remained cold.

But did that place ever leave a legacy. You know, having visited the park once or twice while it was in operation, I'm glad it got shut down. The place was a veritable death trap. Everything—every single thing about it was subpar, from the rides to the concession stands, to the people who frequented the place.

For starters, the Heights was in a rough neighborhood. Assuming you got to the Heights without getting stabbed to death, its attractions threatened to finish the job. Mind you, this was back before there were rules for proper restraints and safety inspections. It had two rollercoasters, both made of wood, built in the twenties. Looking back, I remember those things swaying whenever the wind blew. It's a wonder they didn't topple under their own weight. Hell, some of the holes that dry rot had bitten into their timbers were as big around as my fist.

Which is not to say you were safe on any of the other rides—one time, a girl got her hand caught in the machinery that ran the carrousel. The gears mangled her hand so badly you couldn't tell it from ground beef. Another time, a passenger in the big swing got killed when the chains supporting his seat came loose while the ride was going full tilt. They found his body lying in a crumpled heap on the roof of a dry cleaner's two blocks away. And then there was that rumor about some crazed killer named the Jersey cannibal who supposedly bedded down each night in the tunnel of love. They never caught him, but he supposedly killed five people. I never bought into those rumors about the cannibal, and the police didn't either. It was all an urban legend, as far as everyone was concerned.

Wild rumors aside, injuries and deaths occurred pretty regularly at the Heights, not that any of this ever made the news. Oh no— moneyed interests controlled the park, and they were too invested to let bad press get in the way of admission ticket sales.

Back when I used to write for the historical society, I interviewed the son of the guy who owned the park. His name was Ron Lattoure, Jr. People don't speak about them much anymore but back in their day, the Lattoures had money. Ronnie's dad owned Lattoure Chevy just outside of Newark, and he was easily the richest man in the county.

The park was a side venture for the family's primary business. Just weeks after purchasing the Heights, Lattoure realized that the park was more expensive to operate than he'd been led to believe, but he was in too deep to simply bow out. To keep the place running, he had to siphon his dealership's profits into the failing park, putting his family's fortune at risk.

Then, sometime during the park's 1964 operating season, a virulent rash of botulism poisoning broke out. Between the summer heat and the rapid-onset digestive tract failures, people were dropping dead in their homes. It got so bad that the Center for Disease Control was called in to investigate. Using the data they compiled in interviews along with statistical research, they made Venn diagrams of the affected neighborhoods that showed Stratosphere Heights was ground-zero for the outbreak. The culprit in every case: its infamous Jersey Bomber hot dogs.

With health authorities literally making a federal case out of the unsanitary condition of the park's eateries, the Lattoures could not escape scrutiny. The Heights closed in the middle of '64, promising new attractions coming in 1965—a log flume and a glass house among them. These never materialized. Unbeknownst to anyone except the Lattoure family's inner circle, the Heights had been sold to the New Jersey Roadway Authority for pennies on the dollar. The cost of keeping the park afloat had all but depleted the family fortune, but selling it to the state had staunched the bleeding. Unfortunately, the last-minute sale proved to be too little, too late. The Lattoures did not recoup enough in proceeds to keep their dealership running during a lean 1965 sales year, and in March of 1966, they shuttered up that business as well.

Knowing that it was only a matter of time before the bulldozers came for the park, I took my camera and drove out to the Heights, looking to snap some photographs before demolition work could begin. I was stopped at the park entrance by a policeman who threatened to arrest me for trespassing if I didn't turn around and go home. The officer was noticeably on edge—and rightfully so, as those were tense times, what with talk of a deranged cannibal terrorizing the neighborhood. I got back in my car and drove off, and that was the last time I saw the Heights in person. Nearly a year to the day after the Lattoures sold the land, the wrecking ball made quick work of the park, leaving the ground perfectly flat and clear so that the on-ramp could go up in its place.

I tell you, I was sad to see the park go. There was so much history there. I don't mean just personal history either, though some of my fondest childhood memories were formed at the Heights. If memory serves me, I visited there every summer until I was well into my twenties. The place stood for seventy years; that's plenty of time to deserve its own place on the stage of history... and to garner secrets.

You see, before the park was demolished, I managed to sneak in and take photographs. I've got an album full of photos back home. Once the Heights had shuttered up for good in '64, the park's owners didn't think to hire a security guard to keep people out. Stingy bastards—they were easily the richest family in the county and yet they didn't spare a few bucks to post a guard out front.

Oh, about that: it's a little known fact that the Heights was owned by the Lattoure family—that's right, the same family that owned Lattoure Chevy outside of Newark.

You knew that? Oh.

Well, in any event, I jumped the perimeter fence one night, armed only with my camera. The lights were still on inside — the Heights was in a rough part of town, and its owners thought it would deter vandalism if they kept the lights on all night.

The park was in a sorry state. The garden between the front gates and the ticket-taker's booths was reduced to a mound of weeds and wilted annuals. A pile of splintered wood lay at the center of the gazebo where its roof had at last succumbed to the elements and collapsed. It had taken out one of the four support beams in its fall, leaving the remaining three looking like a deformed hand reaching skyward for help that would never come.

It was eerily quiet. Despite knowing I had the park to myself, I could not shake the feeling I was being watched. Rumors had cropped up around this time about a lunatic called the Jersey cannibal. While I never placed much stock in urban legends, these tales were printworthy enough for the tabloids that ran them with gusto every week.

I hopped the turnstile and pressed on. My paranoid thoughts vanished once I was inside the park. I was the proverbial kid in the candy store. With all the wonderful memories I'd made here, having the park all to myself made me giddy with excitement.

Dead ahead stood the grand carrousel, its burnished bronze aglow under the incandescent floodlights, its menagerie of animals frozen in a manic race that bore out no winners. My heart raced as I approached the carrousel's sole ostrich and stroked its bald head lovingly, with an almost holy reverence that is reserved solely for the relics of the greatest of saints. Vandals had defiled my trusty steed's body, having carved obscene marks into her flank with pocket knives. And yet despite the years and abuse, here she was, having faithfully abided these ignominies to await the return of her rider.

Before I was too sure of what I was doing, I stuck a foot into her stirrup and slung myself into the saddle. All at once that very moment, the dark of night was swept away, replaced by the brilliance of the rose-tinted afternoons of yesteryear. The Wurlitzer organ came to life with a bright and lively rendition of John Philip Sousa's *Sabre and Spurs*. I hugged the ostrich's neck to my chest with both arms and shut my eyes as the carrousel platform spun ever faster.

The music ended in time with the ride. I reopened my eyes and my heart skipped a beat on seeing Stratosphere Heights once again in its prime.

Was this a dream?

Was I reliving a memory?

It didn't matter. It was real enough for me.

The glass house stood intact and gleaming as new in the sunlight. The big swing spun, its chairs a blur against the rosy afternoon backdrop. The Ferris wheel turned in regal and mighty revolutions, its gondolas packed to bristling with smiling faces. The air was full of laughter and balloons and the scent of fresh-cut grass and—I sniffed the air again, unable to believe what my nose was telling me—Jersey Bombers. In the stand across the way, hot dog links sizzled by the dozen on electric flat grills alongside buttered buns lined up like ready war planes on an aircraft carrier.

And then, suddenly, from out of the tunnel of love there came a light like a train's headlamp. The light rolled out from the tunnel's entrance, growing ever brighter as it spilled out into the park, engulfing everything in its brilliance. The light swept wide to the sides—first the left, then the right—and in that moment I could not help but liken the shape they had taken to a pair of gleaming wings.

A shape emerged from the light between the wings. It was a face as white as alabaster, and as smooth as the finest marble. It had two eyes as fiery blue as the brightest sapphires, and yet with all the vibrancy those eyes contained, they held within them a profound and inexplicable sadness.

The face drew close, fixing me to the spot with those mournful eyes.

It smiled.

Then its lips drew apart, and the face breathed a whisper so softly that only I could hear.

It said: "Forget."

And that's all I know about the Lattoures.

Oh, Stratosphere Heights?

Heh, heh.

That's a funny name.

I can't say I know of any such place, though.

You might want to ask the Lattoures. They were a pretty important family around here back in the day.

Mr. Lattoure, Ron was his name, he owned a Chevy dealership and was the richest man in the county...

About The Author
Antonio Simon, Jr.

Antonio Simon, Jr. is a best-selling author of several books. He began writing professionally in 2013. His debut novel, an adventure/comedy titled *The Gullwing Odyssey*, achieved critical and commercial success in 2014. Since getting his start in fantasy, he has branched out into other genres. His work has been published alongside masters of horror Stephen King and Guy N. Smith. His non-fiction delves into obscure and esoteric topics.

Mr. Simon holds a law degree from St. Thomas University. He earned simultaneous B.A.'s from the University of Miami in Political Science and History. His writing has won the prestigious Royal Palm Literary Award, the International Book Award, and the Florida Authors & Publishers Association's President's Book Award.

He is one of the founders of Darkwater Media Group and serves as its Head of Business Development. Within the company, he is known as "the duke," although whether he is in fact royalty of any place real or imaginary remains anyone's guess.

DERBIGNY HOMESTEAD, VERMONT

BY: APARA MOREIYA

March 29, 1936.

You who find these papers, gather them up and turn back now. It's my hope they will serve to warn you and others of what happened to me.

I was a pilot for an aerial land surveying company. We held a state contract to modernize Vermont's land title recording system. I was hired to take aerial photos we'd later piece together into a complete map of the state.

One day, while out on assignment, my plane got caught in a storm. I'm still not certain what happened, and my memory grows hazier by the minute, but that storm downed my plane.

I crash-landed into a bog. By the time I came to my senses, the front half of the fuselage was buried in the mud, with the tail sticking out in the air. I was hurt—my right kneecap was a twisted, bloody mess.

I crawled out of the wreck and patched myself up with gauze and splints from my first-aid kit. There was a largish piece of dead wood nearby; I used this as a crutch and set out in search of help.

It was impossible to tell what time of day it was when I crashed. The bog was an expanse of dusky green twilight. No sunlight made it through the tree canopy above. I had to rely only upon the lightning bugs and the occasional swamp gas flare for light.

After what seemed like forever, I pushed through the overgrowth and found myself in a clearing about fifty yards across. Ahead of me was a dry sinkhole. Ringing the depression were concentric circles of scorched land. The burn marks grew in severity the closer you got to the hole—brown at its furthest extent and black nearest the center. As I had a bad leg and didn't want to risk backtracking through the marsh, I pressed on into the cleaning, thinking it would make for easier travel.

That was a big mistake.

As I rounded the depression, some of the ground I tread upon sluiced away from under my feet. I slid down into the hole, crashing feet-first against a bizarre stone that sat half buried at its middle.

The stone was gray with green blotches that were not moss. It was mostly round except for where it bore shallow craters the size of dinner plates. It was about the size of one of those orange dock buoys people use to keep boats from crashing into piers when the sea gets choppy.

Suddenly, the rock began to let up an electrical hum. I panicked, scrabbling with hands and feet to get out of the hole. Once I was safely out of the depression, I saw smoke seeping out of cracks on the rock's surface, followed by shafts of green light. The light swept the breadth of the clearing and struck me. There was an instant of blinding pain, like my insides were being cooked, and I fell.

When next I woke up, I was still in the clearing. The stone in the pit was dark and cold. I doubted whether I'd actually experienced the strange goings-on of a moment ago, but when I checked myself for injuries, I got all the proof I needed. A large triangular swathe had been burned into the front of my shirt. Beneath it, my chest was hairless—all the hair singed off—and the skin red, sore, and covered in tightly-packed blisters that wept clear fluid.

I got to my feet with the aid of the bough I used as a walking stick, and pressed on.

I walked for what felt like forever. As I had no idea where I was, heading in any direction was as good as any other. I walked in as straight a line as I could from the site of the wreck to make it easy to retrace my steps later.

I came upon an old house. Dilapidated wooden eaves frowned onto a dark front porch. I hobbled to the front stoop and glanced through the window, which was covered in such a thick layer of dust and damp that the glass was opaque. No lights burned within.

I banged on the door. When this got me no response, I tried again, and that netted me a shout from within.

A grizzled old man emerged from the house's shadowy recesses. He was bald and sported an Amish beard that was filthy, unkempt, and stark white, except around his lips where tobacco juice had stained it brown. His jaundiced yellow eyes sat at the bottom of wrinkled dark pits in his face. He shoved his plug of tobacco to his opposite cheek, revealing a mouth that was a checkerboard pattern of missing and present teeth. He wore flannel and denim overalls that were more patches and holes than fabric.

After glaring at me in silence, he introduced himself as Cleophas Derbigny and let me inside.

The man was a hermit, though for what reason he would not divulge, except to say that he treasured his privacy. He sat me down on a moldy divan in his living room and fetched me a bowl of greasy stew. I would have declined, but I had gone too long without eating, and my next meal wasn't guaranteed. It was a squirrel broth—I could tell by the tiny bones—locally sourced, as the occasional shotgun pellet in my meal led me to believe. Disgusted by the whole affair, I ended up eating half and leaving the rest of the slop in the bowl.

We spoke. Cleophas was the sort who valued personal liberties above all else, and the right to privacy was foremost among those freedoms. He lived off the land, with no phone, no electricity, and none of the modern conveniences we take for granted.

When he said he kept hounds in a shed out back, I asked him if he was a breeder, just to make conversation. He shook his head vehemently and reiterated that he simply kept hounds; he neither bred nor raised them, which I found odd.

I brought up the sinkhole and the strange rock at its bottom. At the mention of this, the old man became agitated, calling the stone his "treasure rock" and running through a litany of justifications as to why he thought it was rightfully his: the bog had been his family's homestead since time immemorial; the land was his from the core of the earth to the heavens; and anything that should happen to land on his property was, by extension, also his property. He planned to sell the rock and make a fortune, once he figured out a way to remove it from its resting place.

Then he seemed to recant, as though realizing he'd made a mistake in expressing the value the rock held for him.

Our conversation became strained at this point. I stood up from the couch, thanking him for the meal and his hospitality, and then I promptly sat back down. My head was spinning.

Cleophas rose from his seat and went as though to catch me from falling, but couldn't move fast enough. He stood before me as I slouched into his ratty divan, shaking his head. He went to the kitchen, returning with a glass of water and a pair of morphine tablets, and the offer that I should stay the night.

I declined but he insisted, pointing out how swollen my knee had become from bearing my weight. It was only a few hours until daybreak, he'd said. In the morning, he would see me off with a meal and fresh bandages to stave off infection, but for now, all there was left to do was rest.

A thick sweat had broken on his forehead. His eyes seemed to jitter, as though he were anxious. He was plotting something, I knew — it was apparent on his face, and as much by the fact that he'd drugged my food. Nonchalantly as I could muster, I prodded my index finger into my injured knee, and the pain this caused jerked me awake the first few times. But once the drugs had begun to take effect in earnest, this tactic rendered less by way of results.

I took him up on his offer to stay the night. Injured as I was, I could offer little resistance. Smiling, he proffered the glass and tablets with nervous, shaky hands. I palmed the morphine and raised my hand to my lips, making as though I'd popped the tablets into my mouth. Then, as I drank the water, I discretely slipped the tablets into my pocket. Laying the theatrics on thick, I yawned and stretched my arms, all the while relating how tired I felt. My host bade me a good night and departed as I lay down on his smelly couch and pretended to sleep.

Sleep came easily enough, thanks to the sedatives, although I wasn't quite out when I heard a rustle come from the next room over.

Cleophas entered the living room with a wheelbarrow. He brought it up alongside me and tipped it forward, then grabbed me underneath the arms and hauled me into it. For such an old man, he was surprisingly strong. I continued to feign unconsciousness as he pushed the wheelbarrow out his front door and around to the side of the house. He set it down in front of a ramshackle shed that was little more than a lean-to made up of boards and metal siding. The old man fumbled with a ring of keys and, finding the right one, jammed it into the shed's padlocked entrance.

Once inside, he struck a match and held it up to an oily rag draped over a stick that served as a wall sconce. The fire caught on the rag, illuminating the shed's cramped interior.

Running the length of the shed were pens made from large wooden milk crates. Their bottoms had been cut out and the vertical joists in their corners sharpened into stakes which Cleophas had hammered into the turf to anchor the pens. Strands of barbed wire were looped over their tops to deter their inhabitants from leaping out.

Something stirred in the pens. First came the sound of frenzied movement, and then quick, ragged breaths, like an exhausted spaniel at the end of a hunt. This was, without doubt, where he kept his hounds, but why would he have brought me here, and drugged at that?

Cleophas took a broomstick from a shelf built into the wall and beat against the crates until the hounds quieted down. Then he came back out and pushed the wheelbarrow into the shed. Curious to see what breed these hounds were, I shifted my head slightly, so Cleophas wouldn't notice, and looked into the pens.

I honestly wish I hadn't. There are some things mortal eyes are not meant to behold.

I screamed and leaped out of the wheelbarrow, upending it, sending me to the floor of the shed. Cleophas stumbled backward and landed on his rear.

I sprang to my feet and leaned over the nearest crate, unable to believe my eyes.

It was no dog that was inside that pen. This thing he called a hound was completely hairless, covered in pink skin that looked too human for comfort, except that any semblance it had to humanity ended there. Its face was an elongated muzzle full of overly-long yellow teeth that jutted beyond its lips in either direction. It had no nose, but instead had two slits for nostrils. Its big brown eyes were the size of my fists and had no sclerae. Its paws ended in clubbed digits that vaguely resembled hands. It had sallow, runny skin that hung off its bones, which showed through the flesh. It stood on all fours, watching me with a dour expression, growling, gnashing its malformed mouth of twisted teeth at me.

Cleophas had not one of these creatures, but four of them, one to each pen. Only the fifth pen, at the far end of the shed, was empty.

I leaped onto Cleophas before he could stand and grabbed him by the collar, demanding to know the meaning of all this. By now, the morphine had worn off, and fresh adrenaline brought my senses to razor precision. He wasn't forthcoming at first, but a solid backhand to his face got him talking in short order.

The things he said... I was convinced the man was senile—at first. Only later did the meaning behind his words start to become apparent.

Several weeks ago, he was awoken in the middle of the night by an explosion. When he went to seek out what had caused the disturbance, he came upon the sinkhole I had run into the day before. Only, it is technically not a sinkhole. From one day to the next, the stone just appeared where it lies now, seemingly having fallen from the heavens despite that he had never conceived of such a thing in all his eighty years alive.

The night he discovered it, the rock was letting off steam as though it were extremely hot. It had scorched the earth at the point of impact, and small fires still burned here and there around the pit. Suddenly, a surge of green light shot from the stone. When Cleophas saw this, he turned and ran for home, and never went back.

I asked him whether the light touched him, and he shook his head.

Since then, he had encountered others trespassing on his homestead. For the most part, he had chased them away with his shotgun. Other times, though, people would show up at his doorstep pleading for help with their injuries. Nearly all of them were local hunters and trappers.

A swamp is a dangerous place, what with its quicksand, venomous snakes, malarial mosquitoes, and alligators, but Cleophas was a man of the wilds, and he knew how to deal with the perils that could befall one traveling through the marshes. And yet, he was not prepared for the injuries these strangers presented. Their wounds resembled burns—reddened skin, inflammation, blisters. When asked how they got those injuries, all of them said the same thing—a green light from Cleophas's "treasure rock."

As private a man as Cleophas was, he still clung to old-fashioned ideals of hospitality. He offered his visitors food and let them stay the night in his home before seeing them off in the morning. That was how he learned of the "changes."

Those things he called hounds, each and every one of them, were once men.

The next day, his visitors were worse for wear, complaining of intense muscle pain. The red welts at the site of their initial burns had formed a ring and had grown outward. Sallow, hairless skin sagged on their bodies within the ring of blisters. Their teeth grew long and sharp. One of them had an eye tooth that had grown so fast overnight, it had torn through his face and poked out through his lip. Their hands shriveled, their fingers hooking into fists that they used like a second set of feet when they went about on all fours.

When first Cleophas had seen them like this, he could not help but think they looked like hounds. It was apt to call them that, because by the second day they were growling and barking like wild dogs. He tried talking to them, but they could no longer reason. He tossed them some snake meat he had drying on a hook on the wall, thinking that might appease them, and indeed, that did. With a little time and training, his hounds proved capable hunters and loyal companions.

In time, more people would show up at Cleophas's door complaining of similar burns. Knowing the inevitable outcome of their injuries, he took to drugging his visitors and training them once their changes were complete. In Cleophas's mind, it was the most humane act he could perform, given the circumstances.

In a patronizing tone, he asked me if I agreed, patting my head and rustling my hair like I was some sort of lapdog. I batted his hand away in disgust, but deep down, some primal part of me liked the attention and longed for more. I tore myself away from him and hobbled off into the night as fast as my injured legs could carry me.

My bad knee throbbed with fierce hurt, as did my major joints — my wrists, ankles, and elbows. My body was on fire with fever. Sweat poured off my steaming body in sheets.

I felt as though my body were being molded into a new form from the inside out. I could feel my ribcage move, my hips shift. Walking upright became difficult, painful. Then I remembered those morphine tablets still in my pocket from last night and popped one into my mouth. I chewed it dry with awkward motions of my jaw — it didn't hinge where it was supposed to anymore, and some of my back teeth had grown so long that I couldn't close my mouth fully. Before I was too sure of what I was doing, I was on all fours, pawing at the ground like a dog. My first thought was to attempt to stand, but I put this notion aside. I covered ground faster on fours than I did upright, and I was pressed for time.

Eventually, I arrived at the crash site. In the hours my plane had spent in the mud, it had sunk so low that it was practically consumed by the swamp. Its tail stood at vertical, with only the rudder showing.

I scrounged the wreckage for my logbook and a fountain pen, and began taking down the notes you have in your hands presently. When I'm through, I'll jab the pen into my arm. I'll cut a straight line bisecting a large V and a small V at their vertices, fill it with ink and then seal it up with medical gauze — a makeshift tattoo resembling the wings and body of an airplane. Maybe, once I become one of those hounds, there will be enough of the old me left to look upon it and remember what I once was.

Already I can feel the changes taking hold of my mind.

It's getting harder to make sentences.

This is the end.

You who have read this, turn back now.

Take my notes to the police.

Warn people.

Stay out of Derbigny Homestead.

Stay away from the old man.

Stay away from the strange rock in the crater.

Stay away from the hound with the blue marks on his arm.

Because that would be me.

And I am not your friend.

I am Cleophas's friend.

Cleophas pats my head.

Cleophas is good.

I like Cleophas.

He gave me food once.

Maybe he has more.

I will go see.

ABOUT THE AUTHOR
APARA MOREIYA

Thrill seeker. Unbridled optimist. Sushi aficionado. Lover of terrible jokes. Free spirit. Friend to all. Sporting an outlook on life as unique as he, Apara writes equally distinctive poetry and fiction, and from time to time delves into the genres of fantasy and horror.

Apart from being Darkwater Syndicate's unofficial mascot (and unintentionally running up the company's fire insurance premiums), he is an associate editor working closely with Antonio Simon, Jr.

BISHOP,
MASSACHUSETTS

BY: STEPHANIE KELLEY

The bitter smell of ammonia and chemicals woke me. Or maybe it was the beeping of the machines. I wasn't exactly sure. It took me a few moments to orient myself.

A white-tiled hospital room was not where I had last closed my eyes. As far as I knew, I had fallen asleep in my tent listening to the sound of the waves and forest creatures. How or when I'd become the victim of an uncomfortable hospital bed had yet to reveal itself in my memories.

I shifted to alleviate the pain in my arm. The plastic-covered mattress protested as the tangle of cables and IV's became effective tethers.

My second attempt at moving was no better. The heart monitor belched its piercing sound into the tiny room as panic gripped me. There were restraints on my wrists and ankles.

Just then, a nurse walked in.

"He's waking up. You're not needed. He's fine." A gruff voice echoed off the wall behind me. That rough, mid-baritone growl belonged to my brother.

Even if his voice betrayed his annoyance with the current situation, it was a comfort to hear that familiar sound. It was hard to see him in the shadows, dressed in his black suede shearling lined jacket. He wore that thing everywhere lately, no matter the weather.

"I'll be the judge of that," the nurse snapped, moving toward me.

Courtney turned from the window, his steel gray eyes nearly glowing with the fluorescent lighting. His short-cropped, dark hair was slicked back out of his face. The shadows caught his high cheekbones, making him look a bit more menacing.

"Actually," he ground out, "the doctor already cleared him. I suggest you leave us alone so I can speak to my witness before you contaminate his memory."

"You're not—"

"Do I have to call your boss?" My brother still hadn't bothered to look at me.

"No, no sir. But I will tell his doctor that he is awake." There was a tremor in her voice that I didn't like. What had he threatened her with while I was passed out?

"Yeah, do that," he growled, fist clenching at his side. I could see the outline of his gun holster on his hip. My chest tightened.

I waited for the latch on the door to click before I spoke. "Thanks, Court."

My big brother grumbled as he turned back toward the window without looking at me. "What are you doing here, Alexis? My jurisdiction doesn't extend to Massachusetts. I can't keep doing this for you. They'll pull my badge."

So, he had been throwing his weight around again. I opened my mouth to extend my thanks, but he was right. There was no need to keep pulling him into my mess. "I'm sorry, Court. I don't remember calling you."

"You didn't. I'm listed as your emergency contact. That's the only reason I'm here. Are you going to tell me just what the hell you were doing up here looking for Bishop, Massachusetts?"

Courtney had not been a fan of me digging into our family's history in New England.

"I needed to get away. You know that." I forced the words, my head spinning as I fought down the rush of panic. I shifted uncomfortably on the bed, but couldn't move far. My stomach turned sour as I tugged at the restraints again. "What the hell,

Court? Why do they have me restrained? Not like I was in a position to just up and leave."

My brother snorted, turning from the window to look at me. "The only reason you're not tucked away in a psych ward right now is because I managed to convince them you hadn't tried to kill yourself."

"What are you talking about?" I snapped. I'd be the first to admit, I'd been depressed and testy since my last relationship fell apart, but suicidal, no. That wasn't the case.

"You had a rope tied around your neck, noose style. I managed to convince them it was from getting tangled in the debris from a ship you were on."

"Jedi mind trick again, huh?" I interjected, waving my fingers. Hot pain ran along my bones and deep into my shoulder on my left side.

"You're not funny."

"Gotcha, so bullying with a fake badge it is then," I said with a heavy sigh that rattled my body. I still felt like I was breathing the damp air of that island.

"Was I wrong?" He fumed. "What the hell were you doing in the water?"

"I wasn't." I hadn't been in the water.

Or more appropriately, I hadn't remembered being in the water.

Courtney shook his head at me, raking his fingers through that short brown hair, his eyes hard. A frustrated grumble poured from him in unintelligible syllables. Grandfather had taught us Welsh when we were children, but I remembered none of it. My brother, on the other hand, liked to slip into it when he was angry with me.

"English, Courtney, English," I mumbled, trying to adjust my position on the uncomfortable hospital bed.

Anger flashed on his face, his jaw tensing as he chewed the inside of his cheek.

"Say what you want, Alexis, the facts are what they are. Hikers found you on the beach. You were tangled in seaweed and rope on the mainland side of Buzzards Bay," he said. The fury in him bubbled just beneath the surface of his words. He thought I was lying. Probably the only things holding him back from tearing into me verbally were the shadows of the nurses lurking outside the door.

None of what he was telling me made any sense. I found myself staring at him, unable to provide him with any answers.

"So, you don't remember how your arm got tore up by that whaling hook? Alexis, it was impaled on your bone. It had to be surgically removed. What trouble did you get yourself into this time?"

I swallowed hard. I'd only been hiking and looking for the small village our ancestors had settled in the seventeenth century. There had been no one else with me. "I... I don't know, Court," I mumbled. Maybe it was the drugs the hospital had given me, or maybe it was just the trauma, but I couldn't get to the memories. My stomach constricted, making me nauseous at the thought of missing time.

"Fine. I'll come back when you're ready to go home. I'm not sticking around waiting for you to decide to quit lying about what happened. Call me when you're released."

He stormed out, the door slamming shut behind him, glass vibrating in its casing. Courtney bellowed some commands at the nurses, presumably throwing around his non-existent authority to try to keep me from going anywhere.

I threw my head back against the pillow in frustration. My life had gone a direction even I hadn't imagined it could. Taking stock of my body, I felt like I'd been hit by a truck. The skin on my neck itched where the gauze covered it; rope burn was the most likely culprit according to what Courtney had told me. It hurt to breathe. Tape and gauze chafed my skin beneath the hospital gown. There were probably more stitches and staples, too. I grimaced as I used my foot to push myself back up the bed.

Taking a deep breath, I tried to think back, to remember what I'd supposedly forgotten. The muscles in my arm twitched, making me wince. The tiniest sliver of thought crept into my mind regarding the extent of my injuries. I'd had surgery to remove a whaling hook? I wasn't sure I even knew what a whaling hook was. One by one I managed to move the fingers on my left hand, forming a weak fist through the pain. It wasn't much, but it was a start. I could work with that. I wasn't ready to give up my new-found love for mixed martial arts; it was better than a career I had managing our parents' occult bookstore.

How long had I been out? It couldn't have been more than a day or so, could it?

The whiteboard on the wall gave me minute details such as the name of my nurse on duty and my attending doctor. There were a few other things scribbled there, but no date. The wall clock was broken, or maybe the battery was just dead, but it didn't help.

The sound of my own breathing slowly overtook my thoughts. I tried to settle myself as fresh waves of pain flashed through my body. With the pain came a rush of adrenaline. The incessant beeping of the monitors sped as my pulse raced, the blood thundering in my ears. The IV drug pump by my head gave a soft click and a whir; then the pain faded away as I slipped back into sleep.

Red and orange leaves poked through the evergreens as I made my way through the forest on the island. I'd left my car on the mainland and had taken a ferry to Nashawena Island. It was a forested bit of land tucked between Buzzards Bay and Vineyard Sound, off the coast of Massachusetts. The ferry boat captain had been uneasy letting me wander about the island by myself, but there was little he could do to stop me.

My backpack was full of supplies and gear. I was ready to camp and get back to nature—and look for the village my ancestors had founded nearly four centuries ago.

The last few months I'd poured over seventeenth-century maps, gathering what little information I could find about the village that had long ago disappeared. I had attempted to overlay the maps I'd found with modern maps. My best calculations had led me to an island in the North Atlantic, not far from Martha's Vineyard.

The small village had been settled by my great-great-something-or-other-grandfather and about fifty other immigrants in the 1630's. Bishop Ravendahl had moved to the New World seeking the promise of a better life with his new bride like so many others had. His real first name had been lost to history somewhere around the time he'd gotten on that boat. There had been a storm the first week at sea, and he'd led the passengers in prayer, earning himself the name "Bishop" and the honor of the village being named after him. The rumor was that he'd originally been a member of the clergy but realized that life was not for him when he met Amelia Taylor; but without knowing his real name, we'd never been able to confirm it.

Despite Bishop's former association with the church, he was also known as a healer and a witch. He'd left many recipes for spells and potions in his leather-bound diaries that had been passed down through the generations. Many were familiar recipes that my parents still followed and sold in their occult store as single-use spells or potions. One generation says witch, another herbalist. I wasn't sure what to classify it all as, except as something I did not want to do the rest of my life.

Family lore praised Bishop's accomplishments in the village along Buzzards Bay, such as erecting a lighthouse on the rocky shore, raising a church and town hall. And again, while Bishop had no official church affiliation, the townsfolk didn't care. He had protected them from the storm, and for them, that meant he'd held sway with God. But nearly thirty years later, the town was gone, its remaining inhabitants scattered to the four winds without a reason why.

I had been immersed in digging through my family's archives when my girlfriend left me for another lover. The only thing that prevented me from testing my newly acquired fighting skills on her new bedmate was knowing my efforts were better spent discovering what had happened to my ancestors.

I hiked until my feet hurt, finding myself at the edge of the rocky beach. The North Atlantic water smelled cleaner, saltier almost, than it did back home in New York. Checking my watch, I realized twilight was quickly approaching. It was time to make camp and settle in for the night. I had three days before the ferry returned, and there would be time to explore when the sun rose again.

The next morning, my breath condensed and hung in the air as the sun lit up the fabric tent wall, bathing me in orange light. Birds sang in the distance; meanwhile, the rhythmic crashing of the waves threatened to lull me back to sleep. I lay there listening, anticipating that at any moment I'd wake from the dream to the incessant low rumble of constant vehicles and beeping of horns back home in New York City.

I set out, and by about lunchtime I had managed to find the remains of a neatly stacked stone wall, marking what I assumed had been the village's border. I followed the wall, picking my way through the overgrowth, careful not to stumble over what Mother Nature had already reclaimed. Through the trees, I maneuvered my way along compacted paths that were just beginning to bear the green marks of regrowth, but when I stumbled onto what appeared to be the town square, I had to blink a dozen or so times — I couldn't believe what I'd found.

Nestled among the trees were the broken and moss-covered remains of a few of the main buildings in the center of the village. Piles of stone and broken wood jutted from the tangle of green that tried to tame it. I stared in wonder at the structures. Three and a half centuries later and they were still there. I fumbled through my backpack for my camera, as no one would believe me without evidence. I'd filled one memory card by the time I'd made it through the fourth partially-standing building. Shock seized my lungs as I looked past the next ridge of piled stones where once a building had stood.

There, rising from the green and fallen leaves, was the village graveyard.

I meandered through the tombstones, beside myself with excitement and disbelief. I kept telling myself that this could still be any settlement — I had not yet found proof this was the village my ancestor had founded. Most of the names on the tombstones were so worn it was hard to read their surfaces. There were a couple of Smiths, a few Adams, and one name that was unmistakably Norwegian. But as I picked my way through the fallen leaves and moss-covered gravestones, I saw something that set my heart racing.

Before me was the first tombstone marked: Ravendahl, 1665. I knelt down before it for a better look. Beside it were three stone markers, all bearing the same last name, and all bearing a date of death within the same year. The names matched up with those I'd found in the family archives. I located them one by one. Amelia, Bishop's wife. Thomas, Bishop's youngest child, who'd died at the age of five. Christopher, the middle son. And Faith, Bishop's daughter-in-law, though it took me a while to find her amongst the other Ravendahl tombstones, as the letters were badly worn.

Digging in my backpack, I found another battery pack and memory card for my camera so I could document the stones to add to the family archives. It occurred to me then that one important member of the family was still missing. Faith had been married to Bishop Ravendahl's oldest son, the man from whom my family line had descended.

Elsewhere in the graveyard were flat grave markers set flush to the ground. I shifted away the leaves that had settled atop them, but could not find Bishop's grave. Aside from these, there were two stones that had overturned. I was hesitant to right them, but I did so anyway so I could read their inscriptions.

He wasn't there either.

At the very edge of the graveyard nearest to the woods, set apart from the main bank of weathered stones, was a solitary marker. The letters were barely visible from wear and the passage of time, and I had to squint to make them out, but at last I found where my answer lay. I made my way across the dense undergrowth for a better look. My knees gave out and I took a seat in the leaves in front of the tombstone.

There, written in an Old English script with the carved edges worn round by time, was the ancestor I'd been named after: Alexis Alexander Ravendahl. I could have been staring at my own tombstone; all that was missing was my father's surname of Wynn. I'd been given the name in homage to our ancestors who had spent

193

nearly four centuries on this continent, since my mother had been the last of the Ravendahl line.

I couldn't stop myself, my fingers roamed over the letters, tracing each one with a solemn reverence. There was no further inscription, just the name. If there had been a date, it had been worn away by time. How long had it been since anyone had seen these graves? It was only by luck that I'd found them.

Time slowed as I sat there. The shadows twisted and danced through the trees. The green around me became brighter, the air heavier. The sharp crack of wood and falling branches drew my attention to something moving in the forest.

Tucked back behind the collapsed structure of what may have been the lower portion of a barn was a charred tree with rusty metal at its base. The ground around the tree for a five-foot radius was hard and compact, a circle of black soot obscuring the earth. It smelled fresh, of smoke and sulfur, but there was nothing fresh about this. All the ash was long gone, all that remained was the blackened surface, stark against the evergreens that surrounded it. The bark had been stripped away by the fire, only the hardened wood of the tree remained.

And it beckoned to me.

I went to it, my trembling hand extended to touch the past. I couldn't stop myself.

I had no way of knowing how old this tree was, or why it had not yet been reclaimed by nature. Beneath my palm, the smooth wood felt warm, as if the fire had been recent. I tried to play it off as the sun warming the blackened surface, but it was an overcast day. Switching hands, the tree was now ice cold. None of it made sense. I snapped a few photos of the tree and the ground surrounding it. With a heavy sigh, I turned away from it, my mind set on photographing the remaining gravestones.

Stepping outside the ring of charred earth, a stiff wind blew through the trees, rattling the leaves. My skin bristled with goose

194

bumps. A crack of thunder sounded on the back of the wind. I needed to find shelter, and fast.

A heavy rain started as I ducked into the nearest stone building. I huddled just inside the doorway, beneath some thick logs that served as a makeshift roof now that the floor above had long ago collapsed. It was a futile attempt to stay dry, but it kept the worst of the rain off me.

I stood there, huddled away from the storm, watching sheet upon sheet of water fall around me. The deluge brought down the last of the dried leaves, stripping the trees bare. Puddles formed in the hard-packed earth. The air was heavy and alive with the press of static electricity. The hair on my arms stood on end, prickling my skin. I took a deep breath, the oppressive dampness filling my lungs. It was a wet cold that chilled you from the inside out. I shivered.

White light filled my vision. Then, a heartbeat later, everything went black.

The little village that I had found myself in was gone. I was flat on my back, soaked and muddy, the ground solid and cold beneath me. Sitting up slowly in the dark, I took stock of my surroundings.

The waves crashed on the beach, but I could see nothing. There was no moon. No clouds. Only the ink black sky lit with tiny pinpricks of starlight. The storm had passed, revealing the clearest night sky I had ever witnessed. The pine trees swayed above me, enticing me to stay with their whispers.

As my eyes adjusted, I realized I wasn't far from where I had made camp. My body ached as I stood. My camera was gone, and so was my backpack, which also meant my phone was gone. I had no way to search for it in the darkness, but I did have a spare flashlight at camp.

195

And dry clothes.

I trudged back to my camp, my mind trying to make sense of what had transpired. A minute ago I had been standing in a doorway watching the rain. Then lightning had struck — had it struck too close? Could it have affected me somehow?

My stomach rumbled, reminding me it had been quite some time since I'd eaten. I tried not to think about my hunger as I pressed through the brush, occupying my thoughts instead with the promise of gorging myself on the food I'd packed. Only, when I arrived at the spot where I expected to find my camp, it was not there.

Was I on the wrong part of the beach? There was no way for me to be certain. I'd made an educated guess on where my camp lay judging by the bit of shoreline I could see through the trees. Apparently, I had guessed wrong, and was now faced with a choice: I could keep searching, or I could find a safe place to wait out the night.

Wood smoke drifted downwind to me as I weighed my options. In the distance, an orange fire flickered to life, licking up the sides of a stack of wood.

It didn't make any sense. This island was uninhabited except for me, and yet, here was this bonfire. Shaking my head, I tried to blink the orange light out of existence, but it remained, real as ever.

The terrifying thought hit me that I was no longer alone. How long had I been lying in the mud? Was the person who built this fire the same person who pulled me from the ruins? Were there more people?

I reasoned that, at the very least, I ought to make my presence known. Perhaps they were hunters — if that was the case, I would not want them to mistake me for a deer or whatever there was to hunt on this island.

As I trudged on, my ears perked to an odd sound. It was hard to describe, sounding like wood smashing into rocks. I could see next to nothing in the dark, even as I approached the fire, and so I could not even guess what was making that noise.

Eventually, I found myself standing at the edge of the bonfire. The flames towered well over my height. It was strange that there was no one tending to a blaze this size.

The noise rang out again, clearer this time—a sickening *thunk* of something soft hitting stone. The sound came twice more, each time softer and a bit less hollow.

Then I smelled it.

Blood.

I smelled blood over the salt of the ocean.

A stiff wind blew in from the waterside, and the bonfire roared in response. A jet of flame sprang from the last of the piled driftwood that had not yet caught fire, casting light out onto the waves. The waves lapping at the shoreline were darker; they left a red stain behind on the wet sand. The sea foam was pink, and in other spots, wine red. Littered among the rocks on shore were the boards of broken boats, and at least a dozen bodies.

Some of the bodies, the fresher ones, floated on the waves. Others were dashed upon the rocks, which chewed them up and ripped them apart each time the tide flung them onto the shoreline, only to drag them back out and do it again. The one closest to the fire was nearly impaled on a flat boulder with a jagged edge.

My eyes grew wide when I saw this. My stomach clenched into a tight ball and I doubled over and threw up onto the shore.

"No, please, I beg you! Mercy!"

The high-pitched plea drew my attention back to the water's edge. Someone was still alive.

Just outside the bonfire's edge, awash in unearthly orange light and shadows, was a man thrashing in the surf. He was fighting the current to get to his feet, but something was keeping him from standing upright.

197

And then I saw him. Another man was beside the first, except this one stood erect, half-submerged in the water. He had a hand around the other man's collar, holding him down so the waves could beat down onto him. In his opposite hand was a metal hook that gleamed in the orange light, its sharpened point hovering inches from the other man's throat.

I couldn't believe what I was seeing—was this all a bad dream? I quickly put that thought aside. I wasn't in Neverland, and that wasn't Captain Hook.

He wore a shirt with billowy sleeves tied at the wrists, his wavy hair held at the nape of his neck with a ribbon. His boots were nearly knee high, his dark canvas pants tucked into them. His victim was dressed in a similar fashion. Taking a quick glance at the other bodies that had washed up, I noticed that none were dressed in modern clothing.

"Mercy!" the man thrashing in the water sobbed.

"Hey!" I yelled as I took a step towards the pair, unsure of what I could do to help. I had to try something.

Oblivious to my cries, the attacker raised his arm. I yelled again, this time breaking into a sprint toward the two men, but I was too late. A wet sucking noise resounded as the man sunk his hook into his victim's neck, plunging it into the flesh behind the voice box. Then he yanked it forward, ripping out the man's windpipe. The flailing man's hands went to his throat as he let out a wordless, gurgling scream. I skidded to a halt, frozen in terror at what I had just witnessed.

My knees gave out and I landed on my ass on the wet sand, my eyes still glued to the scene before me. The scent of blood hit me again, turning my stomach. I fought to keep my composure as I watched the killer rummage through the pouch that hung on the dead man's belt.

He tossed the bag aside and clasped a gold hoop earring in his victim's ear. The man yanked it roughly off the dead body, tearing through the flesh to free his prize. He then drew up his foot and unceremoniously punted the body back into the waves. One by one, he did this to all the bodies floating in the surf. The ocean accepted the bodies, pulled them out to sea in back and forth motions, much like a mother might rock her child to sleep on a restless night.

The man turned, then started for the bonfire.

My eyes locked with his and I froze. I could see little more than his outline in the fire's light now, and his glowing eyes. His face came into greater detail as he drew nearer. Even with the mask of blood that had spattered across his face, I could recognize familiar features. I knew those cheekbones, those metallic gray-blue eyes. It was like looking in a mirror, but one that showed the past. I saw myself in that face. That monster was family.

My body twisted, my stomach readying to purge itself of its contents again, as the murderer headed straight toward me. I rolled over onto hands and knees and vomited what was left of my last meal. My heart felt on the verge of stopping as the man high-stepped out of the waves and walked past me. He flung the hook to the sand beside me. I cupped both hands to my mouth to keep from screaming.

From the woods came a deep, hollow baying.

His head jerked in the direction of the forest as the sound came again, those pale eyes narrowing as he scanned the tree line. His hand settled onto the grip of the knife at his waist.

"Come out, come out, wherever you are, *puppy*," he whispered. I barely heard the words above the crackling of the fire.

Following his line of sight to the trees, the shadow of a large canine creature wove between the conifers. Shadow seemed to meld into and around the creature while its dark eyes glowed with the reflection of the fire. The creature stalked closer, its lips pulled back in a snarl. Those lips were blacker than its sooty fur, made darker by its alabaster teeth gleaming in the light. The gangly canine's tail twitched as it stalked toward the man, its fur bristling.

"I've told you before, it's not my time," he hissed at the creature. "But if you want a fight, then it's a fight you'll have, hound."

The hound strode onto the beach, its claws digging silently into the soft sand. The beast's ears flicked toward me for a brief moment as I remembered to breathe.

I swore those snarling lips curved in a bit of smile as the beast launched itself through the raging bonfire and onto the man. Riding him to the ground, the canine snapped at the man's throat but missed, clamping onto the man's arm instead as he defended himself. The crunch of bone filled the air, though the man didn't scream, only laughed. He slashed at the beast with the knife in his other hand, lopping off half of one of the hound's pointed ears. Snarling in anger and pain, the hound violently shook its head, attempting to yank the man's arm from his shoulder.

I locked eyes with the hound in that instant, its eyes alight with the glow of the bonfire. Then, inexplicably, the hound threw its head toward the sky and bayed again to the open plane of stars.

A wave of dizziness washed over me like the rain had. The fire was snuffed out at once, taking the snarls and grunts of man and beast with it. All was darkness.

I blinked, then rubbed my eyes. There was no trace of anything that had occurred in the space of the last ten minutes. The bodies were gone. The fire was gone. I was beside my tent, the stars obscured with clouds. I wanted to puke again, but I sat up and put my head between my knees as I tried to make sense of what I'd experienced.

It was dawn before I dared to move again, my body stiff and aching from lack of sleep. Nothing had made sense, but with the light of day coming I needed to find my lost equipment. I sighed and stretched, wishing for a real bed.

"Time's up."

The one-eared hound leapt from the shadows, pinning me on my back in the sand. It tore at my chest with those heavy paws, pain like fire spreading across my ribs where its claws scored my flesh. I dug my hands into the ruff of fur at its throat, trying to keep it off me. Its hot sulfur breath washed over my face. The pain in my chest was replaced with the stinging bite of stiff, coarse rope as it coiled around my neck and tightened. My breath came in trembling gasps as the rope cinched tighter.

The hound leapt off of me and lunged at my attacker, its claws raking my torso. It moved so quickly that it was merely a flying streak of black fur as it took down the seaside killer. The man dropped the rope, which slackened, allowing me to breathe. I scrambled to my feet as man and beast wrestled.

The rope yanked me back down to the ground, pulling my head at an odd angle as I spilled back onto the sand. I struggled against the rope, but it bit into my fingers as I tried to pull it away from my throat. It tightened around my neck as I struggled.

Then there was a white-hot flash of pain in my left arm. The hook the man had used to tear out the throat of his victim last night was buried in the flesh of my bicep.

With a grunt, he heaved me toward the roaring ocean. I fought for all I was worth, pulling against the rope and kicking my heels into the sand, but with each mighty tug the man dragged me closer to the shoreline. The sand rubbed my skin raw.

My sight grew dim as asphyxiation threatened to take me. I lay on my back, semi-conscious, as the man stood over my body. He kicked at my shoulder to free the hook from my arm, and I hardly felt the pain — it was little more than a dull ache. Thankfully, he let the rope go slack. As I lay in the sand, gasping for air like a fish, I could feel my strength returning.

He swung the hook again; the impact shook my whole body as it impaled itself deep in my bone. Darkness washed over me; no pain this time, just a blanket of warm, sweet darkness. I felt the rope tighten around my throat once more as he started to drag me towards the water.

The cold water shocked me back to my senses. I reached for his leg, but instead brushed against four furry paws that leapt about in the water around me. I tried to stand, but was shoved back under the water when the hound sprang onto to my chest. A mouthful of fangs closed on my shoulder. Instantly, the cold water became warm with the outpour of my blood, and I lost consciousness again.

I awoke gasping for air, clutching at my arm where the teeth had bit down. My racing heart settled when I realized I was no longer in the water. I was dry, somewhere far removed from the man and the beast.

"You touched the tree, didn't you?"

I shot my brother a mean look, then attempted to sit up in bed, but the restraints kept me from moving. Courtney sat in an upholstered chair. He had moved it so he could prop his feet on the end of my bed. His leather jacket was strewn over him as a makeshift blanket.

"There were a lot of trees, Court," I said.

"Fine. I'm going back to sleep then."

I kicked his foot, wincing at the shock of pain that jolted through my body. "Yes, I touched the charred tree. What of it?"

"You triggered the place memory."

I groaned. I'd unknowingly pushed play on the ghost equivalent of a recording that had been trapped in the wood and stone of the past.

Except things had gone farther than just a simple viewing of past events.

"I told you to leave it alone when you started looking into the family history," said Courtney, "do you understand why?"

"I would have been better off if you'd just come out and said, 'Hey, Alexis, that place is haunted, might want to let it alone.'"

"What fun would that be?" he asked, his tone loaded with sarcasm.

I growled and kicked at my brother's foot again "You're pissed I came up here. I'm in a hospital bed all stitched up. Tell me what you should have told me three months ago when Lynne left me and I started looking into this."

Courtney blew out a sigh as he sat up. "One of his children, the man you were named after, was given the nickname 'Priest' by the privateers he sailed with."

"Privateers?" I asked.

"Pirates," he clarified. "It was meant as a jab to his father, since Bishop didn't approve of his son's line of work. Priest came home from a journey and found his wife with his brother."

I closed my eyes to let it all sink in. The man I'd watched kill that poor bastard was my namesake.

I snorted. History had almost repeated itself. "Guess I should be thankful Lynne doesn't care for you."

He huffed at me. "Your girl is bottled lightning, and I don't just mean because of her white hair. She will be the death of you. Let her go, Alexis."

I probably should, but I was never good at listening to my older brother. "There is more, isn't there?"

He nodded. "Priest killed both of them. It was just the start of his madness."

"So why the damn tree, Court?"

"What? You didn't see that?"

"No. I watched a wolf—dog—something jump through a fire, trying to tear out that man's throat. I didn't see what happened with the tree." My words were more hurried than I anticipated. I could hear that creature baying again. I shuddered. The heart monitor beeped faster to match my racing pulse.

"Keep it up and the nurse is gonna come back," my brother teased, eyes focused on the monitor's screen.

I settled back down, and he continued.

"The hound didn't kill him. The villagers caught him that night. He was on the shore, waiting for another ship to crash into the rocks."

"Yeah, Court, I saw that. I watched him kill the shipwreck survivors."

My brother shook his head, and then shifted his eyes out the window to the full moon. Had I really been asleep for nearly two weeks? It had been the last night of the new moon when I'd been dropped off on the beach by the ferry.

"They caught him, and chained him to that tree," he went on. "Days passed while they waited for the magistrate to show up. The day he did, a storm blew in from the ocean. Some swore they heard it howling like a hound that had treed a raccoon. Lightning struck the tree, killing him and setting the tree on fire. Town was quiet for a few months. Then those of his bloodline starting dying one by one."

"That's why there were so many Ravendahl gravestones tucked away with the same year of death." I frowned at this and diverted my eyes from my brother. Our lives were anything but normal—witchcraft and ghosts were in our family line, but stepping back into a place memory and being dragged under the icy waters of the North Atlantic made me question my sanity.

Courtney cleared this throat, bringing me back to reality. "Bishop took his grandchildren and what was left of his family, and headed for what was New Amsterdam at the time."

"Which became New York, where Mom's family has lived for almost three hundred years," I added.

He nodded. "Once the last Ravendahl moved beyond the ghost's reach, the family curse ended, and the one-eared hound disappeared. That is, until you decided to come chasing the past."

"If you would have told me, I wouldn't have gone."

Courtney raised an eyebrow at me. We both knew my words were the farthest thing from the truth. I would have gone sooner had I known the story.

"You touched the tree," Courtney said dryly. "He's claimed the rest and thinks you're dead. Don't tempt him again."

My brother let out a long sigh as he settled back in the chair, pulling his hat back down over his face. "No more poking around Bishop, Massachusetts, Alexis. We're going back to New York in the morning."

I stared out the window, unsure of what to say to my brother.

It had been the hound that had yanked me from the cold water. I hadn't saved myself.

I didn't want to tell Courtney that the hound had been following me since Lynne had left me.

History was bound to repeat itself.

It was just how things happened in our family.

ABOUT THE AUTHOR
STEPHANIE KELLEY

Stephanie Kelley is a thirty-something sci-fi geek who wishes *Firefly* was never canceled. She has a degree in Journalism from Lock Haven University of Pennsylvania. She enjoys writing in the urban fantasy and horror genres.

Steal the Sun, her debut novel, is set in Alaska and centers around a family of supernatural hunters and their gold mine. The novel was released February 13, 2017. *Touch the Moon*, the second in her *Alaskan Hunter* series, is out now. Book three of the series, *Hang the Stars*, is scheduled to be released in late 2018.

EXODUS
ARKANSAS

By: Thomas Vaughn

"You got my money?"

I remember the embarrassed look on Rick Riley's face. As head youth pastor at the Apex Baptist Church, he probably didn't participate in too many illegal cash transactions like this one. I don't know if it was the way I was brought up, but for some reason the art of subtlety just isn't in me. I tend to say what's on my mind.

He dug around in his wallet, fished out five one hundred dollar bills and put them in my hand. I stuffed them in my hunting vest and calculated that I had just earned a month's worth of groceries and a few small luxuries.

"I want to thank you for your help, Mr. Fultz," he said as the two college kids caught up to us at the chain link fence. He was trying to make it sound like we were friends and I was just doing him a favor, but that wasn't the way it was. I was just there for the money.

I unslung my .30-06 and leaned it against a post while I pried a section of the fence from the frozen ground where I had weakened it three years earlier. "Ain't no skin off my ass," I replied. "You paid your money so you deserve a look. I don't know what you expect to see up there. Most of the buildings have crumbled to the foundations."

"But the church is still standing?"

"There ain't much of it, but it's there."

The youth pastor hesitated for a moment, then got down on his back while I held the chain link. He was a handsome devil—trim, blonde and athletic. Apex Baptist Church was no backwoods

207

operation. It hosted an eight thousand member congregation in a stadium size building about forty miles to the north, close to the Missouri state line. I had never been inside, but I had heard it had a spa, a coffee shop and an ATM machine. The head pastor drove a BMW, so I didn't feel too guilty about lightening Rick Riley's pockets a little. Even though he was just a youth pastor, he still made six times the average household income for folks in Madison County.

As he sprang to his feet, I noticed his brand new hiking boots and perfect teeth. He didn't look like any of the preachers around here. At the Apex Baptist Church they didn't use hell and brimstone to fill the seats. Up there, it was all about looking like a winner. You could tell who was right with the Lord by the car they drove.

"Who's next?" I asked the two kids.

There was a boy and a girl, both journalism students at one of the local Christian colleges. The girl was really pretty.

"You go first, Megan," said the boy, who seemed like a nice enough kid, though he was a little dumb. It was pretty clear he was trying to get himself a sniff, the way he made cow eyes at her, but the girl was all business. I hated to tell the kid that he had about same shot of getting in her panties as a terrapin did of crossing Highway 62 without being flattened.

She wriggled under the fence, taking care not to damage her camera. When I saw the way that the youth pastor dusted her off I knew the kid had some serious competition.

"All right, Dillon," said Rick Riley. "Come on through and watch the pack."

If you include the portable lighting, they must have had five grand in equipment with them. I watched the skinny kid slide under the fence, trying to look smooth. But God had other plans for him, because a cord got hung on the fence and Rick Riley had to help him. The boy flushed with embarrassment as the youth pastor scolded him to be careful, all while the girl watched.

I didn't make any pretense about looking smooth as I floundered my way under the fence, but then again I was beyond proving anything to anyone. I couldn't tell if the fence was getting lower or my gut higher, but I figured it was the latter. Once I was on the other side, I retrieved my Jack Daniels hat and gun.

"Is that really necessary?" asked Rick Riley, pointing to my rifle.

"Well, I don't know if it's necessary yet, because we ain't got there. You folks ready for the tour?"

It's funny how people are different like that. He thought it was strange that I would bring a gun along. I thought that it was equally strange that a man would go into unfamiliar woods unarmed. After I had hiked up my trousers, we started up the hill under a heavy winter sky, our feet crunching dead, frost-tainted leaves.

Back in 1935, Reverend Uriah Peale thought he had it all figured out. He wanted to get the hell away from all of the godless drunkards, degenerates and Darwinists, so he and his congregation retreated to the most godforsaken hilltop in the whole county to wait for God's final trumpets. The problem was that God seemed to be running on a different schedule than the reverend. Rather than getting discouraged, they just set down roots and decided to wait the good Lord out. They called this new province "Exodus" because they expected to depart at any moment. As it turns out, the name was more than prophetic: in the fall of 1943, a postal carrier noticed that the mailbag hadn't been picked up in a couple of weeks and ventured up to the settlement only to find it deserted.

Seventy-three souls had vanished without a trace. Whether or not they just up and walked away was hard to say. No one paid much attention with the war going. By then, the God-fearing folk of Exodus had severed most of their connections with the outside, so it wasn't as though they were really missed.

"Maybe we could have a brief prayer," said Rick Riley. The two teenagers linked their hands in his. They stood in a semi-circle, watching me expectantly. It took me a moment to realize they were waiting on me to join.

"You all go on," I replied.

The pastor looked at me reprovingly, then closed their circle and said aloud, "Dear Lord, we ask that you watch over your flock. We ask that you bless our bodies to become vessels of your will. We ask that you use the video we are about to shoot as your instrument. These things in Jesus' name we ask. Amen."

He was a slick one all right. It was the way he locked eyes with the two college students while maintaining a grip on their hands, the faintest trace of a soulful smile on his face. You could always tell a slick pastor by the way they made eye contact.

Once they had gotten their praying done, we started up the hill. I let them walk a little ways ahead of me, enjoying the crisp bite of the January air. It was just this side of freezing, and one of the few times of the year you could come out here and not get eaten alive by ticks.

"Why does the county keep this hilltop fenced-off?" asked the girl as she eyed the cedar thickets suspiciously.

"They say the ground is poison," I answered.

"Do you believe that?"

"Nope. I've been up here a hundred times and it ain't made me sick."

"So why do you think they fenced it off?" she persisted.

"Because they don't want trespassers like us up here. But as far as the *real* reason goes, I guess that's what you're here to figure out. You're the journalist, not me."

I had been leading expeditions to Exodus over the past three years. I didn't make a whole lot of money as a part time janitor, so the extra cash was welcome. I made a show of hiding the cars from the dirt road that ran a mile to the south, but it wasn't necessary. I had a permit of sorts, since I gave half of what I earned to the county deputy. Besides, there really wasn't much to see. I don't know what it is about places like this that attracts people. Maybe it reminds them that, while home might look permanent, it's not.

But this group was different. They were working on some kind of church project. The youth pastor was making it seem like this was a sacred place, like the folks that used to live here had been *miracled* off the mountaintop after all. I couldn't tell if he believed that load of horseshit or not. But then again, it really doesn't matter with that type. Whether the preacher gets in your head or your pocketbook, you're just as screwed either way.

"Uriah Peale was certainly a man of vision," Rick Riley said. He was the type of man that liked to hear himself talk. "Why do you think he chose a place like this, Dillon?" He didn't ask it like a real question, but like a teacher that already knows the answer.

"Well," said the kid. "I guess he wanted to get away from the sinful world, like you were saying."

"Yeah, what else?"

"To test their faith," interrupted the girl. "This is a hard place to live. The Lord needs to know that your faith is strong before he will bless you."

The youth pastor beamed at her like a star pupil while the boy looked a little disappointed. "That's right," he said. "If you leave the

211

world behind and come way out here, you are telling the Lord that you are ready to serve him in any way possible. You are saying that no task is too much for you. Imagine the courage and faith it took to leave their families behind so that they could be closer to God."

About halfway up the hill we started coming across random pieces of debris. Rusted metal and piles of bricks were strewn about, making it difficult to find good footing. As we passed an upturned handcart, the girl asked, "What's that?"

"That's the real reason Exodus was built on this mountaintop," I answered. "There's a zinc mine up here. There ain't no mana from heaven in these parts. When it came to bountiful blessings, the Lord kind of overlooked this part of the world. The folks up here had to make a living somehow."

"You make it sound like they were unhappy," said the boy.

"Well, I don't know about that, but I can tell you the closest railhead is ten miles. They had to cart the ore out of here by the wagonload. Would you want to spend your days carting wagonloads of rock down this hill every day?"

He shrugged. "At least they got away from all the sin." He was even dumber than I thought.

"I'm not sure it's any less sinful up here than it is anywhere else." I knew better than to argue with people like this, but they were irritating me. There had always been something about that Christian certainty that bugged me. If there was a God, he sure didn't give a shit about the four of us.

"What about all the babies that are killed?" asked the girl. "That's sinful. We saw a film at our last youth group about how there are over 40,000 babies killed to feed the abortion industry every year. The doctors trick these poor women who have been abused into giving up their babies. You don't think that's sinful?"

I paused before answering, taking the time to shove a plug of tobacco into my mouth. I had a nice little numb patch just inside my right cheek where I liked to keep it.

Then I noticed that all three of them were waiting for me to respond.

For some reason, my mind went back to the day my daddy caught me dipping for the first time. He made me stand on top of the doghouse while he shot holes in it just beneath my feet. Any time I flinched, he would shoot a little higher. I got real good at not flinching when someone pointed a gun at me.

"I figure there's worse things than not being born," I said and left it at that.

When we got to the top of the hill, they forgot all about me. We'd arrived at where they wanted to go, so I wasn't of much use to them anymore.

The town of Exodus had been comprised of about twenty residences, four barns, three stables, two wells, and a church. Most of the houses had been reclaimed by nature. You could just make out the square patches where the structures had once stood. There were a few beer bottles lying in the leaf clutter with the remains of wasp nests in them, proof that we were not the first interlopers. All told, the hilltop community covered no more than an acre and a half. The main road was gone, but the remains of the collapsed houses lay in heaps along a pathway that was still visible. The structures that remained were little more than havens for mice and hibernating snakes.

"Is that the church?" asked Rick Riley, pointing to the largest structure in town.

I nodded, and then watched as they gathered in front of it. At one time, it had been painted white, except that now that paint was a weathered gray and flaked off in the breeze. Its steeple loomed above us, just past the level of the treetops. Judging how it hadn't yet collapsed like the other buildings in town, I guess the good people of Exodus put more care and effort into building their church than their own homes. That said, it was only a matter of time before it succumbed to nature as well. The roof was bowed in the middle like the backbone of an old man, and there were sagging holes in the shingles where the rainwater poured in during storms. Great clumps of moss and lichens were plastered to the shingles like age spots.

"This is a great place to shoot," Rick Riley exclaimed. "Dillon, get the camera rolling. Megan, start on your intro."

His excitement infected the two students like the Spanish flu. The girl composed herself in front of the church, making sure that her hairband had restrained every strand of her long brown hair. Meanwhile, the boy aimed his camera, searching for the best angle to shoot. I sat down on a stump and laid the rifle across my legs, pushing the snuff a little deeper in my cheek.

"We are blessed to have found ourselves in a place that few people get to see," she began. "This is Exodus, Arkansas. In 1935, Reverend Uriah Peale brought his flock to this hilltop to wait for God's judgment. These people built a city devoted completely to God. Eight years later, they vanished without a trace. The secular authorities would have us believe that they simply abandoned their homes."

Here, she shook her head with mock incredulity.

"But we are here to find the real answer. With God's help, we may catch a glimpse of the truth and share it with you."

A few seconds after her theatrical pause, Rick Riley clapped his hands. "That was great, Megan! Perfect! Did you get that, Dillon?"

"Yes sir," said the boy, and they huddled around the camera to review the playback.

A noise caught my attention. I looked up to see a pair of hawks circling overhead. They were scanning the ground for prey. I always had a thing for hawks and did not tolerate people who shot them. They circled next to each other in opposite directions, slowly drifting with the air currents. I always wondered what the world would look like from up there.

214

Then something strange happened. Just as they soared directly overhead, the hawks abruptly dove to the west. It was like they were startled by the sound of their own voices. That's when I realized how quiet it was. I knew it was winter, but even during this time of year you would expect to hear a few foraging birds or squirrels. I thought back to my other visits to the hilltop and it seemed to me that the whole place was one big grave.

"Mr. Fultz?" Rick Riley was standing in front of me. "Is it safe to enter the church?"

"Probably not, but that don't mean you can't do it," I said, getting to my feet. My legs were sore from the climb.

"By the way," he added. "Do you ever smile?"

"I wouldn't know since I don't look in mirrors too often. You tell them two to watch where they put their feet. There's rats and possums nesting under the floor. You put your foot through a floorboard and you're likely to catch a nail. You'll be getting a tetanus shot for your trouble."

I stood in the doorway as they fanned out in the old church, looking up at the patches of daylight coming through the roof. The pews lay in a clutter on the floor along with torn hymnals and patches of excrement, both animal and human. The air had that sweet smell of rotting wood. There was remarkably little by way of decoration. Reverend Peale's pulpit was a simple podium carved from wood, with no embellishments. The boy peered behind it and asked, "Where did they get baptized?"

"They didn't baptize people indoors in those days, Dillon," Rick answered. "They went to the nearest river, just like John. Where is the closest river, Mr. Fultz?"

"The White River is five miles, but there is a pond on the other side of the hill if you feel the call."

Rick Riley took the camera while the boy held a portable lamp. I was surprised by the amount of light it put out in the dim interior. I looked up at the naked rafters and noticed deserted birds' nests and dirt dauber hives. The camera followed the girl while she narrated their adventure, talking about how the community would gather in this place to ask the Lord for guidance. It looked to me like it was going to be a pretty boring film, but I didn't see any harm in it. The irony of the simple room was lost on them. I wondered what their head pastor would say about bringing his ministry to a humble place like this after preaching to television cameras in a vaulted dome for so many years. I just made sure they never pointed the camera in my direction. I was hoping we could get out of there once they were cold and hungry, but no sooner had they exited the church than Rick Riley pointed to one of the few residences that was still standing.

"Do you know who lived there?"

"They say it's where the reverend lived," I answered.

The house was six hundred square feet, and sturdy. It had a sandstone washing rock propped against the front and a narrow eave jutting out from the roof.

"Look at that, guys," said Rick Riley. "That's where Reverend Peale lived with his wife and seven children. Can you imagine living with seven children in a house like that?"

"I thought it would be bigger," said the boy.

"I want a big family," said the girl. "But it needs space to grow. I want to work until my husband is established at his job, then devote myself to my children."

Rick Riley patted the girl on the shoulder, letting his hand linger for a while. "We should be thankful that we have such nice houses today. Reverend Peale always preached that a woman should submit to her husband so long as he walked with Christ."

"I know this kid at school," said Dillon, trying to get Megan's attention. "His mom makes more than his dad. Can you imagine that? I wouldn't allow that in my house."

Rick Riley nodded. "That's wise, Dillon. When a woman makes more money than her husband, it breeds marital discord."

This time they didn't ask, but picked their way across the broken mason jars and decaying plywood toward the reverend's house. I shook my head and moved my rifle to the other shoulder. As they disappeared through the partially collapsed front door, I muttered, "Darryl, old buddy, you are sure earning your money today."

A little breeze kicked up from the west. I rested against a hickory and scanned the ground for pig tracks. Then I heard a piping sound. It was one of the discarded liquor bottles lying crossways to the wind. I had always liked that sound. As I scanned the debris for anything of interest, I had a weird feeling. I stood and walked to where I could see around the side of the reverend's house—out toward the mine. It almost seemed as though there was a piping sound coming from there as well, like it was answering the bottle at my feet. It didn't make sense. The bottle wasn't loud enough to create an echo, and besides, the topsoil in these parts didn't really reflect sound.

"Mr. Fultz!"

I turned and saw Rick Riley poking his head through the house's front window.

"Can you help us with something?" he called out.

It didn't take a genius to see how excited he was. I had been in the house a few times, but couldn't imagine what would get him all worked up like that. I sauntered over and peered inside the dim room with its faded aqua blue paint.

"In here, Mr. Fultz," said the girl with excitement.

"What is it?" I asked, not really wanting to squeeze my large frame through the doorway.

"I need you to give us a hand," said Rick Riley.

I sighed and lowered the rifle, checking the doorway for exposed nails. Then I ungracefully shoved my way through. Once inside, I saw that they were looking at a satchel caught in the rafters.

"Looks like the ceiling rotted out and exposed the attic," I said.

"Help me give Dillon a boost," said the youth pastor.

"You want that satchel?"

"It may contain answers."

I wasn't too sure about that, as I had thought that everything of any value would have been carried off by now. Here sat an antique leather satchel like what you would see in a museum. After some more cajoling, I found myself grabbing one of the boy's legs while the youth pastor took hold of the other, and together we hoisted him into the air. It took him a while to wiggle the satchel free of the beams, and I got a face full of plaster and mouse droppings.

"Jesus Christ, shit on a stick!" I cursed and shook my head.

The girl gasped, looking like she was going to die from my effrontery. I wondered what these kids were going to do if they ever strayed from the protection of their church. If you flinch every time you hear a cuss word, well, the world is going to eat you alive.

As for the boy, he may not have been too bright, but he could climb like a spider monkey. When he had hold of the satchel, we lowered him to the floor. I had only just started wiping the debris out of my eyes when I heard the girl scream. All three of them were carrying on like they were having some type of evangelical fit. Then I realized what was happening. I grabbed the boy and knocked the black widow from his left shoulder. The satchel fell to the ground and came open, spilling its contents on the floor.

"Would y'all be careful," I warned. "Those things hibernate in places like this during the winter. You don't never stick your hand in a box that's been put in storage without having a good look first."

Soon, they were busy stepping on the sleepy spiders as they tottered across the floor. The girl tensed up and said, "I freaking hate spiders. Are they poisonous?"

Given the trash pile I had grown-up in, I could speak from experience on the matter. "Those sons-of-bitches will cramp you up like nobody's business."

After the excitement died down, Rick Riley dug through the satchel, only this time he was really careful. It was empty. As it turns out, the contents had been dumped with the spiders. The girl reached down and picked up a worm-eaten book that lay amid the decaying rags and papers.

"What's this?" she asked.

The youth pastor took it from her, studied it and opened it to the first page. "It's too dark in here. Let's go outside."

When we emerged into daylight, the already-short winter day was starting retreat. "It's gonna be dark in about three hours," I warned, but the three of them were too focused on their treasure to listen.

"My God," said Rick Riley. "I think this is a journal. This is Reverend Peale's diary."

"Cool," said the boy.

That got my attention. I wondered how much Gladys, the shriveled mummy who ran the historical society, would pay for such a thing. Soon my mind was working on a way to claim it without creating too much fuss.

"What does it say?" asked Megan.

"It's hard to tell. The pages are so brittle I am almost afraid to touch them. There are holes in it, and some kind of webbing."

"What are those specks?" asked the boy.

"That's mouse shit," I answered.

"The first part is almost unreadable," the youth pastor complained. "It's gotten wet or something."

"Just read the last few pages," the girl suggested. She had the look of a bloodhound that had caught a scent.

The youth pastor donned a pair of stylish reading glasses and squinted at the yellowed pages. "Okay. Here is the third page back. It says it's from October 13, 1943. That's about the time they disappeared."

"You mean up and left," I corrected.

He studied the page for a moment, and said, "I don't think so, Mr. Fultz." He waited a moment longer, then began to read.

"It is a glorious day in our community, for truly it can be said that the voice of God speaks to us. I am convinced that Brother Stiles and Brother Ambrose are right. How could I have been so blind? Why did I assume God's word would issue from the clouds when he is equally able to speak to us from the ground? I myself have heard the voices in the mine and I am convinced they are the sounds of the angelic choirs. For so long I have been waiting for the gateway to open in the clouds, and here it is in my own backyard."

He lowered the book and looked into the distance, trying to work out the puzzle in the words he'd read aloud.

"They heard voices coming from the ground?" asked the boy.

The youth pastor nodded. "Apparently, yes, they did." Then he turned back to the book and continued reading.

"On this day, we shall gather in the mine to sing and pray. Everyone shall assemble before the heavenly gate, young and old. We shall praise God Almighty and beseech him to rescue his servants from this sinful plane in which they have been imprisoned. We shall go down to meet him where he dwells and pray that he scourges the earth for its iniquities."

Then he closed the book and removed his glasses.

"What else does he say?" asked the girl.

"Nothing. That's the last entry."

I thumbed my chin-stubble and spat the exhausted wad of tobacco onto the ground. "So they were plumb, batshit crazy."

The pastor glowered at me. "You're so sure of that?"

"Well, they're hearing voices coming out of the ground. What's that tell you?"

He furrowed his brow. "Don't you believe in God, Mr. Fultz?"

I shifted my weight a little. "I don't really see how that's any of your business." The truth was, I really didn't give it much thought. If there was a God, he sure didn't take much interest in me.

"Well, I do," he replied. "He speaks to me. When I pray, I feel his presence. He comforts me when I am troubled."

That's when I got pissed. "That's because you ain't had no troubles," I shouted. "Look at you. There's not a scar on you. Of course you think there's a God. I would too if I went through life never having to work for anything. When's the last time you went to bed hungry?"

He didn't break eye contact with me, and I thought he was getting ready to argue. Instead, his eyes just kind of glazed over. I started to wonder if he had suffered a stroke or something when his face suddenly went wild.

"My friends, the Lord has just spoken to me," he said in a loud voice, joyful tears forming in his eyes. "He tells me that we must go to the mine and pray. We must go to the mine and pray as our brothers and sisters did so many years ago. He will reveal his glory to us and heal Mr. Fultz of his bitterness."

"Whoa, now," I said, putting out a hand. "You leave me and my bitterness out of this." Before I knew it, the two college kids were saying "Hallelujah" and "Praise the Lord" with the same type of glazed expression as the pastor.

"God-damn it! Now cut that shit out," I barked. It made me nervous when church folks acted that way. "There ain't no way we are going to that mine."

Rick Riley locked eyes with me again. There was something fanatical in that gaze that I didn't like. It was right then I made a resolution not to bring any more church groups out here.

"Mr. Fultz..." he began, his tone deceptively calm. "We are going to the mine with or without you. If you want to return without us that is fine. As for us, we may be on the verge of something great. In any case, we are not leaving this place until we have seen the mine."

I sat back on my heels and thought about the situation. I didn't really have it in me to take them down the hillside at gunpoint.

221

Besides, that was kidnapping. Then again, if I left them here and something happened, I might feel bad about it. The slimy bastard had me in a corner.

"All right," I said. "You say your prayer, take a picture, and we beat it. Got it?"

Before the words had finished leaving my mouth, the girl was hugging me. I was not a man given to physical intimacy, so I tensed up to keep from jumping out of my skin.

"You're doing the right thing," she said. "It shows that God dwells everywhere, even inside of you. Remember, you are with friends, and Jesus is holding the light to guide you."

"Yeah, well the only reason my fist is not dwelling on your face is because you're a girl. Now how about you let go of me so we can get this over with?"

She stepped back. "Why are you so angry at the world?"

"If you have to ask that question, it probably wouldn't do you any good to hear the answer."

"You could always pray," she said earnestly.

I could tell from the look on her face that she actually believed what she said. Right then, my mind went back to the day some older boys caught me behind the service station and beat me up. They dragged me to the pumps and sprayed gasoline in my face, trying to get the nozzle in my mouth. After the owner chased them off, I lay on the ground, choking, my throat and stomach on fire. I really thought I was going to die. When I opened my burning eyes, the owner asked, "Who's gonna pay for my gas?"

"No," I told the girl. "I really can't pray. Now, if you want to see that mine, you best get your asses moving."

The mine shaft lay about forty yards behind the reverend's house. The county had come in and put bars across the entrance a while back, but two of them had been dislodged in a rockslide, so there was more than enough space to wriggle through.

"Is there anything we need to be aware of in terms of safety?" asked the pastor when we arrived.

"Well, it's an abandoned zinc mine. You don't want to get it in you. Just keep your hands out of your mouth," I said, though the truth of the matter was I had no idea what the safety concerns were.

Rick Riley took the lamp from the boy. I retrieved my flashlight from my vest.

"I pictured the mine with a track in it," said the boy.

"Laying track costs money. They were pulling the rocks up in buckets and handcarts."

"It must have been hard."

"Hard like you can't believe. But that's what you can do when you got a labor force that's willing to work for free."

I stayed in the rear, keeping my light shining at the girl's feet so she could find her way. Rick Riley and the boy went first. The shaft was just tall enough for me to walk stoop-shouldered. Water was leaking through the porous limestone ceiling, creating wet patches on the floor.

"The walls are green," she said marveling at the sparkling ore.

"I thought zinc was blue," said Rick Riley.

"It corrodes in the open air," I answered.

"Oxidation," added the boy, who seemed pleased with himself.

"Stay close to me, Dillon," said Rick Riley. "I need the lamp."

We had ventured some ways into the darkness when the youth pastor paused. "There are branching passages through here."

"That's how you mine this stuff," I said, looking at the pick marks in the rock face, thinking about all the suffering that it took to dig these tunnels. "You just follow a vein until it runs out, then you pick a new one."

I was a little surprised to find cave crickets on the floor. Even though it was warmer underground, I figured they would be hibernating. Right about the time my tour guests were starting to get their fill of adventure, the lamp caught a bright reflection on the wall. It was a strange type of ore that shone bright red when the light hit it.

"What's this?" asked the youth pastor.

"It's dazzling," said the girl, and she was right. I had never seen a natural ore reflect so much light. I ran through the list of substances that it might be, but couldn't come up with an answer.

"I can't say," I replied. "Maybe a mercury vein? I don't think copper would do that."

"This must be the gateway," suggested the boy.

He had a point. You could tell where the miners had hit the vein, then carefully chiseled around it instead of digging it out. It gave the impression that of some type of door was sitting at the end of a long chamber.

Rick Riley touched the deposit. "It's warm," he said.

I stepped back, wondering if it was some type of uranium. I didn't bear the three of them any ill will, but I was glad to have them between me and whatever it was at the end of the tunnel. Maybe it comes down to how you are raised. They weren't afraid because they had never experienced real threats. I knew the world for the rabid dog it was because I had been bitten plenty of times. The world wasn't run by a supernatural being, but by the savage clockwork of a universe that didn't care whether you lived or died.

"I think we should sing a hymn," said Rick Riley. "Mr. Fultz, would mind holding the camera?"

"If I do, can we get the hell out of here?"

"It's a deal," he replied and handed it to me. "Megan, Dillon, let us kneel in the place where our brothers and sisters went before us."

The three of them knelt before the reflective wall like it was the altar of the Holy Sepulcher. I framed them in the shadows of the lamplight. I was not much of a cameraman, but at least I knew that the record light was on. I stood there, blinking like a cow in the slaughter chute.

I had never heard their song before. I had only been to church a couple of times when I was a boy and I didn't know any of the new hymns. Their voices were reedy at first, but then Rick Riley exhorted them. It wasn't much of a melody. It just kind of rose and fell. The words seemed to be asking God to speak. I figured the song was not altogether inappropriate. Even though they had faith, they still wanted something more tangible than an imaginary voice in their heads.

After about a minute, I felt a change come on. I felt it in my feet first. It was a vibration deep in the earth, coming from that vein of red ore. Who knows how deep it ran?

Soon the vibrations became audible. At first it was just a single tone, but then the tone began to separate. The three singers looked at one another in amazement and redoubled their efforts. As the tone separated, I could hear voices, tinny at first, but growing stronger. Their song was activating some memory in the earth.

My jaw dropped when I realized the rocks were singing back at them, except it was a different song. It was one of those thumping ballads from the old church. It sounded like a full choir. The iridescent wall was vibrating like the magnetic plate in a speaker. My three companions joined hands and began swaying, ecstatic smiles on their faces as they sang their hymn in counterpoint to the voices coming from the wall, and I had no doubt that we were hearing the people of Exodus awakened from whatever obscure fate had devoured them.

Like I said, sometimes it's the way you're brought up. The way I was raised, I knew trouble when I saw it. Every part of me was telling me to get the hell out of there. I didn't want to leave them, especially the girl, but I could tell there was no reasoning with them at this point.

I placed the camera on the ground and began to back up the shaft. I can't say I'm proud of running out on them like that, but when the vibrations started flaking off chips of limestone from the ceiling, I turned and ran for all I was worth back up that passage. Behind me, the group had finished their song, and I could hear Rick Riley telling the kids to say the Lord's Prayer. The last thing I heard from them was: "Our Father who art in heaven, hallowed be thy name," and then their voices were lost. It was the prayer that finally triggered it.

It came fast. I had only just scuttled through the exit when I felt some terrible force roaring through the passage behind me. I ducked to one side and scrambled to get my rifle sighted on the hole. You could almost see it. It was like a ripple in the air on a hot day. It shot out of the mine and across the valley below. There was an unfortunate crow sitting on a tree limb in its path. When that sound wave, or whatever it was, hit it the bird, it melted away in a blue flame. It was there one moment and then it wasn't. I listened as that pulse of energy shot across the hillsides, gradually losing steam as it faded into the distance.

I stood up and looked at the entrance to the mine. I couldn't imagine what had happened to the three of them sitting so close to that vein when it discharged all of that energy. Maybe the saddest part was they had almost solved their mystery. I wondered if my companions were now recorded deep in that subterranean archive along with those other dead voices. Their bodies must have been obliterated in an instant—burned alive by their own faith.

Slowly, I turned and made my way back down the hillside, inserting a plug in my mouth and adjusting it until I found that sweet, numb spot. It's hard to say what they woke up down there. I don't think it was God, nor was it some demon come out of hell. It was the same as everything else in the world. It didn't care what you did or thought. It didn't care who your daddy was or where you went to church. It just did what it did. The world don't take sides.

About halfway down that hillside, I stopped feeling bad for the three of them, even the girl.

What was her name again?

Anyway, the fact was they were gone and I was still here. Beyond that, it didn't really mean much. One thing was for sure though: I would never again doubt the power of prayer.

ABOUT THE AUTHOR
THOMAS VAUGHN

Thomas Vaughn is a refugee from the debris field of rural Arkansas. When he is not writing fiction, he poses as a college professor whose research focuses on apocalyptic rhetoric and doomsday cults. He began submitting speculative fiction for publication in 2018 after writing in the secrecy of his bone cave for a number of years. He has several stories appearing in various magazines and anthologies this year.

Blackwell, New Jersey

By: Jill Hand

The four of us were pumped up from finding a section of fence flattened by a fallen tree, allowing us entry into Blackwell. Once inside we celebrated with a round of high fives.

Pranesh turned to Tyler. "The Scooby-Doo crew explores the mysterious abandoned village! Are you ready, Shaggy?"

"I thought you were Shaggy," Tyler replied. "I'm Fred, obviously. Handsome, well-dressed…"

"Dream on," Pranesh scoffed. "You got those pants you're wearing at a garage sale run by an old lady who was selling her dead husband's clothes."

"Double-knits are making a comeback," Tyler said, unperturbed. He unzipped his backpack and took out a GoPro, panning it slowly from side to side, taking in the wooded landscape and the cluster of buildings in front of us. "You're going to wish you had pants like these."

The pants were a startling shade of orange, bell bottoms, with lime green and dayglow blue stripes. Tyler claimed they'd prevent him from being shot by a hunter mistaking him for a deer.

"Don't tell me I'm supposed to be Velma," I said.

Mason flipped her glossy chestnut hair. How did she get it so thick and shiny? When I used the same conditioner she did my hair just got stringy. "Velma's nice. She's much nicer than Daphne. Besides, your glasses are sort of like hers. It's not an insult if we call you Velma."

"That's easy for you to say. Nobody would ever call you Velma," I told her.

We'd parked at the Kittatinny Point Visitor Center, and gone inside to get maps of the hiking trails before unloading our equipment. Besides our cameras and tripods we had granola bars, flashlights, water bottles, insect spray and, in Pranesh's case, a little plastic figure of an obscure superhero called Action Clown Man.

Clown by day, crime fighter by night, Action Clown Man accompanied us on all our explorations. Pranesh would pose him in some unlikely or amusing spot—peeking out from the crescent moon on a door of an outhouse in the Pine Barrens, for example -- and take his picture, which he'd post online. Action Clown Man had his own Facebook page, with some 3,000 people following his adventures.

Our gear unloaded, we set out. It was a crisp fall day with puffy clouds drifting in a pastel blue sky. The temperature hovered at around 65 degrees. It was a good day for a walk in the woods.

Or so we thought.

We hiked for miles through a forest of towering oaks, birches, and maples, occasionally passing ancient stone walls and foundations of ruined houses before emerging into a clearing. Before us was the abandoned village of Blackwell.

We could hear birds calling and some small animal—a squirrel or a rabbit perhaps—rustling through the underbrush. Other than that and the sound of our voices, it was deathly quiet.

We were in the Delaware Water Gap National Recreation Area. Locals called it the "rec area," or simply the "rec." Its name comes from where the Delaware River cuts through a gap in the Appalachian Mountains northwest of where we stood, high-fiving and exchanging quips about the Scooby-Doo crew, whose antics we'd grown up watching as part of the Saturday morning cartoon lineup. The rec covers 67,000 acres, taking in parts of eastern Pennsylvania and northwestern New Jersey, ending just over the state line at Port Jervis, New York.

We were in New Jersey, but it looked nothing like the way people imagine New Jersey to be whose only familiarity with the state comes from watching *Jersey Shore* or *Real Housewives of New Jersey*. It wasn't congested with traffic and urban sprawl, like Bayonne or Fort Lee, or stinking like rotten eggs, the way it does at Exit 13 on the Garden State Parkway. The beach towns with their rollercoasters and chili cheese fry stands might as well have been on another planet.

Out in the rec it was as unspoiled as it gets and still within easy driving distance of Manhattan. It's a naturalist's paradise, home to a diverse variety of plants and wildlife, including deer, bears, foxes, and timber rattlesnakes, a remainder of the forest that once covered the entire eastern United States. To this day it's still part of the largest temperate deciduous forest on Earth.

The air had the spicy, cinnamon scent of fallen leaves, and of rich, moist soil. Over on the Pennsylvania side of the river, torrents of silvery water plunged through gorges formed from dark grey shale. The largest is Bushkill, a dramatic series of eight waterfalls known as the Niagara of Pennsylvania. Others have picturesque names like Silverthread, and Deer Leap.

I'm not going to disclose how to get to Blackwell. When you're done reading you'll understand why. We figured it out by following clues we picked up from threads posted online by hikers and birdwatchers. When Blackwell was mentioned at all it was simply as a deserted village. Only this and nothing more, to quote Edgar Allan Poe.

Our self-appointed mission as urban (and rural) explorers was to document places before they were gone, worn down by the elements, destroyed by vandals, or demolished to make way for a strip mall or a subdivision filled with McMansions.

The four of us had explored lots of abandoned places, among them Jungle Habitat, a Warner Brothers theme park in West Milford that closed down in 1976, and Greystone, a former psychiatric hospital in Morris Plains. The latter was a hulking, gothic monstrosity straight out of a Hammer horror film.

Greystone's gone now, demolished a few years ago. To give you an idea of its size, before they built the Pentagon it was the largest structure in the United States.

That's part of what intrigued us: the history behind the places we sneaked into. The other part was the weird things we found.

The beauty salon at Greystone was especially freaky, with its row of old-fashioned standing hair dryers and mirrors made of polished metal. I suppose that was to prevent patients from breaking them and stabbing someone. On one of them somebody had spray-painted INSANE IN THE BRAIN in dripping red letters.

The crumbling walls had faded posters on them of women with beehive hairdos and Jackie Kennedy bouffants. Standing on the filthy, lumpy linoleum floor, trying not to breathe too deeply of the stale air that stank of rat urine, I imagined patients sitting under the dryers, their hair in curlers, eyes staring, mouths slack, getting beautified after undergoing shock treatments or lobotomies.

Sometimes there were fences to climb to get to where we wanted to go, but they were nothing like the fence surrounding Blackwell. That fence meant business: chain-link, nine feet high, topped with a double layer of razor wire. It was the kind of fence you'd expect to see around a prison yard, keeping the bad boys in.

There would be no convicts prowling the streets of Blackwell; squirrels and chipmunks yes, and the occasional raccoon or fox. From our research we knew the residents had been forced to leave in the 1960's.

So why the need for such a formidable security fence?

"Some politician probably had a friend who owned a fence company and he got a kickback. That's how it goes; the taxpayer always gets screwed," Tyler said, sounding like a grumpy senior citizen instead of a college kid.

Tyler is Mason's cousin. He and Pranesh go to Rutgers in New Brunswick. Mason works at a day spa, convincing rich older ladies they could have skin as dewy and flawless as hers if they paid hundreds of dollars for a series of facials and expensive lotions. I've known Mason since middle school.

I'm Jenn, by the way. I work in customer service for an insurance company. The best I can say about that is it pays just enough to prevent me from quitting and moving back in with my parents.

This is probably a good time to relate the official version of how Blackwell came to be deserted. It goes like this: Back in August of 1955, around the time Danny and the Juniors were proclaiming rock and roll as being here to stay, Connie, a Category 4 hurricane with winds of up to 100 miles per hour, slammed into the eastern seaboard. It swept north up the coast, leaving a swath of destruction from North Carolina to Massachusetts.

Connie was followed five days later by Hurricane Diane. In eastern Pennsylvania an estimated two feet of rain fell, further saturating ground that was soaked by Connie. Water levels rose in the river valleys, creating some of the most destructive floods the area had ever experienced. Dams burst, producing a surge of brown water that took with it bridges, trees, roads, houses, and anything in its path.

Near Analomink, a resort town in the Poconos, there was a campground owned by a Baptist minister named Leon Davis. Reverend Davis rented cabins overlooking Brodhead Creek to members of his congregation as a place for them to go and prayerfully reflect on the natural beauty of their surroundings.

Forty-three members of Rev. Davis's flock were at the campground on the night of August 18, 1955. They took refuge in the attic of a house on the property, praying and singing hymns as rain pounded on the roof. Within a space of fifteen minutes Brodhead Creek overflowed its banks and rushed through the house, sweeping it away, along with everyone in it. Only six people survived. Most of those who drowned were women and children. The youngest was two. Their bodies were found the next day, wedged in the branches of trees.

By the time the floodwaters receded, the back-to-back storms left 184 people dead, 99 of them in the Delaware Valley.

Congress responded by commissioning the Army Corps of Engineers to review a 1930's study that proposed constructing a series of dams throughout the Delaware River watershed. It would create a lake roughly forty miles long and a mile wide. At its foundation would be a giant dam made of earth and rocks, 160 feet high, running across the Delaware at the southern tip of Tocks Island. It was to be the largest dam ever built east of the Mississippi.

Blackwell, population 214, was in the project's crosshairs. Its residents would be among 600 families to be removed from the reservoir zone under orders from the federal government. Some of the families had deep roots in the area, having been there since before the Walking Purchase, when a man named Edward Marshall walked 55 miles within an 18-hour period on September 19, 1737 in order to claim the entire west side of the Delaware Valley from the Lenape Indians.

Residents staged protests, outraged by the loss of their homes. They were joined by environmentalists concerned by the threatened loss of wildlife habitat. The outcry, coupled with the growing cost of the war in Vietnam, put an end to the Tocks Island project. It was officially declared dead in 1975. The families that were forced off their land relocated elsewhere, bitterly, in most cases. As the years passed, Tocks Island became just another unpleasant memory from the 1970's, like Love Canal and Three Mile Island.

That's the official version of what happened. We were to find the truth was very different when it came to Blackwell.

We walked single-file over the section of fence that had been flattened by a fallen pine tree, our arms held out to the sides for balance. It hadn't been long since the tree fell. The dirt was fresh around its exposed roots and sticky sap was still oozing from where the trunk had split.

The chain-links flexed beneath my boots. We always wore boots on our explorations, the rugged steel-toed kind, even Morgan, who ordinarily favored stilettos. Those were fine on the dance floor or for sashaying down the street, attracting admiring glances. In the woods there were snakes and ticks and poison ivy, not to mention rotten logs and holes in the ground.

Once inside, we waded through knee-high grass toward a cluster of houses. Trails were cut through the grass, the kind made by deer. So far we hadn't seen any. I made a mental note to check myself later for ticks. It had been a bad year for Lyme disease.

A rusted red tricycle lay on its side on the frost-heaved front walk of a bungalow, next to a blue and white girl's Schwinn nearly buried beneath a tangle of poison ivy.

At the house next door, a wooden plaque was fastened beside the front door. It was warped by exposure to the weather but you could see it had a picture on it of a girl in a blue sunbonnet watering some flowers. Underneath it was printed, "The Holcombs. Come on in and sit a spell!"

There were still curtains hanging in the windows. I went up the steps onto the porch, walking cautiously in case the boards were rotten. Pulling a tissue from the pocket of my jeans, I used it to clear a semi-circle in a dirt-streaked front window.

There was furniture inside, including a TV with a screen no more than eighteen inches wide in a wooden cabinet. Facing it were a couch and a pair of easy chairs, their flowered upholstery shredded by rodents and stained the color of tea from leaks in the ceiling. Spiders had been busy over the half-century they and the rats practically had the place to themselves. Webs draped the furnishings like ghostly dust sheets.

I got out my digital Nikon, thinking about how to caption the pictures when I posted them online, maybe something like: "Somebody got a little behind on the housework."

On the coffee table was a scattering of mail and a woman's purse.

That's when I had the feeling something wasn't right. Why didn't the woman take her purse with her when she left for the last time?

"Why didn't they take their stuff?" I asked the others. They were gathered around, cameras raised, taking in the eerie living room frozen in time to when Lyndon Johnson was president.

"Maybe they refused to leave and the government went in and dragged them out by force. Eminent domain, orders to evict and all that," Pranesh said. He was considering going to law school, although we tried to convince him New Jersey already had too many lawyers.

"Yeah, but her purse. She'd need her purse. Her driver's license and her credit cards would be in it," I said.

236

Mason lowered her camera. "Maybe she didn't drive and she didn't have any credit cards."

Tyler chimed in. "Maybe her husband wouldn't let her drive or have credit cards. He could have been like, 'Woman, you ain't going nowhere. Get in the kitchen and make me a sandwich.'"

The sight of that dusty room made me thirsty. As if by unspoken agreement we took our water bottles out of our backpacks and drank. The water in my bottle was lukewarm and tasted of plastic. Mason asked, "Does anybody want to see if the door's unlocked?"

She didn't sound too keen on that idea. The boys glanced uneasily at each other. Nobody made a move to try the door. I didn't want to go inside. I wondered what would happen if the lady who owned the purse was still in there. What if she was upstairs taking a nap and we woke her up?

I pictured a middle-aged woman in a pink nylon nightgown lying on a bed. Her eyes would open at the sound of someone entering the house. They would be solid black, with no trace of humanity in them. She'd smile, exposing teeth like needles. Then she'd sit up and swing her legs off the bed...

I pushed that image aside. "Let's go over there," I said, pointing to a building with a false front, like the ones in Western movies. "Dodd's Store" was painted in fading white letters on the side. There were two gas pumps outside, a red one and a white one. Both were pitted with rust. The red pump was for Gulf. The white one was for something called Gulf No-nox.

"Thirty-one cents a gallon. That's cheap. The last time I got gas it was two dollars and thirty-nine cents a gallon," Pranesh remarked.

"That's about the same as what it costs now, when you adjust for inflation," Tyler told him.

Pranesh looked dubious. "Are you sure? That doesn't sound right."

Tyler said he was sure.

"If you say so. Let's see if we can get inside. I want to get pictures of Action Clown Man with some old-time merch, if there's any still in there," said Pranesh. He removed the plastic figure from the front pocket of his hoodie.

Action Clown Man had floppy yellow shoes and a red rubber nose. His buff, muscular body was encased in a blue bodysuit that had a wide white belt with the initials ACM on it. Action Clown Man was ridiculous, which is why Pranesh liked him.

He took off at a run, shouting, "Power up for action, honk-honk!" That's what Action Clown Man always said when he transformed from a clown into a superhero, the "honk-honk" being the sound his rubber nose made when it was squeezed.

As we ran after him I noticed more trails where the grass was trampled down to the bare dirt. We still hadn't seen any deer. I wondered how they got in. Deer are good jumpers, but unless they were being chased by a bear or a pack of feral dogs, there didn't seem to be any incentive for them to risk getting tangled up in the razor wire on top of the fence, and they must have jumped the fence in order to get in. We'd only been able to get in because we found the place where the tree fell. Before that we walked completely around the perimeter of Blackwell—almost two miles according to my Fitbit—and found no other means of entry.

"No Trespassing" signs were posted on the fence every hundred yards. We ignored them, just as we ignored any similar signs we encountered on our explorations.

At one point on our search for a way inside we discovered a closed gate wide enough for a truck to drive through. A dirt road led away into the woods. The gate was equipped with a brushed chrome keypad lock. I was fairly certain those hadn't been invented yet when Blackwell was evacuated. Like the fence, the lock provided more security than seemed necessary to keep trespassers out of an abandoned village in the middle of nowhere.

Maybe the deer got in the same way we did, I thought. I could have been wrong about the pine tree having fallen recently. It could have happened weeks or months before we got there, but that didn't seem likely. The needles on its branches were still green.

The springs on the store's screen door squealed as Pranesh opened it. Behind it was a wooden door. It was unlocked. Pranesh went in, followed by Tyler, then Mason, then me. We looked around, shocked by what we saw.

The shelves were fully stocked.

"It's still here, all this stuff. Why wouldn't they take it away when everybody had to move out?" Mason wondered.

We didn't have an answer to that, nor did we have an answer for why all the lights were on. If syrupy instrumental music had been playing, the way it does in old TV shows where there's a scene in a grocery store, we might have turned tail and ran, but the only sound was a low buzzing coming from the fluorescent tubes hanging from the ceiling.

To our right was a wooden counter with a chunky brown cash register on it. It had round, pastel-colored push buttons. Whoever made the last purchase got a five-cent refund, according to the amount displayed behind a clear panel on top.

Before us were aisles filled with merchandise—assorted canned goods, health and beauty products, boxes of cereal—the usual sort of things you'd find in a general store.

Everything was immaculately clean. The linoleum floor sparkled. If we hadn't known better we would have thought it was still open for business.

I picked up a cardboard box containing something called a "Toni Kit" from a display at the head of one aisle. It had all the necessary ingredients for a do-it-yourself permanent wave. On the display was a picture of two identical, coy-looking women with puffy hairdos. The ad copy beneath asked, "Which twin has the Toni?"

"Check it. Big Swinger 3000. Groovy, baby." Tyler held up a boxy camera made of gray plastic. "This thing on top is a flash cube. It took four flash pictures before it was used up. Then you had to put on another one. They were instant pictures, too, sort of. This was cutting edge, back in the day."

Pranesh put Action Clown Man on top of the Big Swinger and took a picture with his digital camera.

Mason and I wandered through the aisles, examining the items on the shelves. Boxes of Jell-O were seven cents. Tuna was priced at three cans for eighty-nine cents. Two bottles of ketchup cost fifty-nine cents.

I was looking through a rack of old comic books, wondering if any of them were valuable, when Mason called, "Jenn, come over here."

I found her in the aisle where the cereal was. She was holding a box of Himalayan Balance Sports Nutrition protein bars and frowning. Her voice sounding strained, she said, "It was here on the shelf. The expiration date says June 17, 2018."

There were four more boxes on the shelf, each containing twelve protein bars. They all had the same expiration date: June 17, 2018, eight months in the future. They couldn't possibly have been there since the 1960's. Did they even make protein bars back then?

Her brown eyes wide, Mason asked, "Who do you think put these here?" She glanced toward the back of the store and lowered her voice. "Jenn, the refrigerator cases in the back have cans of soda in them. *Cold cans!* And orange juice, and milk, all with sell-by dates that haven't expired yet. Why are the lights and the refrigeration working when nobody lives here?"

That was a good question. It creeped me out. Why was the power still on in a store that hadn't had a customer since before the Apollo 11 moon landing? Who were the boxes of protein bars for, and the fresh milk? I thought of all the horror movies I'd watched and got a bad feeling.

I was about to say we should get out of there, fast, when I remembered the gate in the fence and the road leading into the forest. I relaxed. The answer was obvious.

"It must be rangers from the park service. This is probably one of their outposts."

Mason gave a relieved smile and put the box back on the shelf. "I thought it was Bigfoot."

"Bigfoot?"

"Yeah, I thought one got captured and they were keeping it here, you know, studying it. That's why they needed such a big fence, because Bigfoot's really strong."

She was serious. I started to laugh.

"You think Bigfoot eats protein bars?"

"Why not? It's possible."

"Well, he's not in here. Maybe he's at his Zumba class," I said, making her chuckle.

We found the boys standing outside on the cracked concrete apron in front of the store. I wanted to start back. We had a long walk ahead of us but the others weren't ready to leave yet. Tyler and Pranesh said they wanted to check out a building they'd spotted on top of a small rise. Its cedar shakes might once have been painted a cheerful bright red, but they'd faded to the color of liver. There was a square tower on top with a bell inside. Off to one side we could see swings and a seesaw.

Pranesh ran a hand through his spiky black hair and adjusted the straps of his backpack. "It's a genuine one-room schoolhouse. In the olden days, teachers used to spank kids with a wooden paddle when they were bad."

"Spank me, Miss Teacher, spank me hard. I've been a naughty boy," Tyler squeaked in a falsetto voice. He grinned and rubbed his hands together. "I wouldn't mind getting spanked by a hot young teacher."

241

Mason told him he was disgusting. She suggested we look at the schoolhouse and then start back. I was relieved. I wanted to be gone before the park rangers returned.

"Let's go have a quick look and get out of here before the rangers come back. Mason found some of their stuff inside," I told the boys.

"They're not coming back yet. It's not even three o'clock. They're still out looking for guys fishing without a license," Tyler said, as if he knew their schedule.

Pranesh agreed. "Even if they come back, all they'll do is tell us to leave. The signs didn't say they prosecute trespassers."

Mason turned to face him. Hands on hips encased in size 2 jeans, she said, "Just because it didn't say doesn't mean they won't. Can't they fine you for trespassing? I think they can even send you to jail."

"Trespassing's just a disorderly offense, no biggie. You worry too much," Tyler told her. "It's not like rangers are real cops. They won't do anything."

We followed one of the trails worn into the grass up to the school. It was wider than the others we'd seen, the dirt packed solid underneath. There were no hoof prints, or deer droppings. I knew from Girl Scouts that deer leave round droppings like rabbits, only bigger. In one place the ground had been muddy and then dried out, leaving the imprint of a shoe. It was a large shoe with a waffle sole, at least a size 16. I pointed it out to the others.

"Big park ranger, huh? Dude must have been almost seven feet tall," Pranesh said, studying it.

"Unless it was Bigfoot," I said, looking at Mason.

"It wasn't Bigfoot. Everybody knows Bigfoot doesn't wear shoes," she said.

I caught a flash of movement in the bell tower on top of the school. Whatever it was, it was light colored and ducked down

242

below the open windowsill before I could get a good look at it. I thought it must have been an owl or a hawk.

We reached the playground. Mason and Tyler tried out the seesaw while Pranesh filmed them with his GoPro. The metal hinge beneath the wooden board groaned as they went up and down. Tyler sank down on his end, leaving Mason suspended in the air, legs dangling, shrieking in mock terror.

He made as if to jump off and send her crashing to the ground, causing her to scream louder. "Don't! Let me down gently. I swear, Tyler, if I break my tailbone I will kick your ass."

Tyler laughed. "You won't be able to, not with a busted tailbone."

"Just watch me," she said grimly.

Pranesh shut off his GoPro, saying, "Seesaws are dangerous. It's a good thing they don't allow them on playgrounds anymore. And see how it's paved with asphalt instead of woodchips or rubber? Old-time playgrounds were hardcore."

Tyler let Mason down and hopped off. "Let's have a look at the schoolhouse."

We walked around to the front and tried the door. It was unlocked. We went in and looked around, our boots clumping on the bare wooden floorboards.

We were in a foyer. A line of coat hooks was set low on one wall. Over them were six names printed in block letters on strips of masking tape: KAREN, GEORGE, LINDA, DODIE, MIKE, PAUL.

The foyer led to a classroom with large windows along two sides, letting in the afternoon sunlight. Facing a desk that must have belonged to the teacher were two rows of three wooden desks with hinged tops. Schoolwork was still on them, as if the bell had rung for recess and the children had gone outside and would return shortly, their cheeks flushed from playing. Except the last bell for recess at Blackwell Elementary School rang over half a century ago.

Above the blackboard behind the teacher's desk was a line of cards with the letters of the alphabet written on them in cursive, upper- and lower-case. The blackboard really was black, not green like the ones when I was in school. On it someone had written in white chalk: "There is a finite upper bound on the multiplicities of entries in Pascal's triangle, other than the number 1."

Beneath it, in someone else's handwriting, was: "True. The upper bound is 12."

I studied it in puzzlement. This wasn't a math problem for kids. I didn't even know what kind of math it was.

Tyler came up behind me. "Combinational number theory," he said, surprising me. I'd suspected his slacker persona was a pretense and he was actually quite bright, but I'd never even heard of combinational number theory.

"What's that?"

He leaned in closer, examining another series of letters and numbers written on the board. Sounding abstracted, he said, "Number theory is devoted to the study of integers."

Mason flipped her hair. "That clears it up. Integers. Yep. Of course."

Tyler tapped his finger against the blackboard. "If I'm not mistaken, somebody solved Gascard's conjecture. It's stumped experts in algebraic K-theory for a long time."

Pranesh groaned. "Stop. You're making my head hurt. So somebody really good at math came in and wrote on the board. Big deal. It was probably one of the park rangers, showing off."

"Like the genius janitor in *Good Will Hunting*," I said.

"Matt Damon," Mason said, nodding her head. "Robin Williams was in it, too."

A worksheet on one of the desks caught my attention. Labeled "February Fun," there was a red construction paper heart Scotch-taped to it. The paper had yellowed over the years, as had the tape. The heart had been angrily X'ed-out with black crayon. Someone had scrawled: "That's not what a heart looks like. Mrs. Holcomb's heart looked like this."

There was a fist-shaped human heart drawn in brown and red crayon. It was accurately done; veins, arteries, the whole deal.

Holcomb. That was the name on the house where the woman's purse was.

It was a sick joke, it had to be, but suddenly I didn't want to stay there another second.

"Guys, let's go," I said.

A door beside the blackboard opened and a man stood there, filling the doorway. He had a tangled white beard and was bald, except for two fluffy white tufts over his ears. His big, impassive face was blotched with purple skin cancers. He was old but he looked strong. His arms bulged out of the cut-off sleeves of his flannel shirt. He took a step into the room, slapping a thick, knobby piece of wood like a club against his left palm.

"You were screaming on the playground," he said in a deep, gravelly voice. "The playground's not for screaming. Mrs. Holcomb was very strict about that."

In a high voice he trilled, "No screaming on the playground, children. Screamers on the playground will go into the *Thinking it Over Room*."

Then, back in his normal voice he added, "That's what Mrs. Holcomb called the room back there by the stairs leading up to the tower, the Thinking it Over Room." He jerked his chin over his shoulder to indicate its location. "After we took Mrs. Holcomb apart to see what was inside her we changed it to the Screaming Room. Everything screams in there: people, rabbits, even frogs. I bet you didn't know frogs can scream, but they do, under the right circumstances. They scream loud."

He grinned, revealing big yellow teeth. He took a step closer, swinging the club. We backed away toward the door leading to the foyer, and the outside. Once outside we'd make a run for it. The

245

man not only looked strong, he looked fast, like one of those bulked-up football players who can run like the wind. I'm not a fast runner. I could feel my heart slamming in my chest. I'd never been so terrified in my life.

"We're leaving now. Sorry to bother you," Pranesh said. He plucked Action Clown Man off the teacher's desk.

"You're not leaving; it's playtime," the man said, taking another step closer.

A voice spoke up from the doorway leading to the foyer, "Goody-goody gumdrops. I love playtime!"

A tall old lady leered at us with one bloodshot eye. Where her other eye should have been was a puckered red hole. Her gray hair hung to her waist in ropelike tangles. Bizarrely, this hag was dressed like a schoolgirl in a pleated skirt that came to just above her knees, white knee socks, and a dirt-streaked white blouse with a Peter Pan collar. On her feet were black rubber boots. As a final creepy touch her wrinkled lips were outlined in dark red lipstick, a generous amount of which was smeared over her teeth.

She was blocking the door to the outside. Like the man she looked strong. Even worse, there was another man looming behind her. He was old like the others, and every bit as large and threatening.

"Girls, Dodie!" he said happily, catching sight of Mason and me. "Two girls!" He rubbed the crotch of his tattered blue jeans and leered at us.

We were trapped. My cellphone was in my backpack, but even if I could get it out and managed to call 9-1-1 there might not be a cell signal out here, this deep in the woods. Even if there was, it would take a long time for help to arrive.

Since flight was out of the question, it would come down to a fight. There were three of them and four of us, but none of us were any good at fighting. Action Clown Man was, but he was five inches tall and made of plastic.

I looked around for something to arm myself with. The desks were too heavy to pick up and throw, but there was something I could use: an American flag on a wooden pole stood in a tarnished brass holder next to the teacher's desk. No wonder Mrs. Holcomb's purse was still in her house; they'd killed her. In the Screaming Room. No way was I going in there, not without a fight.

I yanked the flagpole out of its holder and shook it at the man and woman in the doorway. "Back off. Let us out."

The man let out a howl of outrage. "Put that back! Dodie, make her put it back. She's disrespecting the flag. It's not supposed to be used to hit people with. It's for saying the Pledge of Allegiance." He pronounced it as if it were all one word: *pledjaleegints*.

Tyler held up his hands. "Nobody's hitting anybody. We'll leave and forget we were ever here, okay?"

The man with the club slammed it down on the teacher's desk with a resounding crash, making Mason cry out. He roared, "This is our place. Outsiders aren't allowed in but you came and looked at our stuff and screamed on the playground. Nobody screams on the playground. It's against the rules."

He was breathing hard, getting himself worked up. He'd charge at us in a minute.

"Whack 'em, George!" urged the man standing behind the woman he called Dodie.

George. Dodie. Those were two of the names above the coat hooks in the foyer. Could these freaks have gone to school here? All the residents were supposed to have been evacuated. What were they doing here, besides torturing animals? More to the point, if they'd killed their teacher, why weren't they locked up? Maybe they *had* been locked up, in some kind of juvenile facility. They could have been released and come back here, but how did they get over the fence, and where did they get the fresh food that was in the market? Somebody had to be helping them, but who?

While I brandished the flagpole, the flag swaying back and forth as if I was leading a parade, Pranesh held up Action Clown Man. "See this? It's got a transmitter in it. I summoned help. They're on their way. You'd better leave us alone."

The man who'd encouraged George to whack us craned his neck. "What's the brown boy got, George?"

George curled his lip. "It's just a stupid toy clown, Mike. The brown boy's making fun of us. Let's see if he's laughing when I bash his brains in."

He raised his club. Pranesh shrank back, still clutching Action Clown Man.

From outside came the sound of revving engines, followed by a squeal of brakes. An amplified male voice rang out. "Attention! We have you surrounded. Come out with your hands up."

Dodie stamped her foot in irritation. "Darn it, there goes playtime."

"Come out slowly, one at a time. Don't try anything; we're armed," the voice said.

The one called Mike turned and shuffled away, his hands raised. He was followed by Dodie, then George, who dropped his club and gave us an evil glare. Mason, Tyler, Pranesh, and I stared at each other, nonplussed. My knees were shaking. What now?

"Action Clown Man saves the day," Pranesh said, his voice trembling.

"We're not safe yet. There are people out there with guns," Tyler reminded him.

Mason wrapped her arms around herself. "They can't be any worse than George and Dodie and Mike."

The voice boomed, "Who else is in there? Come out, slowly. Keep your hands where we can see them."

The police, I thought with relief. At that point I wouldn't have cared if they charged us with trespassing and made us pay a fine, or even if they threw us in jail. Jail would be infinitely better than playtime with Dodie, George, and Mike in the Screaming Room.

Six men and a woman stood next to a pair of black SUV's with darkly tinted windows. They wore camouflage. There was no insignia visible, either on their uniforms or on the vehicles.

"They're not cops *or* park rangers," Tyler whispered to Mason. She shushed him.

Six of them were pointing chunky-looking objects with pistol grips at our former captors. At first I thought they were guns but then I recognized them from TV as tasers.

Dodie must have recognized them too, because she shrieked, "We'll be good! We promise! No stingy things!"

The one with the bullhorn seemed to be in charge. He had a shaved head and was built like a weightlifter. He turned to the others. "Pair off. Take them to their quarters. Keep your distance. If they make a move toward you, zap 'em."

They paired off, each pair warily conducting one of the three old people past the abandoned houses and around the corner.

"Okay," said the man with the shaved head when they were out of sight. He put the bullhorn in one of the SUV's and took out a tablet. "Let's see some ID."

It didn't seem like a good idea to protest. Wordlessly we handed him our driver's licenses, which he scanned into the tablet and handed back to us. Frowning, he said, "This is government property. How did you kids get in here?"

I'm twenty-seven. It felt insulting to be called a kid.

"It's part of the recreation area," I said. We were out walking and we noticed part of the fence was down and we were curious to see what was in here, so we came in. That's all. We didn't think we were doing anything wrong."

He shook his head, his lips twisted in disgust. "You didn't think you did anything wrong," he repeated incredulously. "This entire area is posted against trespassing. There's a huge fence with razor wire on top, and you guys didn't notice? You thought you'd stroll in and have a look around, is that right?"

When we didn't reply, he pointed to the ground. "This, right here, is not part of the recreation area. It's government property. *Federal* government property, got it?"

We nodded.

He turned and indicated the schoolhouse, the abandoned homes, and the store. "All this belongs to the federal government. It's a highly sensitive area. You kids could have been killed. Hand over your cameras, all of them."

He deleted the video files and then gave our cameras back to us. Sounding less angry he said, "You say the fence was down? Where? Show me."

We showed him. He took in the fallen tree and the leveled section of fence in silence. Then he unclipped a radio from his belt. The belt was made of green webbing and held an array of items including a flashlight, a baton like the ones police carry, and an egg-shaped thing I was fairly certain was a grenade.

He spoke into the radio, "Salad Bar, this is Green Light, do you copy?"

A woman's voice crackled from the radio. "Salad Bar here."

"Are the three Mouseketeers buttoned up nice and snug in their quarters?"

"Yessir."

"Good. Now get a repair crew on the horn. Tell them a tree took down part of the fence in sector Bravo. Tell them to get out here on the double and fix it."

"Yessir," the voice replied.

The bald guy went to place the radio on his belt, but paused. Lifting it to his mouth again, he spoke into it.

"And Salad Bar?"

"Yessir?"

"Next time one of the perimeter motion sensors goes off, make sure it gets checked out. I don't care if it's 3:00 a.m. and pissing down rain, don't assume it's just a deer or a goddamn woodchuck or something. Send somebody to check it out. If nobody's available, you roll out of the sack and check it out yourself. Do you copy?"

"Yessir, copy that," she said, sounding abashed.

He put the radio away and squatted on his heels, examining the fallen fence, shaking his head and muttering.

Pranesh cleared his throat. "Um, Mr. Green Light? Who were those old people? How come they're here?"

He rose to his feet and narrowed his eyes. "First of all, my name's not Mr. Green Light. You can call me Brislow. Just Brislow. Don't try to look me up online because you won't find anything about anyone by that name connected to this place, *capiche*?"

"Got it," Pranesh said.

"Good." Brislow put his hands on his hips. "What I'm about to tell you is not to be repeated to anyone. Not to your boyfriend, not to your girlfriend, not to your dear old grandma. Don't blog about it, don't tweet about it, don't do whatever the hell it is kids do now, Snapchat or whatever. Just STFU about it. You understand?"

We murmured that we understood.

"I'm gonna give you the abridged version. You kids know about the Cold War? They taught you about it in school?"

Mason said, "You mean like the Cuban Missile Crisis? With John F. Kennedy and the Russian dictator, Gorbachev? Kennedy went, 'Mr. Gorbachev, tear down this wall,' and he did."

Brislow's stunned expression said he didn't know quite how to respond.

Tyler spoke up. "We know the United States and the former Soviet Union were allies in World War II, but then things got bad between them. The space race, spying, proxy wars, the Domino theory, we know about that, at least in general."

I'd read about some of the things that went on during the Cold War, crazy things like experiments in mind control using LSD and attempts at remote viewing through telepathy and at moving objects simply by concentrating; psychokinesis, it's called. Had something equally weird gone on in Blackwell?

Brislow leveled a steely brown gaze at us. "You have to imagine what it was like back then. We had the bomb, but so did the Russians. People were scared shitless, expecting the world would go up in flames at any moment. Even if nobody pushed the button, it looked like a land war between the superpowers was inevitable, one that would make what was happening in Vietnam look like a barn dance. For that we'd need soldiers. Not just G.I. Joe dogfaces, but killing machines. Big, strong, fearless guys who *enjoyed* killing."

"Like Vikings?" Mason asked.

Brislow shook his head. "Worse than Vikings. The Vikings at least had a religion and some kind of moral code. Not these soldiers."

He went on to explain that in a secret government laboratory, a team of scientists led by a former Nazi set to work on a formula that would turn ordinary soldiers into monsters. Brislow said there were dozens of Nazi scientists brought over from Germany after the war, given immunity from prosecution in return for helping us beat the Russians.

"They should have known better," he said. "But desperate times call for desperate measures. They came up with a formula they tested on dogs. From what I heard, the dogs went from tail-wagging, stick-fetching, friendly mutts to fucking nightmare hellhounds. Excuse my language, girls," he said, looking at Mason and me.

A deerfly buzzed in my face. I brushed it away. I was beginning to get an idea about where all this was going.

Brislow continued, "They knew it worked on dogs. They were going to try it on chimpanzees next, but in the meantime they hit a glitch in the form of a budget cut. Thank God for that budget cut. I wouldn't like to think what the formula would do to chimps. The dogs were bad enough. I heard it took twenty rounds of ammunition to put one of those mama-jammers down. It kept coming, teeth bared, going nuts, despite being torn apart."

He went on to explain how the formula, in the form of chewable tablets, was packed into stainless steel containers with screw-on tops and loaded into a Jeep to be taken to Picatinny Arsenal, the military research facility in Morris County. On the way, one of the containers rolled off the back of the Jeep and onto the shoulder of a road near Blackwell, where four kids out picking blackberries discovered it. They unscrewed the top, found what looked like candy, and ate it.

"Kids will eat anything that looks pretty, like Tide Pods. You guys shouldn't eat Tide Pods, by the way. They're poison," Brislow said, as if we might be inclined to do just that.

We had no intention of eating Tide Pods, but we nodded solemnly.

Brislow sighed, then continued his story. The tablets the kids ate had a side effect the scientists hadn't anticipated. Not only did it make them stronger, it also increased their intelligence dramatically. They went from being normal kids to geniuses, practically overnight. Their teacher was flabbergasted. She got in touch with somebody at Princeton University, who reached out to someone at the Institute for Advanced Study, who caught the ear of the CIA.

The end came quickly. The four kids who ate the tablets murdered their classmates and their teacher, Mrs. Holcomb, the lady who strongly disapproved of screaming on the playground. They killed several more people in Blackwell before the village was evacuated. The reason given to the public for the evacuation was that it was part of the Tocks Island project.

The "Blackwell Children," as they became known in top secret circles, were kept in the deserted village, where they were studied,

253

supplied with food, and prevented from ever leaving. One of them, Karen, died of cancer in 1981. Dodie, Mike, and George were the remaining survivors of a group of kids who'd gone into the woods one summer's day in 1965 to pick berries and had been turned into monsters.

As we stood there, stunned, a truck came rumbling up from the direction of the village. Like the SUV's, it was unmarked. Three men dressed in camouflage jumped out and proceeded to unload panels of chain-link fence. They saluted Brislow, who returned their salutes with a brusque gesture. Then he turned back to us. "That's the story. Now get the hell out of here."

We went, practically running, anxious to put Blackwell and everything in it far behind us.

ABOUT THE AUTHOR
JILL HAND

Jill Hand writes time-travel adventures based on bizarre true stories. Her novels, *Rosina and the Travel Agency*, and *The Blue Horse* follow the adventures of a young woman rescued from a railway accident in 1889 by a mysterious twenty-fourth-century enterprise known as the "Travel Agency," which is in the business of time-travel tourism.

Her work has appeared in eight anthologies so far. She writes science fiction, fantasy and speculative fiction and is on her way to becoming a cyborg, having artificial lenses in both eyes and a spine made up mostly of titanium.

DOLVIN, MISSOURI

By: Richard Beauchamp

I first heard about Dolvin from my dad, as it was where he worked. It wasn't on any map I could find, yet according to him it was only an hour away.

He used to work as an HR consultant for Bantor, one of the largest agricultural chemical companies in the world. It was his job to make sure the people living in places like Dolvin were happy, or content at least, and made good on their contracts. They also hired private security details to act as local constables, in order to do civilian checks and make sure everyone living within the legal boundaries of the community followed the rules, which they were very, *very* strict about. He had never talked about his time working for Bantor or Montane until the legal case blew up. I know there was a lot of controversy regarding Bantor's farming practices, and he was forbidden to talk about what he did on the job, which I always thought was a little odd for an agricultural company. But I soon found out there was much more going on than that.

I remember coming home from school one day, and he was sitting in front of the TV, crying. I asked him what was wrong, and he just sat there looking at the screen, tears rolling down his face. My mom was perched in the corner, regarding him silently. It was a bizarre situation, and at the time I didn't understand why he was crying.

On the television was a newsfeed ticker announcing a landmark lawsuit being brought against Bantor & Montane Corporation. I saw snippets of the subtitles and grew nervous. *Horrendous human rights violations... Over thirty confirmed communities... Paid to keep quiet... Awful deformities... Coercion...*

Finally, my dad laughed, and then looked at me, an unhinged expression on his face.

"The truth is finally out there. My god, they took it to the bastards. The world will know about the monsters who provide them their food. We will be judged."

After all that had happened, I didn't think he would agree to come back. But after a few discussions with my editor and my dad, he agreed right off the bat. Next thing I know, we were riding along in his old pickup, driving down winding back roads for over an hour. Finally, after feeling convinced we were lost, he pointed the sign out to me. It was riddled with buckshot. Strung around the metal post were three catfish heads, decayed to the point of mummification. It was a backwoods omen if I had ever seen one. I squinted to read, and I could just barely make out the letters.

DOLVIN, POPULATION: 338
A BANTOR & MONTANE COMMUNITY

The land we travelled to get there was hilly and forested, but as soon as we came along that straight shot of the highway with the sign, it flattened out perfectly for miles around. It was like we were at the bottom of some giant bowl, a fertile valley surrounded by bluffs on all sides.

It was a sea of gold and green, miles and miles of pristine laser-leveled farmland, with combines and tractors lazily crawling along the landscape. The town itself may have been condemned, most of the residents forcibly evicted and taken into protective custody, but the farmland was too good to leave idle. With the world population approaching eight billion, you couldn't afford to condemn the land, even if what had gone on there was part of one of the biggest conspiracies in history.

In the distance I could see the tops of a few buildings, but what immediately caught my attention was the large skyscraper that stretched to the heavens like some epic monolith. It looked wholly out of place in this quiet farming village. We drove further down the road, and that's when I saw the first of the houses.

My jaw dropped in surprise—they weren't houses, they were *mansions*, huge plantation style homes that, when we drove up close, were dilapidated, falling apart from lack of care and maintenance. I realized then, that this place wasn't your typical one stoplight farming township at all.

As we drove into the heart of the village, my dad locked the doors.

"There're still a few hard-liners living out this way, and most of them don't like visitors. They might think we're press. Keep an eye out, and keep your camera out of sight."

It wasn't long afterward when we saw our first Dolvinite. I couldn't help but gawk at his appearance. It was one thing seeing them on TV, but in person, Jesus Christ.

It was in the mid-1980's when my dad got drafted onto one of the lower echelons of the B&M board, something called a "sustainability initiative." Many companies were making significant breakthroughs in GMO technology at the time. The problem was, the EPA and FDA were tying up all the patents due to consumer and worker safety.

Bantor's talented legal team figured out a way around the bureaucratic red tape. At the time, Bantor was the leading agrichemical company. They sought help from Montane, who was the foremost biological agricultural company, the latter owning huge stretches of land throughout the world. Pooling their resources, the two corporations bought massive swathes of private land, creating whole new townships in the process. The end result was the founding of several communities where the corporations wielded complete control over their citizens' daily lives — and where they could test new agribusiness products without government intrusion or oversight.

You would think carrying out this sort of operation would be illegal, but no — Missouri already had laws in place allowing them to do this, and Dolvin was one of the first of these progressive new communities to be unveiled. In each new jurisdiction where the companies operated, they took advantage of similar legal framework or pushed for advantageous changes in legislation.

Still, despite that what the companies did was legal, it just wasn't right, especially considering how everyone who lived in Dolvin had to sign non-disclosure agreements about what went on there. And even with the agreements and court-issued gag orders, news of blatant human rights violations occasionally surfaced.

Most people were willing to turn a blind eye to the abuses. Back then, we were facing a worldwide food shortage. Global famines brought starvation death tolls to an all-time high since the middle ages. Supermarket shelves were empty, governments imposed emergency food rationing. There were riots. People were scared, hungry, and desperate.

To most people, the Bantor-Montane partnership was a godsend. Their merger allowed for the development of radical new fertilizers, growth enhancement hormones, herbicides and pesticides that produced exponential gains in crop yield. All of a sudden, places like the frigid wastelands of Siberia, the arid plains of Africa, and even the great American deserts could be turned into highly productive farmland. It was nothing short of a miracle when the company carried through on its mission statement: "A better future through agriculture."

But no miracle as great as the one Bantor & Montane had brought about comes without a price. Working at communities like Dolvin, the company's scientists and engineers had produced real results, on real crops and real people—some amazing, and some horrifying.

We were on the main street now, where I saw what I'm sure was once a picturesque rural thoroughfare. A row of brick and mortar buildings in that old-school 1950's look that had all the essentials: Randy's Hardware Store, JJ's Restaurant, Dolvin Food Co-Op and Grain Supply, Billy's Auto Repair, all deserted and derelict, the windows busted out, some covered in graffiti. They had a billiards center painted eggshell white with tinted windows; it was called Cock 'n Balls, can you believe that? They even still had their old specials placard out in the gravel parking lot: *Friday night 8-ball tournaments, grand prize $200, $8 catfish baskets and $3 rails.*

In that parking lot stood a man who looked ghostly in appearance. My dad apparently recognized the guy, because they waved to each other; and the man, who had just been... *standing there...* in this empty parking lot in this weird dead town that didn't make any sense, lights up at the sight of my dad and runs over.

What the camera doesn't show you, what they don't really tell you on the news reports, is that you can literally *see into them.* They're literally like those transparent cave toads you see in National Geographic. The guy, Herman Davis, apparently knew my dad well, and the two were good friends. We pulled into a parking space and I got out, feeling incredibly freaked out by the whole thing. The news reports made it sound like these people were only a step above feral animals, but Herman seemed friendly enough.

Herman and my dad shot the breeze for a while, their conversation eventually shifting to the topic of Herman's wife. His face went stolid as he related that his wife was the one who kicked off the latest investigation into Dolvin. She posted a video to YouTube about how the company was forcing residents to either get sterilized or abort their pregnancies.

Herman's wife hadn't been the only one who'd tried to get the word out about Dolvin. Other residents had also tried, and all of them had their videos taken down. Coincidentally, they all either "fell sick" or committed suicide shortly thereafter.

A lot of money was sunk into the smear campaign the Bantor & Montane PR staff used to discredit the residents' claims. It worked too, and most people didn't pay attention to these strange video confessions. It was through sheer luck that Norah Davis's video caught the attention of Krista Gosling, a Missouri social worker for the state Children's Welfare Service. Her video showed something vaguely resembling a human infant in a few frames. Gosling, having seen the video, was legally obligated to investigate the matter. As a result, the video was flagged for possible child abuse before the corporation could take it down.

It was her investigation that lifted the veil from Dolvin and the other Bantor & Montane communities. Her startling exposé revealed that all of Dolvin's residents, since 1989, had developed the same horrendous skin condition not seen anywhere else in the world.

Herman and my dad talked for a while. It seemed they were on good terms, despite that my dad worked for the company that caused so much harm to this community. I had not seen many by way of Dolvinites, but if Herman was any example, then what the company had wrought here was freakish by any measure. He was skinny to the point of emaciation, had no eyebrows or hair, and was dressed in only ripped jeans and a sleeveless John Deere T-shirt.

He must have thought my dad or I was staring, and so he took his shirt off to show me the extent of his condition. I could see his spine, his ribs, and the lattice work of veins and nerves in his system; the purple and red and greenish blobs of his internal organs; even the flow of his blood. It was disturbing and disorienting at the same time, and I had to look away. I thought I was going to be sick.

Herman seemed none too bothered by my reaction. I guess he was used to it by now. Before he could put his shirt back on, I did manage to snap some clandestine photos of his body.

Herman's condition arose from the use of a pesticide blend called Dichombenaise Mo-2. It was a big seller for the corporation, and one of the most effective pesticides to date. This blend made crop losses due to insects a thing of the past. Before its release to the buying public, early research and development had revealed human contact with the compound resulted in dermatological manifestations identical to those found in Dolvin's population. But by the time Dichombenaise Mo-2 hit the market, B&M had learned how to minimize the side effects in humans. This compound was the first major stride toward solving world hunger. Naturally, progress came with costs, and the residents of Dolvin paid more than their fair share for these advances in science.

Herman invited us back to his house, a grandiose mini-mansion like the others that stood in Dolvin, dotting the sea of grain like a backwoods archipelago. The inside of the massive house was as tasteless as its exterior, chock full of things only a middle-aged billionaire bachelor farmer could want—which of course included an indoor bowling alley and movie theatre. And yet, standing in that house, you forgot you were surrounded by barren nothingness, row upon row of abandoned mansions whose previous owners helped save humanity from the brink of starvation, who were now either dead or relocated to strange places and treated as pariahs. In his home, you felt like you were a part of a normal, albeit eccentric community, not a ghost town with an infamous past.

After giving us a tour of his home, he showed us some old photos. In them were some of the first crops they grew with a hormone called SNb231—tomatoes the size of bowling balls, corn the size of skateboards, crop yields which back then would have been unheard of. Then he showed us pictures of his family, of him, and of Norah, who, despite her skin condition, was a beautiful woman in her own right. After that came a photo of Herman standing beside Norah with a swaddled figure in her arms. This photograph had been taken at an odd angle that obscured my view to the newborn, but from what I could see, the child's face looked odd somehow, as though flattened.

Herman paused here, photo album on his lap, no doubt picking up on the trepidation coming off of me and my dad. Then, before he could convince himself against it, he handed us another photo.

My god, what it depicted was worse than anything I could imagine.

As I said before, part of my dad's job was to check up on the people of Dolvin, both to ensure that they were kept reasonably comfortable, but also to keep them from making too much noise. Keep in mind that the town's first residents were not from around here—they consisted entirely of out-of-state farmers who had been vetted for their loyalty to the company and the extent to which they could be bribed to keep quiet.

Right from the start, these people were told that they would be exposed to previously untested chemicals, and that they might experience adverse medical reactions as a result. But in exchange, they were promised a home and a stipend well beyond anything they could ever dream of making as farmers. B&M, being the "exemplary corporate citizen" its internal PR department thought it was, also reinforced the notion that these brave farmers' sacrifices would save millions of lives from the global famine.

All went well for a while—I mean, well enough despite the horrific side effects like the people in Dolvin experienced—until something happened that no one had anticipated: the people in these communities started having babies.

It was such a basic part of life that it shocked the company how no one in their legal or corporate ethics departments had seen this coming. The people who had signed the waivers and NDA's were adults, but no one had accounted for them having children, or what effects the company's new compounds would have on developing fetuses. When the company became aware of its blunder, it turned over its entire legal department—quietly, because if word got out of the mass firings, it would have caused a dip in B&M's stock price.

Despite B&M's best efforts at image control, it could not hold back the truth for too long. Eventually, photographic evidence of Dolvinite babies was leaked to the worldwide media. But the final push against the company's spin doctors came in the form of a shaky video taken with a handheld recorder. It was a clip of a Dolvinite woman giving birth.

The child—if you can call it that—was expelled from its mother's womb in a torrent of blood and afterbirth. Born without anything resembling a skeleton, it was hardly more than a gelatinous mass of floating organs encased in a tissue-thin sac of translucent flesh. In its flattened face were black button eyes and malformed flaps where its nose and mouth ought to have been.

This child, like many that came after it, died during birth. Their skin was so thin and weak that the act of being expulsed from their mothers' bodies tore them open like a leaky zip-top bag full of warm, runny meat. Childbirth often proved just as deadly for the mothers too, as the layers of skin stripped off the newborns clung to their mothers' insides, inevitably leading to sepsis and death.

Once B&M saw that the babies were dying and killing their precious female workers in the process, they immediately banned Dolvin residents from having children. Women who went to the community's hospital exhibiting pregnancy symptoms were forced into having abortions. Mandatory pregnancy tests were administered once a month to all female workers. To quell the outrage the company's decisions had stirred up, B&M raised the residents' stipends. This move was largely effective, although some did still choose to defect from the company town and denounce B&M's activities there. Those few were often never seen or heard from again, except occasionally in the local obituaries, their lives having been taken in traffic collisions or some other freak accident. In every case, there never was any evidence that might tie B&M to the disappearances, although many still had their doubts.

Eventually, the negative press was too much for even a global giant like B&M to control. The government stepped in and condemned Dolvin, declaring it a disaster area. The residents were forced to move out at gunpoint, though some remained, staunchly refusing to give up their homes.

Such was the case with Herman. Looking the way he did, he couldn't live anywhere else. Outside of Dolvin, he might be shunned as something less than human, at best; and at worst, he might be lynched.

Eleven people still live in Dolvin. They had all the money they needed, they had their dream homes, and if they moved anywhere else they would be persecuted as freaks.

Maybe it's human nature, or maybe B&M's PR department was to blame, but once the world learned that people like the Dolvinites existed, their knee-jerk response was to vilify them. In the public's eyes, people like the Dolvinites had sold their bodies to science — these freaks were wealthy beyond imagination because they had no shame in allowing scientists to experiment on them. Having spoken with Herman and my dad, I know better — most of the Dolvinites didn't do it just for the money. The corporation tricked them into thinking they were martyrs, sacrifices in the name of freeing the world from the scourge of famine.

Learning the truth made me feel incredibly sorry for Herman and the rest of the people who lived there. They were prisoners of their own success.

After a few hours at Herman's, we all took a drive to the community headquarters. Don't for a moment think this was a town hall or some other venerated civic institution. Dolvin's headquarters was housed in a skyscraper in the middle of town. Comprised of steel, plate glass and concrete, the building radiated corporate power. Indeed, it was the site from which B&M oversaw every aspect of the town's daily affairs.

The place looked scary as hell, and if what I'd heard had happened in there actually had, then I didn't want to be anywhere near it. But I was doing a story on it for the Saint Louis Post-Dispatch; it was my first assignment as a professional journalist, and I couldn't say no. This story could make my career, especially considering that I had a prime contact — my dad — in one of the most controversial stories of all time.

I didn't want screw this up, so I kept my mouth shut as we pulled up to the gunmetal gray behemoth at the end of a cul-de-sac.

It must have been at least fifty stories tall, looking more at home in the skyline of Manhattan than the laser-leveled farmland of Missouri.

Like much of its environs, the structure was condemned. No trespassing signs were strung in twenty-foot intervals, windows were smashed. Entire sections of the building had been charred black by angry protestors who had stormed the place and thrown Molotov cocktails. This all happened after Gosling's report had come out, but what really incited the residents to violence was the news that she was killed in a suspicious automobile accident — one of the ones I mentioned earlier.

Public outrage ensued, protests broke out worldwide. People flooded these so called "sanctuary communities," attempting to break into the corporate offices and attack the workers. What the protestors hadn't expected was the stiff resistance B&M had prepared. The company generated more money than some of the world's largest economies, and could afford a private security force to rival a standing army.

Shell casings skittered about my feet as I approached the building; in some spots, the casings covered the floor like a carpet of gravel. In other places, where I could see through the spent shells to the pavement, the sidewalk was stained black in splotches several feet across where untold amounts of blood had been spilled.

We cut the padlock off the perimeter chain-link fence security forces had hastily set up during the protests. Once past, we used our wire cutters again to snip through a barbed wire barricade just before the building's front stoop. My dad still had his copy of the master keys to the place. He jammed the key in and turned it, and the huge metal double doors groaned as they cracked open, revealing a lobby that swept wide in every direction. A reception desk sat at the far end by the elevators. At one time, there had been a foyer with couches, but all the furniture had been heaped up in piles at the front of the building to barricade the windows.

My dad crossed the lobby floor and rounded the front desk. Behind it was a door so hidden you could hardly see it against the backdrop in the reception area. The only proof it was there was a tiny metal cylinder that housed its keyhole. The door slid inward unto darkness when he unlocked it. In the faint light that filtered into the chamber beyond was a staircase leading downward.

I knew where he was taking us, and it made my heart race as much with excitement as with terror. Down below was where the killing was done, where the infanticide and sterilization occurred. Armed with my camera, my flashlight and my two companions, I followed them down.

I was immediately awestruck at how huge the subterranean portion of the high-rise was. At the bottom of the steps, we came upon an atrium the size of a small shopping mall. This room branched off into three wings: a walk-in clinic, a trauma center, and a fucked up version of a nursery. A stairwell at the end of the hall led to the laboratories below.

Plastered on the walls were corporate-approved signs on healthy living and proper child-rearing. The graffiti covering them was proof that the protesters had gotten at least this far. I snapped a couple photos of the rooms and some graffiti that caught my interest. One patch of graffiti made me take pause—I meant to photograph it, but hesitated, and in that moment felt a twinge of sympathy for the person who'd scrawled it. It was from the Bible, First Epistle of John 9:1.

But if we confess our sins to God, he will keep his promise and do what is right: he will forgive us our sins and purify us from all our wrongdoing.

Whoever had written it had seen fit to rewrite it across much of the enormous chamber we were in. That passage was written across the triage desk, on the walls of doctors' offices, the floor, and especially in the nursery, where overturned infant beds bore the stains of crusted-over bodily fluids.

Written on the double doors to the nursery, in capitals, one word to each door, was: I'M SORRY. I took a snapshot of this, then noticed something out of the corner of my eye. Along the hallway and past the door was a window that looked in on the nursery. At the depth of the room was a corona of blood at about waist-height, which is where I figured the person who had scrawled all the graffiti had sat before putting a bullet in his head.

Many of the doctors and staff who worked down here had taken their lives once Gosling went public. Although my dad was never part of the team responsible for the abortions or for coercing people into undergoing sterilizations, he had reported several couples to the human relations office whom he suspected were pregnant. It often weighed heavily on his conscience. In his mind, he was no better than the Gestapo reporting families for hiding Jewish refugees in Nazi Germany.

My dad and Herman stood in the atrium for a long while, their flashlight beams slowly tracing over the Bible passages and the discarded legacy of a monstrous world, crying silently, both of them. You know that picture of the two men standing in the nursery, holding hands, tears rolling down their faces? The one that won all of those awards? That was my dad and Herman. It felt perverse to capture that moment. You could tell that those two men, in that scene, were reconciling with two different pasts that would leave their souls scarred until the day they died.

I didn't want to, but I had to capture it all. People needed to see the raw, uncut side of Dolvin.

I let the two men have their moment, figuring this was as good a time as any to search the laboratories downstairs. What I found there was hallway upon hallway of identical workstations — large glass rooms chock full of measuring equipment; shelves laden with various colored vials and beakers, all of which were labeled with complex chemical codes in sharpie on masking tape; centrifuges and other lab gear.

Near the end of the corridor was an office. It was locked, so I carefully punched out the window set into the door, then reached through it to unlock the door knob. Whoever had worked here had left in a hurry. File folders were arrayed in messy stacks across a desk; several had spilled their contents onto the floor. A file cabinet stood in the corner, its drawers slightly ajar. I rifled through it, turning up research notes, internal memoranda, and other data that was not pertinent to my news story, until I found the clinical trial reports for Dichombenaise Mo-2. Knowing I'd hit on something important, I shoved a stack of file folders out of the desk chair and sat down to review my find.

I could hardly believe what I was reading — the reports didn't read anything like what a scientist might report. It was pure horror.

Many more children had been conceived and delivered in Dolvin than anyone had expected. People were having children in such numbers that the company could hardly keep quiet about the deformities — or about the methods employed in the infants' disposal. The newborns were "discarded" en masse, away from their grieving and hysterical parents, in a sterile chamber where several could be asphyxiated at once, and their remains summarily incinerated.

271

All this was typed out in emotionless technical writing, signed off by a man named Dr. Albert Munson. I recognized the name; he was one of the key witnesses in the first round of lawsuits lodged against B&M. After the lawyers had completed his cross-examination in court on live television, he nonchalantly reached into his coat pocket and withdrew a vial that he held up to his lips. Moments later, he spilled out of the witness box and began convulsing on the floor, his mouth ringed in froth. He was dead in seconds.

The evening following his death, a representative of his estate read his suicide note on national television:

You all make us out to be monsters, and we are, I accept that. But what you do not understand is that all progress requires sacrifices. Without the advances in science my team and I had brought about, millions, possibly billions of people would have died from starvation. We saved our planet and allowed the entire species to thrive, yet you turn us into pariahs for the unfortunate casualties that come with ground-breaking research. You should be ashamed of yourselves.

This all brought back memories from years ago. I remembered asking my dad why the man had killed himself, and why my dad sometimes woke up screaming and crying in the middle of the night, waking up the family.

During the B&M trials, my dad was brought into court as a defendant. It came to light that he had been secretly assisting with Ms. Gosling's investigation, which helped get him clemency. His testimony put many of B&M's higher-ups away for a long time, and in exchange, he served only two years in prison. When he returned home, though, he was one of the most hated men in America. On the one hand, people hated him for his complicity in B&M's disgusting experiments. On the other, his willingness to help the prosecution had garnered the ire of many powerful people.

Only later would he explain to me, candidly, that he only worked at B&M because he wanted a better life for our family. That career helped him put my sister and I through college, and more importantly, afforded our family a level of comfort during frightening times. He wasn't alone in this sentiment either—many of his co-workers had families too, and wanted the same things for them. The way he saw it, he and his co-workers were not bad people; they were good people who did bad things.

Fast forward eight years later, and here I am, in Dr. Munson's old office, reading through company confidential memos. I felt dirty after reading them, like I'd unearthed something that should have remained buried.

I went back upstairs to the trauma center. There, I took photos of anything I thought would support my story. I took photos of hospital gurneys that had been outfitted with thick leather restraints. I snapped a picture of a flowchart prepared by B&M that explained the procedure for extracting and disposing of "Series D afflicted fetuses." It called for removal of the children from the womb using forceps, then administering a lethal drug cocktail to ensure an instant, painless death. The final step was depositing the remains in a stainless steel chute that led to the incinerator in the building's lowest level.

Part of me knew that getting a picture of that horrible machine would probably get me a front page feature, but I simply didn't have the heart or the nerve to go to the bottom level. It felt too close to hell. Besides, it was time to go. I had seen enough, and was sure my dad and Herman had too.

My dad cried silently as we made our way back to town. I wanted to console him, but I held back. This was cathartic for him, and he might not get another chance to spend as much time in Dolvin as today.

273

Our car stopped when we came upon two Dolvinite men standing in the middle of the road, blocking our path. It wasn't until they'd plodded toward us some distance that we realized they were carrying shotguns.

Herman instructed my dad to wait in the car as he got out. He approached them with arms raised, palms out, indicating he was no threat. That was when the shouting began.

One of the Dolvinites aimed his gun at the car we were in. My dad shouted for me to get down, but my journalist instincts kicked in, and instead I snapped a few photos with my camera. The man with the gun must have seen the flash go off, because he shouted, "Hey!" just before emptying his double-barrel into our car.

The car shuddered with the blast, then slumped to one side. The Dolvinite's buckshot had obliterated one of our front tires.

Somewhere in the chaos I dropped my camera, but before I could recover it, the men were on either side of the car, shouting at us to "Get out, get the fuck out right now!"

As he reached for the door handle, my dad looked back at me with deeply apologetic eyes. It was the same expression he wore when he was on the witness stand, confessing the atrocities he had taken part in. I remember his haunted look, the way his mouth wrinkled as he frowned, because it was the last time I ever saw him alive.

Before I got out, I made sure to eject both rolls of film I had filled and put them in the back pocket of my jeans. I put a fresh one in the camera—that way, if the men wanted to smash my equipment, the photos I'd snapped earlier would be safe.

I exited our car just as my dad started talking to the two residents. Apparently, they all knew each other. The man shouting at my dad was named Bobby. He was none too happy that my dad had returned after all the negative press he had stirred up about Dolvin.

Before my dad could say anything in his defense, Bobby racked his shotgun and brought it level to my dad's face. I remember him screaming, "You son of a bitch! For all you did, you got off with just a slap on the wrist in court!"

My dad just kept quiet. Everything Bobby said was true, and there was no way my dad could argue against any of it. Instead of speaking, he took a step forward. I yelled at him to come back, but he merely glanced in my direction and shushed me, adding that Bobby was right about everything.

In a way, I think this was how my dad had wanted this trip to end. He never got over what happened in Dolvin, and being put under the spotlight during the B&M trials only amplified his feelings of guilt.

"It's okay, son," he murmured to me before turning back to face Bobby and shouting at him to do what needed to be done.

What came next should not have come as a surprise, but it shook me to the core regardless.

Bobby didn't shoot my dad — it was the other guy, whose name I never found out. Middle-aged and looking more tired than his time alive would put on, he'd been standing stock still the whole time during our standoff, a worried expression playing on his face. My dad's sudden shout had spooked him. The shotgun in his hands belched a gout of fire and noise that opened up a baseball-sized hole in my dad's chest.

I remember screaming, "Dad!" as time slowed to a crawl. My dad fell backward in slow motion as a mushroom cloud of gun smoke and blood rocketed out of his back where the ten-gauge deer slug had exited his body. When finally he hit the ground, lifeless, we all just stood there, staring at each other, dumbfounded by this sudden act of violence.

Then Bobby snapped out of his daze and pointed at me. I knew what he wanted before he could speak a word and clutched my camera to my chest like a woman fending off a purse-snatcher. By

275

the time he found the words to say, "Get that camera!" I had already turned on my heels and started running.

Herman, God bless his soul, did his best to slow them down. If it weren't for him, I'd probably be dead today. As soon as I'd turned to run, Bobby raised his shotgun, and Herman tackled him. The gun went off with a deafening blast, spurring me to run faster still.

Too afraid to look back, I zigzagged through desolate streets, ducking into and out of abandoned homes, hoping to throw my pursuers off my trail. I cleared the village in minutes and found myself in an open expanse of farmland. Not wanting to be caught out in the open, I ran into a sea of waving mutant cornstalks taller than me.

Twice I heard the booms of shotguns go off, and saw whole swathes of cornstalks seemingly vaporize as the men attempted to flush me out like a gopher. I ran at a crouch, blindly charging ahead into this green abyss, half expecting some massive combine to come out of nowhere and mow me down. And if that didn't happen, I was still as good as dead. I was going to get lost in this field while my pursuers, who were probably more familiar with the land, inevitably closed in.

I trudged through miles and miles of corn, choking on a miasma of fertilizer and ammonia tang that made my head spin. By some miracle, I blundered out into a clearing on the shoulder of the only road that led out of Dolvin.

I checked my cellphone, despite knowing I would have no signal out here. There were no cell towers anywhere near Dolvin. On top of that, B&M had strategically placed signal jammers to blot out any Wi-Fi or cellular signals that might stray near the village.

I followed the road out of town for miles until I eventually got a single bar of signal, and dialed 9-1-1.

I suppose I felt obligated, in a way, to do this interview. My excursion into Dolvin netted me shots that have since won me several prestigious awards, in both journalism and photography, but cost my father his life.

The citizens of Dolvin thought him a monster, as did most of the world. Contempt on such a universal scale takes its toll on a man, even one as stoic as my dad. In the end, I don't think he deserved all the blame he took. He was just a man who wanted what was best for the world, and to provide a future for his children.

As of the recording of this interview, in 2017, the world population is yet again approaching unsustainable levels. We are pressed to find new solutions to our old problems. The difference, this time, is that we have the work of people like Krista Gosling, and a tiny township in southeast Missouri, to remind us to take caution when pursuing solutions.

The chemicals developed by Bantor and Montane are beginning to lose their effectiveness. Insects are becoming immune to their pesticides, and the generational effects of their herbicides have both ruined the soil and corrupted aquifers. As the crisis intensifies, it is only a matter of time before people start considering whether the ends justify the same barbaric means as were employed in Dolvin and communities like it across the globe. I just hope that we learn from our mistakes.

About The Author
Richard Beauchamp

Richard Beauchamp is a North American writer who has been writing short form horror and dark speculative fiction for several years. You can find his works in such magazines as *Gehenna and Hinnom Magazine*, *Deadman's Tome Magazine* and several other anthologies, as well as several self-published novellas available on Amazon.

EVENTIDE, SUFFOLK

BY: ADAM MILLARD

I

It was upon a Thursday morning in late February that Charles Jennings, my esteemed colleague, marched excitedly into my office. I had just returned from a sojourn in Dorset, and so was not expecting to see my friend so soon, for he could not know that I had returned yet. Jennings didn't seem to notice me at first, standing there at the corner of the room with a brandy in one hand and a book of architectural images in the other. It wasn't until I spoke that I was sure he was aware of my presence.

"Jennings!" I said, for I have always referred to him by his surname, and he mine, since we are both Charleses. "Good to see you, my friend!"

Jennings brightened further when he saw me. "Ellis!" he exclaimed, then came toward me with his arms wide. We embraced momentarily—I have never been comfortable in the hold of another man, and so broke it off as soon as graciously possible. He went on: "I'm so glad to see you. I had no idea you were back yet. How was Dorset?"

I told Jennings of my trip; that I had visited both Sherborne Abbey and Corfe Castle, but the highlight of my week was investigating the ruined Norman church of Knowlton and its Neolithic henge monument. As I regaled him with the details, he nodded along—as one might expect—but I could sense his distraction.

There was something far more important than my Dorset excursion to discuss; Jennings was simply too polite to interrupt me.

"Your palpable excitement preceded you into the room," I said, motioning to a seat beside my desk. Jennings thanked me and settled into it, and I sat opposite. "What has you so animated this morning?"

I saw in my friend's face something I have never seen before: complete and utter exultation. He could not get his words out fast enough, and it was all I could do to keep up with his ramblings.

"I took a trip of my own yesterday, after receiving a letter in the post from persons unknown," he said. "At first I believed the missive to be a hoax, for it did not address me by name and there was no visible postmark, but after careful consideration I decided to gamble. I could not live with myself had I not packed post-haste and boarded the first train to the destination scrawled, in untidy cursive, upon the note."

"Calm down!" I urged him, for he was almost incomprehensible. "Take your time, Jennings. I'm not going anywhere."

Jennings settled back into the chair, removed a pipe from his breast pocket, and began to tamp it with sweet-smelling tobacco. "What do you know of *Eventide*?" he said, more calmly now.

I had not expected to hear that word uttered in my office that morning, and so it took me by surprise. "The village?" I asked. Jennings nodded, so I told him what I knew of the fabled village. It did not take long; there is very little available information on the place.

"If it *is* real," I said, "it is a plot of land somewhere in this country of ours, no larger than three acres, upon which a village exists in perpetual twilight. Which, might I remind you, is quite impossible."

Jennings lit his pipe and exhaled syrupy blue smoke into the atmosphere. "*Quite* impossible!" he confirmed. "And yet, I was

280

there just yesterday, and it is very much real. I slept in one of its abandoned huts—rather comfy it was too—and had it not been for the sound of distant birdsong, I'm sure I would have continued to sleep for days."

I had a good mind to eject him from my office, for I liked a joke as much as the next man, but this was a little childish for my tastes.

"What are you *talking* about, man?" I said, the derision clear in my voice. "Eventide is a *myth*. Fictional. A fairy-tale. There is no place on earth that experiences perpetual twilight. Even at the poles there are six months of light to counter the six months of darkness. Such a village is beyond the realm of nature and science. Did you perhaps see any hobbits there?"

It was my turn to play the juvenile, for I could not bear to be made a mockery of, least of all by one of my closest friends.

Jennings sat forward in his chair and produced a small, brown envelope from the inside pocket of his jacket. "I know it is difficult to take in," he said, placing the envelope down on the desk and pushing it gently in my direction. "But I assure you, Ellis, I am telling the truth. Eventide is real, and I shall prove it to you."

I picked the envelope up and removed the letter contained within. I held in my hand a single slip of paper with a series of numbers—52.2767, 1.6266—scribbled across its top. Beneath that was the following:

To whom it may concern,
Follow the numbers, and you shall find us.
Eventide.

That was all. There was nothing else obvious about the letter, no conspicuous markings that should lead me to believe it a forgery. I had naught but the word of my colleague and my own gut-instinct to go upon.

"This could have been sent by anyone," I said, examining the slip once more.

"I agree," Jennings said. "And had I not visited those coordinates myself, seen Eventide and its perpetual twilight with my own eyes, I would also remain dubious of its authenticity, as you do now."

Coordinates. Yes, that was what they were. It was the X marking the spot, leading Jennings directly to Eventide. A place that should not—possibly did not—exist, and yet I could not fathom the reason why. Why Jennings? And why would a resident of Eventide compose such a letter? To me, it was making less sense by the minute.

"You said you could prove it to me," I said, tamping my own pipe. "Yet you have nothing but a crude slip of paper in a brown envelope."

Jennings smiled. I could make out the slightly discoloured fang-tooth on the right side of his mouth, incongruous next to the perfect white of its companions. "We shall go there together," he said.

I could not believe my ears, for if this were a trick—and I was loath to think of it as anything other than one—the lengths to which my colleague was willing to go to deceive me were troubling.

"You want to take me to Eventide?" I said, a question I never thought would pass my lips.

Jennings's nod was far too eager for my liking. "Tomorrow!" he said. "We shall catch the first train. Now that I know its location, I shall have no trouble in finding it. I got lost a little yesterday, but that was my own—"

"Eventide?" I said, my booming voice severing Jennings's sentence. "You think I can afford to drop all of my work to accompany you on some wild goose chase, to a place which I'm almost certain is either a figment of your imagination or a cruel jest at my expense? Preferably the former, for there are several good asylums within the borough. You would fit right in at any one of them."

He tapped the smouldering remnants of tobacco from the bowl of his pipe into the ashtray upon my desk and sighed. "It is the only way I shall ever be able to prove it to you," he said. I could see something in my friend's countenance. An amalgamation of hurt and disappointment; I had offended him. It had taken many years, but I had finally offended him.

"If I go with you," I said, "and the whole thing turns out to be nothing more than a malicious prank, then I shall have no other choice but to draw a line underneath our relationship." It hurt to say, but there was no way I could ever forgive him if he made me into a fool. "This is your last chance to call it off," I went on. "Tell me you're not serious, that you are the author of that letter, and I shall forget all about the matter."

Jennings shook his head. "I can't wait for you to see it. I shall arrive at your residence at eight a.m. We have a long journey ahead of us, and—"

"I'll drive us in the Ford," I said, for I did not wish to get stranded in the middle of nowhere, reliant upon the trains, which were haphazard at best. "I'll be at your residence at eight sharp. And Jennings?"

"Yes?" he said, almost at the door.

"Not a word about this to anyone else, okay?" I said. Not because I was concerned our impossible discovery would be unearthed by another party before we had a chance to investigate thoroughly, but because I didn't want it getting around the university that I, Charles Ellis, was as gullible as a con man in love. "The last thing I want is Dean Hendricks catching wind of this. You know how he likes to impose himself and accept credit for our discoveries."

Hendricks was a crooked dean, the kind of man liable to stab you in the back with your own knife, if you weren't careful.

"Our secret," Jennings said, before leaving my office in precisely the manner in which he had entered.

I sat at my desk for a while, feeling as though a tornado had just been and gone. And yet, something niggled at me like a sore tooth, for even after I had offered Jennings the chance to retract his claim, he had persisted. Perhaps, I thought, there was a morsel of truth in his assertion somewhere.

I didn't have to wait long to find out for myself.

II

The journey was long. More than halfway across the country we travelled and, for much of the duration, something continued to trouble me.

If Eventide *was* real, how was it that no one — other than Jennings, apparently — had discovered it yet? And who, in this place of perpetual twilight, had written the note? Not only that, but who had then hand-delivered it to Jennings's residence? It was an awfully long way to travel just to leave a cryptic slip of paper in a mailbox. What if Jennings proved unable to figure out the coordinates? What then? A wasted journey, it would seem.

"How much farther?" I asked, for I knew not where I was going. Beside me, with a large map unfolded upon his lap, Jennings grunted something. "What was that?"

He lifted his head up. "Just a few more miles," he said. "Not far past Dunwich. There was a sign hanging upon a gate advertising fresh eggs. I'll know it when I see it."

Great, I thought. Out in the country, where even those with the severest of chicken phobias owned at least three roosters and a brace of hens, and we were looking for a sign peddling free-range eggs.

"Who do you think sent the letter?" I asked of my colleague. "Do you think there are people living there? In Eventide?"

"If there are," said Jennings, following a red line on the map with his index finger, "then they failed to make themselves known when I stayed over the night before last."

"But someone sent the letter," I pressed. "Which means someone, at least one person, knows of Eventide's existence."

"It would appear so," said Jennings.

"And that someone knows your home address."

"I never thought of that," he said. "Quite scary, when you put it that way, is it not?"

And it *was*. For if it was I who had received the letter instead of Jennings, I would have marched it straight down to the police station and ordered them to dust it for fingerprints.

"Then we should be on our guard," I said as I dodged a fresh road kill. A badger, perhaps, although the way it was painted to the road made it difficult to be sure. "We don't know what we're walking into, or whether this mysterious third party will, at some juncture, be making an appearance."

I must admit, I was somewhat terrified at the thought of it, and yet I couldn't fathom why. I should have been excited, and I was, but I was also anxious. What were we getting ourselves into? And what might happen should things go awry? No one knew where we were going. We would simply become two missing persons, sketches of our faces taped to telegraph poles throughout the town, our loved ones none the wiser as to what had become of us.

We drove on in silence for several minutes. Jennings glanced thoughtfully down at the map, grunting occasionally as we passed signs on the side of the road. I took it as confirmation we were still on the right path.

A mile past Dunwich, Jennings called out, "There!" He pointed off to the left, to where a sign hung askew upon a rotten wooden fence. "That's the sign! Take the next left, and prepare yourself. Things are going to get very strange from this point."

My friend was not wrong, for no sooner had I turned left—into what appeared to be an empty field—than the light began to fade. But that could not be, could it? I was still of the mindset that Jennings was playing me for a mug, so when the sky became even darker the further across the barren field we travelled, I was terrified.

"It's just the clouds!" I said, stooping into my seat so that I might get a better look at the sky overhead. However, to my surprise there were no clouds up there. There were stars. A trillion pinholes in the dark blanket of a sky. There was even a moon, bright as can be, but no clouds.

"I told you!" Jennings said, hammering his palms against the glove box in excitement. When he next spoke, his voice wavered, such was his exhilaration. "It's Eventide! The village that should not be!"

As much as I wanted to argue with my friend, to tell him how ridiculous it all sounded, there was very little I could come up with to explain the sudden blackening of the day. "I don't... I don't understand," I said, for my pocket-watch—which had not lost or gained a second in ten years, perhaps even longer than that—told me it was not even lunchtime.

And yet, off in the distance an owl hooted plaintively, and was that not the keening of a pair of foxes, either mating or fighting or both at the same time? Foxes and owls in the middle of the day? The chittering of nocturnal insects before the clock strikes noon? It was all I could do to keep the car moving forward in a straight line.

"It is a magic place," said Jennings, folding his giant map down into a square no larger than his hand. "I told you, did I not? Didn't I tell you, my good man? Now, we must keep on going straight. At the edge of this field, we shall have to take to foot. There is a large wooden stile, which we shall have to climb, and if I'm not mistaken, just through those trees there we will arrive at the village proper."

My heart was beating so fast and hard within me that I wondered if I would make it over the stile and through the trees to Eventide, or if I would drop dead at the edge of the field, a look of surprise upon my face, for the last thing I would see is that impossible night sky. A dark, star-pocked blanket which had only a moment ago been the blue-grey of a dismal mid-morning.

As I pulled up at the edge of the field, turned the engine off, and climbed out of the car, I felt wash over me a strange sickness. So nauseated was I that it was all I could do to keep my insufficient breakfast down. My mind swam with the impossibility of it all, and I was one moment deficient in saliva, and the next spitting it out as quickly as I could, lest I choke to death.

"I need a moment," I said, and even that would not be enough. Jennings humoured me, however, allowing me all the time I needed. He was a good friend, old Jennings, and would never deign to make me feel foolish, even when the opportunity was right there on a plate.

After several minutes, I straightened up from the bent-over position I had adopted and said, "Okay. I think I am ready."

I wasn't, but we couldn't stand in that damned field all day — night? — long. We could, I thought, get back into the car, head back across the field and onto the road we had been driving along just a few moments ago. What was the worst that could happen? I would never know whether Eventide was real, would have to take my colleague's word for it, which wasn't such a bad thing, was it? For there are some things which a person can go throughout their life without discovering.

"Are you sure?" Jennings looked at me with what amounted to pity. At least, that was how I interpreted it.

I took a deep breath, glanced up toward the moon that should not have been there, and said, "I'm intrigued, if nothing else. Let us get to Eventide, before fear gets the better of me."

"I do not believe there is anything to fear," Jennings reassured me as he scrambled over the wooden stile first.

Out of fear, I was barely a second behind.

III

We emerged from the trees—a forest of gnarly, leafless branches and thick black roots, which I'm sure reached up for us as we walked over them—breathless and wet from the rain. My mind was yet to acclimatise to the strange new atmosphere, and so I could not shake the notion that this was all just some surreal nightmare from which I would waken shortly.

As we climbed over an identical stile, I thought we had, somewhere along the line, lost our bearings. That we had gone around in a circle and returned to the very place we had set out from. I expected to see the field, and the Ford parked there a few metres along the tree line. So, when I glimpsed the first ramshackle hut—perhaps held together only by the termites—it came as quite a shock.

There were at least a dozen cabins, each a facsimile of the next, scattered about the 'village'. I could just about discern, through the ever-increasing darkness, the shapes of doors and windows, the unmistakable contours of long-neglected carriages, knotted tree branches limned by the moonlight. It was all very disconcerting.

"Eventide," Jennings said, not much more than a whisper. "We found it. One of the greatest discoveries of recent times, and it will be ours."

I shook my head, for that was not true. Eventide had already been discovered. We were here in response to an invite, a letter sent by Lord knows who. I shuddered at the thought.

"Where did you sleep last night?" I asked, motioning to the cabins all around us.

Jennings shrugged. "I think," he said, turning and squinting into the darkness, "yes, I think it was one of these." He pointed to three huts off to our right. "It was, as I said yesterday, relatively comfortable. However, might I suggest that we do not spend the night on this occasion? We should compile our report on this very day, make the announcement of our discovery tomorrow."

"It is not *our* discovery," I had to remind him. The rain became even more torrential, and I could not stand to feel its icy needles beating upon my face and hands any longer. "Come on. Let's get out of this—"

Just then, something moved through the darkness to our left. Jennings saw it, too, for we both turned at the exact same time. Indeed, I watched as a tendril of something grey and, dare I say, rotten, disappeared behind one of the cabins.

"Did you see that?" I asked, my own voice now little more than a whisper.

Jennings nodded. "I saw *something*," he said. "Crepuscular creatures are no doubt ubiquitous in Eventide." He scratched at his stubbled chin and shrugged, and I wanted to take him by the shoulders and shake him roughly, for how could he be so calm? How could he possibly maintain this air of fearlessness in this mysterious place? "One can only assume what we just saw was the tail-end of a badger, a fox, a—"

"It was *none* of those things," I said, for I was certain that what I saw had been carried along on two legs. Two legs at the very least. "I believe, Jennings, that we are not alone here tonight."

Tonight?

This morning?

I no longer cared.

"I fear you may be right," whispered my colleague. "But I have to show you Eventide in all its glory. You must see every inch of it to appreciate its unobvious beauty."

There was, as far as I could see, nothing beautiful about Eventide. It was derelict, and dark. So, so very dark. I had never wanted to leave a place so keenly, never to return. I was just about to articulate something to that effect when, up ahead, three more shapes darted through the gloom. This time I saw legs and arms, and yes, more tendrils of dark grey flesh trailing behind them as they moved.

"We have to leave!" I said, my eyes fixed upon that spot in the distance through which the creatures of Eventide had just pranced. "We have to get out of here now! Something is not right!"

Jennings, in a fit of either terror or denial, shook his head and said, "I saw nothing last night. I was utterly alone, of that I'm certain."

A howl pierced the night, and damned if my heart didn't stop beating for a moment or two.

I could feel them all around us now. Hidden creatures, whose refusal to step into the clearing was not for lack of courage, but rather a clever tactic. They, whatever they were, had us surrounded. This was their lair, *their* Eventide, and woe betide anyone who trespassed. I found myself pondering the origin of these things. Had they always been here, or were they once people like us, explorers and pioneers searching for undiscovered worlds? Were Jennings and I about to join their ranks?

Finally, I was able to move. I turned and made my way past three ruined shacks, ignoring the pleas of my colleague: "Come to your senses, man! This is the find of the century!"

That was when a second voice announced itself from somewhere I couldn't quite place. It seemed to come from all around and nowhere at the very same time, but I recognised it almost immediately.

"I didn't want to do it," said the voice. "They made me do it."

Stopped in my tracks, I turned to find Jennings standing there, glancing all around in search of the disembodied voice. We didn't have to wait long for the mystery speaker to step out of the shadows.

Tall, emaciated, and looking bedraggled — as if he had spent many years dragging himself through mud and raw sewage — Dean Hendricks emerged from one of the huts at the end of the street, if one could call it that. If not for his voice, I might have been unable to recognise him. I was used to seeing him dressed in dark, funereal suits, not the oversized robe draped over him now.

"They said they would release me," he groaned. "If I delivered two to replace me, they would let me go." Behind him, two disfigured bipeds bounded across the path, their tails whipping at the air, their pure-white eyes only visible in those instances they glanced our way. Hendricks didn't seem to be frightened of them. And why should he be? He had upheld his part of the deal.

Here we were.

The replacements.

"*You* sent Jennings the letter," I said, just as something bolted past me. I felt the wind as it moved inexorably through the night, but when I turned to see, there was nothing there. And yet I knew they could take us in a heartbeat, should they so desire, and there would be nothing either Jennings or I could do about it.

"I *had* to," Hendricks said, approaching us slowly, cautiously, his hands held out in a placatory fashion. "I'm not yet meant for other worlds. The things they do, the amount of people they have butchered here... I just... I didn't want to be one of them, and so I made a deal. I promised I would furnish them with two bodies, and in return they vowed to release me."

"How very noble," I said, my voice drenched with sarcasm. I wanted him to come closer, just a few more steps that I might swipe him hard across the face.

Jennings had backed away and now stood at my side, both of us staring into the darkness, looking for the creatures intent on slaughtering us. "This is my fault," he said. "I did not ask the right questions. I was blinded by... by all of this, and I leapt into this mess. Not only that, but I brought you with me."

I silenced him with a wave of the hand. "You weren't to know," I said. I did not blame my colleague in the slightest. If anything, he had revealed to me something that I had spent a long time searching for. *Proof* of Eventide. That the place even existed was a miracle; that it had its own food-chain, well, that was not something foretold in the legends. But some things never are, are they?

"I must leave now," said Hendricks, his gaunt face turning this way and that, making sure the creatures were satisfied with him before breaking into a run.

He came in our direction, and that was when Jennings removed from his waistband a dagger. I had seen this particular blade before — Japanese, ceremonial, sharp as hell — but I had never seen it wielded by Jennings with such intent. "Go!"

I stood there, frozen in the moment, and it wasn't until Jennings repeated the command that I understood. But I could not leave him at the mercy of those shadow-dwellers, whose tails looked apt to rend flesh from body and whose inhuman speed suggested it would not take long to do so.

But Jennings was not giving me a choice, for he rushed toward Hendricks and they both dropped to the muddy ground, where they began to wrestle and grunt and struggle to gain the upper hand.

The creatures were closing in now. I could feel hot, putrid breath upon my neck, could hear them whispering to one another, their sibilance likely to drive me insane if their appearance failed to.

I watched as Jennings plunged the ceremonial dagger into our former superior's chest, and then as seven, eight, nine dark shapes lunged from between the cabins, landing upon my friend and the wheezing coward, Hendricks.

I turned and ran.

Jennings's final scream came as I was halfway through the forest, with its arthritic branches and ravenous roots reaching for me as I went, and by the time I had the car started, there was only an unbearable silence, punctuated occasionally by my own mad whimpers.

IV

It has been several weeks now since those horrific events of Eventide. I can only assume that Charles Jennings and Dean Hendricks were devoured by those unspeakable creatures, whose village we had fortuitously stumbled upon. I am terrified of most things now. The darkness. The things concealed within it. Travelling to places unknown. I seldom venture beyond that which I already know to be safe, for fear of accidentally discovering another Eventide.

It is no way to exist, but exist I shall.

The policemen came to me again today, asking the same questions they have been asking since Jennings and Hendricks went missing. I am at a loss for what to tell them. Should I confess? Indulge them in tales of villages forever existing in twilight? Should I concede that, yes, I do know where my colleagues are, and that, yes, they are most likely dead by now, consumed by unearthly beasties not too far from here, and yet in a wholly different world?

I no longer sleep for more than an hour at a time, for even the darkness at the back of my eyelids is enough to send me spiralling inexorably toward madness. I often wake screaming, drenched with sweat, searching the well-lit corners of the bedroom for things that should not be.

I shall take Eventide to my grave, and hope that no one ever pays that godforsaken place a visit again, accidentally or otherwise.

There is already so much darkness in the world.

As I stare down at the slip of paper, the words and numbers scribbled upon it by a coward whose office now sits empty just a few rooms over, I realise that my world—what remains of it—will never be light again.

I think I hear something. A rapping somewhere in my office, or just beyond its paper-thin walls. I hear it most nights now, but it is forever growing louder, coming closer, and closer. I will not go searching for the source of the approaching sound.

I will wait for it to come to me.

And then I will go into the darkness one final time.

ABOUT THE AUTHOR
ADAM MILLARD

Adam Millard is the author of twenty-six novels, twelve novellas, and more than two hundred short stories, which can be found in various collections, magazines, and anthologies. Probably best known for his post-apocalyptic and comedy-horror fiction, Adam also writes fantasy/horror for children, as well as bizarro fiction for several publishers. His work has recently been translated for the German market.

EVERYTOWN ADVENTURES RESORT, SOUTH CAROLINA

BY: DAPHNE STRASERT

I don't know why you reporters still want to talk to me. You already know what happened. *Everyone* knows what happened. The cops are done sifting through it, so what more is there to tell? I mean, Jesus, you could just watch the documentary. All I did was find the damned place. What am I supposed to know that no one else does?

It was just an Internet rumor, one of those things people post about on Reddit, but no one ever actually believes is real. Everyone jokes that the EveryTown Corporation secretly runs some dark empire. Between the kids' movies and theme parks, they put on a show like they're all family-friendly and sunshine and shit, but there must be something in the Kool-Aid. I mean, no one is *that* happy.

Anyway, the rumor was that they built this huge luxury theme park in middle of nowhere, South Carolina. They wanted it to be an immersive experience. Families would stay at their resort hotels and eat in their restaurants and play in their theme park. It would be the EveryTown Experience from start to finish with nothing but the resort for miles. I found some promotional materials put out in the late eighties. It was supposed to open in 1993, but after '92, there was no mention of it anywhere. The tickets never went on sale.

That's not too weird. Parks go under, projects get abandoned. I didn't actually consider going there until one of my subscribers suggested I check it out. He said that his sister was hired to work there, but she couldn't arrive before the staff training started and the company terminated her contract. She's probably glad for that now. I mean, she's lucky she never met Peter Blythe.

I didn't expect much from my trip there, just a cool walkthrough for my YouTube channel. Abandoned parks are catnip for urban explorers, after all. EveryTown Adventures, though, it wasn't just abandoned; the EveryTown Corporation had wiped it off the fucking maps. The road that led there didn't even exist anymore. I took my Jeep as far as I could, but I still had to hike through ten miles of forest to find it.

When I got there, I didn't see any "No Trespassing" signs. That should have been my tip-off. Corporations don't want you snooping around their property, sure, but they always hang signs everywhere. It's part of the legal trappings. That was the first sign this place wasn't... normal.

See, when a company shuts down one of its facilities, they tend to clear out anything of value—merchandise, equipment, supplies, everything. I mean, if they have any time at all, that's what they do. Unless you're looking at a Fukushima kind of situation, nothing gets abandoned. Sure, they'll leave some things behind: things that are too big or too expensive to relocate, stuff that they don't have any use for. They know that people like me exist—urban explorers—and they don't want us to get our hands on anything. Then they lock it up tight, stick "No Trespassing" signs all over everything, and get the hell out of Dodge.

EveryTown Adventures, though... man, *everything* about that place was wrong. Like, deeply wrong. The kind of wrong that your bones recognize even if your brain tries to talk its way out of it. It was winter and drizzly, so just about the worst weather for exploring a rusty amusement park. I've been to some creepy places—you've seen my video from the Salto Hotel, right?—but my soul knew something really bad was lurking here. I've never... my hair never stood on end quite like that. And I hadn't even found anything yet.

The gates were locked. That wasn't exactly unexpected. What *was* weird was that they weren't *just* locked. Chains crisscrossed the rusted bars of the main entrance, held in place by four massive padlocks. Office furniture and rusted lockers lay on the other side of the bars—a makeshift barricade. Barbed wire curled over the top of the gate, the sharp ends still shiny, though the wires were coated in rust.

It was a lot to push through, and not an easy climb, but that didn't deter me. I shimmied up one of the ten-foot stone walls and tossed my pack over to the other side. Frankly, that was my saving grace, the only thing that kept me from dying right then and there. I heard the bag hit something, something that wasn't the ground. That's what made me look before I swung over.

There were spikes—big, wooden spikes—like someone had broken two-by-fours and planted them upright in the ground. And metal—bars or something that still had splotches of paint in different colors. They had been twisted apart so that they exposed jagged ends, rusted through. All of that was pointed straight to the sky, just waiting for me to come down.

Companies don't set booby traps. Someone didn't want people getting in and it wasn't the fucking EveryTown Corporation.

But everything was old. No one was maintaining the barriers. I'm not telling you this because it makes sense, more just because everyone always asks, "Why did you go in?" And that's tough to answer. There isn't really a good reason except that, you know, I wanted to. I needed content for the channel, sure, but I started the videos because I liked sneaking into places I wasn't supposed to see. I guess it just never occurred to me that I could find anything that bad. Maybe a homeless colony. Or like, a *lot* of rats. Not... well, you know.

Anyway.

Once I started into the park, there were no more booby traps.

It struck me that there wasn't any trash. The crews that take out the equipment and merchandise don't normally care too much about garbage left in the park, but this place… it was clean.

I mean, as clean as a thirty-year-old park can be.

The paint was peeling and the concrete had split where tree roots had burst through, but overall, it was still pretty nice.

I wanted to get to the rides, because those always make for the best shots. Character faces overgrown with brush and metal jutting out of the bushes—it's cool shit, man. But I passed a souvenir shop first. Normally, those aren't worth seeing. Most of the time, it's just a bunch of empty shelves, but this one... there were still stuffed animals stacked in the display, looking out with their big, glassy eyes.

That was actually... I guess that was the first time I saw the graffiti. You know what I'm talking about; they named the documentary after it.

"The Magic is Real."

God, it sounds so stupid, but I swear it still gives me the chills.

It was on the front door of the souvenir shop, right next to the window, in black spray paint. Not freehand, so I guess graffiti isn't quite the right word. It was made with a stencil, in the corporate font and everything, with little stars surrounding the words.

I didn't think about it all that much. It isn't odd to find vandalism in old, forgotten places. At the time, it was kind of reassuring, thinking that someone else had made it here before me.

The door to the shop was unlocked, like they were about to open for the day. Everything inside was laid out just like a normal store. Everything was covered in a layer of dust that was inches thick, but the merchandise was still on the shelves—glass snow globes and journals and stuffed toys and a whole wall of those headbands with the ears on them—all set out, all perfect. I got a good dozen pictures of that place, with the little stuffed mascot leaning against the side of the cash register and everything. There were thousands of dollars of vintage merchandise in that store. No one had ever come to collect it.

The front of the park was set up like the Hollywood version of a small town. There were lampposts and trash cans and that All-American vibe that works wonders when there are thousands of people packing the street. I mean, there were park maps in the

301

shops—faded and a little fragile, but just fine nonetheless. The only thing that looked out of place was the foliage. With no one to tend to the bushes and trees, they had grown out of control in the intervening years. Roots choked the cobblestones and the branches intertwined overhead, making everything just a little darker. That... and the graffiti. The deeper I got into the park, the more I saw that graffiti.

"The Magic is Real."

I found the carrousel first. It was this big, old-fashioned thing with dozens of horses and tigers and zebras. And, you know, while I never thought carrousels were fun, they never freaked me out. This one—I feel stupid saying this—all the animals looked like they were screaming. It wasn't anything I hadn't seen before, just standard stuff, but the tigers' eyes were wild and the horses' hooves seemed just a little too sharp. There were all these things that looked like they should be moving, but they weren't. With the peeling paint and cracked mirrors, I actually scared myself shitless walking around that thing. You know how you get when you're all by yourself: sometimes, you're your own worst enemy, and paranoia does you in.

I was standing by the chariot—the only thing on the carrousel that wasn't connected to the gears—setting up a shot with the zebra and lion in line with a kiosk in the background, and I swear something moved just out of my field of vision.

I swear to God. I know that sounds ridiculous. I might not remember it right. Maybe I'm just letting everything else that happened screw with me. Maybe it was my own damned reflection in the mirror or maybe there was a rabbit. Still, fuck, I saw *something move*, and I hightailed it away from that thing like it was on fire.

That right there tells you just how edgy I was feeling. I do this for a fucking living, okay? I've visited the Island of Dolls. I stayed overnight in an abandoned wing of Trenton State Psychiatric Hospital. My audience wasn't going to be impressed with the half-hearted spooks I'd found so far, so I gave myself a little slap and went on the hunt for something really interesting. That was when I found the rollercoaster.

I know they mentioned the rollercoaster in the documentary, but I feel like it got overshadowed by all the other stuff. Which... well, the other stuff is worse, don't get me wrong, but the rollercoaster really rattled me. That was the first time that I thought that maybe something *had* actually happened here, in the park, and that there was something more to those Internet rumors.

The ride entrance was set up for a long line. Concrete paths wound through probably a mile of landscaping, then through indoor character exhibits. But the guardrails—those metal things that keep people from skipping ahead in the line—were missing. They'd been cut out, sawed off at the ground, and the underbrush had grown over their stumps completely. Then it occurred to me—that's where the staff got those metal spikes that I'd almost jumped into back at the park entrance.

Later, I would come to learn that the spike pits went all around the park's perimeter. And the staff didn't just take the rails from the rollercoaster's queuing line. They pried up safety fences, stair railings... even the bars that kept people from falling onto the rollercoaster track. They'd cut out all of them, just cannibalized the metal from the whole damned park to keep the rest of the world out.

I made my way to a shack at the front of the line. Here was where park operators would seat passengers into the rollercoaster cars. I had to be careful getting there, though, because some of the boards that made up the stairs had rotted through. And, like I said, there weren't any safety railings.

The inside of the building was covered — *covered* — in that graffiti.

"The Magic is Real" and "We are the Magic" was written everywhere — on the walls and floor and ceiling, all of it set in perfect alignment, a grid of spray paint.

The coaster car sat on its tracks, ready to take off. In each and every seat sat a stuffed animal, one of the EveryTown characters. They were strapped in like they were about to go for a ride, their beady little eyes looking straight ahead in anticipation. I took that picture, the one that ended up on a lot of the news broadcasts. As far as what I found later, the network stations didn't air any of the other pictures on television. In fairness, I don't think the FCC's decency regulations would have allowed that anyway.

Stuffed animals were arranged in like manner at the other rides — the swings, the teacups and so on — all of them buckled in, ready to go. Some had survived the years better than others. Years of exposure to the elements had left some all but rotten. A few had been picked apart by birds for their nests. Still, just about everywhere I went, one of those things was staring at me.

And of course, there was graffiti. It grew like a patch of parasitic moss, leeching off of whatever goodness this place might once have held, and becoming thicker the closer I got to its center.

Eventually, my investigation of the park brought me to the administrative building. I could tell immediately that this structure was not meant for the public to see. It was devoid of the bright colors and embellishments that were reserved for park visitors, and was instead done up in generic corporate white—at least, initially.

Nearly every wall surface was covered in the same graffiti I'd seen since coming here, stenciled so compactly that hardly any of the original paint could be seen.

"The Magic is Real."

It was here that I found the PA room. And this was the weird thing: it was open. I don't mean that the door was unlocked; I mean the room didn't *have* a door. It had been taken off its hinges. Clean. Not broken. Someone had come in and—very professionally—removed the door from the frame. I don't know if you've ever worked in AV, but that's not something that happens. You need the door there to keep out the extra noise.

As I'd come to expect by now, the walls were covered in graffiti. I could barely make out the words, they interlocked so much, but a few of the stars still showed. Inside was the PA desk, with handwritten notes and announcements, and a tape recorder for premade messages. I turned the desk chair around to sit, but it already had something in it—another one of those fucking character dolls. It was wearing the AV headphones.

I looked through the papers, but found nothing too interesting. Most of it had to do with park operations. Among these things were park maps and staff guidelines, and a poster announcing the park's grand opening.

I remember that poster really fucking clearly. It was printed on a huge piece of poster board. In it was a picture of a family—the real nuclear ideal: blonde parents with two kids—standing on Main Street at the front of the park. But here's the kicker: someone had scratched out their faces. Instead of painted-on smiles, their faces were just blank. The poster's white backing showed through where their faces ought to have been. Under the company logo, someone had written "The Magic is Real. We are the Magic." Seeing that made the hair on my arms stand up, and I didn't even know what that meant... yet.

I mentioned the tape player, right? You've heard the recording, right? Of course you have. Everyone has heard it by now. Let me tell you, if I had known beforehand what had happened in there, I never would have pressed play. I still hear that shit when I'm trying to sleep. That... *voice*. I guess in any other context it wouldn't be so creepy.

You know which one I mean. It's the one that says: "Good morning, cast members. Who's ready for another *magical* day?"

Considering how things ended, you have to wonder: did the staff wake up to that message every morning? And on the last day, did they know what was going to happen, or was it just business as usual?

I mean, we've all heard about what happened with Peter Blythe. Every news network has done an exposé on him since it all came to light. But hearing his voice, how fucking cheerful he sounded, knowing that he —

Fuck.

Anyway, the PA room was like a control center for the entire park. Posted up on the wall was a map laying out all the attractions and the administrative buildings. Behind the park's HQ were the staff dorms. As this was the next building over, I figured I would head there next.

A thought occurred to me while I was on the way there. Just say to yourself: "staff dorms." This wasn't some mining town or army base where you'd expect employees to live on the premises, this was an amusement park. What were they thinking?

Okay, so maybe that was unfair of me to say. The park required hundreds of people to operate, it was in the middle of nowhere, and there wasn't anywhere nearby for the employees to live.

The dorms sat at the outer edge of the park. Things were decidedly less touristy there. Promotional posters hung from walls, each of them with the families' faces scratched out. There were

307

stuffed characters everywhere—sitting in trees, on beds, behind desks, all of them shriveled and ragged from the elements.

There were no doors anywhere in the building. Not at its entrance, nor at the residences inside, not even in the bathrooms. The dorms looked lived-in. It was unnerving, because the rest of the park was in decay and yet these rooms looked like their owners had just stepped out to do groceries.

Then there were the photos. They were everywhere, covering the walls of the rooms and hallways. They were all taken at the park and showed three or four staff members at a time, always wearing the park uniform, always smiling super big and bright like they were competing in a beauty pageant. In all of those hundreds of photographs, there was one person in common—Blythe. Just the sight of him made my skin crawl. He looked like a god-damned televangelist, for Christ's sake. A person like him, and what he was capable of, you would expect him to look like Charles Manson, but no—here he was, smiling, giving hugs and shaking hands like he was running for senate.

The room at the end of the hall was different from the others. There were pinholes in the wall where thumbtacks had supported a myriad of photos like out in hallway, except that in this room, the walls were bare. Someone had spray painted "Protect the Magic" on the wall above the bed. The mattress was covered in black plastic wrap and duct tape, looking like someone had torn up trash bags to wrap the mattress with. A character doll sat by the headboard, cotton stuffing bleeding out of holes where its black button eyes had been ripped out.

I'd done some research on EveryTown since heading out and discovered this had been Marcy Keen's room. Marcy was one of the few who had seen the writing on the wall. She knew this place was devolving into little more than a cult and tried to stop things before they went too far, but Blythe got to her first. He had her ousted from the group—no doubt evidenced by the character doll with ripped out eyes placed on her bed. But this came after his goons had slit her throat on her mattress one night — which explained the black plastic wrap. There were several other bedrooms arranged similarly, which meant Marcy hadn't been the only one who had disagreed with Blythe, though they likely met the same fate.

I found Blythe's room next.

I could tell it was his because it was the only one with a door. That says something about the man, doesn't it? He wouldn't let anyone else have their privacy, but insisted on it for himself.

Blythe ran the park's PA system. He was the ubiquitous voice in the sky, something more like a constant presence than a man. He wasn't even a manager, though according to reports, he was very charismatic. He was also extremely obsessive.

Like the other rooms I'd seen on the way here, his dormitory was covered in photographs, except these were different. For starters, the photos were of him. Also, in all of them — hundreds of them — he had replaced the faces of the people accompanying him with tiny cutouts of the EveryTown characters. The room was filled with a myriad of cartoon faces — all except his. His image was untouched. He had created a little world where it was just him and the characters, no people to mess it up.

The last place I visited was the castle. I guess that's the part you really want to hear about. It's what everyone asks to hear about. I've told the story a thousand different times, but everyone wants to hear it for themselves.

Nothing inside the park had been locked, so when I crossed the drawbridge to the castle, you can bet I was surprised that the door didn't open when I pushed. I retrospect, I should have taken that as a sign not to press on any further.

It took some time to break the lock, but even then, the door wouldn't budge. Something was blocking it from the inside. I kept pushing until I'd cleared some wiggle room, then squeezed through. I didn't get far. All sorts of junk had been stacked against the door to keep it shut. I'd managed to get inside, but then I had to maneuver over a pile of trash twenty feet high.

The lighting inside was dim. The only windows were narrow and positioned high on the walls. If the park had opened, the place would have been lit up by the huge chandeliers that hung from the ceiling, but the electricity sure as hell didn't work anymore, probably hadn't for decades. Thankfully, I'd brought a flashlight.

The castle's entrance was a massive reception hall with thirty-foot high cathedral ceilings. Built into a balcony at the depth of the chamber was the throne room, accessible via stairwells on either side that led to the second-story mezzanine.

Once I'd clambered past the barricade at the door, I heard the rattle of empty plastic bottles. I'd inadvertently stepped on a few as I made my way through the chamber. The floor was littered with them, and in places they were so thick you couldn't get by without kicking them out of your path.

Honestly, I didn't know what to make of it at the time. The barricade at the door and the bottles on the ground, I mean. It wasn't until I got upstairs and pushed open the door to the throne room that it all came together.

Jesus, nothing prepares you for something like that.

The door offered some resistance. As at the castle's entrance, there was something behind it keeping it from opening. I put my shoulder to it and gave a shove, and nearly fell headlong into the room when it finally gave.

The floor was covered in a carpet of mouldering bones. I remember staggering backward in shock, my mind unwilling to take in the horror of the place. I refused to accept these were people's remains—in my mind they were Halloween decorations, although part of me knew better.

Littered among the skeletons were more plastic sports drink bottles. Several of them were still clutched within bony fists.

That was when it hit me—they'd poisoned themselves.

Later, after listening to the audiotape from the PA room, did I realize what had happened that day. Blythe's voice had come on the speakers, crisp and cheery as ever, instructing his staff to assemble at the throne room. There was an element of command to his voice, despite how polite he sounded. And yet, there was also a sense of urgency. His announcement ended with: "Remember, the magic is real. We are the magic. Protect the magic."

God, can you imagine? To be so obsessed with your job that you cut off ties the whole world? Thinking that if you let outsiders into the park, it would ruin the *magic*? These people died for that. They died so tourists would not ruin the *experience*. They believed that shit, what Peter Blythe told them.

Forty-one people. Forty-eight if you count the staff they murdered beforehand. And the company just fucking left it there, claimed all the employees were let go. They didn't even tell the families that something had happened until I took the photos to the police. That's the crazy part. How fucked up do you have to be?

But people don't blame EveryTown. Not for the conditions that led to the cult, or for cutting off the park when things went bad, or for never going back to check what happened. Instead, everyone fixates on what Blythe did.

I remember seeing his skeleton. At the time, I didn't know it was him, as it would take the police weeks to identify all the bodies in that mess. But I had a hunch it was him, and it turned out to be correct.

Seated upon the throne was Blythe's skeleton, the headband ears still fixed over his skull and the stuffed character sitting on his lap, staring out at the piles of bones that were once his cast and kingdom.

ABOUT THE AUTHOR
DAPHNE STRASERT

Daphne Strasert is a horror, dark fantasy, and speculative fiction writer from Houston, Texas. She was a semi-finalist in the 2017 Next Great Horror Writer Contest and has several stories to be published in 2018. You can find out more and read some of her writing at www.daphnestrasert.com.

BLACK BRIDGE, NORTHUMBERLAND

By: Richard Ayre

August 4th.

I pulled up outside the old pub in the middle of the village green and switched off the engine, the heat belting into me as soon as I got out. It was a hot summer. The hottest since 1976, which I still remembered. As a kid that summer had been magical, but for a man now approaching his mid-fifties, the constant heat of the last few months had become tiresome.

A few tourists were sitting outside the pub, sipping beers, and I thought this would be as good a place as any to ask a few questions. I made my way inside.

An empty fireplace sat forlornly to the right as I entered. A long wooden bar lay straight in front, and a lone punter leaned on it with his feet hooked into a bar stool; an old, hard looking guy, in shirtsleeves and flat tweed cap. He glanced at me as I approached the bar, and I nodded to him.

The barman appeared, a fat man, also in shirtsleeves, damp stains under the arms. He didn't ask me what I wanted, but instead waited for me to speak.

"Pint of cider, please," I said, and he started pulling some from the pump. "Could you tell me, am I far from Black Bridge?"

He looked at me for a second, but said nothing.

I sighed pointedly as he handed the drink over, but he just put out his hand for the money. He gave me my change and went through a door in the back silently.

I shook my head.

"Friendly," I said to the old coot at the bar, tipping my head at the doorway where the barman had gone. The guy just looked at me.

Jesus, I thought, taking my drink outside and finding a shady umbrella. I got the map out.

If I was right, the place I was after was only a few miles to the north. It was marked on my map, but marked only by me. Black Bridge did not officially exist. The map just showed an area within the Northumberland National Park, an unnamed lake situated where the village should have been.

I sipped my cider and stared at the words I had scrawled on the map; BB. MOD, 1982. BB for Black Bridge, MOD for Ministry of Defence, and 1982 for the year the lake was formed. The year, if I was correct, when something very strange happened there. Finding out what that strangeness had been was the reason for my visit.

More than two years since Chloe's death, I was at last beginning to live again, not just survive. My wife's passing had been swift and brutal, the cancer destroying her within months, leaving me bereft. Those two years had gone by in a cruel, tiresome montage of just getting through each day, and enduring each night. Those long nights in an empty house, with half caught visions glimpsed from the corner of my eye, where, for a split second, I forgot she was gone, the greeting I was about to speak to her drying in my throat. The smell of her slowly fading from my life.

The realisation that she was gone, the *reality*, had eventually sunk in, and the struggling had turned to managing. And now, I thought, the managing was once more turning to living. I took up my long-abandoned idea of writing a book. So, with the holidays upon me, and with nothing else to fill my time, my interest in Black Bridge had brought me to Northumberland.

It might make an interesting chapter. Stories told of an MOD facility, far away from prying eyes. Set up during the Cold War, all sorts of experiments and tests were alleged to have happened there.

According to the rumours, Black Bridge had been the Porton Down of the north.

But in 1982, something had happened. With indecent haste, the valley had been flooded and the village was soon under fifty feet of water, drained from the nearby river and held there by a dam. According to the stories, the houses, and even the graves in the cemetery had been left, unlike the village of Plashetts under Kielder Water, a huge, man-made reservoir situated only a few miles away. There they had dug up the bodies and re-buried them elsewhere. The village had then been levelled before being submerged. But this, apparently, had not happened at Black Bridge.

This threw up a few questions. Why had Black Bridge been flooded when there was a reservoir only a few miles away? Why had it been flooded in such a short time? And what had happened to the people who lived there?

I looked up as a shadow fell across the map.

The old guy from the bar was standing at my shoulder, staring down at my scrawls. His eyes slowly turned to my own.

"What's your interest in Black Bridge?" he asked me, suspiciously.

I paused, and then stood up, holding out my hand.

"Jim Kelso," I said. "How do you do?"

He stared at my hand for a second, and then shook it. His own hand was hard with callouses that pressed into my soft skin.

"Wally Green," he muttered, his eyes turning back to the map. "And I'll ask you again. What's your interest in Black Bridge?"

I indicated for him to sit at the table, which he did, begrudgingly.

"Just curious," I lied, in answer to his question. "I heard about a flooded village up here and I thought I'd take a look. Sounded interesting."

Green pulled a face at this.

"Interesting!" he repeated. "That's one way of putting it."

"What do you mean?" I asked as innocently as I could. "Haunted, is it?"

I smiled at him, indulgently, as if we were sharing a joke, but he just shook his head.

"No. Not haunted as far as I know," he said. "No ghosts there. Nothing at all there."

Despite the sun on my back, a slight shiver ran through me from the look on his face. I sipped my cider to cover the feeling.

"So, do you know why it was flooded?" I asked him.

Green sipped his own drink; a dark, evil-looking bitter.

"You police?" he asked.

I laughed.

"Do I look like the police?"

I decided that honesty might be the best policy here.

"No," I went on. "I'm a teacher, actually. Well, a lecturer. Down in London. Modern History. I'm researching stories about the Cold War for a planned book. I heard about some strange things going on at Black Bridge thirty odd years ago, so I decided to investigate."

Green didn't look impressed. In fact, he looked downright disappointed.

"Oh," he said slowly. "Then you can't help."

He got up to leave, but I stood with him and touched his corded forearm to stop him. It was like holding a bunch of steel cables. He looked at my hand pointedly, and I hastily withdrew it. Old he may have been, but I reckoned he could have booted me clear across the beer garden without breaking a sweat.

He was indecisive though. I knew this because he didn't leave, just drained the rest of his beer.

"Can I get you another?" I asked.

He nodded quickly enough, and I knew I had him. I went back into the pub and got two more drinks from Happy Golightly behind the bar.

Once back outside, we sat again.

"You know, my publisher will pay good money for any information about what happened at Black Bridge," I said, and from the sudden interest in his eyes, I knew this was the tack to nail him with. I doubted whether the publisher would pay a penny for any story I might come up with, but since Chloe's death, I had become used to lying, as much to myself as well as others who asked me how I was doing. I'd become quite good at it.

I could tell he was interested. He took a long swallow of his beer, took out the makings of a rolled up cigarette, and had smoked half of it in silence before he began to speak.

"I was part of the goings on in Black Bridge, back in '82," he said eventually. I felt a small frisson of excitement flash through my body. I nodded at him to continue.

"The village itself was small, only a few houses and outlying farms plus a manor house. Place didn't even have a pub!"

He shook his head at this thought, as if it was the worst crime in the world.

"Anyway," he continued, "I was a farm hand in those days. No money and no real future. The manor farm had been taken over by the army, or the government, or whatever, since about 1949. There were stories. All sorts of stories. I grew up with them."

"Stories about what?" I asked, pulling out my phone to record him. I showed it to him and he nodded, acquiescing to the interview.

"All sorts of crazy things," he continued. "I never paid them no heed. Then, one day, I heard they were hiring at the manor house."

"The manor house?"

"Aye. That's where the complex was. On the edge of the village. The army had taken it over, like I said. They put wire fences around it. It grew over the years. Lots of buildings there by the time I started working for them. Always soldiers with dogs. Patrolling, you know? Spotlights, guard towers and God knows what else. Anyway, me and my mate, Joe Dawson, heard they were hiring.

There were a lot of animals, you see. I think they used them for experiments. Cows, sheep, even chickens and geese. They wanted people to look after them and to deliver them when they were needed. So, me and Joe went down there, and we eventually got the job. It paid well, the hours were good, and as long as we delivered the animals on time, we were pretty much left alone. We had to sign that, what's it called? That paper that says you can't talk about anything?"

"The Official Secrets Act?"

He nodded.

"Aye, that was it. Nondisclosure, and all that."

He sniffed. I was going to remind him of what that document meant, but I caught him looking at me.

"You're wondering why I'm telling you this," he said. "That they'll throw me in prison if they catch on?" He chuckled. "Don't make no difference to me anymore."

He held the cigarette out in front of him.

"I've been to the doctors. These things have already killed me. No Official Secrets Act can get me now." He laughed softly, bitterly.

I felt tears pricking behind my eyes as his words brought back memories of Chloe, but I blinked them back down and took another drink.

"Anyway," he continued, "Joe and me had been there about five months, when things went... wrong.

"The manor house, on the edge of the village, was wired off, like I said. Me and Joe worked in the farm complex. But there was another ring of fence, inside of this, surrounding the house itself and some other buildings. We never got to go inside there. Whenever we delivered the animals, we were stopped at a gatehouse and they were taken away. We were never allowed inside the Inner Sanctum."

"The what?"

The old man smiled, but it was more like a grimace.

"That's what we called it. The Inner Sanctum. It seemed to fit. We never knew what went on in there."

I took another sip of my cider.

"Go on," I urged. "You said things went wrong?"

He drained his second pint so I wasted another few minutes getting him another.

"We'd delivered a couple of sheep to the gatehouse," he continued. "But when we got there, we saw that the gate was open and empty. Well, we didn't know what do. The guard house was usually crammed full of soldiers. We stood around for a bit, and shouted 'hello' a couple of times, but no-one answered. The whole place seemed deserted. Then we heard gunfire coming from one of the buildings inside the fence."

"Gunfire? Are you sure? Perhaps it was a car backfiring?" I suggested.

He scoffed at this.

"This was automatic gunfire," he insisted. "I've had cars backfiring on me all my life, and I know the difference. No. This was a machine gun. Sounded like it was spraying everything in sight."

"What did you do?"

"Well, we just stared at each other. Too surprised to do anything. Then we saw them."

He took another hasty gulp of his beer and rolled another cigarette, lighting it with shaking hands.

"Who?" I asked eventually.

He still didn't look at me. His gaze was fixed on the forest along the horizon, as if he could see beyond it into the past.

"The soldiers," he said eventually. "They came running out of the building. Sprinting out. And they were screaming. Screaming like devils."

Another shiver coursed through my body.

"What happened then?"

Green looked at me for the first time since starting his story. He suddenly looked like a very old man indeed.

"There were about thirty of those young lads," he said, "all of them carrying rifles. Their faces!" He shook his head slightly. "I've never seen a look like that on anyone's face before or since."

He took another long gulp of beer.

"What do you mean?" I asked.

Green licked his lips.

"They looked terrified," he continued. "Like they'd seen something horrible. One of them pointed his gun at us and started firing. Automatic fire, you know? I felt something hit my chest, and I was knocked backwards into an old water trough that stood there. By the time I got myself upright, wiping the water from my eyes, the soldiers were on us."

Here, Green rolled and lit yet another cigarette, inhaling greedily.

"One of them was standing over Joe, who was lying on the ground. He'd been shot at least twice. Blood was pumping from him. Without hesitating, the soldier stuck his bayonet right into Joe's stomach. Again and again. He was in a frenzy. I saw the light go out of Joe's eyes. But even when it was obvious he was dead, that young soldier kept stabbing and stabbing. Like... like he wanted to be sure."

Green gulped his beer.

"Then the soldier looked at me, and I thought my time was up. I thought he would do the same to me as he had to Joe. But his eyes sort of skittered around me, and he ran off, catching up with the others who had all ignored me too."

"What did you do?" I whispered.

Green took a long breath and let it out in an equally long sigh.

"I climbed out of the trough, the pain hitting me as I did. I found out later that the bullet had gone clear through my upper chest. It missed everything vital by inches, but it tore out quite a chunk of me. Look."

Here, he opened a button on his shirt, and high up on the right side of his chest was a puckered scar.

"The back's worse," he muttered.

"So what happened after that?" The afternoon seemed to have become brooding and silent, so engrossing was his story.

"I legged it as fast as I could up the hill, collapsing in the bushes as the pain really started to get to me. I could see the whole village from there."

He shook his head at the memories.

"God, the things I saw that day."

"Tell me," I said.

"The soldiers ran into the village. The people had come out to see what all the fuss was about. They... they slaughtered them. They slaughtered them all."

"The villagers? The soldiers killed them?"

He nodded.

"I saw one of them grab an old fella, Bernie Gresham was his name. I sort of knew him. Must have been ninety if he was a day. This soldier threw him to the ground. Then he stamped into his face. Stamped and stamped. Until Bernie's head was nothing but red meat. Flattened. The soldier was screaming at the top of his voice. They all were.

"Another soldier fired into a group, a family I think they were. Fired and fired at them. One of them was a young lad, maybe eight or nine. He was shot so many times his arm flew off, and his legs, they sort of bent backwards. Then his head... it just exploded."

Green seemed to cuff something from his eye at this memory.

"They killed the rest of the lad's family too. Shot them to pieces. They killed everyone. Every single person in that village was murdered. Shot, stabbed, hacked to death. There was blood all over the road."

I leaned towards him, elbows on the wooden table.

"But that's impossible," I said. "There's no record of anything like that happening. I've been looking into the history of Black Bridge for a while, and there's no mention of any massacre."

Green nodded and smiled grimly.

"Believe me or don't believe me. It's no skin off my nose. I don't care."

We sat for a while in silence.

"Well, what happened to the soldiers?" I eventually asked.

Green stared at me for a while, then decided to finish his story.

"They were killed," he eventually said.

"Killed how?"

"Other soldiers. I had managed to rip the sleeve off my jacket to make a kind of pad for my chest and back. It took me about half an hour to do this because I could hardly move from the pain. I was just finishing when I heard a noise, and a helicopter swooped down over the hills to the north of Black Bridge. It was one of those big things, with two rotors on the top. Anyway, this thing came in, and before I knew what was happening, a door opened and a gun started firing. Knocked the soldiers on the ground down like ten pins. Killed them all in seconds. They didn't even try to run away. Just stood there and were chopped to bits by that huge machine gun.

"I decided I needed to get away, no matter how much pain I was in. But before I did, the helicopter landed, and people came out. They were carrying guns, so they must have been soldiers, but they were all dressed in white suits, with hoods and clear visors."

"Chemical suits?" I asked.

Green didn't respond to this, but just continued his story.

"I went straight to see Yvonne Armstrong. She was an old woman who used to live here. Long dead now. She patched me up. She told me never to mention what I'd seen. Not to anyone. And for thirty five years, I haven't.

"By the time I had recovered enough to leave my bed, the place had been flooded. The dam wasn't put there until about a year later. Black Bridge is in a natural bowl, you see. They didn't need the dam at all. It's not even a real dam. Just big, curved walls of concrete that were slotted in to *look* like a dam. I know that much because I watched them do it in the spring of '83. It's my opinion it's just there to make it look like a reservoir, which it isn't. Because, if you'd been here three weeks ago, you'd have seen that the water of Black Bridge was brackish. No fresh water at all."

"What do you mean, three weeks ago?" I asked.

Green looked at me with frightened eyes.

"Because it's dried up," he said. "The village is there for all to see. This summer. The heat, you know? The water has completely gone."

August 5th.

I listened to the recording of Wally Green's interview over and over.

It didn't make sense. Surely, if what he'd said was true, something would have got out. Some stories would have leaked. But then again, what about the scar he'd shown me? I'm no expert, but it certainly looked like it could have been caused by a bullet.

His revelation about the lake drying out was alluring. The summer had been long and hot, the temperatures regularly rising into the high 30's. There were hosepipe bans all over. There might never be another chance to see what usually lay beneath Black Bridge Reservoir. I waited until the darkness of early morning, then I set off.

I had a hell of a time finding it, but eventually, I parked the car by the side of a small gravel track and climbed a low hill, crouching in the bushes at the edge of a forest overlooking what had been the lake. I wondered if I was in the same place that Green had described where he'd watched the soldiers carry out their massacre.

I'd noticed the glow as I climbed the hill, and now I saw where the light was coming from.

A single arc lamp illuminated the scene, and in its light, figures moved. At least one thing about Green's story was correct, anyway. There was no reservoir here. The water was gone and those distant figures walked the ghostly ruins of what had once been a village.

A small chapel stood at the far end of what I assumed had been the single road through Black Bridge, close up against the wall of the "dam." The road itself could not be seen as it seemed to be covered with sandy silt. That silt enveloped everything in the depression in which the village sat. The only reason I could tell the building here was a chapel was because the spire still stood, although black shadows cast from the arc lamp showed gaping holes in its slate roof.

Down the road lay a row of houses; slime covered, broken-doored, the windows all gone. But houses all the same. One of them even seemed to have a stiff, mud-encrusted curtain hanging limply in its frameless window.

326

At the end nearest to me was what I assumed had been the manor house that Green had mentioned. A rusting chain-link fence reared in places, although most of it seemed to have been flattened into the silt, and concrete structures still stood inside what had obviously been a compound. Like the houses in the street, these structures were windowless, but this was because they'd never had windows. They were big, square, featureless blocks of concrete with double sized doorways as the only entrances. The doors still seemed to be intact, and they were all closed. They looked to be made of metal, because I could make out rust streaks on them from my vantage point.

The manor house itself would have been quite impressive in its heyday. A big, Georgian affair, it was three stories high, and had several wide steps running up to the double fronted doors that now showed only a shadowy blackness within. Like the chapel and the houses in the street, parts of its roof had collapsed, and I assumed the wooden floors inside must have completely decayed after decades of being under water.

A greenish slime covered every surface of Black Bridge, giving the newly revealed village a ragged, bearded appearance. It was a sad sight to behold.

I turned my attention to the moving figures down below.

There were about twenty people down there, and they all seemed to be bending down and taking samples, or looking through the viewfinders of mysterious tripods and jotting things down. They looked busy.

I pulled out my camera and started clicking away furiously, taking everything in. Using the camera's zoom feature, I got my first close ups at some of the people in the village, and I gave a start when the photos confirmed that they all wore white chemical suits.

Jesus, I thought. *Was Green right? Had he been telling me the truth?*

After a while, I noticed some of the figures were not scurrying about like the majority. These were spread out, mainly around what was left of what Green had called the Inner Sanctum. I zoomed in on one of them, and noticed an automatic rifle hanging at his back.

Were these people soldiers? What about the ones doing the work? Scientists? This would explain the chemical suits. Whatever they were, it looked like the soldiers were there to protect them, although, with their guns on their backs, it seemed they were not taking this duty too seriously. What were they protecting them from?

I stayed in my little bush at the crest of the hill all night, watching the strange figures down in the village, until, as dawn began to orange the sky, the figures climbed into a couple of black vans that had been parked beside the arc lamp. The ones with the guns then dismantled the lamp and packed it away. Within an hour, they had gone.

Now was my chance. I scurried down the hill and took my first, tentative step inside Black Bridge.

My foot sank about three inches into the silt, and immediately, a dank, sour smell wafted up. This smell haunted me as I made my way towards the nearest building; the first of the row of houses. I hesitated outside the doorway, peering inwards. God knows how dangerous it was in there. The floor was probably completely rotted, and anything could fall from the upper rooms and roof space. I took my time.

Sunlight shone in through the doorway, and my eyes slowly grew accustomed to the gloom.

Straight in front of me was a sitting room, with a ruptured staircase to the left. Sagging and bloated furniture still sat in that room, a slime covered TV in the far corner. Something was sticking half out of the silt that covered the floor, and I tentatively pulled it free. It was a glass framed photograph that must have once hung on a wall. After wiping it as best I could, I saw it was a family picture; a man, a woman and two children. One of them was a young boy, and I wondered if this was the lad Green had spoken of in his interview. I hastily threw the photo onto the dilapidated sofa.

The floor was stone flagged, not wooden, and this made me feel a little safer as I moved into the kitchen, its cupboards full of mould-covered tin cans.

I took more photos. This was crazy. It looked like the house had been evacuated, then flooded immediately, along with the rest of the village. Nothing had been removed, nothing taken.

I left that dank little dwelling (how good it felt to have the sun warm my face again) and stepped into the one next door. Same story here. I moved from house to house, and all told the same tale. Each one was ruined and putrefied, but still kitted out with TV's, radios and furniture. All abandoned. All forlorn.

I eventually made my way to the chapel at the edge of the village, peering inside cautiously. As I walked, I noticed small excavations in the silt. I assumed this was where the figures I'd seen had been digging things up. I wondered what those things might have been.

Inside the chapel, rows of mildewed pews provided a silent congregation for the dilapidated altar at the front. A big, wooden crucifix stood, embedded drunkenly in the thick silt in front of the altar, its roof fastenings long since rotted. I took more photos, but did not venture inside.

It was then that I noticed the small cemetery at the side of the chapel. The headstones lay tilted and scattered like crooked teeth. I wondered if the bodies were still there, forgotten like everything else in this desolate place. A breeze whistled through the village and found me, causing a shiver to run down my spine. I turned away and made towards the manor house at the other end of the street.

I found a section of fence buried in the silt, and gingerly stepped over it. There were more excavations here. I climbed the wide stairs of the Georgian fronted ruin and looked in the doorway. And here, my breath caught in my throat.

Straight in front of the doorway was a staircase that had once been elegant, but was now slime-covered. Like the houses in the street, furniture still squatted in the silt. But this furniture looked more like it had belonged to an office than a private house. A large desk sagged to the right of the staircase, with an old fashioned dial telephone still standing on it. There was a chair on its back behind the desk, half submerged in the silt. A sofa slumped against the wall in a far corner, and a metal filing cabinet stood opposite the staircase. I wondered if there was anything in that filing cabinet, but realised that, even if there was, it would have turned to mush long ago. A chandelier lay on the floor behind the desk, smashed and mildewed like everything else.

But it was not the furniture that made me gasp. It was the mound of bones and rotted clothing that lay heaped in the middle of the floor.

For a second, as my eyes adjusted to the gloom, I didn't know what I was looking at. But then shapes started to define themselves;

a leg bone here, a mouldy skull there. The bones looked like they had been thrown together; no rhyme or reason to their shape. Draped over some of them like shrouds were rank, stiff rags of what must have once been clothes, but the material had split and disintegrated, making it difficult to understand which of the skeletons they had belonged to.

Now I knew what those indentations had been that I had seen in the street and in the compound. Those figures had been digging up bodies! They had placed them here, bits and pieces at a time, in a pyramid of the dead.

I turned away from the horrid sight, a hand grasping at my mouth to stop a scream from emerging.

Green was telling the truth! The people had all been killed and the bodies, along with the entire village, had been flooded and covered over. But why? What had happened?

Eventually, I recovered enough to turn back to the door and started taking more pictures. I wanted evidence of what I was seeing. It was through my camera's viewfinder that my shocked eyes took in more detail. I saw how some of that ragged clothing had insignia stitched onto it. A sergeant's stripes, the metallic pip of an officer. I also recognised the barrel of an automatic rifle sticking out of the silt like a pipe.

Some of these people, then, had been army personnel. Were they the ones who had instigated the massacre in Black Bridge?

Eventually, I turned from the manor house, and my eyes alighted on the concrete buildings that dotted the area. And I noticed something then. Something that couldn't be seen unless viewed from the manor house itself. The door to one of the buildings was open.

I swallowed hard as I gazed upon that black entrance. Was this the building those soldiers had ran from thirty five years ago, screaming incoherently? Before they killed Joe Dawson? Before they murdered the entire population of Black Bridge? I did not want to go inside that building. I even told myself not to go near it, but before I knew what was happening, my legs had carried me to the entrance.

Even with the sunlight streaming through the doorway, five feet into the interior it was as black as night. But luckily (or unluckily, take your pick), I'd brought along a torch. I switched it on.

I was in what had once been a corridor, with broken doors sagging on either side along its length. As I unwillingly moved forward, I heard things crunching under the silt beneath my feet. They sounded like glass vials or test tubes breaking. And I ignored that noise. God forgive me, I ignored it. I carried on, peering into doorways as I went.

Most of them seemed to be small offices, with rusted typewriters and metal cabinets leaning drunkenly in corners. One of them seemed to be a menagerie of sorts. Rows of small, rusted cages lay against one wall, many with tiny bones scattered within them. I looked closer. The skull of some rodent, perhaps a rat, stared back at me from its eternal prison. I shuddered and moved on.

Eventually, I found myself in what I believed had been the heart of this structure. A large room stood at the end of the corridor. It also contained cages, although these ones were empty. A wheeled trolley with a spongy foam covering was tipped onto its side. I took a photo of this as it seemed to have rotted leather manacles attached to it. Had they tied people down on this thing?

A huge, hinged light, like the lamp of an operating theatre, still hung from the ceiling, and it looked like the trolley had once stood under this lamp.

I looked all around that suddenly terrifying room, and rubbed a hand across my jaw. I shook my head. I'd had enough of Black Bridge. Something, maybe some primeval warning system, was screaming at me to get away, and I heeded its advice. But I was far too slow.

I made it outside just as the squeal of brakes and the roar of an engine informed me that a vehicle had pulled up at the manor house. I peered around the side of the concrete building, and my heart thumped in my chest as I saw an armoured personnel carrier disgorging white-suited and hooded soldiers. My fear ramped up when I heard a muffled shout from one of them: "The car's just over the hill, so he must be here somewhere. Fan out. Find him."

Shit! They'd found my car! Had they been patrolling, or had that fat, miserable bastard back at the pub phoned them? Or had Green?

It didn't really matter. My immediate problem was that I was on MOD property, with a camera in my pocket. An entire village had been murdered here. I doubted they would be bothered about adding one more person to that number.

And here I was. A fifty three year old lecturer, hoping to evade a dozen soldiers, more than likely Special Forces. I didn't stand a cat in hell's chance.

After a second or two of sheer, blind panic, I tried to work through my options.

The car was out. They'd found that, so they'd probably left someone to guard it. The bushes where I'd hid earlier? Possibly, but I'd be exposed all the way there. It was doubtful these guys would miss me puffing up that hill.

No. There was only one option. The soldiers were heading towards the village. They didn't seem to be coming near the concrete buildings yet. If I could use those buildings as cover between the soldiers and me, I could make my way northwards. About half a mile away was a thick forest. Get through the forest and then find somewhere to get another car. A hire place or something, I didn't really know. All I did know was that, if my plan was going to work, I had to act now, before they turned their attention to where I cowered.

I ran.

Christ, I was terrified. My feet slipped in that bastard silt as I scrambled up the incline towards the distant forest. My breath was wheezing in my chest before I'd gone a hundred yards. I had once been a fit man, but the last two years had seen me drinking far too much. Without Chloe to keep me in check, I had used alcohol as a companion to dull the grief. But I was paying for it now. I could almost hear Chloe whispering "I told you so" as I ran up that slope.

I eventually reached the crest, and freed myself from the silt. However, I was now in full view of the soldiers down in the village. All they needed to do was turn around and they would see me pelting across the moorland towards the forest. *Five more minutes*, I thought. *Don't turn around for five more minutes*. I was already tiring. Unused to such exercise, my legs were shaking and the sweat was pouring from me.

The hope for more time was dashed as I heard a cry behind me. I started so much at this that my shaking leg juddered and gave way. I scrambled over onto my rump, my lungs heaving. They had seen me! They knew where I was! There was no escape.

A sudden lethargy came upon me as I lay there, panting. I simply watched them down in the village. I had given up. I couldn't go on. I remember wishing that I was a religious man, because then I would at least have the comfort of knowing I would soon be with Chloe. But I wasn't. Never had been. Chloe was dead. And soon I would be too. There was no other equation I could come to. They had kept this village a secret for thirty five years. They would not change their minds now.

However, as I lay watching those soldiers, a frown appeared on my face. They were not looking at me. The cry had come from one of them, yes, but it seemed it was a cry for help, rather than a cry of discovery.

One of the soldiers was bent double, hugging his stomach. The others all seemed to be staring at him. Suddenly, he sprinted towards one of the other soldiers, a banshee-like shriek rising from him. There was a moment's hesitation, then the others opened fire.

To me, two hundred yards away, it looked like red flowers had suddenly blossomed on the white of the soldier's suit, then an invisible wire seemed to yank him sideways and he was flung down into the silt. He didn't move.

By now, one of the other soldiers was screaming. No. Two of them!

Suddenly, the valley was alive with gunfire, and I saw four of the soldiers go down, one of them screaming incoherently as he fell to his knees. Another shot seemed to spray the inside of his visor with red, and he was smashed backwards.

Within seconds, only two of the original soldiers were left alive. They seemed to stare at each other as if they couldn't believe what had happened. One of them tore off his hood.

The other one said something, but the first shook his head.

"Makes no fucking difference, does it! Didn't stop it getting them!" He waved his arm in an arc at the dead bodies. After a second, his companion removed his own hood. And it was as he did this that he saw me on the hill, staring down at him. I wasted no more time, but jumped to my feet, and sprinted once more towards the distant forest.

I risked one backwards glance as the forest eventually loomed nearer, and, with a gasp of fear, saw that they were both almost upon me. They were young, fit, and, by the looks on their faces, in no mood to take prisoners. I was doomed. They would be on me in less than thirty seconds.

It was an unholy screaming that alerted me to the fact I might get away.

A second glance showed me one of the soldiers bent double and clutching his stomach, just like the one down in the village. His companion had also stopped and was staring at him, fear etched into his hard, young features.

"No, Dixie!" he shouted. "Fight it. Fight it!"

It was too late. The soldier named Dixie screamed again and ran at the other soldier, his arms outstretched. I had never seen such a look on anyone's face.

His eyes bulged from his head like marbles, and his mouth was stretched downwards in an expression that showed absolute, naked terror. His lips were drawn back, exposing his gums. His scream was high-pitched. Even in my own frightened state, it set my teeth on edge. I could only stare as he rushed towards the other soldier. There was a bang, and Dixie's head exploded in a red fan. He was thrown backwards and lay still, spread-eagled on the grass.

For a second, the other soldier just stared at the corpse, then he turned his head towards me. He started trudging towards me.

I couldn't move now. I had witnessed eleven people being murdered. I couldn't handle it. I just stood there, panting like a dog, as that soldier approached me.

He stopped in front of me. He was breathing hard too, but not as uncontrollably as myself.

"Hold this," he muttered, and thrust the rifle into my startled hands. He unzipped the chemical-suit and wriggled out of it.

"Hot as fucking hell in there," he mumbled, then took the rifle back.

"What... what's going on?" I managed to ask him, but he shook his head.

"No time," he replied tightly. "We have to get away."

With that he set off towards the forest. I hurried to catch up after eyeing the corpse of the other soldier for a second. I grabbed his arm once I was alongside him.

"What the hell's going on?" I asked him again. "What happened to your men?"

He shrugged off my hand and carried on walking.

"The same thing that happened here thirty five years ago," he said. "It was a leak. They were working on something. It got out."

We walked a little further, eventually entering the gloom of the forest. I tried to engage him in conversation, but he was short of answers.

"All I know, is that my unit was posted to guard the scientists as they did their tests," he said. "We were told that the hot summer had dried the reservoir out. The government wanted samples and to collect the bodies for examination. A lot of the records of what went on here over the years have been lost. But whatever happened in '82 was because of a secret biological warfare programme. Some sort of virus that caused hallucinations. The idea was that, in the event of war, this stuff could be released and the population would do the army's job for it. They would kill each other. No need for nukes. But, from what I can gather, there was a leak. That's why the unit here went on the rampage. The stuff got out, and the government covered it up. Literally. Swamped the whole place underwater. But apparently, the virus was still live."

He looked at me. "That's what I think, anyway," he murmured. "It's still alive."

He was wrong in this assumption. But neither of us knew it at the time.

"But the suits…" I began.

"Useless," he replied, scathingly. "Like everything else about the fucking government."

We walked in silence. I wondered why he had told me everything he had. But I think it was because he knew the game was up. I think he knew it didn't matter anymore. Eventually we came to a break in the forest. The river trickled wearily between its banks, barely six inches deep.

"So where are we…?" I started, but was broken off by his scream.

I jumped, staring at his wracked face, but at the same time, I felt something in my own stomach. It was like someone had stuck a screwdriver into my guts, and I screamed too. I managed to look up at the soldier, but saw instead a creature so horrific that my brain could not fully comprehend it. Green-skinned, slime-coated. It was hump-backed and saw-toothed and hook-clawed. And it screamed at me.

A raging thought suddenly seemed to throw itself into my head. I had to kill this beast. Kill it before it killed me!

The monster was too fast though. It lunged at me, and I felt something tear into my shoulder. My foot slipped on the bank of the river, and I tumbled down, hitting my head on a rock and rolling into the freezing water.

I lay there, half submerged, half stunned, as that creature leapt down the bank.

But, as that cool, clear water washed over me, the creature wavered and flickered and dissolved, disappearing. The green skin turned into the green cloth of an army uniform. I rubbed my eyes, the pain in my stomach gone as if it had never existed.

The soldier looked about the river bank. He stared straight at me, but his eyes did not seem to see me. An errant current swished the river nearer to him and he jumped back, his face terrified. Finally, with another scream, he ran off, back into the woods.

I lay in the river for a few more minutes, but then managed to drag myself to my feet. I splashed across to the opposite bank and sank down, holding my head in my hands.

I inspected the cut in my shoulder where I assumed the soldier had stuck me with a knife or a bayonet, but it was superficial. My fall had saved my life. Literally.

Eventually, I reverted back to my original plan. Find a village, find a car, and get the fuck away from Black Bridge.

September 1st.

The screaming outside stops me. I sit, fingers poised over the keys of the laptop, as that screaming ululates in the night. It sounds like it's coming from a couple of streets away at least. But it's getting closer. The city is desolated and no longer safe.

I wonder, idly, who will read what I am writing. Will someone, at some distant point in the future, read my words? Will they take heed of my warning? Or would it be known to them already? Doesn't matter. It has to be done. I have to finish. Someone needs to know about the water. It may be too late for me, but someone needs to know about the water.

The water saved me, you see? For the same reason the flooding of Black Bridge had saved everything back in 1982. Something in water stops the infection if it's caught quickly enough. The infected are fearful of water. They can't even see anything in it. This was why Wally Green had not died. He fell into the water trough. He became invisible to the diseased soldier, so he survived. I fell into the river, and it washed the infection from me.

It still amazes me how something so simple, and so abundant, can halt the infection. No-one else seems to know. What's left of the government evidently does not. The flooding of Black Bridge was not done because of this knowledge. They just wanted something quick, to hide their mistake. It was a simple fluke that they chose water. And it would have worked forever too, if it wasn't for a nosy, idiot lecturer crunching his way through unseen test tubes in a concrete laboratory and releasing the virus once more.

It's not every day you get to realise you've killed the world. But that is what I have done. And in this never ending summer, things are only going to get worse.

I pick up the tumbler of single malt, sip, and start writing again. And in the echoes of that screaming outside, I pray for rain.

ABOUT THE AUTHOR
RICHARD AYRE

Richard Ayre was born in Northumberland, Northern England, and now lives in Newcastle upon Tyne where he continues to write horror fiction. At an impressionable age he fell in love with new wave heavy metal and rock music, and at the same time read his first James Herbert novel. The combination of these two magnificent things led him to write *Minstrel's Bargain*, a tale of music and horror.

Minstrel's Bargain is the first novel in the *Prophecy Books*. Richard has also written *Minstrel's Renaissance*, the second of that trilogy, and *Point of Contact*, a sci-fi chiller, as well as the short story anthology, *A Hatful of Shadows*. When not writing, Richard can be found zooming around the Northumberland countryside on his motorcycle, Tanya.

Spirit,
Ohio

By: Robb T. White

Indiana proved to be a colossal dud. None of its dozen ghost towns offered me anything interesting for the book, but I felt obligated to include a couple of them besides abandoned grain silos and overgrown railroad tracks. I waited three hours in the abandoned Elizabethtown Cemetery for one decent shot at sundown. The goal was to capture the sun's longer rays bursting through overhead branches of maple trees illuminating the rows of mossy, slanted gravestones in a picturesque, if not eerie, exposure. It wasn't going to happen. Thick, black cumulus clouds loomed above me. I was about to get soaked.

"Sorry, Indiana," I said, packing up my equipment. "Dunn will have to represent." A mere grain elevator and a general store with weeds sprouting through the boards out front were all that remained of that ghost town.

I was moving on to Ohio, my home, to finish the book even though I'd begun with Western Pennsylvania. When I started this project as a photojournalist, I reminded the acquisition editor in New York there would be a few photos of people in my selection of ghost towns. Unlike the abandoned mining towns out West during the manic silver and gold rushes, modern ghost towns still retain some populations. Most disappeared off the maps; they got incorporated, washed away in floods or catastrophic fires, ruined by drought, or the economic conditions changed so drastically the towns disappeared almost overnight.

I drove toward Smith's Landing on the Ohio River. It has no coordinates; it's just a state marker off Highway 52, with a lone historical marker noting "Utopia Community" for the few residents that still lived around there. Its past is what intrigued me, however, being that it's one of those communal experiments made famous by socialist writer Charles Fourier.

Some believers in the Fourierist *phalanstére* settled there in the 1840's and called it "the Clermont Phalanx" for the county, but it failed and was renamed Utopia. Members were invited, paid a fee to live there, all believing a 35,000-year epoch of peace was about to occur in the world. The sect's goal was to achieve enlightenment through communal living. It took only three years for the experiment to fail; then the land came under the ownership of Josiah Warren, the anarchist, who believed in private property and a free-market economy. That experiment also failed and was followed by a group of Spiritualists led by a man named Wattles. Little is known of him, but he must have been a headstrong man because he was warned by other settlers in the region along the Ohio not to move the town hall too close to the river's edge.

Yet that is exactly what he did. His followers moved the structure brick by brick to the bank just days before one of the worst floods in Ohio history. People left their houses as the waters rose and fled to the town hall for safety. That night, a party was being celebrated just as the back wall of the building collapsed under pressure from the rising waters, overfed by a warm weather and an early thaw. Most of the Spiritualists drowned or died of hypothermia. Nothing is known of any survivors.

I was eager to speak to some longtime residents of Smith's Landing to see what stories I might glean to enhance my photos. A tradition that rich ought to have folk tales, family stories—maybe superstitions—in the communal memory. That had proved to be the case in the other states I'd covered so far, especially in Wisconsin, which hummed with paranormal activity at some of the places I had snapped for the book. I spoke with a paranormal expert in one ghost town, who showed me his gadgets "for detecting ectoplasm" at a farmhouse where four children and a mother had been murdered by the axe-wielding father in 1919. That man claimed he spoke directly to God and God told him to do what he did.

I'd done research in advance of setting out on my six-month project. One afternoon a month before setting out for Erie, PA, the commencement of the book, I ran across a diary in the special collections of Gannon Library. How it wound up there, I don't know. It was a diary of an educated farmer named Elias Hammond from Hoffmeister in the Adirondacks, who arrived with Joseph Smith and his band of followers when they fled persecution in New York State. Smith had one of his visions commanding him to establish a congregation in Ohio close to Lake Erie in tiny Kirtland.

Pure coincidence, of course, that I was born in nearby Chardon in a house on the Euclid-Chardon Road. I was a teenager when Jeffrey Lundgren declared himself a prophet and led his Reformed Latter-Day Saints paramilitary cult movement to settle in Kirtland. Lundgren, a self-professed Prophet who also spoke directly to God, made national news when he ordered five members of the Avery family in his own congregation to be murdered one at a time; they were buried in a pit in a barn that belonged to the farmhouse Lundgren rented on Euclid-Chardon Road five houses down from my home. Again, mere coincidence, but the Southern Ohio Correctional Facility where Lundgren was executed in 2006 is located on the Ohio River in Lucasville about a three hours' drive from where I planned to begin my search for the remnants of Utopia.

My plan was simple: snap some shots, chat up a few locals for tidbits, and motor on beside the Ohio to Cheshire in Gallia County, which is right across the bridge from notorious Point Pleasant, West Virginia, made famous in the 60's and 70's by UFO sightings, not to mention the famed Mothman with his fiery red eyes and massive wingspan, seen by dozens of residents — so they say. Cheshire made my list as ghost town with nothing as flamboyant; the town's power plant spewed sooty residue polluting the town in a milky chemical fog, and that was what drove the residents off.

When the special collections archivist laid the thin leather booklet in front of me in her white-gloved hands, she removed the slip that noted "Diary of Elias Hammond, 1836 — 1837" and gave me an extra pair of gloves and a flat stick like a doctor's tongue depressor for turning the pages.

"The paper is a little feathery at the edges owing to age," she said, "but you can use this."

She showed me how to maneuver it inside the booklet without damaging the delicate paper. I thought of my ninety-six-year-old grandmother in a nursing home and the blue veins of her hands.

Hammond's diary was full of his fear — mainly fear of God and displeasing Him. He spoke glowingly of Smith, "the true Prophet," in terms of rapturous sanctity, but he mentioned "Brother Brigham" only once and then only to praise Young's carpentry skills during their mutual Ohio period. When he wasn't quivering with fear over the wrath of God, he recounted the Saints' mundane struggles in the Ohio wilderness: much of his commentary was preoccupied by the weather (temperature fluctuations duly recorded with date and time of day in the upper right-hand corner), the prospects for a good crop, copied out hymns from his boyhood, and prayers composed partly of celestial yearning and his desire to be "beaten to a purer form on the anvil of God."

It sounded like depressing, not to mention ho-hum, stuff—that is, until the last three pages when Hammond seemed to slip a few more cogs, mentally speaking. He spoke of the "strange children" who had come among them with a batch of new followers. He didn't say where or who or how many. He had mentioned an influx of "new followers" eager to join Smith's Saints that had arrived that winter, but their children were the object of his concern. Hammond interjected dreamlike phrases in his descriptions, such as describing them "with faces blue" and how they "came dancing, dancing out the forest." They seemed to acquire a dangerous aspect for Hammond and he observed them from a distance with trepidation, even warning his own family to have nothing to do with them. I guessed the poor man was undergoing some trauma brought on by his own religious dread and zealotry.

On the final page, he reversed his early enthusiasm for the new arrivals and quoted one biblical text after the other, castigating them as "evil spirits" and declaring them "messengers of the Dark Spirit." The library's air-conditioning was kept at morgue temperature, I assumed, to protect the priceless volumes and illustrated manuscripts in the collection; however, Hammond's last sentence added an extra degree of chill to the air: "They seek to devour my soul, God save me," he wrote. The final pages of the diary were blank except for some Latin phrases, one of which I recognized: *Dies Irae*. Day of Wrath: Judgment Day.

It was beginning to look like Indiana all over again, another bust. The granddaughter of the oldest resident in the vicinity told me her grandmother often spoke of "a gypsy camp" out in the fields miles beyond Old Coshocton Road.

"What kind of gypsies?" I asked.

I had an image in my head of painted caravans drawn by horses, bearded men strumming violins around campfires, casks of red wine, and hordes of happy children speaking in a strange dialect.

"My grandmother never said," the woman replied.

I had interrupted some serious baking, judging from the pleasant smells wafting my way from inside the house. She spoke through the screen door while I stood at a respectful distance on the porch and didn't expect to be invited inside. Way out here in the boondocks, she was wary of strangers—who isn't nowadays?—and obviously wanted to get back to her kitchen.

"I'd love to visit her," I said. "Can you give me directions to her nursing home?"

"It wouldn't do you any good," she replied. "She suffers from severe dementia."

Still, the woman had given me reason enough to linger before heading off to my next ghost town.

She told me where Old Coshocton Road used to be located.

"Used to be?"

"Oh my, yes," she said. "That road's long gone. Probably not much more than a cow path by now."

She was right. The asphalt had crumbled away to dust. Nature had taken over as the decades passed; gravel turned to dirt, dirt became a pockmarked, rut-filled trail. Overhanging trees waged a war with their opposite numbers to extend their own branches across it. Small, dusty, spear-shaped leaves interlaced among the battling twigs and blocked out most of the sun. I was losing daylight as I bumped along the trail, looking for any abandoned landmark or artifact that I could use for the book.

About three miles in by the odometer, I was becoming desperate. This jungled-over canopy of wilderness was untamed. No plow blade had furrowed ground here in generations, not a cow or a babbling brook in sight. I felt ashamed of the fact I was chasing my tail out here, wasting time trying to promote a lost, tragic village into a *son et lumière* show for my future book sales.

I hit the brakes in disgust, performed a three-corner turn, and gunned the accelerator. The sooner I was back to civilization, the better, I thought. Then reality hit: I was going nowhere, literally spinning wheels. My rear tires were churning in a slurry of soft, rank-smelling mud. I did what any frustrated driver might do: I jammed my foot on the pedal harder — and sunk deeper. My nostrils were filled with swamp decay and burning oil. I lay back against the seat to think. The Garmin I had installed for the trip mocked me with its blinking cursor out here in the middle of nowhere. And here I would stay until I made a move.

I grabbed a water bottle and my insect repellant from the back seat, hung my back-up camera around my neck, and piled everything else into the trunk. Even if I didn't get a shot, I wasn't about to leave a $2,000 Canon and all my expensive gear behind. Now the only question remained was: go back or go forward — which to choose?

Pushing my luck, I kept going down the remains of Old Coshocton Road.

I walked for hours until the declining sun dipped to the tree line — that is, whenever I was afforded a clearer view between the thick branches arching over the path and shrouding every step I took in a dappled light. The insect repellant seemed to attract mosquitoes rather than repel them. I itched everywhere, especially on my sunburned neck. I'd drunk the last of my water an hour earlier. I wondered: Was this what it was like to be lost in the woods? At first, the thought amused; now, I worried. If it weren't for the trail snaking ahead, I'd probably have been walking in circles. I'd have been grateful to spot a barbed-wire fence, if there were any out here. My cellphone was useless.

I had time to think, though; the granddaughter's words struck a chord with what I had been hearing in dribs and drabs whenever I'd stopped for food or gas on my journey along the Ohio. When Indians lived along its shore, it must have been an impressive sight with waters clear and wildlife everywhere. A muddy brown soup where barges pushed up and down with or against the current, debris bobbing along the shoreline, and the symbol of our current existence's wastefulness regarding the environment: ubiquitous, one-use plastic bags snarled in every other twig and branch sticking out of the water like torn pennants. I thought of those poor souls washed away in the terrible flood of 1847.

Hammond's strange little journal kept popping into my head for some reason. His overwhelming fear of God displaced by an irrational fear of the children, whose curiosity and strong-willed behavior seemed to pose a threat to his peace of mind. He attributed an unnatural clairvoyance to them.

I'd heard of "indigo children;" children possessed of high intelligence, born with a sense of entitlement and having a strong innate spirituality. Children born with a "blue aura" who are empathetic and even touched by a spiritualism that gave the supernatural abilities of prophecy; these "star children" can channel spirits. New-age California wackadoodle nonsense, I always suspected. One more legacy of the hippie generation besides Charley Manson. More likely, I thought, it was supported by parents whose children were autistic or afflicted with ADHD to compensate for the heartache or havoc they produced in the family.

Hunger pangs and weariness sapped my strength with every passing minute. The last final rays of the setting sun were gone, and a breeze replaced the suffocating heat but did nothing to dampen the stench of the wetlands I was passing by. Invisible small varmints scuttled into the cattails whenever my footsteps snapped a twig or kicked a stone. Insects chirred all around, the late-summer grasshoppers that whip through tall grass and the electric buzz of cicadas. All of it increased my unease and reminded me of my predicament. My mind played tricks. What if I collapsed? The deer flies that bit with every landing on exposed skin were the worst.

As I walked, I wondered: Would these same bugs come to feast on my carcass? I shivered at the thought. I'd started my career as a crime-beat journalist years ago in Fayetteville, Arkansas. I'd been allowed close to a crime scene once by a cop with a morbid sense of humor; he moved the wad of tobacco from one side of his jaw to the other and pointed at something in the weeds. "Lookie yonder, kid," he said; "you can take all the photos you like of that, if you want to. That is, if you think your newspaper will print 'em." Lying crumpled like a broken doll in the thick dockweed was a murder victim, long dead and cored from anus to gullet by a family of possums. I've never been comfortable with nature ever since.

It would be full dark in minutes. My choice to forge ahead was looming larger in my imagination. I decided discretion was indeed the better part of valor. I turned around to go back to my car and sleep overnight. In the morning, I'd make the embarrassing trek back to the highway I'd turned off and call for road service.

How I got mixed up in the dark, I don't recall. I seemed to be sleepwalking, taking baby steps in my exhaustion, one foot gingerly in front of the other. At some point, when the blackness reached a palpable, coal-mine thickness, I felt tall grass slap at my legs. That was odd because I didn't recall anything like that on the path. It wasn't possible to take bearings. If I'd had any stars to see, I could determine a direction. If you film outdoors at night for any length of time, you tend to get familiar with the nighttime sky. Blackness in front of me, above me, all around me. The noise of the night insects grew by several decibels and the temperature dipped by more than a few degrees. Autumn was closer than I had realized.

I stumbled in the dark, my hands extended like the Frankenstein monster, hoping to touch something solid, preferably a tree thick enough to spend the night curled up against.

Sleep eluded me. My mind exacerbated my nervous, exhausted state with irrational fears, such as coyotes sneaking up on me and dragging me off to their den. Then it was a battalion of nocturnal spiders, poisonous snakes, stinging critters; whatever slithered, crawled, or scuttled through woods at night. I laughed at my own stupidity but was determined to remain awake until dawn. I could make up for the lost sleep in the car, I told myself.

But sleep I did—and dream, too. I was caught in a flood as the river rose. I awoke at one point trying to lift my camera out of the rising floodwaters that had reached my waist. When I snapped to and realized I had been dreaming, I wanted to laugh but I was filled with fear. My eyes wouldn't stay open. I was dreaming again of children with blue faces running toward me from burning cane fields. Black, greasy smoke billowed up from the petrochemical plant beyond where the sea and land met. I watched from a window while they cavorted and howled like berserk creatures, not even human. With flaming torches in their hands, they ran pell-mell in every direction until I no longer saw them. I heard chanting as they got closer, some unintelligible gibberish—and then they were there, in my house, confronting me with their evil smiles.

Flashlight beams blinded me. I instinctively put my hands up to shield my face, but the light reached through my fingers and stung my eyes. I heard words—English. *Oh thank God...*

"You okay, fella?"

Coming up from the depths of that last dream was like climbing a rope out of a deep well.

"I'm—I'm fine," I said.

"He must be lost," someone else said.

"No shit, Sherlock," another, older voice replied.

Hearing that jaunty colloquialism of my youth, I relaxed. I was saved. Maybe the woman I had spoken to had called out a search party for me. *No, not possible*, I remembered. I never told her where I was going when I left the porch.

Strong hands pulled me to my feet. Adults were in this group. I couldn't tell how many at first. Their flickering beams darted around in the blackness, bounced off the trees and ground, and swept over me. It was like being caught in one of those old-time prison movies where the police dragnet closes in on the escapee.

But no dogs, thank God. Just a bunch of men and older boys. What they were doing out here they never said, and I didn't ask. I was grateful to be rescued from my own incompetence. I made a weak joke about regretting not joining the Boy Scouts. They didn't seem overly curious, and I didn't elaborate on my explanation other than to say I was a photographer working on "a nature book."

They led me to a clearing where four-wheelers were parked like horses at a hitching post. I was told to get on one and hold tight to the rider because "we got us a ways to go yet." I asked my rider what that meant when he throttled the engine and drowned out my voice; his machine joined the ear-splitting din of the other riders revving theirs. We tore out of there at a speed I never would have thought possible considering the nature of the ground I had been tramping through half the night. But they were taking me back to civilization, and that's all that counted.

Except that they didn't. The few times I risked leaning my face out to see where we were heading, I detected nothing but a rutted path that petered out as we bounced over rough ground. My driver was forced to swerve around sudden curves he only seemed to recognize. I hung on for dear life. After traversing in this zigzag fashion for several more miles, we entered a wide open area, and I detected lights winking in the distance.

The other four-wheelers closed the distance around my rider like planes in formation; we rode abreast of one another toward these distant lights at a much slower speed.

My rider brought us to a stop with a fishtailing, figure-eight flourish that caused me to grip the fabric of his jacket so hard I thought I'd tear pieces off in my hands. When we stopped moving, I relaxed my grip and slowly stepped off and felt the earth under my feet once more. My legs trembled at the knees and for a few steps I walked with an old man's hitch in my gait. My ears had a constant buzz, a crashing timpani, from the high-pitched whine of the machines.

When I looked around, I made out the boxlike structures of old-fashioned trailers. My first thought was a depressing one: *Some kind of redneck trailer park...*

"Welcome to Spirit," my driver said.

People came out of trailers to look, none smiling, mostly women and a few older children. *Was lost and now am found.* The words of the famous Protestant psalm came to my mind just then, I'm not sure why. My Bible-thumping grandmother in the bedroom next to me sang it all hours of the day and night to the point I jammed a pillow down over my ears to sleep. My father had her carted off to an Alzheimer's clinic and I'll never forget the wild look in her smeary blue eyes.

They handed me bottled water, gave me blankets and took me to a place to sleep in one of the unused trailers. It was packed with muddy farm implements and tools, which was odd because all around the trailers were sumac and climbing vines. Not a sign of any landscaping or gardening.

This small travel camper came with a portable toilet but no shower hookup. Washing up would have been bliss. I was thoroughly tick- and mosquito-bitten. But sleep, glorious sleep, would do for now, I thought. I was safe, out of those dark woods, and that was all that mattered. My head no sooner hit the small red pillow one of the men handed me than I zonked out. My weary brain couldn't handle more stress.

In the morning, someone awoke me with a knock. A plate of bacon and eggs was handed to me along with some coffee by a teenaged girl who looked about seventeen.

"Here ya go," she said. "I'm thinkin' you're half-starved by now."

"Not half," I replied, "all the way. I could eat everything in the woods on four legs."

"You a hunter, too?"

"No," I said. "I only shoot with a camera. Do you get service out here?"

"What did you say?"

"Cell service, you know. By the way, have you seen my camera? It was hanging around my neck when we drove in."

"No, but I'm sure it's around here somewhere," she said and gave me a bright smile. "That pillow comfortable enough?"

353

I looked at it for the first time. It was something you'd see at a yard sale. It had the words *Biker Chick* on one side and a German cross on the other.

I laughed. "It was better than a goose feather pillow," I replied.

She was pretty but so very pale. I wondered if she was anemic. *Not a vegan*, I thought, *unless this bacon is made of soy*. I didn't waste another second thinking about it. I tucked into my food and could have gone through a couple more just like it.

She smiled, watching me eat.

The bacon was pig bacon, all right; and I was glad things were returning to normal after my little adventure in the woods. Her name was Rebecca. She took my plate and left.

When I stepped outside the camper, I noticed the only people around were women and children. No men. All the four-wheelers were gone. I hadn't heard them leave.

Two children were squatting in the dirt playing with sticks; they seemed to be threading them into a pattern, making teepee shapes.

"Hello," I said, approaching. They sat side by side, working with their little piles of sticks. "Are you making birds' nests?"

"No," the little girl said without looking up at me.

"What are they?"

"Devil-catchers," the little boy said; he too did not look up at me when he spoke.

"Cyrus! Evie!"

One of the women called to them from the doorway.

The children scooped up their stick toys and ran into the trailer. I made eye contact with her. She was trying not to be obvious about eyeing me, too. She looked about thirty, bore a strong resemblance to the teenager who had brought me the food, maybe a big sister.

"Miss," I began, "can you tell me—"

She retreated into her trailer and slammed the door. I noticed her trailer, all the trailers, in fact, looked like they'd been rescued from a dump site. They were patched in places with pieces of tin or

354

cardboard. It looked like a miniature Slab City, that bizarre, lawless land in California where people lived off the grid.

Now the alarm bells were starting to ring. No signs designating a campsite. It certainly wasn't a village. Nothing but these rundown trailers, a ramshackle camper filled with tools, and an aged Jeep Wrangler on cement blocks. Daylight revealed some egg-shaped structures behind the trailers that resembled WW II Army munitions igloos. Vines and creepers had completely covered them over. I saw graffiti scrawled across the metal door of the nearest one, but I was too far away to read what it said. An old man walked up seemingly from out of nowhere. He brushed his palms off on the front of his slacks and offered to shake hands. I accepted. He introduced himself as Ezra but gave me no last name.

I was on the verge of asking Ezra for a ride back to my car when a girl screamed, a loud wail that cut through the early morning sunshine and made me jump.

"He's bleeding! He's bleeding!"

The woman who had avoided me came out the door in a panic. The little girl who led the boy with his arm raised in the air was about his age, six or seven. A small cut on his forearm was bleeding, although the boy was being brave and only whimpered when the woman grabbed him and hustled him inside. Ezra left me to follow her.

I could hear the little girl crying.

"Oh, Luisa, I told you to watch your brother!"

More doors opened. A dozen women and girls poured out like bees communicating with the hive and headed straight for the trailer. It seemed to be an incredible overreaction to a little boy's cut arm but maybe it was much deeper than it looked, I thought.

I went back to the camper to gather my thoughts. I didn't want to leave without my camera. Waiting for the men to return seemed like my best option.

Knocking on the three trailers at the other end of the line produced nothing. Maybe they were all tending to the wounded boy in the last trailer, although that seemed ridiculous. They must be off working, I thought. Maybe they were transient labor. I thought of the "gypsy caravan" the woman from the highway had spoken to me of. I assumed these trailers were hauled up the Old Coshocton Road, so it must widen out to meet a highway. As the crow flies, I wasn't more than fifteen miles from the houses just beside the Utopia marker.

Lightheaded, probably from my dehydration, and still tired from my vigil against the tree, I decided to go right to the trailer where all the people were. My legs felt gimpy going up the three metal steps. I knocked and waited.

Rebecca came to the door.

"I need to speak to one of the adults inside," I said, smiling.

"Go back to the camper," she said. Her eyes were wide with fear. "I'll be right over."

"But I need to go—"

"Please, mister," she hissed.

Someone inside shouted her name.

She slammed the door in my face.

What the hell was going on around here?

I went down the steps and headed back to the little camper. I sat on the air mattress they'd given me and tried to suppress the anger eating at my placid mood. I owed these people some courtesy for rescuing me, but I had places to go, people to meet, as they say. Besides, I was irked that my camera was gone; it should have been strapped to me. The film had photos I wouldn't be able to replace.

A knock.

"Come in."

"It's me, Rebecca,"

"I could have guessed."

"Are you being sarcastic?"

"Yes, I'm sorry. Look, I didn't mean to be rude, but I need to get back to my car," I said. "I'm on a tight schedule, you see."

I wasn't, but it was a harmless lie.

She didn't know what to say to that.

She was even paler than I first thought. Her skin was translucent, lightly dabbed with freckles across her nose. By the standards of the average teenaged female today, she looked anorexic. I doubted whether a Moon Pie or a glass of Kool-Aid had ever crossed her path.

"How's the little boy?"

"He's still bleeding," she said simply.

"I'm sorry to hear it. Shouldn't they take him to the hospital — you know, for stitches?"

She looked at me again with that blank stare as if I'd just spoken Tagalog.

"You're in trouble, mister," she whispered. "They saw the photos on your camera."

"What?"

"Them photos," she repeated. "That other stuff in your car — "

"My car?"

"They think you're going to tell about us."

My blood chilled. I thought I'd stumbled into some Jonestown cult or some large-scale marijuana grow operation. The latter seemed more likely with all the men on four-wheelers and trailers. They weren't out here in the middle of the wilderness for recreational ATV driving. That woozy feeling I had when I left the trailer came back in a rush. My hands were trembling.

"It's just a book about places," I told her. "Photos of towns — towns that disappeared across the Midwest."

"Spirit ain't disappeared," she said. "Other places, maybe. Not us. We see things, we know things — "

You know that fight-or-flight syndrome people speak of that's supposed to be lodged in the reptile brain somewhere at the base of the spine? Well, mine was doing the full-tilt boogie just then. The quiet way she spoke only made her words that much more astounding. I wasn't sticking around to hear more. I pushed past her to the door—and stepped right into a pipe wrapped in duct tape. The swing caught me beneath the jaw and knocked me backward into the camper; my left arm flailed, knocking Rebecca to the floor beside me.

I was dazed, and my eyesight was quickly fading to black, but I could still hear them speaking.

"Becca," the man who had hit me uttered, "what are you doing in here with him?"

I distinctly heard him pronounce her name in his rage: *Rebecca Hammond.*

Rebecca Hammond. Elias Hammond's diary... the children from the fields...

Coming to was a long, strange, slow process. I felt like one of those mall rock climbers crabbing at pegs up a rock face with my fingers outstretched for the next purchase, straining to lift myself higher.

"He's comin' round," someone said above me. A gravelly voice.

"You out of practice there, Hosea. You didn't give him enough of your bug juice."

Bug juice. It sounded like convict lingo.

I blinked against the sunlight streaming through the tiny window. Four or five men were standing around the mattress looking down at me. My head pounded like a bongo between my ears. I jerked my head to the side fearing I might choke on my vomit if I threw up.

"Told you I give him enough," the one called Hosea said.

"I—I need to go," I gasped.

Someone above me laughed; it sounded like a horse's nicker.

"You ain't goin' nowhere, Mister Camera Man."

"Where am I?" I choked out.

358

"Done told you last night," the voice I recognized said. "Spirit."

They left me there. My hands and wrists were secured by nylon rope tied off to eyebolts drilled into the camper. I must have been out for a while. *Not good*, I thought, *if I'm concussed as well as drugged.*

I gave up struggling against my bonds. I lay there for about an hour before the door opened again and Rebecca came in. Ezra, the older man with white hair, followed her inside and stood off while she lifted a bottle of water to my lips and tilted it.

"Drink," she said.

I shook my head and spat out the liquid that poured down my face.

"It's only water," she said.

"Leave us, Rebecca," the man said.

She hurried past him without a word.

"Are you the leader of this hillbilly outfit?"

"I can understand if you're angry," he said. Almost sadly. "I understand completely."

"What do you understand? Tell me, because I don't understand shit!"

"Language, sir, language," he said.

"You're kidnapping me, after drugging me and clobbering me with a pipe, and you're worried about my language?" I was hoarse, virtually screaming through the veins of my neck. "Cut me loose! Right now!"

He was in no hurry to respond. He upended a plastic milk crate and sat on it.

Calmer, thinking more clearly, fear settling over me, I pleaded: "Tell me what's going on."

"That's better."

"What—what are you going to do?"

"That's not a question you need to be concerned about right now," he replied. "In time, you'll have your answer."

"What are you?"

"Ah, now that's a better question. I shall try to answer it to your satisfaction."

He did—but not to my satisfaction. He spoke for about twenty minutes. I interrupted to ask questions, but that seemed only to annoy him, and he refused to reply to anything that required him to justify himself or his actions.

They weren't the descendants of the Spiritualists of Utopia but the Mormons who had left Joseph Smith's congregation back in Kirtland. They'd splintered off because the larger group did not share their fixation with apocalyptic, world-ending visions; and because they were descended from "another, finer race," according to Ezra.

"It sounds Heaven's Gate bullshit to me," I said. "The dope you sell keeps you from having to panhandle for donations, but you're still crazy."

"I don't think you're in any position to judge us."

"Look, man," I said in desperation, "I'm just a photojournalist who took a wrong turn! I'm doing a book on ghost towns. I don't give a damn about your weed farm or your messed-up religious beliefs!"

"Ghost towns. That's interesting. What is your name, by the way?"

"Why? Do you need it for a grave marker? What's it matter now?"

As soon as I said it, I realized how close to the horrible truth my instincts had drifted. My head was splitting. It felt as if every nerve ending in my head had been touched with a cigarette lighter.

"Not to me, but to the Lord God it does surely."

It wasn't an *either-or* cult I had stumbled into but a *both-and*. What he said had me thinking I was in some parallel universe, not the real world I had lived in all my life before this place. They were a religious cult, and they did grow marijuana to support themselves; they'd even found a religious justification for it in the

Bible, according to Ezra: "Everything is permissible for me—but not everything is beneficial. Everything is permissible for me—but I will not be mastered by anything."

Thanks to my crazy, Bible-spouting grandmother, I could quote Corinthians, too. "Whatever happened to: your body is a temple of the Holy Spirit, who is in you, whom you have received from God, Ezra?"

I wasn't prepared for what he hit me back with.

"Be sober, be vigilant," he replied, "because your adversary the devil walks about like a roaring lion, seeking whom he may devour. That's Peter, Mister Jones, and his words are most apt, don't you think? I mean, since you are here among us. But we are prepared."

He left me reeling not only from the pain in my jaw but the words he'd quoted. To him, I was the incarnation of the devil, a demon to be expunged while I was in my earthly disguise.

These people, incredibly, were the actual and spiritual descendants of Elias Hammond. After getting kicked out of the Mormon congregation, they'd drifted downstate until they'd reached the river and settled here, taking over from the failed communities before them, the Utopian Fourierists and the anarchist community led by Josiah Warren—a secret society wrapped in other secret societies, like one of those wooden Russian nesting dolls. They'd not only survived, unlike the others, but they stayed remote by living off the land. It wasn't until they were faced with extinction that they broke their isolation somewhat. Marijuana must have seemed like a godsend to them, with all the money it brought in. They prospered, expanded their community, and adapted to modern times.

Worse for me, Ezra's mishmash of their early Mormonism had somehow merged with an apocalyptic vision aggravated by communal isolation. Their end-of-the-world fears were heightened by what little they had come to learn of the modern world, and that, God knows, was grim enough: nuclear war, a long-overdue asteroid collision with the earth, global warming, unchecked population growth. Hell, here I was running around the Midwest looking for ghost towns when every day the world was inching closer to becoming one big ghost town of a planet. Even Stephen Hawking felt the Earth was doomed, giving humanity a hundred years until it would all be over.

If it weren't for my condition, I would have seen the signs of things out of whack: the total absence of cellphones, the separation of the men and women, and the uncanny similarity of the features. That could mean only one thing: incest. I thought of the furor over the little boy's bleeding, and a long-ago chapter in some history book about interbreeding among families that produced hemophiliacs.

I don't know how long I lay there, itching and squirming from bug bites and immobility, the skin around my ankles and wrists chafed raw. My throat felt like a blast furnace.

The door opened and Rebecca entered.

"Here to give me more drugs? What's on the menu — marijuana brownies?"

In fact, if she'd offered some dope for the pain, I might have gone for it.

"No," she said, "just water and some salve for your insect bites."

She gave me sips of water. Right then, I would have traded diamonds for that bottle of tepid water. I lay silent while she ministered to me, their homemade salve from a bowl over my bites and under my neck where the sun had baked me.

I kept my voice even as I spoke, worried she'd see through the ruse: "Rebecca, please, my wrists are on fire. That stuff feels good."

"You shouldn't try to escape," she said, but applied more salve on the bruised skin around the ropes while I tried to distract her with questions. "When are they going to release me? I told Ezra I had no intention of reporting him to the police."

"The council is meeting right now to decide. I'm sure they'll let you know soon."

"What's to decide?" I protested. My voice quavered despite my attempt to keep it light. Her choice of words had alerted me to my danger. "You know, Rebecca, kidnapping is a whole lot worse, don't you think? If you cut me loose now, I'm gone from here and you'll never see me again."

She didn't say anything but offered to pour more water in my mouth. A man I didn't recognize came into the trailer just then and stepped around Rebecca to grab a pair of shovels. He didn't say a word, or even look at either of us, but just grabbed the tools and left.

A few seconds later, we heard four-wheelers fire up and take off. I didn't like the way Rebecca hunkered over the tray, pausing to listen.

"What are you doing?" I asked her.

"I'm praying for you," she said.

"What is it?"

"They've decided. I've got to go."

That didn't sound good.

"Go? Go where?"

In my gut, I already knew the answer. The man fetching shovels was my gravedigger. Those shovels were going to be put to work some distance from here. I was going to disappear. The irony of it walloped me like a punch to the solar plexus: the author of a book on ghost towns was about to become a ghost himself.

We see things, we know things...

Rebecca's words came back to haunt me. Had that predilection for clairvoyance Elias Hammond recognized in the Kirtland congregation come down with him and the other renegade Mormons?

Strange how a greater fear will knock out the pain sensors. A fox will chew off his paw in a leghold trap to escape what it knows to be certain death. I curled my hands into fists and began twisting them back and forth, ignoring the pain, working that greasy salve beneath the rope fibers a millimeter at a time. I lost all feeling in my fingers, but I never stopped for a second. I gasped for air and sweat rolled into my eyes, blinding me, but I worked on until I felt I had some slack around the skin, and a new part of my flesh was being abraded. That meant progress. The thought of two men out there digging my grave provided all the incentive I needed to keep going.

I was practically in a fugue state by the time my right hand slipped free. I rolled over to use my fingers to free my other hand, but they were too numb to work. I sobbed and then laughed at the cruelty of it. I lay back on the mattress, panting. I'd given up. Then, as if the gods had decided they'd had enough sport for a while, sensation returned to my hand. It burned like something on fire. Gradually I could wiggle my fingers.

I tugged at the rope, yanking with all my strength until I had a space. I pulled to get more salve into the rope and jerked at it. I was that wild animal for a time. Those last seconds of confinement were absolutely the worst, purest mental torture I had ever known. If Rebecca or one of the others had come in just then to see what I was doing, it would have been game over, lights out — and trust me, I'd have preferred a death blow with a mattock or shovel than to have been dropped, maybe alive, into a grave and covered up.

I had the remaining ropes off in seconds. I was on my feet, dizzy, weakened from the hours-long struggle to free myself, but damned well alive and ready to do what my limbic brain had been urging me to do for a long time: get out and get out fast! I cracked the door and peeked out — a few children playing in the dirt with their "devil-catchers." No doubt, I was the inspiration for that little cottage industry going on.

I stepped out, prepared to bolt. No sign of the four-wheelers. Even that battered Jeep had been removed from its blocks and was gone. I hoped they were far off cultivating their grow patches.

Slowly, I walked down the steps. None of the trailers had curtains. I walked toward the children who scattered like fish once I was spotted. Women and girls appeared in the windows. I felt like a rat walking past a gauntlet of owls. But no one came outside, no one tried to stop me or raise an alarm. I hadn't prayed since Bible school, but I offered one now in the hope that even walkie-talkies had been banned as the devil's instruments like cellphones and the Internet.

I kept walking and tried not to show panic. For all I knew, the women weren't privy to men's doings or were confined to women's work like the Amish. I kept my gaze fixed on the narrow clearing where the men had brought me just a day before, what felt like a lifetime ago. As I was approaching the end of the last trailer in line, I saw it: an unmanned four-wheeler. My heart hammered inside my chest already thick with the blood of fear. No rider or anyone else nearby.

I went right to it. Giving it a quick once-over, I didn't see anything wrong; tires looked solid, the battery looked new, and the cables secured. The distant whine of ATV engines reached the encampment on the breeze aloft. Not one or two but several, all coming right toward me. I no longer hesitated. I jumped aboard and hit the button, silently thanking my long-dead parents for the 110 cc ATV I had relentlessly nagged them to buy me for Christmas when I was sixteen.

I was off in a blue curl of smoke, dirt, and gravel spitting up behind the rear tires in a rooster tail of debris, slewing from side to side in panic until I eased off the throttle. The old skill of riding an ATV over rough ground finally seeped back into the right memory cells. I only hoped my head start was sufficient.

I blasted through the underbrush and skirted around stunted trees and thorn bushes and shrubbery with ease, but I recognized none of this terrain. It was too dark when the men drove me here. I pushed these thoughts aside. Escape was the only thing on my mind—that, and the posse of men riding up to kill me. I had no sense of time or even motion, all attention fixed on the ground flying up to meet me at every twist and turn of the handlebars. The compass in my head and however much gas remained in the tank were all that could save my life now. I leaned into the handlebars and drove like a bat out of hell, in a way I wouldn't have dared even during that reckless time as a teen. I took chances that no small branches or rocks lay in my path. As I approached the wetlands, I tried to recall how long I had walked parallel to it that long day under the sun.

Remember, remember, I told myself. *See the ground ahead – watch it!*

Too many times I was nearly bucked off when I had to make a fast dodge around an obstacle like a clump of rock jutting up from the ground and obscured by underbrush. I banged my sore jaw on the handlebars ducking beneath a trio of stunted crab apple trees; my face was lashed and whipped despite last-second swerves to avoid branches. The fear of what was behind me was greater than the dangers of crashing. Straining to hear, I heard nothing above the staccato whine of my four-wheeler and the wind blasting me in the face.

Little by little, the ground smoothed out and the path widened. I had no hope of seeing my car where I'd left it. Rebecca had as good as told me it was looted and gone by the time they came to get the shovels to finish the job of making me disappear. I bore down and increased the speed to full throttle. Speed alone could save me now.

Remember this, remember this—I kept demanding my memory to alert me to familiar signs in the terrain I was hurtling over. But nothing came to mind. My speed was too fast, and my vision blurred. I passed the spot where I remembered leaving my car— nothing remained, as I suspected. It was probably gone before I had finished that plate of food Rebecca brought. I didn't let the realization I had been a lamb being led to slaughter diminish my speed. I hit that path with a tunnel vision that never wavered until the path opened up to become a gravel road, and then that road became the torn-up asphalt I recalled, and finally the pavement of an old highway.

Made it...

I didn't let the bent sign proclaiming Old Coshocton Road deter my speed, either. I kept going right past the Utopia sign and the farmhouse where I'd spoken to the old woman's granddaughter — right to the first gas station I came to where I told the wide-eyed store clerk to call the police, the sheriff, the state troopers, the FBI, and every cop in a fifty-mile radius. I must have been babbling, hysterical, but I was overjoyed, giddy to be alive, and still jolted by the adrenaline rush of my escape from Ezra and his band of loons.

I can't tell you how much, in the hours and days that followed, I looked forward to seeing Ezra and his disturbed clan of misfits being rounded up. I remained in the county longer than I needed to, in fact, but it proved useless. The Clermont County Sheriff coordinated a search with the Franklin Township police that scoured the woods with tracking dogs, helicopters with thermal imaging cameras, and teams of volunteers from several police agencies. Not one person was found in those woods. The trailers were empty, abandoned, not even food supplies left behind. No four-wheelers, no men, women, or children. No Rebecca, although I'd described her right down to her freckles. One of the deputies kept slapping at mosquitoes on his neck and showed me one of the stick figures the children had left behind in the dirt.

"This one of them things you told the sheriff about?"

"Yes."

"Don't look like much to me," he said.

I was beginning to look and sound like some kook, an outsider. My Ohio credentials had long since expired from years of living in the East.

"New York City, huh?"

I heard that a lot as if that sufficed to explain my story of being kidnapped by a band of religious freaks. Even explaining my ghost town project seemed to add to the impression I was some whack job looking for free publicity. In the end, the only thing that kept the sheriff from filing charges against me was the fact they found some marijuana plants—just not enough to justify a massive search for more, he said.

"Probably some kids growing marijuana out there," the sheriff told me.

"What about those trailers?"

"Squatters," he replied.

"They didn't drive themselves out there, sheriff," I reminded him.

"We'll haul them off. Cost the township a fortune to do it. I wouldn't keep my dog in one of them shitboxes."

Zero, zilch, nothing. Protesting I had almost lost my life made me sound worse than hysterical. The purple bruise on my jaw wasn't proof of anything. I could have done that on the four-wheeler, which—the sheriff took pains to explain to me with a sneer in his voice—had been stolen from Fly, a little resort town on the Ohio east of Clermont in Monroe County. I was afraid he was going to charge me for felony theft, so I dropped it.

My uncle in Chicago wired me money to take a Greyhound to Columbus. I flew home to Long Island the following day. My ghost town book was abandoned soon after, lost, like my car, gear, and cameras. I didn't have the heart to go back. I repaid the publisher's advance and tried to resume a normal life.

My dreams are settling down. Every so often, though, I'll have a flashback. My nightmare of that time in the woods always starts the same way: a pale-faced girl with freckles splashed across her nose brings me a plate of food. Before I take a bite, I look up to see her grin at me. But it's no human, feminine face staring back. It's a face like a Halloween mask, something to frighten children with. Sometimes it resembles Ezra's face, sometimes it's a face you might see in a painting by Hieronymus Bosch.

"Eat," the Ezra-demon commands.

Stupidly, reluctantly, tears streaming down my face, I do so.

Two claw-like hands remove the mask from its face, and I behold evil, pure evil. The face widens to a leer, its pointed canines glow like phosphorescence in the dark. I am paralyzed and wait for the first bite into my flesh. I am being devoured in the demon's bloody jaws like Saturn eating his son in Goya's most terrifying of the demonic Black Paintings.

ABOUT THE AUTHOR
ROBB T. WHITE

Robb T. White was born, raised, and still lives in Northeastern Ohio—although he did get to China for two weeks once. He writes noir, crime, and hardboiled stories featuring series character Thomas Haftmann. He is the author of the noir/crime novels: *When You Run With Wolves* and *Waiting on a Bridge of Maggots*.

Special Collections won the New Rivers Electronic Book Competition in 2014. *Dangerous Women* is a recent collection of stories. Crowood Press published *Perfect Killer*; another UK press, Fahrenheit, is publishing *Northtown Eclipse*, a hardboiled novel featuring a new series character.

SILER, LOUISIANA

BY: DAVID CLARK

Holy shit! my mind screams as panic and adrenaline take over. Every nerve ending in my body fires at the same time, sending a message back to my brain that every single inch of me is in pain. It feels like I've been scrubbed with sixty-grit sandpaper from the top of my head to the bottom of my feet. The remaining senses—hearing, sight, and smell—feel muted. I feel separated from reality.

Something is holding my eyes shut. I can feel the thin tissue of my eyelids stretching and starting to tear when I attempt to force them open. My arms are not working. Wait, I *can* move them, but some great force is holding my hands down. I need to fight against this and get free!

"Arg...!" I try to scream as searing pain explodes through my body when I try to move my arms, and yet hardly a sound emerges. Any attempt to scream is interrupted with the feeling of razor blades cutting the inside of my throat.

My fight or flight instinct kicks in hard. I have to get free at all costs; fight now or die trying. I thrash my arms and legs against their restraints, all the while ignoring the lightning bolts of pain shooting from every extremity into the core of my being.

Suddenly, I feel a hand on the center of my chest trying to hold me down. Fighting back even more violently than before, I hear someone's voice trying to sooth me.

Through the fog, the voice starts coming in clearer. "Mr. Whelms? Mr. Whelms, please calm down."

It is a female voice, muffled and calm. Who is she and why the hell does she want me to calm down? Protesting against her instructions, I try to scream and achieve a stifled yelp.

"Mr. Whelms, you are only going to hurt yourself further. Please don't try to talk. You have a tube down your throat."

I what? I try to ask her what she means, but only a parched murmur leaves my mouth. My throat is so dry it hurts; it feels raw.

She puts a hand on my forehead. "Just hang on, Mr. Whelms."

Using her gloved thumb and forefinger, she pulls ever so slowly on something connected to my right eyelid. Soon, my eye is free, and then I feel whatever it is she's pulling start ripping at my cheek with shooting pain.

Tape, I reason. She is removing tape from my eyelid.

"Mr. Whelms, keep that eye shut while I remove the tape on the other side."

As the last of the adhesive lets go, taking a few pieces of flesh with it, I feel her hands move to apply pressure to my eyelids. She is holding them shut.

"All right Mr. Whelms, I am going to let you open your eyes now. Take it slow, things might seem a little bright."

With that, I feel the pressure lift off of my eyes. I find myself staring up at the rectangles of a drop ceiling and embedded fluorescent lights. Soon the face of a middle aged, curly-haired redheaded woman wearing no makeup or jewelry comes into view, but only through the visor of the hazmat suit she is wearing.

"Mr. Whelms, can you see me? If so, just nod."

I nod in response, staring back at her with what must have been a look of panic.

"Mr. Whelms, in a second I am going to count to three, and on three I am going to want you to blow as hard as you can." She pauses while messing with something around my mouth; I cannot see exactly what she is doing. "Okay, ready? One, two, and three — blow... blow. Okay, good."

I feel a tube sliding up my esophagus and out of my mouth. She turns to place the apparatus on a table to her right and returns with a cup of water. "Before you try to talk, take a quick sip of this." She holds the cup just below my mouth and tips it toward my lips. I feel the cool water running in my dry mouth and down my rough and abused throat; it's so cold it almost burns as it goes down.

"Thank you," I croak with a hoarse and painful voice.

She does not acknowledge my reply and instead turns to put the cup on the table to the right.

"Where am I?"

As she turns back from the table and starts to check the IV's in my arm, she replies, "You are in Dallas General. You have been here for four weeks."

"Four weeks?" I shout in alarm, and just as quickly pay for it— my throat suddenly feels like I drank a cup of broken glass. I'm pretty certain I tore something down there.

"Yes, Mr. Whelms," she explains. "You were brought in here four weeks ago. We were starting to wonder if you were ever going to wake up."

"What happened to me? Why can't I move?"

"We were hoping you could tell us what happened. You were brought in like this. As for why you are restrained, right now it is for your own benefit."

Trying to comprehend what she just said just makes me even more confused. "Wait, what do you mean? What is wrong with me?"

"Mr. Whelms, the doctors will be in shortly to talk to you. Just try to relax. You have been through a lot." She moves out of my line of sight, and I have no clue if she left the room or is merely watching me from the corner.

Have I really been here for four weeks?

What happened four weeks ago?

The last thing I remember is going fishing with Tim and Steve. Steve had finally bought the boat he had been talking about for over fifteen years; a twenty-one foot Stratos bass boat with a 9.9 horsepower kicker motor and a live well. No sooner had he bought it than he was itching to go fishing somewhere, and went about asking the locals where the fish were biting. Everyone pointed him to different spots in the bayou. We were planning to go check a few of those out until we stopped at the local bait shop.

We must have looked like complete newbies—the old timers gave us a hard time, taking full advantage of our lack of knowledge for their own entertainment. They asked Tim what kind of fish we were going for, and he answered, "Big."

As we were leaving, this one guy stopped us at the door. He said, "Son, these guys were a little less than friendly, and I want to apologize for their lack of manners." Meanwhile, his friends were snickering in the background. "Tell you what," he went on, "why not visit my favorite fishing hole? I guarantee you will be the only ones there."

He gave Steve directions, and we set off to the north. I kind of still remember the instructions he gave, but everything beyond that is fuzzy. I don't remember if we caught anything, or what we did after we got back. Everything is just a big black void in my mind.

A voice brings my consciousness back into the room. "Mr. Whelms, I am Dr. Robert Billord. How are you feeling?"

In the room with me is a middle-aged man with dark hair, dressed in a hazmat suit like the nurse before him.

"Confused and in pain," I respond. "What is wrong with me?"

He glances away so not to make eye contact. "Well," he says with a sigh, "we are not yet sure at the moment. All this time, we've been hoping you would wake up and help us shed some light on this."

"Doctor, what do you mean you don't know what's wrong with m—?" Pain cuts my words off mid-breath.

Billord retreats a step. "Mr. Whelms, try to not to move. Can you tell me what you were doing in Siler?"

"Siler?" My brow bunches up with recollection. "Where's that?"

He raises an eyebrow and asks, "Mr. Whelms, you do know where you were?"

I shake my head. "I don't know what you mean. All I can remember is my friends and I were out fishing in this old man's favorite fishing hole. Where are my friends, Tim and Steve? Did you find them too? Are they okay?"

Billord waves my concern away. "Mr. Whelms, please try to focus. The more you can tell us, the better equipped we will be to help you and your friends."

I level a heavy stare at him, drilling into his eyes through the plastic visor of his safety suit. I'm on to him—there's something he's not telling. He's just acting like he knows where my friends are. He didn't actually know I was with anyone else that day four weeks ago until I brought it up.

"Mr. Whelms?" he asks again, drawing me out of my contemplation. "What were you doing in Siler?"

I try to focus on remembering what happened. Dr. Billord has been cagey at best, but if I can recall and share with him what happened back then, there's a chance it might help Tim and Steve—assuming they're still alive.

"We drove up to this spot a guy at the bait shop told us about," I say, almost automatically as the memories slowly start to come back. "It was off of state road 311, just a few miles south of Ardoyne. We parked on the side of the road there and put the boat in the canal and headed west. He told us we would come upon a fence shortly, but that there were breaks in the fence we could pass through. Sure enough, we found a place where the fence looked like it had been pushed down. We had to tilt the motor up, but other than that our boat floated right over it without an issue."

Billord's face is a mask of annoyance. His eyebrows are pitched steeply downward at the inside corners and his mouth is set in a hard line. "Damn it," he says under his breath, then he asks me, "were there any warning signs?"

His question stuns me. I blink, then take a pause before asking, "What kind of warning signs?"

Billord shakes his head. "It's something of a long story, Mr. Whelms, but I'll make it brief. You see, there used to a small town called Siler, but Hurricane Katrina pretty much wiped it off the map. The place was completely flooded."

He takes a moment to adjust his spectacles, forgetting that they are behind his protective hood. Even so, I recognize it for an empty gesture, meant only to buy time.

"What happened next," he says, considering his words carefully, "was never reported in the media, but..." He sighs. "But I suppose you, of all people, ought to be told. As soon as the storm passed, the National Guard was called in to evacuate the town. It took two days, but not a soul was left behind. As soon as everyone was out, the Guardsmen put up a fence to keep people away."

I shake my head, unable to take this all in. "But... why?"

"There is..." He hesitates, drums his fingers against his thigh. "Well, was, a top-secret government facility just north of Siler. It took significant damage during the storm, and, supposedly..." He drums his fingers again, and this time, he breaks eye contact. "Something leaked out."

He must have seen the alarm in my face, because right then he says, "They never said what it was that leaked out; only that everyone had to leave and that no one would ever be allowed back in, ever. After the National Guard left, the Army Corps of Engineers built a berm all around it to contain the contaminated water."

"No," I tell him, shaking my head again as more memories come trickling in. "We didn't know any of that. The old man at the shop said it was a sunken town and that the fish treated it like a reef. He said the fishing was good there. That's all we knew."

Concern darkens Billord's face. He steps away to speak to someone just outside of my field of vision. I can't hear what they say, and can only pick up on a few words here and there. From what I can tell, their conversation is mostly about how the barricade has proven inadequate time and again.

"Mr. Whelms," Billord says, stepping back into my line of sight. He is no longer alone. With him is an older gentleman with close-cropped white hair and a hazmat suit. "In order for us to know what we're dealing with, we need to know exactly where you went. Tell us as much as you can remember."

"Once we were past the fence, we headed straight for a few minutes until we came to the first of the partially-submerged houses. The old man told us to find the first street and follow it to the right, then keep going to the town square. About ten minutes in, we knew we had arrived at the center of town."

Memories flood back so quickly that it is hard to keep up. I speak quickly, eager to recount everything to Billord as I remember it, out of fear that I might forget just as quickly.

In the town square was a half-submerged gazebo. It frame was badly decayed and several of its beams had already collapsed due to the elements. The tops of cars peeked above the water's surface where we presumed the streets would have been. All around us were shops; their painted signs having flaked and faded to the point where they were illegible. We could make out the sign for the grocery store only because it had raised letters.

The grocer's had two large storefront windows, both of which were smashed in. Water had flooded halfway up the building's walls, and above that was a solid mat of black fungus that clung to the surfaces like living shadows The place stank of rot even from outside. Only the products on the uppermost shelves were safe from the water, but that did them little good, because they had fallen prey to the fungus that grew thick and furry on their surfaces.

This was the first of two spots the old man had told us about.

We dropped our anchor beside one of the cars parked outside the grocer's. Our momentum pushed the front of the boat on top of the car's trunk lid, holding us in place. We baited up and cast our lines just where the old man said we should.

We sat there and watched our bobbers in the still water between the cars and the storefront, over what used to be the sidewalk. There was no current to speak of, so our lines just sat there. Steve suggested we create some movement by reeling our lines in and casting them back out. We did, and then immediately saw movement in the water around the store's windows. The fish were definitely there.

We stayed there for about an hour or so and had a few nibbles, but nothing we could set a hook in. There were fish, but they were not interested in what we were selling. That was when we noticed that the fish were actually the only wildlife we saw. No birds, no squirrels in the trees, nothing. I found that extremely odd.

We grew tired of just sitting there with no bites, so we decided to move to the other spot the old man had told us about. We reeled in the lines, but when Steve tried to pull up the anchor, we realized it was caught on something. No matter what angle we tried to pull from, we could not get it loose. We even tried to free it with the kicker motor on full reverse. The line went taut, followed by a loud bang and a quick jerk on the car we had beached on earlier, sending ripples radiating out from it in the stagnant water. Our anchor had somehow managed to wrap itself around the car. Tim wanted to just cut it, but Steve said there was no way he was losing his anchor the first time out with the boat. So, with no other choice, he pulled back up to the car and stepped out on the trunk lid.

Tim and I took bets on whether he would fall right through the rusted metal surface, but it held, so I owed him a six pack.

Steve shuffled his feet along the surface, looking for the edge, and then stepped down off the car, submerging about chest-deep in the water. Following the anchor line with his hands, he found it wedged between the back driver's side quarter panel and the bumper. He pulled a few times and finally managed to get it free. I pulled in the anchor while Steve climbed back in the boat, and then we were off to the next spot.

"Mr. Whelms," Billord interrupts me, "did you notice any odd smells, in particular, any smells coming from the water?"

"It smelled like a swamp. Just like the ones I used to fish in as a kid. There is a salty smell to it." In fact, it occurs to me now, it was exactly like the places where my father took me when I was a kid. The place was dirty, salty; full of debris and muck.

"We headed up what looked like the main street through town," I resume telling them, "looking for the high school. The old man told us it has a pool and the deep end is a nest for fish."

Memories of the place come flooding back, and again, my mouth is in a race to share them as fast as my mind can recall the events.

It was eerie traveling in a boat between buildings, down what used to be a road, with no signs of anyone else around. The air was still, with the only sound being the low hum of our motor. Just out of curiosity we decided to take a closer look of some of the homes we were passing. As we drew nearer, we saw our first signs of life — well, it would be better to call it death instead.

Floating in the water, trapped up against a chain-link fence, we saw what appeared to be the carcass of a deer. There was no way this deer was killed in the flood; too much time had passed since then, and the remains were still covered with fur. There were no signs of decomposition.

Tim felt the deer probably roamed in through a gap in the surrounding fence like we did, and maybe drowned or got preyed upon by something. None of that made sense. The water was only two feet deep or so, and we hadn't seen much by way of fish, or any other wildlife for that matter.

We pulled up to the deer's carcass. The side facing us was devoid of any gunshots or injuries that likely would have killed it. Tim leaned over the side of our boat, and, using an oar, managed to turn the carcass onto its other side. What we saw then shocked us so badly that we nearly fell overboard.

The underside of the carcass had been eaten away — no, not eaten. Dissolved is more like it. There was no hair, no skin, nothing at all but bones stripped of flesh. Everything beneath the waterline had been picked clean as though a school of ravenous piranhas had happened upon the carcass. Its ribcage was completely exposed, and within it sat a disgusting mixture of gelatinous rotting tissue and some kind of black ooze that looked like tar.

We powered on the engines and resumed our search for the school. We knew we were getting close, because off in the distance we could see the lights of the school's football field. Instead of keeping to the roads, we cut through flooded yards to take a more direct approach. It felt weird — despite that the town was deserted, it still felt like we were trespassing on people's property.

We had just barely coasted up to the high school's stadium when Steve began complaining of a terrible itch in his legs. At first, he'd ignored it, thinking they had been mosquito bites. But by this time, he was scratching until he bled. Red splotches covered both his legs up to his crotch, looking like a rash.

Tim said Steve had likely brushed against some poison ivy while trying to free the anchor, but none of us bought that. Poison ivy doesn't grow in water. Without saying so, I reasoned that something in the water must have caused an allergic reaction.

"Hmm," Dr. Billord grunts and shoots a glance at his companion. "What made you think it was an allergic reaction?"

"I couldn't think of anything else it could have been," I reply. "We decided for the rest of the trip that he should stay on the boat, thinking he might get worse if he got back in the water again."

"What happened after that?" Billord asks. The man next to him crosses his arms.

Recollection of what happened after encountering the deer carcass sets my heart racing. I can feel beads of fresh sweat forming on my brow. Billord must have noticed how upset I have become all of a sudden, and he says, "You are safe here, Mr. Welms. Please, try to relax your breathing and continue telling us what happened."

I do as he asks.

It was about two in the afternoon by the time we'd cut through a series of front lawns to arrive at Siler High School. Steve was worse off than before. The red splotches on his legs were now taking on a black and scaly look. His face was pallid and sweaty, and he looked on the verge of going into shock. Suddenly, he leaned over the side of the boat and threw up. Once his heaving spell had passed, he settled back into the boat, and then got up and vomited again.

I insisted that we turn back, and my friends agreed, but I never told them of the red welts that had begun to form on my hand.

Steve moved to the front of the boat, in case he needed to throw up again. I stayed in the back with Tim, who took the controls for our journey home. We were about ten minutes into our return trip when Steve started swaying back and forth. He looked drunk and on the verge of passing out. I went to check on him, but wasn't halfway across the boat when he fell headlong into the water.

Tim immediately shut off the motor and cut the wheel. Our boat coasted past where we last had seen Steve, then banked in a wide circle around the ripples where his body had hit the water. I took a shallow dive off the side of the boat and swam in a furious overhand stroke for Steve. Steve's left forearm broke the surface and I grabbed it to haul him back to the boat. His skin felt different— squishy, like squeezing a disintegrating sponge. By the time I got back to the boat, my fingers were clenched around the radius bone in his arm. All the flesh had sloughed off, as though it had melted off his bones.

I screamed and dropped the arm in a panicked knee-jerk reaction, and it hit the floorboards with a hollow rattle. Raw tendons and shreds of flesh dangled in bloody ribbons from the end where the bone would have met Steve's elbow. The flesh turned black before my stunned eyes, instantly rotting into a sticky tar. I followed the strands of black tar that led up from the bones and realized a mass of the stuff was stuck to my hand. I hadn't even noticed the slight burn on my skin.

I leapt back into the water, Tim screaming all the while to get Steve. This time, I snagged the back of his shirt and was able to haul him into the boat. His head was first to break the surface. Beneath a mostly-intact scalp was a gleaming white skull with two black pits for sockets where his eyes used to be. His body was emaciated— rotted almost instantly away by the ooze that devoured his soft tissue, until nothing but shreds of clothing and bones were left of him. Horrified, I screamed again and dropped his remains. They were swallowed up into the brackish water and gone in a heartbeat.

"You say his tissue just dissolved?" Billord interrupts. He steps forward to examine my arms and legs.

"Yes, doctor," I say in a faraway tone. Steve, my friend of twenty years, was dead. I was so caught up in the moment that it never had a chance to sink in until now. I snuffle, then sob and begin to cry but no tears come, only the burning pain that accompanies my slightest movement.

"Can you describe it a little better?" Billord asks.

"If you have ever felt soggy bread, that is what it felt like when I first grabbed his arm. And as I started to pull him up, my fingers just slipped right through down to the bone."

Billord pauses in his investigation of my limbs but doesn't look at me. "I see," he says. "Go on."

Once I'd hauled myself back onto the boat, Tim stared at me with wide, horrified, eyes, screaming, "What the hell was that? Oh my god—Steve!"

I didn't know how to respond. I didn't know any more than he did.

"Mark, get back in there and help him!"

"There is nothing left to help!" I shout over him. "Steve is gone."

"Mark," Tim said after a long pause, his voice failing. "We can't just leave him."

"We have to. There is nothing we can do for him now." I looked him square in the eyes and said, "Tim, we need to get out of here and go get help. Let's go."

Tim didn't respond, but instead began pacing nervously along the transom of the boat; one step to the left, turn, one step to the right and repeat.

The mild yet persistent burn on my hand had spread to encompass my entire body. Worse, it began to itch. It took all the presence of mind I had to keep from scratching. "Tim, we need to go, now."

This got no reaction from him.

"Tim, we need to go before *that* happens to *us*. I have the same spots on me that Steve had, and look," I said, pointing, "you have them on your legs."

Tim looked down at his legs and stopped dead in his tracks. He didn't say a word and instead just sat down, started up the motor, and accelerated to full speed. Meanwhile, my hand itched furiously. I looked down at it and saw more red spots starting to develop.

Then it hit me — it was the water.

I didn't start to break out in welts until after I reached into the water to pull up the anchor. As for Tim, we created a good bit of wake as we sped down the flooded streets — he likely got splashed a fair amount.

At the corner by the grocery store, we turned left, following the route we came in on. Just then, the boat's engines cut out and we started to drift to the right.

Steve was hunched over the motor, seemingly unconscious. I broke into a run to go help him, but stopped in my tracks on realizing every inch of his exposed flesh was covered in black scales. Drooping skin hung from his face in runny streams as more of the black oily substance dripped from his mouth. His body listed to one side as the flesh on his legs jellied and ran into a pool at his feet, marring his shoes and clothes with black sludge.

This sudden shock put me off balance and I fell over backward into the live well at the center of the boat.

"Was Tim ever in the water?" Billord asks as his companion looks on keenly.

"No, but I did notice the seat he was in was soaked from when Steve sat on it after getting back in the boat."

The two men glance at each other again.

"Please proceed, Mr. Whelms," Billord says.

I was the last of my friends alive. I was going to die if I didn't get out of Siler. With no regard for Tim, I pushed his skeleton out of the boat and took up position at the motor. Twisting the handle as far as it would go, I revved the 9.9 horsepower engine to life, catapulting the boat forward.

It was all about survival now. I could already feel the nausea coming on that had taken Steve when he fell overboard.

As the boat roared down the flooded street, I scanned the water for the house where I needed to make a turn toward the perimeter fence. It had a silver minivan in the driveway. I spotted it and kept the boat at full speed even as I gunned it around the corner.

Nausea made my head spin. I tried to hold down my heaving stomach, but it ended up winning out. I blew chunks onto the floor of the boat along with fair amount of bile. My body was growing weaker, and my eyesight was getting hazy.

The boat struck an obstacle so hard that I was flung to the deck. Whatever it was that I'd hit rattled with a jangling metal on metal sound that I immediately recognized—the chain-link fence. I lay face down, too weak to get up, thinking that here was where I was going to die and no one would ever find me.

"And then," I tell Billord with a throat parched from all the talking, "the next thing I remember is waking up here. I don't remember anything else. Who found me?"

Billord steeples his fingers in anticipation of speaking. "Mr. Whelms, you are a lucky person. Some hunters found you later that afternoon. They heard the sound of a boat off in the distance and then the collision with the fence. They called it in, and an agent for the Louisiana Department of Wildlife and Fisheries called us."

Gratitude wells up in my breast, and again I am almost driven to tears. "Doctor, I would like to thank those men, if you know how to get in touch with them. Maybe I can do that when I get out?"

Billord goes into an uneasy pause.

"So what is wrong with me?" I ask. "How long will I need to be here?"

Billord glances at the man with him, who gives an approving nod before stepping back and allowing the doctor and me some privacy. "Do you know where you are?" Billord whispers.

"Yes, the nurse told me earlier I am in Dallas."

"Yes, you are in Dallas, but more specifically, you are in a secure location at the Center for Disease Control. You came into contact with biological and neurological agents that leaked out of the government facility in Siler. We do not know exactly what the substances are, nor do we know how to treat the injuries they cause."

"You don't know how to treat what?" I yell at him with a throat that feels like sandpaper. "What is wrong with me, doctor?"

The doctor puts out his hands, gesturing that I settle down. "Please, just trust us. We are going to do everything we can to help you. It is just going to take some time."

"I'm on to you—there's something you don't want me to know, maybe it's classified. I don't care! Tell me what is wrong with me!"

Billord sighs heavily, then relents. "All right, fine. Give me a minute," he says. He and his companion back out of the room, returning a moment later with a large mirror in their hands.

"Try to remain calm," Billord says as the two men hoist it over their heads and angle it downward so I can see my reflection.

I have never seen anything as horrible as what I saw reflected in the glass, and it was all the more terrible because what I saw was me.

My skin is gone. I am a mass of pulpy, twitching red muscle fibers and tendons that glisten under the harsh hospital lights. In some spots, there are holes the size of a quarter where even the muscle fiber is gone and I can see straight to the bone. Straps at my head, wrists and ankles hold me fast to a hospital cot.

And then I see my face—gleaming white teeth like those of a clean-picked skull grin back at me in a head that is all red and bloody. My eyes bulge in their sockets, on the verge of falling out, kept in place by ribbons of ragged muscle where the black tar hadn't eaten though entirely.

I scream, and the nightmare in the mirror screams back at me, every sinew in its face twisting and churning with the movement. I want to vomit and run away or at least close my eyes, but I haven't got eyelids anymore, and all I can do is stare as the monster rages on.

The thing in the mirror, the thing that is me but not me, screams and screams and screams. My heart flutters in my chest as my eyes grow dim, and I faint from shock.

ABOUT THE AUTHOR
DAVID CLARK

David Clark is an IT professional by trade and a horror and sci-fi author by passion. He has been working on various writing projects for the better part of the last ten years, mostly for his own enjoyment or small release via various forums and social media outlets.

His writing style takes a story based on reality, develops characters the reader can connect with and pull for, and then adds a twist of surprise to the journey.

In addition to novellas and novel projects, he also enjoys the challenge of short stories and is currently published in three anthologies.

TWIN JESTERS, BRIDGEND

BY: DAVID OWAIN HUGHES

I can hear their harsh, raspy breathing and low snarls mocking me from the shadows as they give chase. They're not racing after me, although it feels like it. They're teasing me, much like a cat does with a mouse.

I dare not stop, not even to wipe the stinging sweat from my eyes. My only hope is to push forward and make it back beyond the border of Twin Jesters.

They may not wander that far from their town…

My mind is a scrambled mess.

The sound of rushing blood pounds the inside of my ears. I cough, stumble and stagger over a small stone bridge with parapets lined with flowers. On the opposite side of the humpbacked structure, I spot a warm glow spilling from a large edifice looming in the darkness. A low hubbub of chatter and laughter floats on the air.

"Goin' to rip your gutsssss out, ssssnoop…" a snake-like voice says from just behind.

"Argh-ugh!" I cry, holding a hand out towards the pub.

Tears threaten.

I stumble again but stay upright.

My laptop carry case and camera bag slap my back as I continue at a jog. I take a fleeting glance over my shoulder, spotting their red eyes that stand out in the darkness like burning match heads, and trip over my feet. I don't go down. Instead, I rush headlong, down the other side of the bridge and slam into the pub's side wall. I bounce off it with force and flop to the ground.

More hissing from the shadows gets me moving.

I don't see them advancing.

I thought they'd stay —

I get on my feet, and a rock sails from out of nowhere, missing me by centimetres. The projectile ricochets off the floor and rattles out of sight. I don't have time to think about it as a shower of stones rains down on me. I cover my face with my arms but it's no use — the rocks strike my head, arms and shoulders. One cuts my cheek, another hits me in the eye, a third splits my bottom lip.

Yelling, I run for the pub's main entrance. Rocks continue to pelt against the wooden tables and chairs, walls and ground as I enter. I crash through the door and slam it closed, then collapse against it.

My actions bring the roaring pub to a graveyard silence. People cease talking and laughing, men playing pool look up and stare, mouths open, whilst darts miss the dartboard and the landlord stops drawing a pint.

"Jesus!" I manage between sharp intakes of breath. My eyes are running. *Don't!* — I shake my head, unable to finish my sentence. *Keep quiet. I don't want to be carted off to a mental hospital.*

"Brandy," I tell the owner. "Make it a double-double, Rodney."

"You've not been out there chasing 'em big, wild cats of yours again, Owen?" he asks, drawing a hearty laugh from the barflies and the men playing darts.

A laugh hitches in my throat as I wipe my face clean with my sleeve. Blood mixed with snot smears the fabric down to the cuff. "Something... like that..." I manage, my breathing coming back under control.

Pool balls begin clacking, darts thump at their black, red, and green beds.

"You okay, matey?" a man at the bar asks, turning on his stool to look at me.

I nod. "Fine, thanks. I took a tumble on my way here."

My hand is shaking, and it takes both to grab my drink from Rodney. The ice cubes clatter against the tumbler's rim, bringing to mind ships caught in a storm. The fiery liquid is in danger of sloshing over.

"You positive you're okay, Owen?" Rodney asks.

"A little shaken," I reassure him. "I went down pretty hard, banging my knees and elbow." I wince, making it look as convincing as possible. I even grimace as I hobble to a corner table, out of sight, out of mind. "A couple of hits of your finest Eight Bells and I'll be as right as rain. You'll see."

Rodney shrugs, goes back to serving his punters.

The chatter and laughter have hit their zenith by the time I've sat down and got myself comfortable. My camera bag, laptop case and weatherproof jacket lie by my side.

Before reaching for my laptop, I drain the glass of half its contents and set the brandy to one side. I gasp, sigh and wipe my mouth. On the table is a glass tube housing a candle which is burnt down to a stump. It offers little light. A faint smell of jasmine rises from it.

The wallpaper is drab and uninspiring; and in the spots where it has peeled off to reveal the bare wall, damp has taken hold. Still, the place is warm—a safe haven—and Rodney is someone I have known for years. If need be, I could spend the night, no questions asked.

I guzzle the last of the brandy and order another.

"Run me a tab, Rod, please."

"Sure thing, Owen."

I take my drink back to my table, hands no longer shaking, and sit down. Placing my glass on a coaster, I set my laptop on the table and switch it on.

The battery is full.

Good, it'll need it.

With my laptop set up, I turn to the carry case and dig out a pile of handwritten notes, files, a pad and pen. I also remove the memory card from my camera, and pause when my gaze crosses the backs of my hands. The skin has been torn off both sets of knuckles. Dried blood has crusted over the cuts. Ignoring this for now, I slip the small plastic card into a port at the PC's side.

I may as well send the images. I don't think this can wait. Besides, if something should happen to me after I leave here, it'll be good to know my information has been passed on to Jim and Sam.

I open a fresh Word document and take a large gulp of brandy, inhaling deep and exhaling noisily.

Where, and with whom, do I start? What about Twin Jesters itself? The people have a right to know about the town, about its chequered past... But is the violence and bloodshed relevant? Of course—it shows how cursed the place is. In that case, I'll start with Sam Enrich.

"Sam Enrich," I say aloud, making me think about the conversation I had with the private eye a week ago.

"Hello, this is Owen Figs, Bridgend News Post. How can I—Sam?" I smile into the phone.

"I need your help, Owen."

"Okay, if I can. What's on your mind? You don't sound yourself. Is everything—?"

"Dandy, mate," Sam cuts me off. "I'm looking for information to help me with a job I'm on."

I slide my legs off my desktop, sit up and huddle closer to the phone. "This wouldn't have anything to do with Twin Jesters, would it?" I whisper into the receiver.

"How—?" Sam stammers. "Doesn't matter. Yes, possibly. They've put you on it?"

"Yes, I'm looking into it. Strange, don't you think?"

"Very. Do you believe the grapevine?"

"And what would that be, Sam?" My grin must be infectious. Sam laughs.

"Look, you scratch my back and I'll scratch yours. Deal?"

"Depends…"

"What will it take to get you up off your arse and out there with your camera?"

"You think I'm crazy enough to go there?" I reply, my voice pitched. "The police have the town sealed off. It's a no-go area. I'd be arrested on sight."

"Then what the hell have you been doing? You're supposed to be a ball-busting journo."

"Sure—talking to eyewitnesses, the police…"

"Oh, really? I suppose you know the army is planning to bomb Twin Jesters?"

"What?" I sit bolt upright. My colleagues turn to look at me; the hubbub in the office dies.

"You heard," Sam grunts. "In the next week or so, they're sending in a team of soldiers to try and eradicate the problem. If not, bombs away."

"Don't be crazy, man."

"You're talking to the best damn snoop there is, friend. I have contacts everywhere, and I paid good money for this information. Now I need some from you."

My hands are shaking. "What?" I choke out, my voice barely audible.

"I need you to get into the town and confirm the problem's existence, Owen. With photographic proof."

"Why?"

Sam hesitates a long string of moments before responding. "Because I believe the problem has spread to another town close by. Like I told you, I'm working a case, and I think it coincides with Twin Jesters. My client seems to think there's something strange going on at a pub by the name of The Lamb and Flag. I've confirmed it. If this truly does connect with Twin Jesters, then we could be sitting on something huge."

I chew my lower lip in trepidation. "Okay, you've got my attention. Tell me more."

"Remember the incidents in Bridgend many years ago, the ones involving the cannibals?"

I almost laugh. "No!"

"Then I suggest you look it up. Connect the dots, Owen."

"But—"

"We've wasted enough time talking. Research Bridgend's history and seek out the murderers they used to call the 'Man-Eating Fucks'. When you do, get back to me after you've been to Twin Jesters."

"I—"

The line cuts to a dial tone.

Grimacing, I drop the phone back on the hook.

A day after the call with Sam I had a meeting with Jim Hengroth, my boss and head editor at the Bridgend News Post. I needed his advice.

After I'd told him in confidence what the P.I. had said, Jim answers, "You're my top reporter, Owen. I'd hate to see you go out there on a whim. Nobody knows for sure what's going on inside Twin Jesters. Do you really want to risk your career — hell, your life! — for hearsay?"

"Isn't that what we do?" I smile.

"I suppose, but this is different. This is outright dangerous."

"If I don't live for the scoop, then what's the point of living?"

He chuckles. "I guess you're right, and I won't stop you. You know that. After all, I have a business to run." He claps me on the left shoulder with a huge, weatherworn and scuffed hand.

That's what happens when you spend your summers as a child, teen and young adult pitching hay on your daddy's farm, he'd explained one drunken evening. *Hard to cry it down, mind — the seasonal work helped pay me through five years of university.*

No amount of Neutrogena is going to soften those babies, I'd ribbed.

But that's where the joking ended with Jim. He was a good man and a blessing to work for, the hands-on sort of boss who wouldn't expect anything of anyone that he wouldn't do himself.

"Thanks, Jim. I'll be careful, promise."

I take another swig of brandy.

"You're going to be one ecstatic snoop when you receive my email, Sam. You too, Jim," I think aloud as I swirl the remainder of the drink in my glass, then finish it off and shout for another. The warm-bodied drink helps deaden the pain in my face, body and hands—especially my hands, which are hard at work typing an email to the private eye.

Dear Sam:

You were right. Merciful God, were you right! It's true. All of it—every last blood-soaked detail from the past to present regarding the Man-Eating Fucks. But there's more, much more, and only you, the government and I know exactly what's going on at Twin Jesters. However, we'll change that. I have the proof you need attached to this email.

Upon escaping Twin Jesters I was followed to the town's borders by the Fuckers, as they've been so grossly named. They almost got me, but I managed to make it to safety, to a pub I know. Still, I fear they are lurking outside, waiting to tear the flesh from my bones and the organs from my body.

I may wait it out here until daylight. The landlord is a friend.

This danger is also the reason why I've decided to email you from my current position. I don't want to die without someone else knowing the truth. After I've sent this, I plan to communicate with my editor, whose contact details can be found at the bottom of this correspondence.

You may want to speak with Jim should something happen to me.

Before I go into what happened at Twin Jesters, I need to tell you what I know about the Man-Eating Fucks and the town itself, for Twin Jesters is steeped in a bloody, violent past.

First, the name: Twin Jesters is an odd name for a town, isn't it? There's a reason for that. And the place is hardly a town — before the evacuations, some 452 people lived there; and now less than half remain. It's said that fifty or sixty of the escapees are in critical condition and won't last the week.

But I digress. Let's get to the history of the place.

The town didn't exist until after the Roman garrison departed the isle in 410. At the time, Wales was divided into a number of separate kingdoms, the largest being Gwynedd in northwest Wales, and Powys in the east. Glywysing, or Glamorgan (Morgannwg) as we know it today, was a much smaller kingdom in modern Gloucester, ruled over by King Glywys.

According to twelfth century sources, after King Glywys died, his kingdom was divided into seven *cantrefs*, and each of his sons received one. These were a form of medieval Welsh land divisions, often ruled jointly by the head of the family or sometimes treated as appenage subkingdoms.

This is where it gets really intriguing, Sam. I never knew so much about Welsh history until I started digging.

Pawl, son of Glywys, settled in the cantref named after him (Penychen), and built a castle there. The land held great economic potential, and Pawl sought to develop it into a market and farming town. Construction was finished in the year 510. He named the new settlement after his twin jesters — Ddu and Coch, which translates to Black and Red. I can only assume their names were derived from the colours they wore.

This pair didn't look like your typical clowns of the day. Most jesters of that era wore brightly-coloured costumes comprising of

397

bells, tassels and three-pointed cloth hats. They looked gaudy and told jokes. Not these two. In the scant records that mention them, they are depicted as looking sinister. Even though it was the medieval period and everything was ghastly and frightful, this pair took the biscuit.

Their black and red costumes were meant to evoke terror and blood. They both wore half-masks similar to the one made famous in *The Phantom of the Opera*, and the halves were said to interconnect when the two were placed together. On the exposed sides of their faces, black daubs of make-up shrouded their eyes, and white make-up was applied over their lips to give the impression their mouths were full of razor-sharp teeth.

Their make-up is worth commenting upon. With modern cosmetics, their look can be achieved with ease, but in the year 510, it was quite a feat.

The two men were said to be brutally strong. When they weren't in costume, they went about bare-chested, exposing tattoos that snaked around their torsos. And instead of a marotte with a carved, smiling head on it, they carried shrunken human heads impaled on a spike.

There is nothing funny at all about the jesters. They looked more like executioners than clowns.

I stop typing and pull away from my laptop.

My brandy sits untouched. I pick it up and take a small sip. I'm starting to feel light-headed. Replacing the glass on the coaster, I sort through the files at my side and fish out the blown up image of Ddu and Coch.

A fresh shiver rips a path down my back.

I resume typing.

There's hardly any information to be found on the jesters. I don't even know if they were real twins. All I do seem to know, which I've taken from history books and the local mythos, is how they came into Pawl's care, what they did, and their fate.

By all accounts, Pawl was a generous and sympathetic ruler. He is said to have found the twins in the wilds just outside the settlement that would become Twin Jesters. At the time, Ddu and Coch were youths, and Pawl, thinking them to be orphans, took them in and raised them as his own.

Then, for reasons which have since been lost to history, the twins are believed to have gone on a killing spree. In the span of three nights, the pair is said to have slaughtered half the town's population. Among their victims was Pawl himself. Grisly as the murders were, the killings had been conducted in such a way that conclusive evidence could not be raised against the twins. Furthermore, a desire among the ruling class to "sweep things under the rug" helped ensure the twins would not be brought to justice.

Clwyd, Pawl's cousin, was next to rule over Penychen, which meant that the youths fell to his care. There was peace over the next ten years, though the town never fully recovered from the massacre.

A curse had descended upon Twin Jesters.

Crops fared worse from season to season until eventually the yields were not enough to support the population. Each generation of calf was thinner than the previous, until at last the livestock failed to produce live births. Calves emerged stillborn from their mothers' wombs.

Eventually, the town came to be shunned. People wouldn't go near the place for fear of the curse attaching to them.

It was not long before trouble struck again.

Over the course of a week, there had been a rash of house fires that had resulted in several deaths. The guilty parties were never identified. This was going on in the midst of mysterious infant deaths — children as young as the newly-born were found murdered in their baskets where they slept, their throats cut. The terrified villagers demanded justice, which came swiftly enough. Just as tensions were approaching a boil, Ddu and Coch were caught in the act of starting a barn fire. In the minds of the townspeople, evidence of the twins' recent crime was enough to make them responsible for the previous arson attacks as well. In addition, the depravity of their offenses made it a foregone conclusion that they must also have been responsible for the infant murders.

With the evidence stacked against them, the twins were summarily declared guilty of their crimes. Clwyd ordered their deaths by hanging in the town square. Their bodies hung from the gallows for a week, at which point they were cut down and their heads were impaled on pikes with a message nailed to their foreheads:

DYMA BETH SY'N DIGWYDD I LOFRUDDIAETHWYR
(THIS IS WHAT HAPPENS TO MURDERERS)

Their heads remained on the spikes for carrion birds to peck away their flesh, eyes and tongues, until at last their bones weathered, cracked and fell apart.

But even in death, the village would not be free of the jesters' curse.

Almost as soon as the twins' rotted remains hit the earth, the town was beset by all manner of disasters: swarms of rats, floods, disease, famine—death. Not even Clwyd, who had ordered the jesters' executions, was safe from the curse. Within months, he was found dead, his severed head impaled on a pike.

The string of disasters proved to be too much for the townsfolk to bear, and the village of Twin Jesters was ultimately abandoned. It remained that way until the tenth century, when Gruffydd ap Llywelyn used the ghost town as a garrison during his conquests against the English, and later, his home. Legend has it that he chose to settle here after a vision in which he beheld a pair of jesters who persuaded him that the town would be the site of a great victory.

He saw it as a blessing, Sam.

A fucking charm, of sorts.

Gruffydd ap Llywelyn had thought he'd been touched by God.

Goddamn idiot!

When I looked into Gruffydd's life, I turned up some interesting information you won't find in most history books. The official story is that Gruffydd allied himself with Ælfgar, son of Leofric, Earl of Mercia, who had been deprived of his earldom of East Anglia by Harold Godwinson and his brothers. They marched to Hereford and did battle against a force led by the Earl of Hereford, Ralph the Timid. Gruffydd destroyed them, then sacked the city and crushed its motte-and-bailey castle. Shortly afterwards Ælfgar was restored to his earldom and a peace treaty was concluded.

What the historians won't tell you, however, is that two jesters were often seen on the battlefields, helping Gruffydd and his army defeat the opposition. Wherever the jesters were spotted, the battlegrounds were always a scene of great bloodshed, even by medieval standards.

By 1056, Gruffydd had seized full control over Morgannwg and Gwent, along with extensive territories along the border with England. After another victory at Glasbury, the English finally recognized his sovereignty as the King of Wales. Gruffydd then returned to Twin Jesters to rule over his newly-acquired dominions.

By this time, though, Gruffydd was a changed man. The town—or perhaps the influence of its jesters—was turning him into an overconfident warmonger. All he could see was power. Gruffydd was blinded by it, and through his victories, he'd started believing his own hype.

Some five years after establishing his rule, Gruffydd received another vision from the jesters. Following their advice, he reached an agreement with Edward the Confessor, but the death of his ally Ælfgar in 1062 left Gruffydd vulnerable once again. In late 1062, Harold Godwinson obtained the king's approval for a surprise attack on Gruffydd's court at Rhuddlan. The general consensus is that Gruffydd was warned of the attack in time and escaped out to sea before he could be captured, but that's a lie. Gruffydd was slain at Twin Jesters during Harold's surprise attack, his head impaled on a pike in the town square. With his death, the land of Wales fell and was annexed into England.

The rest is history, as the kids say.

People will believe what's been recorded in books, of course, but local Welsh historians will tell you otherwise. And, from what I've witnessed tonight in Twin Jesters, I believe the rumors, Sam. I'm not easily spooked, but I'm positive on this one and I hope I can convince you.

Others, too.

There's darkness at work, here. Twin Jesters is cursed by Ddu and Coch, who still roam, their reign of terror unending after Gruffydd's death.

Harold Godwinson, who orchestrated the attack on Gruffydd, died in Pawl's castle at Twin Jesters. He was murdered, his body mutilated nearly beyond recognition.

The town was destroyed in a massive fire one hundred years after Harold Godwinson's conquests. It lay in ruins for two centuries, then was rebuilt by a businessman who sought to exploit the surrounding natural resources. The atrocities started back up again: murders, rapes, plagues, deaths... the jesters' doings? I think so. There are reams of blood-drenched stories about the place the historians all disregard as local myths.

You're probably wondering why I'm telling you all this. Tonight, with my own two eyes, I saw the fools of yesteryear, and I believe they've brought the threat you spoke of to Twin Jesters, a town that's seen peace, bar for the odd incident here and there, for the past five hundred years.

Why has it started again? While I can only guess, here goes.

This year, 2010, marks the town's fifteen-hundredth anniversary. The townspeople have begun celebrating with street parties, fun and games. Even the local brewers got in on the action by brewing a new beer for the festivity: Weeping Fools.

Plus, the restoration of Pawl's castle has been completed.

When two jesters turned up for a party, one wearing black, the other red, nobody suspected a thing—that is, until the killing started.

A few days ago I spoke to one of the survivors, a Mr. James Gogwin, who's currently laid up in the hospital with minor injuries. He told me the week leading up the festival, which had been planned to span from late Friday evening through to Monday afternoon, was "pleasant and peaceful. Nothing seemed out of the ordinary."

"It was your average working week," he continued. "When Friday rolled around, and the party kicked off, everything ran smoothly. And then, on Saturday afternoon, as people took to the streets to continue enjoying their town's activities, a pair of fools strolled into Twin Jesters with a bunch of naked people caked in mud and leaves. They looked like feral cave-dwellers."

I didn't have to push Mr. Gogwin for answers.

"At first, we stood about, laughing and joking, thinking the jesters had been hired by someone from within the community. We didn't think anything of it, you know? The nakedness was inappropriate because there were small children present, but I thought it was part of some strange act. Besides, you couldn't really see their privates—the filth and greenery hid their modesty. They were led by these clowns, who were juggling flamin' daggers whilst riding unicycles. When they themselves got closer—and I don't mind telling you this—I almost soiled myself."

Before I could ask why, Mr. Gogwin continued.

"They were—dead—behind the eyes, I mean. There was no colour to their faces, even though they wore make-up. The laughter all around me turned to gasps. The children started sobbing, screaming and pointing, as the jesters snarled and snapped their teeth, which looked like needles; hundreds upon thousands of needles, all stained red. Then they started throwing their burning blades. Mrs. Salls, who was standing next to me holding her granddaughter to her chest, caught two daggers in her eyeballs, which exploded like water balloons. A third, fourth, fifth and sixth, thunked into Olivia, the child, pinning her to her grandmother as she wailed, bled and burned. Pandemonium ensued. A stampede erupted, as burning bodies hit the ground one after another: men, women, children... When the jesters ran out of knives, they unleashed the cave-dwellers, who started attacking people by — *eating* — them. Flesh, tongues and eyes were torn from people. Their skin... *devoured* — "

Here, Mr. Gogwin broke down, refusing to speak further. I had to find others willing to open up, thinking it would be easy, but most refused, except a young widow, a Ms. Peterson, who'd come face-to-face with the "cave-dwellers."

"I wouldn't call them cave-dwellers," she told me. "They looked more like cannibalistic freaks to me — things that live deep in the woods or underground. They snatched my Lilly from my hands — "

I discovered Lilly was Ms. Peterson's six-year-old daughter.

"They tore the flesh from her face. One of them ripped her leg off — it took me days to — wash — her blood from my — my hair."

I didn't want to push her, but she continued once she'd composed herself and stopped crying.

"There were loads of them; fifty or sixty. Maybe a hundred. I don't really know. The streets became chaos, and I found myself ankle-deep in bloody water that had body parts, organs and party food floating on it. It was like something out of a horror film. When I got to the town's border, I saw the police arriving — they had a helicopter in the sky. I was told by others that the army would eventually turn up, but I'm not sure."

After getting all I could from Ms. Peterson, I went to the police station for more information, but didn't turn up much — they were tight-lipped about the whole thing. They also denied the army's involvement, even as they escorted me off the premises. I was lucky to escape their clutches with my camera, notepad and laptop.

I stop typing, my fingers aching. As I sip my drink, which will be my last, I read through my email, making sure all information is present and correct.

"Another, Owen?" Rodney yells over.

I look up, startled, and shake my head. "I'm feeling dizzy."

This rouses a few titters from the men propping up the bar.

I ignore them and go back to my PC.

These "cave-dwellers" are your "Man-Eating Fucks," Sam. I found pictures of them in old newspaper clippings at the library. Do you think the jesters brought the tribe back to life? What if they can't be stopped? Are there more? Maybe the jesters conjured up a new clan of Man-Eating Fucks based on the history they know about Bridgend?

Whichever may be the case, you were right about us sitting on something huge!

Don't bother returning my email, Sam, as I want to speak with you face-to-face. I need to get everything straight and down on tape if I'm going to write about it in the paper; I might leave out the part about seeing ghosts.

Having said that, I could mention them and say that someone could be masquerading as Ddu and Coch — that a couple of local nutters want people to believe the history. Then again, do I want a straitjacket as an early Christmas present? Leaving the jesters out is for the best.

Anyhow, I need to tell you about what happened at Twin Jesters tonight.

Again, I stop typing.

Maybe I'll have that brandy after all, Rodney, I think to myself.

I get the barman's attention and ask for a double.

"A double-double?" he calls back.

"Please, Rodney." My voice wavers, and I fail to see the rotund landlord walk over to me and clamp a meaty hand to my shoulder.

"Are you fine there, lad?" Rodney asks.

"Ye—"

"I've never seen you this…"

"This what?" My guts knot and I fear they'll fall out of my anus if I don't clench.

"Like—like you've seen a ghost. You're as white as a sheet, Owen."

"It's nothing—"

"You never put brandy away as you're doing this evening. Is something troubling you? Is someone giving you trouble?"

I shake my head, take my drink and swig a mouthful. "I promise you, everything's okay."

"Well, if there *is* anything I can help with, yell. You've been a loyal customer over the years, and I'd hate to see anything bad happen to you."

I give a half-hearted smile, even though I'm genuinely pleased by Rodney's concern. "Trust me, please."

The man nods and lumbers to the bar. As I watch him go, I notice some of the barflies looking in my direction. They're smirking.

Nosy fuckers.

I give them an aloof, distasteful look, before shaking my head and dropping it back to my laptop. My eyes travel along the last

407

few lines I've written. I take a small hit of brandy and place it to one side.

The shakes have subsided.

The ice-vipers that were nestled in my guts have melted and burned away.

I take a deep, shaky breath.

I have to admit, I wasn't going to go tonight, Sam. I saw it as a wild goose chase. Not only that, I was worried I'd get myself into a heap of shit. But hell, how could I not? I'm a journalist. A "hard-nosed" one at that, remember? In my twenty or so years of covering news stories for various papers, never, ever have I seen or heard of anything like I have tonight. Hell, I've never taken such a risk before.

I've wished for excitement, even thinking about moving to a large city —

Ah, I've gone off on a tangent.

I went to Twin Jesters with an open mind, putting the eyewitness reports down to some sort of mass delirium or madness that had been contracted from a gas leak or virus that had wormed its way into the town. I even swept aside what you'd told me, Sam.

How wrong I was! I'm also glad I decided to pick up my reporting equipment and head out there — even if it ends up costing me my life.

The army are out there.

Or were, rather.

My first thought was to walk to Twin Jesters, but I decided against it last minute, thinking I might need a fast get-away. I'd almost laughed at that. The smile was soon wiped from my face when I was met by armed soldiers blocking the town's main entrance.

"This is a government zone now, sir—you'll have to turn around and go back," I was told. Normally I would have pushed, tried worming my way in with a silver-tongued response, but I felt threatened by the G.I. Joe wannabe, who had three others with him.

They loomed over me, Sam, and the one who'd spoken to me kept his hand on his holstered pistol the entire time. I didn't utter another word. Instead, I left and searched for another way in, but was met by the same resistance.

I had one option left: I ditched the car and used the night as camouflage. When someone wants to gain access to somewhere badly enough, they'll find a way. And so I crawled through a sewage pipe like a rat, popping up in the middle of Twin Jesters.

The lengths we go to…

A genuine laugh escapes me. It feels good, even though it attracts the attention of Rodney and the bar bozos. I gulp some brandy and avoid eye contact.

Even though the stench of shit was overpowering, I could still smell the charring of flesh, which is unmistakable to me as I worked four summers at my dad's crematorium when I was younger.

It was all around me, filling my nostrils.

Tears stung my eyes.

The heat within Twin Jesters was staggering.

Within seconds, my shirt matted itself to me, my forehead was like a burst dam from the sweat.

I shot to my feet, unloaded my camera, and started sneaking around. It didn't take long for me to locate the bodies that had been burned by the army. Some were still alight, others were burned-out husks.

I feel sick thinking about it.

I'm not ashamed to say that I vomited all over a flaming corpse.

Hell, when I was being chased, I wet myself, and that's a hell of a thing for a grown man to admit. But I think anyone would have, had they come face-to-face with what I did.

After following a trail of scorched remains, I came across the soldiers doing the burning. They were kitted out in suits that made them look as though they belonged on a space programme, with flamethrowers in their hands and petrol tanks on their backs.

It was crazy.

There were five of them in total, and they were guarded by three soldiers brandishing automatic weapons.

Sound like something out of a film, doesn't it?

Believe me, it's not. I was there, and I probably still smell to high heavens of human waste and smoked barbeque.

That's probably why I'm getting such strange looks here at the pub.

Twin Jesters looked war-torn. Cars and buildings were riddled with bullet holes. I even saw a tank stalking the streets. Craziness.

Had I been caught, I fear I would have been shot on sight. Hell, if we go public with these pictures and stories, I could end up in jail. I'm not sure what scares me more — the fate of Bridgend as a whole, me dying, or being incarcerated for treason. They'll probably throw me in a deep, dark hole beneath London to rot.

If you don't hear from me in a day or so, make sure you get all this out there — don't let me die in vain.

Once I'd captured enough images of the soldiers participating in body burning, I moved around the town as stealthily as possible. Where no soldiers roamed, the place was a ghost town — hollowed-out buildings and empty houses with smashed windows and missing doors. Some structures had even collapsed, spilling their bricks and mortar into the streets.

A thick-as-soup dust hung in the air and the multiple fires cast searing, wavering and bottomless shadows. I heard their snarls, the Man-Eating Fucks, I mean. I was terrified, Sam, but nothing could prepare me for the sight I was about to witness.

Towards the back of Twin Jesters where the land runs out and a river cuts through, soldiers were digging a mass grave. Bulldozers were ploughing dead and burned bodies into it; there must have been fifty or sixty being dozed.

I've also included those photos.

Before the soldiers could finish burying the townspeople's remains, the Man-Eating Fucks attacked. They came out of the darkness all shadows and teeth—and tore through the military before they could react, let alone get a shot off.

In minutes, the bulldozer and digger sat idling, their drivers devoured. And when they were finished...

I grab my brandy and drink the remainder greedily. Some of it spills out of my mouth and splashes into my lap.

...they were led into the heart of the town by Ddu and Coch.

I swear. I saw them.

It wasn't a trick of light or anything such, Sam. They were there, with God as my witness, and they led the charge like a pair of demented dragoons minus their horses. I even took photos.

Ddu and Coch saw me, too, even though they were stood at an impossible distance, when you consider I was shrouded in blackness. They pointed their fingers and let out a deafening cry, wail, screech—no human has ever produced a noise like that—which I took as a battle cry.

Blood trickled out of my ears and nose, the shout was that powerful.

And as I retreated, taking as many snaps as I could, I saw more and more Man-Eating Fucks spill out of the foliage at the backs of those advancing. It was as spectacular to watch as it was terrorizing.

I ran, screaming, with piss trickling down the legs of my jeans.

When I bumped into soldiers, they tried stopping me, which, by then, I was a gibbering, crying wreck, trying to warn them.

They soon lost interest in me as shots rang out from behind.

Somewhere in Twin Jesters, a siren began to wail.

"Here they come!" someone bellowed.

More gunfire.

The reek of cordite was choking.

Before making a dash for the bridge at the town's edge, I stopped and looked back. The carnage was horrendous. The Man-Eating Fucks, which I could then see plainly, were hideously disfigured—monsters. There's no other word for them, and seeing them in full fight, with blood, guts and gore decorating their chops and chests, was far-fetched, but I was witnessing it.

Flesh was torn away, along with privates and eyeballs.

And the screaming, Sam; God, the screaming—it'll haunt me forever.

When the remaining soldiers were torn up and torn through, the jesters and Man-Eating Fucks set their sights on me, and that's when I fled to this pub.

They didn't follow.

I had a gut feeling they wouldn't, but why? Are the jesters trapped there? If so, why did the Man-Eating Fucks stop? After all, you've seen them elsewhere, which brings me back to an earlier point—did the jesters reanimate the Man-Eating Fucks of yesteryear? The ones killed in the articles you told me to read? If that's the case, then we're dealing with spirits. There's food for thought!

How do we explain that if nothing's found in Twin Jesters tomorrow morning? Will the bodies of the soldiers have disappeared? Will the government then level the place with bombs and explain it away as a gas leak or some such tripe?

Before I sent this email to you, I read through it and realised I waffled far too much, but I needed to tell someone all this. I was worried I'd take the knowledge to my grave.

Anyway, I'll be in contact soon.

Best,

Owen.

I pack away my laptop and camera, suck the dregs out of my glass and return it to the bar to settle my bill.

The barflies give me a fleeting look.

Outside, I glance at the bridge. My nut sack shrivels and I pull my coat's collar around my neck that bit tighter.

I hear their hisses and cat-calls from beyond the darkness.

"Going to pull your tongue out through your arssse, sssnoop!"

The icy threat cuts me to the marrow. I turn from the pub and make my way towards home.

Sam Enrich rolls over in his bed, the morning light coming through his window blinds having grown too strong to be ignored. Groaning, he plods to the folding table where he'd left his laptop powered on. Wiggling the mouse to kick the PC out of low-power standby mode nets him a view to his desktop and its cluster of icons. A new email sits in his inbox. He opens it, already knowing who'd sent it without stopping to read the addressee line. A grin crosses his lips—he knew he could trust Owen with this job. The newsman's snooping has paid off in spades.

He sits, hunched over his laptop's tiny screen, devouring Owen's message word for word. Minutes later, at the stroke of eight in the morning, his PC goes into a fit of stuttering chirps as new emails flood his inbox. He ignores them, as he knows these are from the various newspapers to which he's subscribed—information is a P.I.'s stock in trade, after all, and newspapers were often good for leads.

Eventually, he can ignore them no longer. The insistent notification beeps and alert boxes piling up along the right side of his screen demand his attention. He turns his gaze to the headlines, and his jaw drops in the sort of awe and terror that can clench a man's guts to the size of a tangerine.

"Twin Jesters Destroyed by Fire."
— *South Wales Media.*
"Town Detonated by Terrorists."
— *The News Corner.*
"Mysterious Murders & Mayhem: What Are You Hiding?!"
— *Herald.*
"Award-Winning Journalist Found Dead in River."
— *Bridgend Mail.*

ABOUT THE AUTHOR
DAVID OWAIN HUGHES

David Owain Hughes is a horror freak! He grew up on ninja, pirate and horror movies from the age of five, which helped rapidly install in him a vivid imagination. When he grows up, he wishes to be a serial killer with a part-time job in women's lingerie…

He's had several short stories published in various online magazines and anthologies, along with articles, reviews and interviews. He's written for *This Is Horror*, *Blood Magazine* and *Horror Geeks Magazine*. He's the author of the popular novels *Walled In* and *Wind-Up Toy*, along with his short story collections, *White Walls and Straitjackets* and *Choice Cuts*.

Four Beasts Gate, China

By: Johanna Vandredi

My brother was practically leaping out of his skin with excitement when he got word that our tourist visas to China were finally approved. I was thrilled too, but more so for him, as he was the Sinophile of the family. He'd been into Chinese culture since we were in grade school. But what we both had in common were our passions for hiking and mountain climbing, and this trip promised the climb of a lifetime.

The target of our excursion was Mount Huashan, in central China, which rises to an elevation of 7,000 feet. Located in the Chinese heartland, the mountain has long been revered as a holy place. Daoists had established a monastery there as early as the second century BC; the monks believing the mountain was where the god of the underworld held his court. Other legends held that the mountain's inaccessible peak was where magical herbs grew that could bestow immortality to those brave enough to attempt the journey.

Regardless of who came to Huashan or their purpose for coming, the mountain greeted all with its stoic challenge, its sheer rock cliff sides becoming graves for those who were ill-prepared, foolish, or unlucky. For those who successfully breached its summit, the mountain graced them with its favor. Perhaps not immortality as in the legend, but at the very least there were bragging rights and some of the most stunning views on Planet Earth.

After a short stop in Hawaii, we took a flight into China. Once we were checked into customs, we hopped onto a smaller jet headed west, then took a hired car to Huayin City. By the time we arrived at our hotel, we were utterly spent. We pulled the blinds and hung the "Do Not Disturb" tab from the door, then slept off the jet lag for the next two days.

We awoke the morning of the third day and decided to soak in the ambiance. Jonathan, my brother, was passably fluent in Chinese, but he'd been trained in the manner of speaking employed in the big cities. Here in the hinterlands, the provincial idioms and pronunciations gave him some trouble, but we communicated well enough with the locals.

In speaking with the residents, we learned that there was a practice among those who desired to ascend to the peak. It sounded like suicide at first, but it was actually rather practical once you thought about it.

The Chinese climbed at night.

You see, at night, it was so dark that you were oblivious to the extreme danger around you. That automatically made you sure-footed, because what you couldn't see couldn't scare you, and if you fell, you'd never see what would kill you anyway.

The footpaths up the mountain—that is, where there were paths—often were so narrow that you had to go up single-file, and sometimes at a grade of thirty degrees or greater. Other times, all you had was a chain nailed to the rock face to hold on to as you shimmied like a crab with a sheer drop off at your back.

Climbing at night also meant that there would be less people on the mountain, which was a boon for making progress up the peak. Since the paths only allowed for one person coming up, if you met someone coming the other way, you had to backtrack until it was safe to pass.

We spent the better part of the morning in Huayin City, then returned to our hotel at noon to get some shut-eye in preparation for the night's climb.

Our alarm went off at two a.m. We wasted no time in slinging on our backpacks and heading out.

Huayin City is built into the foothills of the mountain. It was a short trek from the hotel to the start of our ascent. For the better part of an hour, it was an easy hike. Bucking local custom, we'd brought flashlights with us—our purpose for coming was as much to enjoy the natural beauty as it was to climb it. Besides, the extra light would help us get better photos along the way. We stopped at intervals for an occasional snack and to sip from our water bottles before pressing on, knowing the more challenging sections were yet to come.

We were several hours into our hike when the air started to get noticeably thinner. This was to be expected; we were accustomed to high-altitude climbs. But what we hadn't anticipated was the lack of visibility—our flashlights quickly became useless once the mist settled in. Our torch beams merely illuminated the cloud that enveloped us instead of cutting through it, turning it into a perfectly opaque wall.

By this time, we were breathing heavily, as much from the thin air as from our exertion. The wooden footpath beneath us was as wide as the balls of our feet, and it was steep and slick with condensation. With our chests pressed to the rock face, we had to pull our bodies along using the chain fastened to the cliff face. More than once, my feet slipped out from beneath me and I had to cling for dear life onto that chain, or else risk going over the edge.

We rounded a switchback and found ourselves at the start of another footpath. This one, thankfully, was much wider, designed for foot traffic two abreast, and had guide bars on either side. The ground bobbed beneath our feet, cresting into gentle hills that sank into shallow valleys. The easy terrain was a welcome change, but it did not last long, as this was merely the path that led between peaks. Sure enough, the ground pitched sharply skyward once more, and we were hauling our sweating bodies up the slope with overhand pulls on the chain at our side.

Gone now was the wood plank flooring that had provided us somewhat steady footing. We were relegated to negotiating a rocky dirt path. And as if that were not bad enough, it started raining. The loose dirt beneath our boots became runny mud that shifted and sluiced under our tread.

I'd been on some bad hikes, but this one took the cake. It was pitch black with zero-visibility fog, shaky footing, driving rain, and a constant howling gale that tried its damnedest to snatch us off the mountain and cast us careening into the jagged rocks below. It was enough to make me want to turn back, and I told Jonathan, but he would not be deterred. In hindsight, I think it was the universe trying to tell us that we should not have been there. We should have listened.

Jonathan was ahead of me. I had him square in my flashlight. His foot came down onto the path, which at this time was hardly more than a rocky shelf about two feet wide. The face of the mountain seemed to cave under him and give way. His body dropped straight down, into a sort of vent that had opened into the mountainside, but he managed to cling to the guide chain to keep from plunging the whole way in.

He held on for a moment before his grip slipped off the wet chain.

I saw my brother fall into that black hole and vanish as though the mountain had slurped him up like a mouthful of noodles.

I screamed his name and rushed to him, nearly losing my grip and falling over the edge. Once I got to the crevasse, I shone my light inside. I couldn't see a thing.

I called my brother's name again, several times, and eventually he called back. He was alive, but injured, somewhere within that deep, dark hole. Going against my better judgment, I shimmied into the vent and crawled inside, feet first.

I fell a distance of about ten feet, then hit a sloped surface and tumbled the rest of the way, bouncing off rock shelves like a pinball off bumpers. I came to rest on my back.

"You okay?" I remember my brother asking me. He was already on his feet, leaning against the rock wall with his flashlight beam on me.

Groaning, I stood up and went to him.

He was hunched over, favoring his left foot. He'd turned his right ankle in the fall, and while he didn't have any broken bones, he was hardly in any shape for a climb.

I put my arm around him for support, and together we shuffled further into the cave. Both of us knew, but neither wanted to admit, that we were going to die within that cavern. Still, we put this thought aside—in our minds, we were positive there had to be a way out somewhere. Looking back, I think this mindset is what kept us alive. We could just as easily have given up, but instead we pressed on, hoping against hope that we would find a way back to town.

We walked for what felt like forever in that cave. It was impossible to tell the time down there; my watch had broken during the fall and there wasn't anything else to go by. Eventually, we found an underground fast-flowing river, and this buoyed our spirits, because if the water was moving this fast, we thought it meant it had to be escaping to the surface somewhere. We decided to follow it.

The river led to a cavern whose dimensions were too precise to be naturally-occurring. Shining our lights around, we eventually realized we were in a subterranean grotto. The river snaked through it in S-curves carved into the floor. All around, trees made of fired clay rose to heights of twenty feet and more all around us. They were masterful works of craftsmanship. The trees looked just like fir trees you'd find on the surface, and there were enough of them for a forest. I rapped on the side of one—it rang hollow, but was set sturdily into the floor. It boggles my mind how anyone could produce something like this, let alone hundreds of them, and transport them into the depths of a mountain.

We limped through the clay forest, our path leading through arched gazebos and around reflecting pools. It was a whole other world down there, a mirror-image of something you might find topside. I started getting the feeling that these things were not built above and brought below, but rather, that they were built on-site. But how? There was no light down in that cave except for our flashlights. And why? There wasn't anyone around to appreciate the work.

The path led to a giant stone gate arch carved into the face of the rock. Just looking upon it filled me with foreboding. The gate meant we had reached a different section of the cavern. If we didn't have any business being in the cave, then something about that gate told me we really didn't belong past its threshold. Still, it wouldn't serve us to remain where we were, and so we set foot inside.

About twenty feet past the gate was a sheer drop-off. We stood upon a raised platform overlooking a recessed area of immeasurable breadth. We shone our flashlights across the open space and could not see the far end.

Below us, level to the height of our platform, stood an army of clay soldiers. The way they were armed and arrayed, shoulder to shoulder in strict military discipline, immediately called to mind the Terracotta Army. It was as though an exact copy of that famous art emplacement was built here. They were lifelike in their features, each of them with unique faces, posture and armament. It was almost uncanny. As we made our way across the platform, we could almost feel the weight of their tireless stares upon us; we were not welcome, and they wanted us to know it.

Following the wall that bordered the platform, we passed through another gate arch, this one leading into a chamber where the walls swept upward into a sort of cathedral ceiling that had been sanded into a smooth dome. At the center of the room was a raised dais upon which sat four figures, one at each corner, each of them facing the center. We drew closer, and beheld a staggering work of art unlike anything we had seen in our years alive.

Standing with its back to me was a massive terracotta turtle, its rounded back hunched like the crest of a hill, and each of its legs like tree trunks. Its face was intricately carved to look gnarled and ancient. We rounded the sculpture and stood at the center of the dais to behold the other statues erected here. Even with what little I knew of Chinese culture, I understood what it was I'd set eyes upon.

We stood at the center of the court of saintly beasts: the Black Turtle of the North, the Azure Dragon of the East, the White Tiger of the West, and the Vermillion Bird of the South. I turned in place, looking at all of them in turn, feeling overawed as their empty gazes drilled into me. The dragon was in full form, jaws splayed and fangs barred; the tiger reared back as though bringing down a deer twice its size, its muzzle wrinkled in a vicious snarl that showed all its teeth; the bird swooped down with wings and tail fanned out behind it, its talons in the lead to rend its prey to shreds; and the turtle lunged forth with its beaked mouth to snap at any so foolish as to disturb its home. Each of them was larger than life, standing well over thirty feet, and made of fired clay. Whoever commissioned their construction spared no expense – despite their massive proportions, the artisans who produced them took painstaking care with the finest of details.

The air was heavy here, charged with awe and an unseen energy that threatened to fry my nerves. I backed away, my eyes darting from one beast to another, watching them all as if fearing they would come to life and knowing that simply couldn't happen, though they sure looked like they might. As I crossed the center of the dais, my foot descended onto a section of the floor that sank under my tread – a pressure plate, I came to find out later.

Suddenly, the cavern began to shake. In a panic, we fled in separate directions. My brother pulled away from me, hobbling on his bad leg, but we couldn't keep our footing for long. The cave trembled ferociously, as though the mountain would collapse onto us, and we were knocked the ground. Then there was a loud crack like a static electricity discharge, and the sightless eyes of the four statues lit up with blue fire. The fire leapt from eye to eye, forming a box of lightning in the air above our heads.

There was a flash, and then a surge of lightning coursed from the grotto of the four saintly beasts, smashing into the cave wall ahead of us. The mountainside crumbled away, revealing a view to a baleful moon.

Screaming, I ran in a blind panic for my brother and scooped him up, slinging his arm across my back. Together, we hustled toward the exit, unable to believe our good fortune.

The mountain shook again, and we spilled to the ground, falling face first. Another mighty lightning bolt surged from the four beast statues, this time, headed for the chamber where the clay soldiers were housed. The lightning collected into a ball, then dissipated into the air, seemingly raining down onto the heads of the army, crowning each with a nimbus of blue energy.

That was the last we saw before turning tail and running for the exit. Thankfully, the mountain here offered far more forgiving terrain, and we put a safe distance between us and the cavern in almost no time.

We turned back to watch as the mountain shuddered before us. There was another deafening crack of sizzling energy, and yet another sheaf of vertical mountainside fell away like a stage curtain, revealing the chamber packed to bristling with the soldier statues. A cloud of mist seemed to roll out of the chamber. The air within was thick with blue lightning that darted from one point to another in chains of sparking energy.

Then the earth shook again, but somehow, it felt different than the previous tremors. Before I was too sure of what was happening, a blast emerged from the opening in the mountain, a long, flat note, as if from a hundred trumpets. This was followed by the sound of a million tramping feet taking a shambling first step.

Jonathan was the first to spot what had caused these sounds, and he tugged at my shirtsleeve to direct my gaze at what his eyes had settled upon.

A myriad of tiny blue lights lit up from within the cavern, looking like a crowd of pilgrims on a candlelight vigil. The soldiers' eyes were aglow with miniature blue blazes. The front line of troops shook, taking a shambling step forward on legs that had not bent in ages. Eventually they caught their rhythm, their march accelerating into a rapid lockstep as the army trudged out of the cavern with disciplined efficiency. They poured out of the mountain in an endless stream, taking the paths that led down to the foothills.

We could not believe what we were seeing. A part of me was awed by what was playing out before my eyes—things such as this just aren't possible in the real world. And at the same time I was terrified, because here we were, my brother and I, hurt and stranded while this fantastic army of clay soldiers marched into the valley. At the time, there was no telling what their intentions might have been, but seeing as they were armed, we felt it best to just sit and wait them out, wait for them to leave before moving on.

We spent the rest of the night on that cold mountainside, exposed to the rain and the wind, unable to do anything but watch as the army just kept flowing out of the cave. Day broke over the mountain, and in the faint light that bathed everything in shades of orange and maroon, I could still see soldiers emerging from the cave. They just kept coming without any sign of stopping.

It was around this time, too, that the first of their contingent must have arrived at the unsuspecting city below, for we heard screams the likes of which I have never before heard in my life—the screams of people dying by the thousands, so loud and in such number that their cries reached our ears as crisply as if they'd been standing next to us.

We watched and waited on that mountainside until sundown, by which time the last of the clay army had exited its ancient home. That was when we began our trek towards safety. A return to the city was out of the question, as by now the screams had fallen to eerie quiet, replaced by the metronomic tramping of clay feet that thundered through the hills and valleys in an exorable march of death.

We thought it prudent to travel in the direction opposite the clay army's heading. After two days of traveling on foot, we found a tiny no-name village. The residents patched us up and fed us, and in repayment they took our cellphones — not that they were any use to us anyway, so far out of their service area.

Thankfully, there was a landline phone in the village. It hung on a post at the outskirts of town. The device was ancient, looking like it had been installed in the sixties, but it was serviceable, and we used it to hire a car. A day later, our car arrived, and after a sixteen-hour trip, we were back at the airport.

My brother booked us the earliest flight back to the States — a non-stop to Los Angeles. California wasn't home, but at least it was on the same side of the world as home. Once we touched down in the U.S., we booked a red-eye back home to Colorado.

First thing we did upon arriving home was check the Internet for any strange activity in the Chinese heartland. A whole day spent scouring the Web turned up nothing. In a way, we expected this. China has a stringent policy on what news they release to the world. And yet, by the same token, we were surprised to find the Internet wasn't blowing up with news of a paranormal clay army terrorizing the countryside.

People had died out there. We had heard them screaming from miles away.

It was horrible.

With everything that went wrong for us on that mountain, those screams were the worst of all. Some nights I spring awake in bed from nightmares in which I recall those screams—no sights, no images, just the sound of all those people being slaughtered.

It wasn't until weeks later that the news finally broke, only, what the newscasters reported wasn't what actually happened. The international news community stated that there had been violent demonstrations incited by terrorist factions, and that Chinese military police had quelled the civil unrest with minimal damage or loss of life.

It was a cover-up. I can't begin to guess who might have benefitted from keeping this under wraps, or how, but that's what happened.

I know what I saw. I'll admit, I can't make any sense of it—chalk that one up to the supernatural—but I know what I saw, and Jonathan can vouch for me.

And those screams...

My god, you just can't make up stuff like that.

ABOUT THE AUTHOR
JOHANNA VANDREDI

Johanna Vandredi is a travel writer. As part of her job, she spends more time on an airplane or train than at home, during which time she writes about her experiences abroad. She is from the Catalonia region of Spain, where, during her time off, she writes fantasy from her apartment balcony overlooking Barcelona.

Murmur Mills, Maryland

By: Nick Vossen

It always starts with a wrong turn, doesn't it? Yeah, that's as good an answer as any when I'm asked why I shiver at the sight of sharp, cutting teeth; or why I fall apart at the sound of wolves howling in the night. But that wouldn't be the truth. I never got lost on the way to somewhere else—I drove to Murmur Mills completely of my own accord.

There are stories from the backwoods of Maryland that tell of the mysterious "Plague Lady," a so-called "Banshee of the Woods" around Murmur Mills. My research into the subject turned up that there was indeed such a place as Murmur Mills, despite the entire town having dropped completely off the radar years ago. You can imagine my excitement when I finally located it. I dropped everything and set out to see it in person.

It was late in the evening and raining like crazy when I pulled into a gas station a mile or two short of the town. It was a godsend—my car was running on fumes, and I was in the middle of nowhere. Just getting there was proving difficult. Paved streets had been a thing of the distant past, and the rain had all but washed out the muddy road. But the gas station brought me some degree of comfort—its frowning incandescent street lamps were the first lights I'd seen since leaving civilization.

The filling station was little more than a wooden shack. A light flickered from behind its drawn curtains. I got out of my car and went for the door, but found it locked.

"Damn it," I huffed, heading back to the car.

Back beside the gas pump, I realized that someone—the station's owners, likely—had set a bar across the pump nozzles, no doubt to keep people from stealing gasoline while the station was closed. It took some effort, but I managed to jimmy the bar free. I placed the nozzle into my car's tank and squeezed, getting me nothing but a dry hiss.

"Hey!" I heard someone shout from the direction of the shack.

I nearly leapt out of my skin in fright. It was a man's voice—a big man—sounding like he'd caught on to my trying to steal from him.

The door swung open and the man's silhouette appeared at the shack's entrance. I couldn't see his features—backlit by the light coming from the shack, he looked to me like a giant shadow.

"Hey," he called out again. "You lost or something?"

"Uh, yeah," I stammered. "I'm on my way to Murmur Mills; I'm supposed to meet a colleague there at a bed and breakfast."

"How'd you end up here?"

"I took a right-hand turn out of Weverton. My phone navigation said this should be the right way to..."

"And who told you there was a hotel in Murmur Mills?" he interrupted.

"A bed and breakfast," I corrected him. "Is this the right way to town?"

"It is. But we don't get a lot of visitors. Haven't seen a car pass this way in months." He shifted his weight slightly, then leaned against the doorpost. "You sure your friend is in town?"

"My colleague," I corrected him again. "I met him online. He lives in Knoxville. Maybe he came from the other direction?"

"On where?" He sounded confused. "There's nothing past here but miles and miles of forest. This is the Black Hills, son. You're on the Appalachian Trail. It doesn't run to Knoxville. One way in, one way out, get it?"

The man stepped forward, into the light of one of the street lamps. I recoiled, in spite of myself, when I saw his face. There was a subtle wrongness to it—his features were harsh, especially in the garish orange glow of the overhead lights. His jaw was entirely too square, his nose elongated. He was old, his unkempt moustache and beard growing wild and yellow at the fringes.

"Listen," he went on, "you can't stay out here in the rain. My hut's not really built for more than one, but you can spend the night if you like."

His features softened. If he came across as angry before, he now seemed apologetic.

"Name's Abe Buck, but people around town call me Old Mosquito. I'll help you get to town and direct you where you need to go. When we get there, you can tell me exactly how long you intend to stay and we'll make sure to get your car the gas it needs before then. Sound good?

"That sounds great," I said, smiling, as I offered him my hand to shake. I looked him over from head to toe. "Why would anyone call you Old Mosquito?"

He batted a palm at me. "I'll tell you on the way. It's a good hour's hike still, so let me get us some umbrellas."

Old Mosquito ducked back into his shack momentarily, returning with the promised umbrellas before setting out on the trail through the Black Hills Forest. Along the way, we discussed the history of Murmur Mills.

My research had revealed the village was once a thriving lumber community, except that one day all the traders in the neighbouring towns inexplicably stopped dealing with the residents. Old Mosquito nodded at this, and I took it as a sign to continue. That was when I mentioned the town had dried up. He stopped me there, explaining that some old timers still lived in Murmur Mills, more than my research led me to believe.

He explained that many of the original townsfolk were blood related to the ancient Tutelo tribe, or Yesan, as they were originally known by. The residents of Murmur Mills mostly kept to themselves, partly out of resentment from having been shunned long ago, but also out of the belief that they were a self-sustaining community. They didn't need help from any "outsiders."

As a result of their isolation, many tribal customs, some dating back to pre-colonial times, survived. One of them was the giving of nicknames, which was how Abe came to be known as Old Mosquito.

My companion went into a laughing fit when I told him my purpose for coming. Later, he apologized, explaining that every town near the Black Hills Forest had its own legend or two concerning ghosts, witches, and cryptozoological sightings — the most famous among them being the infamous Blair Witch of Burkittsville, whose story was made into a "documentary" back in the 90's. He reassured me that there wasn't a shred of truth to any of these made-up stories.

My heart sank on thinking that I'd come all the way out here for nothing, but part of me felt there was more to the tale of Murmur Mills's Plague Lady than just campfire stories. There had to be — the Plague Lady was different from the others. There were documented sightings and credible accounts of her existence.

We'd been slogging through the rain for some time when it occurred to me to check my phone. An hour had passed since leaving the gas station; it had been slow-going thanks to the bad weather. Thankfully, though, my phone reception was perfect, which meant that if anything happened to us out here tonight, I could always call for help.

I got the impression that the path Old Mosquito had set us on was taking us through the thickest part of the woods. With the heavy rain and the dark of night fully upon us, I couldn't help but feel claustrophobic, as though the trees themselves were reaching out their branches to strangle me. Eventually, we reached a section where an iron fence had been erected parallel to the footpath. Covered in undergrowth and crowded by a thick stand of trees just behind it, the fence was as see-through as a concrete wall.

I stopped walking when I heard the sound of heavy breathing, the huffing, ragged breaths of a large animal in full sprint. I was about to ask Old Mosquito about it when suddenly, a large black shape hammered into the fence at top speed. I leapt back in fright, and that was when I saw the biggest wild dog I'd ever seen, snarling and barking at me from the other side of the fence.

"Calm down, son," said Old Mosquito, putting a hand on my shoulder. "The fences were put up for a reason, you see. The woods here are ancient and wild. Us in town, we know where nature wants us to go and where we need to stay away, got it?"

"I don't like dogs…" was all I could stammer in reply. Truth be told, I'd always loved dogs, but that encounter had left me shaken. I'd never seen anything so wild, so ravenous, before or since.

"Let's go, town's just up ahead," the old man chimed in.

Before I could turn back I heard it again. Now, closer than ever, I heard the heavy breathing and growling behind me. My skin went ice cold as I felt a row of teeth puncture my arm.

I screamed, panicked, as the wild dog bit down. The way it thrashed, it could very well have torn my arm off.

Old Mosquito was on me in a second, swinging his lantern wildly at the beast.

"Ho! Get off him right now! *Yala! Yalaaa!*"

The dog let me go, and I collapsed onto my backside in the mud, staring straight into its eyes. They were glassy and wild, the eyes of a predator face to face with its prey.

The roar of a car engine behind me caught my attention. We broke eye contact, and the hound quickly escaped back through a hole dug beneath the fence.

I felt faint. Now that the adrenaline was wearing thin, my nerves were getting the better of me. My eyes shut as I flopped drunkenly onto my back, my head coming to rest in a divot of soft mud. I could see nothing, but I was aware of shouting around me.

"Get this man to Doctor Ontkean at once!" It was Old Mosquito's voice. I couldn't make out what the other man was saying. "No, I don't care if you have to get him out of bed, he could be bleeding to death for all we..."

The voices faded to distant echoes and went silent.

I awoke in a doctor's office. It was a small clinic, and its furnishings were somewhat dated, but still, it looked more contemporary than what I would have expected from so isolated a community as Murmur Mills. I sat up in my examination cot just as the door swung open and a kindly-looking gentleman with a goatee and thick-rimmed glasses entered.

"I wouldn't try sitting up just yet if I were you. Ought to give your head some much needed rest."

"You are... Doctor Ontkean?" I stammered, rubbing the side of my head to ease the pounding.

"That is correct," he said, stepping up to shine a light in my eyes. "Follow the light please. How are we feeling?"

"My head is killing me."

"M-hm," he grunted, switching the light off. He scribbled notes into a pad as he spoke. "That old fool should've known better than to take an outsider on a hike after dark." He glanced up from his pad to look me in the eyes. "No offense," he added. "The wild dogs are accustomed to the townsfolk, they respect us as we respect them, as we both respect the land we share. But to outsiders, those with a particular smell about them, they can be vicious."

"It's nice to know they like how I smell," I groused. "Listen, doc, I had a meeting set up with a friend of mine in a local B&B, so if I'm all cleared up here..."

"A bee and bee? Oh! You must mean Old Lady Fara's lodgings. Don't you worry, we've spoken with your friend... Ben, was it?"

"Uh-huh," I grunted.

"He'll meet you for breakfast tomorrow. For now, we need to give you a shot so your wound doesn't get infected."

I glanced down at my arm. Clean bandages were wrapped around the site of the injury. Right then, I got the impression that, for all the urban legends surrounding this place, it didn't seem quite so bad. In fact, its residents had been nothing but polite and helpful. What I could not figure out, though, was how Old Mosquito had missed Ben on his way in. With visitors to Murmur Mills as scarce as they were, more residents should have known of an outsider in their midst.

"Hey doc," I spoke up. "Tell me a little about yourself."

Ontkean tapped the side of a glass syringe and gave it a squeeze to purge it of air bubbles. "Nothing much to say, really. I'm just the village doctor. Grew up here, just like everyone else in town. Studied medicine at the John Hopkins Institute in Baltimore, and after graduation, I came right back."

"What can you tell me about the village itself?"

He smiled. "So, you're big into those rumours too, huh? I'll bet that's why you came—same as everybody else from outside—you heard tales of an inbred community of witchcraft practitioners."

He batted his palm at me. "It's all bunk. We're a close-knit bunch, but we're nothing like what you've heard. You see, our Yesan forefathers worshipped a god called Nahato, a dog-headed entity that bestowed fertility and a bountiful harvest. This part of the Black Hills Forest was thought to be sacred to Nahato because it was inhabited by large packs of wild dogs. And so, to better honour Nahato, our ancestors founded our village here, among the dogs."

"That's… actually really interesting, I did not know," I replied.

"Do you know how the town got its name?" Doc Ontkean asked. "An old Yesan chieftain used to say that if you stand in the middle of the clearing, right where the town square is now, and listen carefully to the wind in the treetops, you can hear the woods whispering."

"How could you possibly hear anything with all those dogs running around and barking at all hours of day and night?"

"The dogs are only aroused when they encounter people they don't know." With an odd grin that I did not like, he added, "They must really have taken a liking to you." He raised the syringe. "So, are you ready?"

"Yeah sure," I replied.

The needle went in and out quickly, but the sensation lingered just long enough to make me feel queasy. The last bit of the syringe's contents dribbled onto my arm. It stank horribly.

"God, that stuff reeks, doc."

"Yeah, well, when it comes to medicine, results are more important than comfort," he responded dryly. "Now, you've had a rough night, and you must be tired. Let's get your over to Lady Fara's. A room has been prepared for you there."

The boarding house was a short walk from Onktean's clinic. On the way, I took the opportunity to soak in my surroundings. There wasn't much to the village, which consisted mostly of a town square, a few small shops, and narrow streets that radiated from the center into residential areas. Off in the distance, I could see the outlines of the old timber mills, now defunct, looming at the outskirts of town.

We were at Fara's front stoop in short order. Dr. Onktean knocked on the door, and we were greeted by an elderly lady. I couldn't help but recoil slightly at the sight of her—like Old Mosquito, there was something off with her facial features; they just didn't meld together. Her lower jaw extended past the sweep of her already too-long nose; her cheekbones were high and cut hard angles. Shadows pooled in the pockets beneath her cheek where the sallow skin drooped concave. Her hair was stark white and tumbled down the sides of her face in a knotted mess.

"Ms. Fara, I presume?" I asked, immediately composing myself—I hoped I hadn't offended her.

She smiled with a mouth of checkered missing and present teeth, then gave a slight bow of her head. Onktean and I shook hands, and then he left for his clinic. Fara led me upstairs to my room. I'd scarcely arrived there when the pain from my wound climbed to unbearable levels. I lay down on the cot, gritted my teeth and shut my eyes, hoping the dull ache would be gone in the morning.

With everything I'd endured this night, I could scarcely have predicted what would come next.

I awoke in the middle of the night, the threadbare sheets sticking to my skin. I was soaked in sweat and burning up with fever. Clutching my aching head, I rose to my feet with a hand against the wall for support.

A howl from outside my window pierced the air and sent a sliver of ice down my spine. That's when I realized—this had been going on all night; I hadn't given the cries much thought as I bobbed into and out of consciousness, but for however long I had been here at Fara's, the braying outside had been a near constant backbeat to the sounds of the night.

I shuffled to the window and opened it. Beastly howls filled the night air from deep within the Black Hills Forest. The cries were relentless and insistent, shot through with an anxious energy that demanded to be acknowledged. They came one after another, incessantly, a solid wall of canine voices that drew ever nearer until the noise of their calls echoed within my meagre four walls so loudly it rattled in my skull.

Something, call it intuition, demanded that I look down, past the frame of my window. When I did, I nearly fainted and fell headlong to the street. A great mass had accumulated down below, looking like a giant black cloud or a gathering of shadows. Streams of black from off in the distance funneled into the mass. All the while, the night air was thick with the sound of howls, rushing paws, and metal fences rattling under a persistent onslaught. I shifted my gaze from the horizon back to the cloud beneath my window, and my eyes, finally accustomed to the darkness, saw what awaited me below.

What I thought was an inexplicable dark fog was actually the massed-up bodies of the hounds. There were a great many of them, all with fangs bared and fur bristling.

I stumbled backward, overcome with fright, and collapsed onto my knees beside the bed. I buried my head in a pillow and sobbed openly out of hopelessness, regretting with my soul having come to Murmur Mills.

The next morning, I awoke in the same position I had fallen asleep in. The hounds were gone without a trace—there weren't even paw prints in the street outside my window. I clutched my temples with both hands, trying to make sense of the situation, and chalked last night up to it all having been a fever dream. Later in the morning, when Dr. Onktean came to check up on me, he confirmed this. He explained that infection was one of the more serious side-effects of an animal bite, and with infections came the risk of high fevers. He gave me another shot, advising me to stay at Fara's and get plenty of rest.

I stayed in my room the whole day until nightfall, when finally I attempted to sleep once more.

The fever dreams continued the entire night. It was already well into the morning by the time I rose from bed, drenched in a cold sweat and with my pulse fluttering. Fara brought me breakfast, which I put down in a hurry, knowing Dr. Onktean would be coming shortly after to check up on me. Sure enough, he appeared at my door, and shook his head at the sight of me. I couldn't blame him—I must have looked as awful as I felt. After checking my pulse and taking my temperature, he gave me another shot and a pat on the shoulder for encouragement. Before turning to leave, he repeated his advice from the previous morning: get some rest, stay at Fara's, and know that it will get worse until it gets better.

I passed the hours pacing that tiny room. Every so often I thought I heard the faraway mournful cries of those wild dogs. Much as I tried to pass these paranoid thoughts off as the product of cabin fever, I could not shake the feeling that the dogs were out there, watching me even in the daylight, waiting for me to come outside so they could tear me to ribbons. The howling was constant now—in the morning, it had begun with a single hound, and others had joined throughout the day, until their nonstop cries filled my ears and echoed in my skull. I jammed my palms against my ears to blot out the noise, but that did nothing, because their voices were already in my head.

Suddenly, I realized the danger I was in. I needed help. In a moment of clarity, I snatched my cellphone out of my pocket but hesitated before dialing a number.

"Ben!" I said aloud. I remembered just then, I was supposed to meet him here. "Ben," I repeated, and the howling seemed to fade.

Several voice messages had funneled into my inbox since the last time I checked my phone. A few were from Ben. I listened to these first.

"Hey dude, I just arrived in Murmur Mills. Locals say I'm the first outsider in months, so that probably means you aren't here yet. I'm staying at Lady Fara's. Give me a call when you get here."

"Thank God!" I rasped. Ben was here, which meant I wasn't alone. But the question remained: where was he? Neither I nor anyone I'd spoken to since arriving had seen him. I clicked on to the next message.

"Hey, are you all right? Word is you got bitten by a dog or something. Place is packed with the rascals so it doesn't surprise me. Anyway, get a good night's rest, I'll see you at breakfast tomorrow."

I got the impression then, that things just weren't adding up. Ben had intended to meet with me this morning, and yet circumstances had kept me from leaving my room. Those circumstances had names: the fever, Dr. Onktean, and Old Lady Fara. But why would they keep me from meeting Ben? What would it benefit them?

I played the next message. "Hey man, something's going on here and I'm not liking it. They say that I can't go in to see you. Are you sick? Dude, I'm in the room next to you. Please come and see me if you can. They won't let me in. I could hear you screaming and scratching the walls all last night. Please let me know if you're okay."

"Oh my God," I spoke under my breath. I *was* right—there was more to Murmur Mills than I'd seen at first blush, and I was learning this the hard way. Ben's next message proved it.

His voice wavered, as if he were on the verge of utter panic. "The mosquito bites you in the night. It lures you from drowsiness and steals what is yours. It is the carrier, the bringer of fresh blood. Get out—get out of there now!"

My hand trembled as I hit the button to silence the phone. Ben—what did he mean? And his voice—it was different somehow, in a way that I couldn't quite put my finger on, but the change was there, as if he was someone else—something else.

One unopened voicemail remained. Teeth gritted, I hit play.

My screen said this last voicemail was from Ben, but it wasn't Ben's voice coming through the speakers. What I heard brought back the all-too-fresh nightmares of a day ago: the savage braying of dogs and the ferocious barking of a pack in the midst of a hunt. I felt the blood drain from my face. My vision rippled and I crumpled on the spot, collapsing onto my backside.

Then came the screams.

Barking and screaming, howling and yelling, growling and hunger, the hunt and the pain.

I couldn't take it anymore. I slung on my clothes and hurriedly stuffed what belongings I could carry into my pockets, then went for the door.

A horrid stench buffeted my nose as I set foot in the hall. The rancid stink clenched my stomach into a tight ball, and I had to brace against the doorframe to settle myself before pressing on. It reeked of faeces, and in that smell was the familiar tang of the stuff in Dr. Onktean's syringe.

Covering my nose in the crook of my arm, I went to the next room over, were Ben had said he'd been staying. When he didn't answer my knock, I jimmied the knob and found the door was unlocked.

Ben was not inside, although his room showed signs of having been lived in. Some of his clothes had been laid out atop his bed and strewn over the back of the desk chair. Despite the urgency of his voicemails, nothing looked out of the ordinary. I shook my head — none of this made sense. Checking my phone, I realized that there were only three voicemails from Ben in the inbox. The other two — the ones that had captured his frantic warning and that infernal howling — were nowhere to be seen.

I pocketed my phone, my hands just as quickly flying to clutch the sides of my face. Had I imagined all of this? Was all this just the product of a fever dream brought on by an infected dog bite?

I shook my head again to clear the cobwebs in my mind. If Ben was safe and healthy, then I could call him to confirm this. I dialed his number, but before I could place the call, I heard footsteps coming from up the hallway.

Those footsteps — those heavy, stomping footsteps — spurred my heart to a gallop. This wasn't some resident coming back to his room. The footfalls were loud and quick, moving with purpose. Accompanying those footsteps were vicious growls and slurps. I had to act fast. The noises were coming from the room next door—my room.

I dove under Ben's bed and shuffled into the corner to get as much of me away from the door as I could. No sooner had I done so than two figures barged in. I held my breath and watched.

I could only see them up to their ankles. Two pairs of feet tramped to the desk. I held back a gasp on noticing my phone was inches from one of those booted feet. It dawned on me then: I'd dropped it when I'd heard the footsteps coming my way. Carefully, very carefully, I inched closer to the edge of the bed. If I could get the edge, then I could reach out and retrieve the phone.

The laboured, raspy breathing of the two interlopers sped up, sounding like a pack of hunting dogs that had been alerted to prey. I froze, not daring to reach out from beneath my cover.

Suddenly, the room erupted in inhuman growling and braying. These sounds—these *animal* sounds—were coming from *them*.

Something like a grizzled paw descended onto my cellphone. It had five hooked fingers that were seemingly human, yet covered in fur and knobby. It lifted the phone up and out of my line of sight, and my heart sank, as that was my only chance to call for help from the outside world.

The room exploded with more ear-splitting howls, brays and snarls. My cellphone clattered to the floor beside the booted foot, then exploded in a splintered mess of plastic as a blade ran it through several times. Then, for good measure, the boot rose and descended like a meteor onto the cracked screen, splitting the phone in two. The same clawed hand I'd seen a moment ago swept up the broken phone and flung it out the window.

Once the deed was done, the two figures headed for the door. As they left, I peeked out from beneath the bed and caught a glimpse of them. Both wore brown hooded robes bedecked with black markings. These did little to hide their protruding snouts, misshapen yellow teeth and drooling canine jaws.

I clasped my hand against my mouth to keep from screaming.

I waited until I could no longer hear their footfalls up the hallway before shimmying out from beneath the bed. My head was swirling—whether from fright, or from the stench in the boarding house, or from whatever Onktean had been shooting me up with, I could not hazard a guess.

I stumbled out the door to Old Lady Fara's place, doubled over and emptied my guts on her front stoop. The throbbing in my head intensified. With each pulse, my field of vision narrowed to pinpoints.

"The fever is going down, you just puked up the bad stuff, you're good," I told myself as I slouched in the doorway, waiting for my stomach to settle down. Meanwhile, the hounds were out in full force—braying, rattling the perimeter fences, growling from parts unseen. I was not safe here. I forced myself to run.

More than ever before, Murmur Mills looked abandoned. There wasn't a light on in any of the windows. Steeply pitched roofs cast stark shadows onto darkened roadways. Going by memory alone, I ran through the narrow streets, looking for the way out of town. All the while, the fog in my mind threatened to overtake me. It dimmed my vision and sapped the strength from my muscles. I wanted so badly just to stop and rest, but I knew it would all be over if I did.

Somehow, I found myself in the woods surrounding the village. How I'd managed to get that far eluded me—my mind was a jumbled mess. I stopped and hid behind a tree when I spotted a line of burning torches marching toward the old lumber mills. There were many torches—it looked like the whole town was out in the woods tonight, and if that was true, then Ben was likely among them. Slowly, I made my way there.

I trailed the line of torches from a good distance away, hoping no one had spotted me. The procession stopped, and I halted to watch them. The group had assembled around the trunk of a fallen tree. This tree had been ancient, judging by its size alone, and when it fell under its own weight, it upturned a large volume of earth, forming a deep burrow. One by one, the procession marched into the hole. Once the last of them had entered, I stayed behind for a few moments to give them some lead, then leapt into the hole.

I fell a short distance, landing in peaty soil that had been stamped flat by dozens of feet. Ahead of me was a cavern, a pitch black throat that led further into the earth than anyone had any right to go. The last of the torches burned some thirty feet ahead. I tiptoed behind them.

The procession passed through a section where metal cages had been laid out in rows along either wall. They looked like livestock pens, each of them rising about as tall as my hip. Some of them were empty, while others were practically stuffed to overflowing with the blood-streaked bones of dead animals.

Something stirred weakly from one of the cages ahead. Whatever it was, it was still alive, though just barely. I gave the procession some lead, then went in close for a better look. In the waning torchlight, I could just barely make out the outline of a human being lying on his side on the filthy cage floor.

"Ben?" There was no way of knowing if it was him, but I had to take the chance.

"It's not real," he croaked, then went into a coughing fit.

"Ben! It is you!" I said, but he cut me off.

"You need to leave!" he rasped with a dry throat.

He did not attempt to sit up as I drew nearer, choosing instead to remain on his side. That was when I saw he had been hog-tied — his wrists and ankles were lashed together like an animal about to be slaughtered. Several of his fingers were missing, and those that remained were mangled beyond use, held together by tendrils of loose meat.

"But..."

"Go before they find you!" he snarled. "And don't believe what you see. It's the mushrooms — none of it is real. Now go!"

Ben's agitated speech must have caught the attention of the procession, because now the torches were headed back toward us.

"Oh no," Ben sobbed. "No, no, no…"

In a panic, I darted from the chamber into an adjoining room. Once inside, I pressed my back against the wall and peeked out from behind cover to watch. Several hooded figures, all of them with dog's heads, dragged Ben out of his cage. They descended upon him with kicks and punches, Ben begging all the while for it to stop, that he would tell no one of this place, and still they beat him mercilessly until he fell quiet.

In the silence that ensued, it dawned upon me: mushrooms — *magic* mushrooms. Whatever Onktean had injected me with had been laced with hallucinogenic drugs. *That* was what Ben had meant, but it still left me pondering the meaning of: "None of it is real." Whatever had beaten Ben into submission was certainly real, as far as he or I were concerned.

My train of thought was cut short by the panting and growling of something beastly approaching from behind me. Biting back a scream, I spun around and came face to face with one of the dog-headed creatures. That was too close for comfort. I dashed towards the tunnel I'd entered through as fast as my legs could carry me, but the dog-headed thing caught up and charged into me from behind, sending me flying against the wall. Before I could react, rough hands were lifting me up by my sides, dropping me onto my back atop the rusty cages.

A sliver of steel glinted in the dim light as the dog-headed thing held its knife out before it. With a running start, it jumped on me with its knife in the lead. I caught its hand at the wrist just as its blade hovered within inches of my throat.

"None of it is real," I murmured into the creature's face.

Either its strength wavered, or I seemed to grow stronger at this affirmation.

"None of it is real," I said through teeth gritted from effort. "None of it is real! *None of it is real!*"

I managed to sit up, earning myself better leverage to push the knife further away from my face. Then, twisting to one side, I shuffled out from underneath the dog-creature. Its momentum carried it forward, pitching it onto its belly atop the cages.

Desperately, I looked around for anything I could use as a weapon, and found a long bone, possibly a femur, that had splintered off to a sharp point at the end. I grabbed it, and in the same motion I lunged for the dog-creature just as it whirled back around to face me. The bone's sharp point pierced the creature's neck, and the beast let up a howl so inhuman and terrible that it froze the blood in my veins. The beast fell over backward, clutching at the bone jutting from its ruined neck, thrashing and kicking at the air until at last it lay still.

"It's not real," I told myself as I drew closer. Before my stunned eyes, the dog head's features seemed to drain out of reality, giving way to a wooden mask that was a caricature of a vicious dog. From beneath the threatening visage came whimpers.

Gathering up all the courage I could muster, I reached for the creature's head and removed the mask. Pulling it off revealed the face of the man who had driven me and Old Mosquito into town after I'd been attacked. His face was waxen and pallid from massive blood loss, and his eyes stared glassily into forever. He was surely dead.

"They're all in on it," I said under my breath. "The whole town."

I rushed out of the tunnels and back into the woods. It was raining hard now, and despite the noise from the downpour, I could hear the woods around were astir with activity. The sound of ceremonial drums reverberated through the trees amid the ghostly chanting of the assembled townsfolk.

I ducked beside a large rock and watched the procession of torches as they marched away from my position. From a safe distance away, I tailed them to a forest clearing.

The townsfolk arranged themselves in two parallel lines, forming a corridor through which Ben, chained, bloodied and beaten, was dragged. The drums and chanting ramped in tempo as he neared the end of his march. They were leading him to a massive log in the centre of their ring of torches. Beside the log stood Abe Buck, Old Mosquito — I recognized him despite his dog-face mask by the clothes he wore.

The mosquito is the carrier, the bringer of flesh blood, I remembered.

The rest of the townsfolk, some wearing masks and some not, closed the circle around Ben and Old Mosquito, standing shoulder to shoulder to watch the action in the middle. Then they started raising and lowering their arms in rhythm with the chant, which ramped in speed and volume. Before long, their chant had devolved into a senseless guttural screeching and howling. Their cries were answered by the calls from the wild dogs in the woods, which drew ever nearer by the heartbeat.

From the crowd emerged a new figure. This person was dressed differently than the others. His dog mask was far more elaborate than any I'd seen so far, and he wore what appeared to be a robe adorned with feathers. As he took up position beside the log at the centre of the clearing, a pair of burly men with dog masks on grabbed Ben and pinned him against the log. The man spoke in a language I couldn't place; but if I had to guess, it would be the Yesani native tongue. Meanwhile, the two other men chained Ben's wrists and ankles to tethers on either side of the log so that he lay face-up, parallel to the log at his back.

When he was through addressing the crowd, the man in the robe raised an arm to the exultant cheers of those in attendance. Then he turned and addressed the two men with a solemn nod. The men nodded back, indicating that they understood it was now time to do what they'd come here to do.

Someone from the crowd produced a giant two-man wood saw, the type professional lumbering crews might use to strip an acre's worth of timber in a week. The men took the saw, each to one side, then arranged themselves crosswise to Ben as the audience fell silent.

Ben groaned as the teeth of the gleaming wood saw prickled the flesh of his exposed belly. Then he screamed as the saw jerked violently to one side. His executioners were taunting him, as they'd hardly put any effort into that pull, and the saw had scarcely cut his skin. The saw went back again, and Ben howled in fright, but as before, the instrument drew no blood.

Scattered laughter rose from the crowd.

In the middle of the third pass, the executioners threw their weight behind the saw and the tool dug a diagonal cut into Ben's belly. Ben howled his throat raw with pain. Driven on by their blood lust, they quickened their pace to the rising chants of those assembled. Working like a machine that was picking up steam, the men drove the saw faster and faster.

The crowd cheered as Ben's broken body slumped into two ragged pieces. Then, from the opposite side of the clearing, two villagers yanked aside a gate and let in a flood of snarling, hungry dogs. Countless dogs of every breed and colour charged through the gate, headed for the centre of the clearing at full pelt. They descended onto Ben's corpse and ate their fill, a clear sign of that the ancient Yesan deity Nahato had accepted the town's sacrifice.

That was the last straw. I spun away from the horrific scene, doubled over and threw up. I felt awful, like my insides had become liquefied, but it was enough to snap me to my senses. I had wasted too much time watching the ceremony when I should have been fleeing.

What came next happened so fast that it's hard to recall now. I remember running from the forest clearing where they had butchered my friend. By sheer luck, I ran into a parked truck one of the townspeople had used to get to the woods. The keys were in the ignition. Muttering thanks to a stack of deities, I turned the engine and drove it as far as I could from there. I drove without any particular destination in mind—anywhere was better than staying put in Murmur Mills. My nerves were so shot that it wasn't until I'd seen the flashing sign announcing Baltimore's city limits that I regained my sense of place.

As you could probably tell from how I started my tale, stories like these never end well. The next morning I went to Baltimore P.D. and gave an account of what happened at Murmur Mills. While the police had the courtesy to file my report, I knew they would never act on it. Hell, I wouldn't have believed my story myself unless it had happened to me. They asked me to take a urine test, insisting it was "standard police procedure" in these sorts of cases, and didn't at all look surprised when my urine turned up positive for hallucinogenic drugs. This, along with my "clearly fabricated" story, was enough evidence for them to detain me for two days on charges of disorderly conduct.

Eventually, Ben's body turned up in the woods. A group of hikers found his remains while on their morning trek. The police called what befell him a "tragic hiking incident" and brushed it under the rug.

It's all bullshit. Nothing ever gets fixed. And in the Black Hill Forests of Maryland, nothing will ever change.

For your sake, you should take heed of the tall tales. They're warnings. Respecting the tales will keep you out of trouble. Even if you do not believe in banshees, witches or ghostly white women, know that something even more terrible, something more human, more real, could always be hiding in the backwoods, waiting to pounce after you've made that wrong turn into someplace you've got no business intruding upon.

ABOUT THE AUTHOR
NICK VOSSEN

Nick Vossen is a creative writer and author from the Netherlands. He prefers to dwell in the realms of twisted fairytales, magical realism and everything strange and bizarre that is caught in between. He has been published in magazines such as *Gathering Storm Magazine* and *Sanitarium*. In 2017, he released his first collection of short stories, titled: *The Fissures Between Worlds: Tales Beyond Time and Space*.

He is currently writing his first full-length novel, *The Eldritch Twins*, a humorous crossover between Lovecraftian horror and conspiracy theory mumbo-jumbo.

Nick is also active in the Dutch film industry where he writes screenplays and works in the art department of several short film projects. He currently lives in the "Deep South" of the Netherlands with his girlfriend and his two cats.

SPRINGLAND MEADOWS, VIRGINIA

BY: MICHAEL WARRINER

Have you ever felt your life was a nightmare you couldn't wake from? Most would answer *yes* without thinking it through all the way; without understanding what the statement means — to relive a continuous horror without end. Those were the cards I was dealt, and nothing more. Reality, after all, can be more terrifying than fiction.

For me, the story began with a missing person. My friend, Brian, stopped coming by. It used to be part of a daily routine. Every day at noon, his rusted sedan would pull into the driveway and he'd step out with a packed lunch for the two of us. We'd talk for hours, take trips around the neighborhood to apply for jobs, and even have the occasional walk in the park. That was our established routine, day in and day out.

But then one day, Brian stopped coming. Calling his number would result in no answer. Something had happened to him, and I had a feeling I knew what it was about.

My life had thrown a series of events at me no one could prepare for. As a result, I was frequently in the hospital. The temptation to take my own life was ever-present, and on more than one occasion I acted on these thoughts to try to free myself from my living nightmares.

During each hospital stay, Brian would visit me. Those visits didn't start well. The disappointment in his eyes could tear down a wall. I'd explain all the thoughts leading up to my attempt, to which he'd always reply: "It isn't real."

He would repeat these words until I would say them back to him. It is hard to explain, but there is something perfect about those three words. Repeating them helped me to feel safer. Once I'd calmed down, we'd then talk about the same thing for hours: Springland Meadows.

It was a town built to help those with mental health issues; a community where those with a psychiatric diagnosis could live independently of family and live-in hospitals while being surrounded by peers. The town offered all sorts of meaningful employment. There were farms for crops and animals; there were workshops where residents could learn trades like carpentry and ironworking. It was mostly self-reliant too—everything produced on its farms or in its workshops was offered for sale at the market in the center of town. Its small church held Sunday services. The school offered its residents GED's and vocational degrees. Its hospital was a state of the art facility. All told, Springland Meadows was a paradise of ideas made real... but like all good things, it met its end twenty years ago.

What was left was a ghost town—derelict buildings crumbling into unkempt fields where the grass grew to knee-height. It shut down so quickly and so quietly that rumors began to crop up about barbaric practices carried out there that needed to be kept hidden from the public eye. And while those rumors were largely falsehoods, they did contain a kernel of truth.

There had indeed been an incident at Springland Meadows. The doctor assigned to oversee the community suffered an accident caused by one of the residents. Or maybe… accident isn't the right word. A dangerous resident suffered a psychotic break and carved the doctor's face off with a knife. It's your prerogative if you want to call that an "accident," but that's how the news chose to report it.

In one fell swoop, the community's reputation was ruined. Before the accident, several leading journals had lauded it as the model of psychiatric care; but afterward, no doctor would dare send any of his or her patients there, out of fear of legal reprisal. The doctor who formerly oversaw the community never recovered from his injuries, and the town languished for lack of management. In the weeks that followed, there were several deaths and residents reported missing. That was the final nail in the experimental town's coffin—Springland Meadows was ordered condemned, and its residents were forced to find other homes.

Each time Brian and I spoke about Springland Meadows, the thoughts of the place filled my mind with excitement. Some days, I'd spend hours online or at the library printing up photos and articles about the place, and tacking them onto my bedroom walls. Before long, every inch of my walls was covered with clippings about the place and the people who lived there. The day before Brian stopped coming, he said we'd plan a trip there so I could see what was left of it with my own eyes.

After the first day he didn't show, I didn't think much of it. There were times he felt sick and couldn't make his usual visit, but he would always call beforehand. After two days without a visit, I phoned him, but could never get a response. Things got really bad after a week. That was when I started seeing things outside my house—things that still haunt me whenever I try to sleep.

I'm not one to believe in monsters, so I don't call them that. A better word for them is *Grotesques*. Beings larger than any person I've ever met stand outside my house every night. One is tall and lanky, another is morbidly obese beyond comprehension; and there is another that sometimes appears, this one smaller than myself. They never speak... nor do I see them move. They simply watch the house. This started after Brian went missing, after we talked about visiting Springland.

I've gone to my mother with this, but she insists Brian's fine and nothing is watching the house. Each night, before sunset, I close the blinds so I don't have to see them, but they're still there. While in my bed, I can hear them moving about in the yard. One has quick footfalls; the others take their time crunching on the leaves outside the bedroom. And while they haven't threatened me with physical harm—yet, at least—I don't like knowing they're there.

They frighten me.

The day at last came when I got fed up with no one listening to me. No one around me had the answers I sought. It was up to me to find them, and I knew just where to look.

I waited for my mother to leave the house for the day. Once she was gone, I grabbed my coat and walked to the bus stop. It was still early in the morning, which played to my advantage. I had only the daylight hours to find Springland and return home before the Grotesques came out at dusk.

The bus was crowded. There were no seats available, and so I stood, hanging on to a support pole and doing my best to avoid eye contact. I glanced over the shoulder of a man who was seated in the bench in front of me, reading a newspaper. The article on the facing page read: "20th Anniversary of Springland's Exodus."

The coincidence made me smile.

As Springland was no more, the bus no longer stopped there. Instead, I got off at a stop in the city a few miles from where the abandoned community lay. I bundled up my coat and tightened my shoelaces in anticipation of the long trek ahead.

In a few hours' time, I found myself at the woods near the city limits. The paved road beneath me turned into a dirt path. Following the path led me to a familiar sedan pulled off to the side of the road.

It was Brian's car.

My heart racing with excitement, I ran over to investigate. The driver's door was left open. Reaching inside, I noticed the leather seats were cold to the touch, as though the car had sat here for a long time. Something wasn't right about all this. The upholstery felt similar to leather, but it was off somehow, as though the cold had damaged the material. The steering wheel had three control sticks coming out of the side; I remembered it having two before.

Stepping away from the vehicle, I noticed a cement sign that was partially obscured in overgrown weeds. It was set to one side of the road and built low to the ground, resembling a gravestone. Brushing away some of the weeds revealed the words carved into its surface: *Welcome to Springland Meadows.*

A vacant guardhouse and roadway gate stood across from the welcome sign. I ducked under the barricade and walked along what seemed like an endless road flanked by trees. Paranoia began to set in.

Where was I? Springland Meadows or the middle of nowhere? It sure felt like the latter, because no matter how far along the road I walked, I felt like I wasn't making progress. Everything looked the same. I could disappear and never be found, and no one would ever think to search for me out here.

A chill breeze swept the treetops. I tightened my coat around me for warmth as I pressed on, and it was then I heard a faint sound coming from up ahead. As I rounded a bend in the path, I saw what had made the noise.

As far as the eye could see, there were wind chimes hanging from the limbs of all the trees. They were as delicate as they were simple, just a collection of seashells strung together in sets of three with fishing twine–a group crafts project, no doubt. Just listening to the chimes and watching them sway in the breeze brought a smile to my face. They made me think of all the trips to the beach I took with mom as a kid.

I heard the leaves crunch behind me. I turned around, and before me stood what I thought was a child in a patient's gown – I couldn't tell for certain because of the burlap sack it wore over its head. The bag had a single hole cut out at eye-level. The child was dirty and frail, its elbows and knees the size of apples, and its limbs like twigs.

"Who are you?" I asked.

The child didn't respond. Instead, it held up three fingers for a moment before turning in place and running off into the thicket, disappearing from sight.

Something changed while I was speaking to the child. I hadn't noticed it while it was happening, and only became aware after the fact. The wind chimes were gone. I couldn't understand how all of them could simply vanish so quickly – even if there were a team of people working in perfect silence, they would not have had enough time to take them all down and leave. Wide-eyed with mounting fear, I shook my head at this, then made my way back to the road.

After walking for what felt like another mile, I reached a break in the trees. Up ahead, a sign hung over the road. It was missing several letters, but what was once written there was clear: *Springland Meadows.*

The arched sign was connected to what was once a white picket fence. A couple sections had fallen over from lack of maintenance while other areas were overgrown with vines. Beyond the sign lay what appeared to be a flatland that stretched to the horizon.

Just beyond the archway, stacked in piles on either side of the street, were the dried remains of rotting crops. A couple of scarecrows still stood among the remains. Their heads appeared to be made of the same burlap material the child was wearing earlier. Like everything else around them, they were in terrible shape. They were emaciated, their stuffing having fallen out of them long ago. They had deteriorated to the point where the birds weren't afraid of them anymore. Crows perched victoriously on their bodies and pecked the straw from their innards.

I kept walking. The road I followed ran through a field of decayed plants. The land was dotted with posts that had once propped up scarecrows which had since fallen off their supports.

The fields gave way to a massive structure. Passing a sign that read *Administration and Educational Center*, I approached the building, which seemed to be made of slick black river rocks. Movement from within one of its upper windows drew my eye. Someone stood behind a curtain, watching me. When I approached to get a closer view, they stepped out of sight.

"Brian?" I shouted, and got no response.

I ran up the cobblestone steps and through the dilapidated door. The door closed behind me with an echoing thud, and what happened next still sends shivers down my spine.

A shrill voice rang out in the abandoned corridor. It sounded like an unnatural gargle, like someone trying to speak underwater.

"Quiet!" the voice yelled in response to the door slamming behind me.

I froze. My eyes struggled to adjust to the darkness. Before me was a reception desk in an otherwise empty lobby. I proceeded into the hallway, my footsteps echoing off the tiled floor.

"I said quiet!" the voice yelled.

My heart raced and each beat grew louder in my ears. After a few seconds, the thumping was all that was audible in the dead silence of the building. I let out a prolonged breath to calm myself.

"I've had enough!" the voice screamed, followed by a door slamming against a wall. Not sure of where the sounds were coming from, I ran down a deserted corridor. Light, but frantic footfalls echoed somewhere behind me.

I ran through the first door I came across and shut it, but there wasn't a way to lock it. I found myself in a dank classroom that smelled of mold. All the empty desks faced a blank chalkboard. Not having time to investigate, I shuffled away from the door and toward the hall windows that looked back into the corridor.

Perching myself underneath the window so not to be seen, I heard the frantic steps slow as they neared the room. When they stopped, a deafening silence took over. I crept up from under the window and peered outside.

It was one of the Grotesques. The shock of the realization froze my muscles. I'd never seen one this close before. It was the small one; standing at half my height. Its head was oversized and gnarled, its face resembling an old woman's, and yet it its limbs were wisp-like, withered to mere tendons. Its skin was dark and leathery, almost as though it had been mummified.

She looked down the hallway in silence, but didn't notice me. She reached for one of the many half-moon spectacles that hung around her neck to place over her enormous hooked nose. Then she squinted her tiny black peppercorn eyes and brushed a strand of hair from her face to scan the hallway for any sign of me.

Standing on her tiptoes, she grasped the knob to the classroom door. I pushed myself against the wall, hoping not to be seen. The door opened a crack. I held my breath as she shambled inside.

Once she was at the front of the room, she grabbed a piece of chalk and began writing on the board.

"Now," she mumbled, "where were we?"

I glanced at the open door, wondering how I might slip by her unseen. I nearly leapt in panic when she slammed the chalk down, the sharp noise pealing in my ears. On the board was written:

$2 + 1 = 3$

"No," she said under her breath, "that's not right."

Quietly, on my hands and knees, I crawled toward the door.

"There's two," she said, scrambling to change out her glasses. She pressed her face up against the board. "But where's...? There's three, but what happened to two...? And one? This isn't right at all!"

I sped up, inadvertently brushing the door with my arm. The Grotesque's face turned away from the board and looked toward the sound. Terrified, I froze once again.

"What was that?" she mumbled.

Fumbling with her different pairs of glasses, she approached, coming within inches of me. She squinted her beady black eyes.

"Feet?" she said, alarmed. She looked upwards toward the door. "Doorknob?! No, no, no! This isn't right at all!"

She threw down her pair of glasses and tried to untangle another from her neck. During her confusion, I crept out of the room. Being careful not to make a sound, I snuck into the hall and turned down another corridor.

I racked my brain as to why there would be something resembling a Grotesque here. What was it? Why was it here during the day? What does it have to do with Brian?

I came upon another room that opened into a vast foyer. A marble staircase rose to a landing halfway up a story before splitting in two opposite directions that led the rest of the way up. The space was filled with elegant furniture that had sat here for a long time, judging by the dust.

The sound of a cello broke the silence. My eyes darted about, looking for the source of the music, but then I realized someone had turned on a record player. Accompanying the cello was an opera singer. I couldn't understand what was being sung, but it brought to mind dark and morbid images.

Along with the music, I could hear a faint tapping sound — footsteps. At the top of the staircase, a man in a suit was descending the steps. He wasn't a Grotesque, but his entire head was wrapped in bandages. Black goggles covered where his eyes should have been. He stood ramrod straight with an arm at his back, carrying himself with a confident posture. He turned to glance in my direction.

"Beautiful," his deep voice resonated, despite being muffled through the bandage wrappings.

I remained silent, watching him. Even with all the bandages the man had covering his face, I could tell that wasn't Brian. He was too tall and thin to be Brian.

"I love this song," he said. "Sometimes, when I need to get away from the world, I sing along…"

And he did. Without missing a beat, he added his tormented wails to the melody.

I backed away and tried to locate an exit. The man danced in place to accentuate his notes. Throwing his head back and arms apart, he bellowed a sustained note at the top of his lungs, then ran his hands across his bandaged face while trying to catch his breath.

"Oh," he let out, "pardon me. I've forgotten myself." He removed a surgical blade from his coat. "Do you have an appointment?"

I ran out of the foyer and down another hallway. With a glint of light guiding my way to an exit, I burst through the wooden door at the end and tumbled down a flight of steps.

No sooner had I rolled to a halt than I was back on my feet again, running. Following a dirt path led to another crumbled road with a steeple peeking out from behind the trees. I leapt over fences and ran through open lots. As the church ahead came into view, I stopped outside its iron fence.

On the far side of the church grounds was a playground overgrown with weeds. The shrill squeak of rusted metal came at regular intervals. I turned to look and found a playground carrousel with the child perched atop it; the same child wearing the burlap sack and patient gown.

The carrousel came to a stop as the child leveled its gaze on me. It held up three fingers once again, then ran into the church. Confused, I glanced back the way I came. Not far off, the man in the suit and bandages was closing the gap between us.

I jumped the fence and plowed through the church doors, then slammed them shut behind me. The blast of the wooden doors hitting the doorframe startled someone within the church—I could see only his outline in that shadowy building, but just by his profile I could tell it was another Grotesque.

Without thinking, I ducked behind a pew and hid. There was a slight rustle as the Grotesque in the front pew turned his head one way, then the other, searching me out. Slowly, my eyes grew accustomed to the darkness and I could pick up on his details. His flesh was dark and petrified, and his eyes appeared sewn shut under the brim of his beat-up old hat. He snuffled, as though he were trying to pick up my scent. His long, bulbous nose bobbed with each sniff.

I felt my eyes narrow and a hot surge of hatred coursed in my veins. The Grotesque was dressed as a priest. I've always hated going to church. The sermons always seemed to end with someone saying demons were influencing me, or that I should be punished for my sin of sloth. As terrifying as the monster before me was, my fear was overpowered by rage.

The Grotesque stood from his seat to his unnatural height; two times bigger than the tallest person I've ever met. His arms hung past his knees. He cracked the joints of his long fingers; each pop echoed in the musty space. Then he turned in place and sniffed again, as though a foul odor had entered his church. He took a few steps in between the rays of light filtering through the boarded windows. Each time he stepped into the light, I saw more of his putrid visage.

The Grotesque used its gangly arms to navigate through the center aisle, sniffing the air with each step. He bent down to sniff near the floor between rows and three cross necklaces slid out from beneath his collar; they jangled around his withered throat. As he lifted his head to continue his search, his stringy hair brushed the floor like a broom. He ran his elongated fingers across each pew before continuing to the next row.

My heart raced as he drew closer to my row. I lay down, thinking to hide underneath the bench. I held my breath as he drew nearer, until finally he was at the bench just before mine. His spidery fingers peeked out from over the top of the bench, and then came his deformed face. He took another stentorian sniff with his massive nose; I felt his hot exhalation rustle my hair.

I was as good as caught. His head dipped lower, closer to where I lay as though he were following my scent. His nose was inches from me. Quickly, I reached back and snatched a bible from its cubby, then hurled it as far from me as I could. The book slammed into a wooden bench with a resounding crack.

"Punish!" the Grotesque roared, springing up to its feet to ferret out the source of the noise. "Unclean! Unworthy! Punish!"

With the monster distracted, I shimmied on elbows and knees toward the front of the church, and stood when I got to the altar. The wooden floor creaked under my weight, instantly drawing the Grotesque's attention. Its head went whipping in my direction. My heart sank into the pit of my stomach. But instead of charging at me, the monster simply took a cautious step forward and sniffed the air. Then its lower mandible came unhinged and its jaw dropped almost to its belly button, revealing a mouth that was deep and dark and wide as a train tunnel. An inhuman groan rose from that mouth, sounding like the winds that blow in hell.

I lost myself in a panic. I screamed, my hands up on either side of my head, fingers threaded in my hair. A split-second later, I'd gathered my wits and did the only thing that made sense.

I ran.

The Grotesque wasted no time in pursuing. As I bolted toward the door, the creature plowed through the pews in its way, shattering the benches and leaving them in splinters. I burst through the door and fell headlong into the dirt outside. Scrambling to my feet, I shot a quick glance behind me. My pursuer was gone. Sunlight flooded the old church, illuminating the specks of dust that swirled in the air.

I rose, brushed myself off and then slumped against the doorway to catch my breath. The child with the burlap sack over its head was back. This time, the child stood next to a concrete building up the way from where I was. The structure rose to three stories and bore the simplistic and functional design cues of a basic workplace.

"The workshop," I said to myself.

I took a tentative step forward, and the child turned and ran into the structure.

A run of about five minutes put me at the workshop's front stoop. As I entered, I felt as though I'd crossed a threshold into a place that time had forgotten—as though, long ago, the world had turned and left this place behind to rot.

The workshop floor was a vast open space. What light there was came through boarded-up windows set high into the walls, just beneath the ceiling. The dust of bygone ages caked onto rows of machines set atop workbenches arrayed in perfectly straight lines. A loud banging noise came from the floor above. Making my way along the depth of the workshop floor, I found a rusted spiral staircase and ascended the steps.

The hammering was far louder on the second floor. Metal on metal pealed like a blacksmith working his anvil. Following the noise, I came upon a deserted cafeteria—and another Grotesque.

This one was enormous in girth and misshapen. The creature's body was so massive its shoulders consumed its neck, making it look as though its head sat directly upon its torso. Its mouth was full of twisted, malformed teeth; some were too big to fit and kept its jaws from closing properly. It wore an ill-fitting business suit that stretched at the seams. The Grotesque's blubbery green skin spilled out of its clothes. Its tiny arms struggled to hold onto a plastic serving tray as it slammed it repeatedly into the queuing rails beside an empty register.

"I need food!" the beast bellowed through its slobber. "Why won't you feed me?"

It threw the tray behind the deserted serving station and wobbled toward the seating area. A lone briefcase sat on top of a table. Groaning as it moved, the Grotesque took a seat in front of the case. The chair cracked under its weight.

It opened the case and licked its lips as it pulled out a blank prescription pad. Then it tore pages from the pad and stuffed its salivating mouth with the paper. It wasn't enough. The creature pulled out folders stuffed to the brim with paper and began an eating frenzy. Papers flew from the table in the chaos. One traveled all the way to the doorway and landed by my foot.

I picked up the paper and gave it a cursory glance. It was an account statement filled with charges: a charge for medications, another for housing, and others for nursing services, doctor's referrals, and companion services. Something about the last one struck me as familiar.

The account statement went on with still more charges, but these were of a ridiculous nature: functionality charges, admin fees of astronomical proportions, oxygen fees, "feeling safe" fees, and to top it all off, a living fee.

All the outrageous numbers on the ledger started with three, but none of them added up at the end. At the bottom, the total read: *Not Enough.*

Holding the paper elicited an unpleasant sensation in me. I can't quite put my finger on it—it was something akin to hunger, as though I hadn't eaten in days. And yet, it was irrational, because I had become hungry for the paper in my hands. Looking down at it, I got the impression I wanted—no, *needed*—to eat this paper, despite that the rational part of me knew it would not provide the nourishment my body needed.

In the moment, I didn't care. My mouth salivated with the thought of eating the paper. My stomach clenched into a tiny knot of anger, reminding me that it was still empty, and that I needed to fill it, fast.

I tore off a strip of paper and balled it up, stuffed it into my mouth and began chewing. It tasted horrible, but before I was too sure of what I was doing, I had stuffed another piece into my mouth.

The Grotesque stopped. Its green eyes glared at me in horror as I pushed what remained of the paper into my mouth. Enraged, the creature flung the table away and charged at me, but it lost its balance and fell over with its first step. Dragging itself along on its belly, it covered ground surprisingly quickly.

I ran back to the staircase, taking the steps two at a time. Looking over my shoulder, I spied the Grotesque as it squirmed in the cafeteria doorway. It was too big to get through. There wasn't time to smile at my good fortune because, suddenly, it made a pained face and its body popped through the door.

I had just gotten to the bottom of the stairs by the time the Grotesque reached the staircase. The corpulent monster took the first step then tumbled headlong, rolling down the spiral staircase like a giant pinball. I broke into a run again without first setting my eyes ahead, and charged into someone who stiff-armed me to a halt. The tall man with the bandaged face blocked my path.

There was a sharp sting at the side of my neck. My hand flew to clutch at my neck, but the world went black long before my hand got halfway there.

Troubled dreams filled my chemical-induced sleep. All of a sudden I was in my therapist's office. We sat in our usual spots, me on her couch and her in her chair. Suddenly, her body was wracked with convulsions as she twisted into the shape of the small Grotesque from the classroom. I leapt out of my chair, screaming. My mother came in through the door, and when she set eyes on us both, she too was stricken as her body contorted into the shape of the Grotesque. I bolted out of the room and into the hallway, the soles of my shoes squeaking as I came to a halt upon seeing all eyes present lock on me.

Everyone in the hall was a Grotesque—each of them identical to the priest Grotesque I'd seen in the church.

Everything was a blur as I pushed past the deformed bodies. I passed a doctor's office with a pharmacy, but didn't dare go in; all of the people inside were the obese Grotesque. Ahead was a friendly and familiar face: my case manager. I pumped my legs

470

hard in a desperate sprint to reach her, but stopped short when the child with the burlap sack stepped into my path. It showed three fingers again.

"Where's Brian?" I asked my case manager. "All I want to do is find Brian!"

"You know he's not coming back," she said. "We talked about this before."

"That doesn't make sense!" I yelled. "How could I lose him?"

"You didn't. The service was lost. It had nothing to do with you."

"Service?"

Before she could answer, she twisted, cracked, and morphed into the priest Grotesque. I stifled a horrified gasp as I backed away. The child stepped forward and removed the sack from its head.

It was Brian's face, but on the body of a child. He looked disappointed, but instead of saying a single word, he held up the same three fingers he'd shown me before.

I snapped awake, feeling completely disoriented. My body felt like it was floating on water. It was a strange and confusing sensation—I wasn't actually in water, but it felt like a current was moving me.

What I thought sounded like water at first transitioned to something else. It was music. As clarity returned to my mind, I recognized the tune as the opera I heard playing on the gramophone earlier.

My vision was shot—I could see only blurs of light. Sensation in my extremities was slowly coming back. I was in a sitting position. My hands were pinned down, though my legs were free. Suddenly, my situation became obvious. I was in a wheelchair with my wrists in leather restraints. The chair was positioned just outside the glow of the surgical lights which filled the room. In front of me, with his back turned, was the bandage-faced man.

He was no longer wearing his suit; instead, he had on a clear plastic apron. He rolled up his sleeves as he sang along with the twisted opera tune. One by one, he examined his surgical equipment in front of a corkboard. I couldn't make out what was pinned to it, but it looked like dried skins.

The light smeared to blurs. His singing faded into the sound of the record player, and these too were overtaken by sounds without origins. I recognized this feeling. I was having a seizure.

My head and legs flailed in place as my arms nearly ripped through the straps holding me to the chair. I don't remember anything beyond seeing flashes of light, until I came to once more. The bandage-faced man with dark goggles knelt in front of me and attempted to steady my head with his hands.

"It's all right," he said. "It's all right. It'll pass."

I fought to keep my eyes open. Saliva ran from my mouth like a waterfall. The man removed a handkerchief from his pocket and cleaned my chin.

"Is it over?" he asked. "Are you with us again?"

I tried to respond, but couldn't form words. My mind was a jumbled, confused mess.

"Not a reaction I usually get from my anesthetic," he went on. "Most would still be asleep. Are you on any medications? An antipsychotic, perhaps?"

Still unable to respond, I strained my eyes to peer down at my pockets. The man reached inside and pulled out an empty pill bottle. After examining it, he chuckled.

"This explains it," he said. "How long has it been empty, I wonder. I'm sorry. I know schizophrenia isn't easy by any means. I understand this better than most." He pushed the pill bottle back into my pocket and straightened up.

"This place used to help others like you, others whom the world had turned its back on." He shook his head. "But in the end, it fell prey to the same sins."

He grabbed the back of the wheelchair and moved me closer to the surgical table in the center of the room.

"Money makes the world go round," he went on. "But unfortunately, few people have money—well, enough money to make a difference anyway. Those few don't care about people like us. The paradoxical thing about wealth is once you've earned enough, the hunger for more gets stronger, and this necessarily leaves the rest of us struggling to grab onto whatever's left."

As he wheeled me closer to the table, I realized that the skins on the corkboard were faces—human faces, expertly removed with precise cuts of a scalpel. Sightless eye sockets stared at me as toothless, expressionless mouths gaped.

"You see," the man said, "to them, none of us have a face. But your face looks familiar. Have you been here before?"

He left my side, headed to the table where his surgical equipment was set out. While his back was turned, I tugged against my leather restraints.

"Oh, here it is," he said, referring to the music. The song rose to a crescendo of torment. The man allowed the melody to take over as he sang along with the record player once more.

My thumb dislocated with a dull pop, allowing my wrist to slide through the restraint. Wincing from the pain, I undid the strap over my other wrist. At just that moment, the man swayed with the music, turning in place to face me as he let out a baritone note. I sprang from the chair and grabbed the surgical light connected to the table. With as much force as I could muster, I threw the heavy lamp into the man's face.

The light bulbs burst on impact. The man stumbled backward, his face in his hands, screaming in agony as electrical current set fire to his wrappings. Without a second thought, I ran out of the room.

Once out the door, I ran down a darkened hallway of what seemed to be an abandoned hospital. The fluorescents above gave an occasional flicker, revealing a stairwell at the end of the corridor.

I flew down the steps, but had to stop and cover my face with my arm from the stench. A mutilated corpse slouched against the wall, its flesh bearing signs of advanced decay. On the wall above it, written in dried and blackened blood, was:

DOCTOR BURMAN IS A SURGEON
WITH THE FACE OF ROTTING VERMIN!

Angry grunting sounds came from above, growing louder by the moment. I ran past the body and down another stairwell. Running footsteps followed me as I burst through the door at the ground level and sped down another hallway. I turned a corner that led to a reception area and vaulted the desk, then hid beneath it, breath held so I could focus on listening for my pursuer. Soon enough, footsteps boomed down the hall. They slowed as they drew nearer to my hiding spot, then stopped, and the room went silent.

I nearly leapt out of my skin when I heard an inhuman cry. It was the man with the bandaged face—he was singing opera again, except this time he was without the accompaniment of his record player.

I waited until the sound of his voice faded up the corridor away from where I hid. Once he had gone far enough, I crawled out from behind the desk, and froze. The exit to the hospital lay directly ahead, and so did a Grotesque.

It was the small one from the classroom. Its long, hooked nose swung back and forth while scanning the area. The creature kept switching between the dozens of pairs of glasses that hung around its neck, holding one pair up to its eyes to test it, then another.

My heart leapt in my chest when I heard a door open nearby. It was the man, I was sure of it—only it wasn't. This time, it was the child, still wearing the sack over its head. As before, it held up three fingers and said nothing.

I returned the child's stare. No doubt it meant to communicate something to me—why else would it hold up three fingers each time our paths crossed?

I thought back to the dream I had while drugged. The Grotesques were everywhere, but something was familiar about them. The child in the dream removed the sack from its head and showed Brian's disappointed face... The number three... The three perfect words... The words that helped me feel safe when Brian visited me in the hospital.

It's not real.

I felt as though I'd had an epiphany. All of a sudden, the day's events began to fall into place. Anytime I encountered the number three, something wasn't right and my mind was trying to tell me. The child wasn't real, and neither was the Grotesque blocking my path.

I started for the exit. The Grotesque squealed and ran towards me.

"It's not real," I whispered, prepping myself for the hardest acting role I could imagine—me, pretending to not be me. Me, pretending to be like everyone else—everyone who was "normal"—who didn't see things they knew weren't there. I pressed on toward the door and ignored the rancid Grotesque running at me. It grabbed at my legs, but the sensation was odd. It was like being hurt in a dream. I continued my stone-faced approach to the door.

The Grotesque screamed and slashed at my legs, but I refused to acknowledge it, even as tears flowed from my eyes. Being careful to not make any noise, I opened the door and walked into the light of the fading sun. The Grotesque let go and retreated, choosing instead to stand at the hospital's threshold and watch me leave. Not wanting to acknowledge it, I watched it out of the corner of my eye. This was all too familiar to me, as though I'd done this before. I hadn't seen this place today, but I knew I was heading in the right direction.

Down the road was a neighborhood of cracked pavement and abandoned homes overgrown with vines. Some of the homes had collapsed into rubble. Under my feet, pieces of the sidewalk were missing and I knew it was because of something I did. One of the houses triggered a memory. All of its windows were smashed. Peering through the fractured windowpane, I could see a Grotesque hiding within, and wanted to chase it off.

Realization struck me then. I had been here before—that was why this place looked so familiar. My blood froze in my veins with my next thought: that was also why the bandaged man recognized me.

My mind went reeling back to the scarecrows from earlier. Had that been straw falling out of their tattered bodies; or had it been their innards dripping with fresh gore? My mind focused to razor precision—those hadn't been scarecrows at all but dead people haphazardly lashed to poles. No wonder the crows wouldn't leave them alone—whole flocks of birds could feast on the countless bodies out in the field. Somehow, I couldn't help but think the bandaged man was to blame. He had done this; he was behind all of it, having torn up those victims and left them to the elements, and he would have done the same to me.

As if in synch with my moment of clarity, the doors to every house on the block swung open at once. From within their shadowy depths emerged the Grotesques of the priest and the obese man until the front yards of every home were packed with them.

I closed my eyes and reflected on the threes I encountered with each, then looked ahead and walked. The Grotesques mocked me and shouted ugly things, while others threw whatever garbage they had on hand at me. I ignored them as best I could. My eyes watered as much from the pain of the hurled garbage striking my body, as from the futility of my circumstances, for I knew I could never escape the Grotesques no matter how hard I tried. And despite everything, I bit my lip and focused, knowing I would be safe.

It wasn't real.

The barrage of hurled trash died down as I neared the outskirts of the neighborhood. The Grotesques hadn't left, but remained just outside of my line of sight. I resisted every urge to look, as I was almost in the clear. The administration building was ahead. I ran the rest of the way.

When I made it to the crop fields, I paused. Seeing one of the scarecrows being attacked by birds evoked a desire to investigate further, but I decided against that. I already knew what was behind the burlap sacks they had for faces.

As I ran to the street surrounded by woods, a police car rolled up. It stopped just before hitting me. The officer didn't delay in jumping out.

"There you are!" he said. "We've been looking for you."

"How did you know where to find me?" I asked.

"Any time your mother reports you missing, you always come here. Come on, let's get you home."

I hesitated before getting into the vehicle. I wanted to tell them about the bandage-faced man, but I was uncertain. Was he real?

I stepped into the police car in silence. I was certain I had done this before, too, despite that I was unable to recall any one prior instance. How long would I retain the memories this time? Did I do anything different than before? When would I wake from this never-ending nightmare?

"Have you been taking your medication?" the officer asked.

"No," I said. "We can't afford it anymore."

"I'm sorry to hear that," he said, frowning. "This never happened when Brian was assigned to you. It turned my stomach hearing you guys couldn't afford his services anymore." Then he looked out toward the community beyond the windshield. "It's a shame this place closed down. It may have been a good fit for you."

Why did Springland Meadows close? In the end, there was never any evidence of mistreatment. They tried to do everything right to create a community where people like me could feel safe and not judged. Was it because a violent man removed its founder's face? Or did it close because of everyone else?

I know this recent trip to Springland was not my first, nor will it be the last. It calls to me, and I must go, despite knowing there is nothing for me there — there never was. Like an open field that runs forever to the horizon, devoid of homes, or hills, my life has become an infinite stretch of flat land, and I am alone.

I experience the Grotesques every day, and in many forms.

How long before I forget to ignore them?

How long before I return to my perpetual meadows?

ABOUT THE AUTHOR
MICHAEL WARRINER

Born and raised in Central Florida, Michael Warriner pursued an early interest in learning music and creating characters in hand-drawn comic books. He began his career working simultaneously in the mental health industry and as a character performer at his local theme park. It was while pursuing his degree in Psychology that he began writing stories "just to kill time." Before long, he had written two manuscripts. This developing interest in telling stories was further driven by his fascination with amateur filmmaking.

By day, Michael now applies his education and training to assist clients diagnosed with mental illnesses. By night, he writes novels, and in his free time he composes music. He draws upon these varied interests to create unique characters and thrust them into memorable stories.

His debut novel, *The Man In The Forest*, is a tale of paranormal horror involving feuding musicians and the curse of an ancient entity that dwells deep in Romania's haunted Hoia Baciu woodlands.

Ullassee Gulch, Alabama

By: A.P. Hawkins

The police officer placed his tape recorder on the table between us and clicked it on. "All right, Ms. Jackson. Please start from the beginning, and be as detailed as you can," he said.

I pulled the blanket they'd given me tighter around my shoulders, trying to ignore the bloodstains on my shirt. "Well, Eddie and I planned this backpacking trip," I said. Then I added, "Eddie Jones," thinking the officer would want Eddie's last name for his report.

"Who's Eddie?"

"An old friend from high school. I moved to California for college, but I've been missing Alabama a lot lately. I told Eddie I wanted to visit, and he said he'd take me backpacking. He's—" I swallowed against the lump rising in my throat. "He *was* a ranger in the Talladega National Forest, so I thought it would be fun to go there."

"Did you fly in to Birmingham?" the officer asked.

I nodded.

"Okay, let's start with the airport, then."

I supposed that was as good a place as any.

I arrived at the airport in the early evening. My excitement for our trip began somewhere in my chest and vibrated down through my fingers. It felt almost like touching one of those electrically-charged glass balls, where the current arcs toward your hand and

481

makes your hair stand on end. I rushed through the airport to the pickup area feeling like the tiniest shake of my head would send sparks flying out of my hair.

"Haley, over here!" a man called as I stepped outside. He was standing in front of a beat-up 1993 Chevy pickup, waving at me. I blinked.

I wouldn't have recognized Eddie if he hadn't called out to me. It wasn't as though I'd forgotten what he looked like, or that his features had changed significantly since high school, but something about the way the shadows fell on his face and played over his bushy black beard distorted his features into a grotesque mockery of what I expected to see. The right side of his face appeared to be sunken, crumpled, his right eye swollen shut. There were shadows in his mouth where teeth should have been.

I know now that I should have left right then. I should have just turned around and walked back into the airport, exchanged my return ticket for an immediate flight back to Cali. Deep down, I think some part of me knew it even then.

But then Eddie stepped toward me, a tiny movement of just a few inches, and the shadows shifted. The horrific features transformed into the familiar, smiling face I expected. It put me at ease. I relaxed, allowing my anxious frown to melt into a smile.

"I thought you said your truck was new," I said as I approached. I reached for him, allowing him to envelop me in his signature bear-hug. "This thing is ancient," I continued, my voice muffled against the broad expanse of his chest.

"It's new to me," he said, chuckling. He plucked my backpack from my shoulders and laid it in the truck bed with his own pack. "What do you think?"

I rapped my knuckles experimentally against the faded blue hull of the Chevy, listening to their sturdy *thunk* against the metal. "Seems appropriate for Mr. Bigshot Forest Ranger," I said, grinning.

"That's what I thought, too. Come on, get in. I already ordered pizza at the station."

I climbed into the passenger side of the truck as Eddie got behind the wheel.

"Our last decent meal for the week?" I joked, thinking of the freeze-dried food packets in my backpack.

"Not to mention our last showers," Eddie said as he started the Chevy.

I laughed and pulled out my phone to text my parents that I had arrived safely.

We stopped for a red light right as we came off the highway into Talladega. An old man stood in the median as we pulled up behind the car ahead of us. He was wearing a threadbare beanie pulled down low on his forehead. Tufts of white hair poked out on either side of the hat, just above his ears. A beard that must have been decades old trailed from his jaw, the hair matted with clumps of dirt. He was holding a cardboard sign that read: "CANCER Hungry Please help GOD BLESS." As the cars piled up at the light, he began to walk down the row, his weathered face impassive.

I reached for my wallet, intending to scrounge up a few dollars for him. Eddie stopped me with a gentle hand on my arm.

"Don't," he said, without looking at me. I frowned and opened my mouth to protest, but the look on his face arrested my words before they could form on my tongue. His eyes had darkened, and his mouth was pressed into a hard, angry line.

As the man drew near enough to see inside Eddie's Chevy, his dull eyes sparked to life, rage igniting in them. His sign hung limp at his side, forgotten, as he glared at us. I looked from him to Eddie, confused, but Eddie just stared straight ahead, unblinking. The old man raised one trembling finger and pointed at the windshield of the Chevy. Tremors radiated up his arm and into his neck, causing his head to bob crazily as he glowered at us.

"That's *sick*," he said, loud enough that I could hear him through the closed windows.

I gaped at him. *What?*

Eddie's grip on my arm tightened. His other hand clutched the steering wheel so hard that the knuckles were pale.

The old man sidled up to the driver's side window, nearly pressing his face against it. His finger jabbed at the glass.

"That's *sick*," he said again, his voice rising into a nearly hysteric whine. "You're sick. *Unnatural*. It's sick. Disgusting, unnatural union."

My heart fluttered in my chest. I wrenched my eyes away from the man as his ranting dissolved into incoherence. I knew that he couldn't get to us through the Chevy's windows, and Eddie had locked the doors as soon as we stopped at the light. But I still felt uncomfortably vulnerable, like I was a fish in an aquarium, put there for him to point and jeer at. I desperately wanted to get away, but the light refused to turn green. I pulled my knees up to my chest and wrapped my arms around them, holding myself in place, as though that would block out the man's raving.

Finally, the light turned green. Eddie accelerated as fast as the car ahead of us would allow. The old man raised his voice as we pulled away from him.

"Judgment will be passed on your wicked souls!" he shouted, his white tufts of hair quivering in the rearview mirror.

We drove in silence the rest of the way to the ranger station. I thought about asking Eddie to turn around, take me back to the airport so I could go home, I don't want to be here anymore, take me back. I should have. Then we never would have found that nightmare in the forest. But my tongue felt like a ball of cotton in my mouth, thick and dry and immobile. It wasn't until Eddie pulled his Chevy into a parking space and killed the engine that I found the courage to speak. Sort of.

"Eddie... does that man... uh..."

"Every time he sees me in the car with a white girl," Eddie said, not looking at me. His mouth was still set in a firm line.

I had already begun to put the encounter behind me, to chalk it up to a crazy man's raving. It wasn't personal for me. But for Eddie, it absolutely was personal. Targeted. Repeated over and over until one day he wouldn't remember what it was like to not have his right to exist in the same space as a white person questioned. And then I realized, like a punch to the gut, maybe Eddie had never known what that felt like. I felt stupid and selfish for not having realized it years ago. I reached out and put a hand on his arm.

"Eddie, I'm so sorry. That's... really messed up," I said. It was all I could say. Tears pricked at the corners of my eyes, but I wouldn't let them fall. Eddie needed sympathy, understanding, camaraderie. Not pity.

He rubbed both hands over his face and sighed, forcing the air out from between his lips in a long hiss. Tension and anger melted off him, and he turned to me with a half-smile.

"Thanks, Haley," he said. "I'll be all right." He pulled his keys out of the ignition and opened the door, unbuckling his seatbelt so he could slide out of the truck. "Let's go inside. Pizza should be here soon."

After we ate, Eddie showed me where I could sleep and shower. A few hours later, I got up to use the bathroom. I crept through the station in the dark, not wanting to wake Eddie. As I was heading back to my couch, I heard a voice behind me.

"So, the boy says you're heading south on the Pinhoti Trail?"

I choked back a scream of fright. An old man was standing behind me in the dark, smiling. He wore a ranger's uniform, the hat tucked under one arm. A clump of white hair sprouted over each

485

ear, but otherwise he was completely bald. He looked harmless enough. I should have known better.

"What? Oh, yes, that's right," I managed to squeak.

"That's my favorite part of the forest," he said. "It's true wild country out there."

He paused. I shifted my feet uncomfortably, wondering why he hadn't turned on any lights when he came inside.

"Hardly anyone heads into the southern part of the forest," he continued. "Most people come out here just to summit Mount Cheaha. Even the real backpackers usually only head north on the Pinhoti, to connect with the Appalachian Trail in Georgia."

"I hadn't realized," I mumbled in response. I took a step away from him, wanting to go back to sleep but unsure how to break away from this dialogue graciously.

"Lots of old trails branch off the Pinhoti out there," he said. "Some of them lead to caves, waterfalls, abandoned coal mines. Hidden gems." He grinned again, revealing several gaps where he was missing teeth. "It's real wild country, the wildest country you'll find in Alabama."

"I'm really excited to explore it. It's been a long time since I've been out here," I said. I took another step backwards.

Before the man could reply, I felt a hand on my shoulder. It was Eddie.

"Haley, what's up? I thought you were asleep."

"Well, actually, I was just talking to..." I hadn't gotten the man's name. I turned back toward him, the question on my lips. He was gone. Ice crawled up my spine, making my hair stand on end.

"Who were you talking to, Haley?" Eddie asked, his brow furrowed with concern.

"I... I don't know," I said, trying to shove the chill aside. "At least, I didn't get his name. Maybe someone on a late shift?"

Eddie's brow furrowed. "There is no late shift. Are you sure there was someone there? Maybe you were sleepwalking."

"I guess I could have been," I said. I didn't quite succeed in keeping the quaver out of my voice.

"All right, well, we really should get some sleep. We're starting early tomorrow."

I nodded and headed back to my couch, but sleep didn't come right away. I stared into the darkness for a long time, waiting for those tufts of white hair to reappear out of the gloom.

We woke before dawn and packed into Eddie's Chevy for the drive to the trailhead. We had decided to start at the base of Mount Cheaha, climb to the summit, then hike down to the Pinhoti trailhead through the Cheaha Wilderness Area. We planned to hike the Pinhoti through the southern Talladega Forest, then loop back around on one of the better-known connecting trails. The whole trip was expected to last about six days, but we packed food for eight, just in case.

The first few days of our trip ran together in a blur of trees, rocks, streams, campfires, and blisters. It was wonderful. We started each day at dawn and set up camp just before sunset. The weather was perfect. The trail was well marked and easy to follow. I couldn't have asked for a better hiking trip, or a better hiking companion. Eddie was just as excited as I was to be on the trail. We were on track to make it back to the trailhead on schedule when I fucked up big-time. That's the worst part. Knowing that what happened was my stupid fault.

It was the beginning of our fourth day, and we had just a couple of miles to go on the Pinhoti before we made it to the connecting trail that would take us back to our starting point. Eddie and I had just started out for the day. I was munching on a granola bar, looking down at my feet, letting Eddie lead the way. The crunch and swish of leaves under my companion's boots assured me that I wasn't far behind.

Of course, I would be the one to trip while looking at my own feet. My half-eaten granola bar went flying as I sprawled in the dirt and leaves. My chin bounced off the ground when I landed. For a moment, all I could do was lie there and groan. I heard Eddie's footsteps stop and the rustling of leaves as he turned to check on me.

"Haley! Are you okay?"

His hands grasped the undersides of my outstretched arms and he hoisted me into a sitting position. I tasted blood in my mouth.

"Unnghh," I groaned, reaching up with one trembling hand to feel my face. Eddie pulled my hand away.

"No, your hands are filthy. Let me see." His hands weren't much better, but at least he could see the open wounds and cracked teeth that I was sure were there. He probed my jawline carefully, then peeled my lips back to reveal my teeth.

"You've got a nasty scrape on your chin and you bit through your lower lip a little, but it looks like you didn't break any teeth," Eddie said with a smile. "How about your legs? Anything broken?"

"Does it look like anything's broken?" I demanded through my swelling lip. Half of me was being a sarcastic asshole, but the other half was terrified of what I'd see if I looked down at my legs.

Eddie laughed. "Well, you're not screaming, so I'd say that's a good sign. But you banged up your knee pretty good. Jesus, Haley, what did you trip over?"

"I don't know. Tree root or something."

"All right. Where'd you put the first-aid kit? We should get you cleaned up."

"Front pocket," I said, jerking my thumb behind me to my backpack, which miraculously had stayed in place as I fell. As Eddie moved behind me to rummage for the kit, I could see the patch of overturned leaves and disturbed loam that marked the space where

I'd fallen. There hadn't been a tree root in my path, or even a rock. Nothing at all that I could have tripped over. Confused, I looked down at my legs.

A red mark encircled my left calf, just above the hem of the wool socks I had pulled up to protect my ankles. Every hair on my scalp stood on end. It wasn't just a single mark. Four red welts stood out clearly against my skin. A fifth circled around my calf from the other direction, not quite meeting its companions. Each welt was capped by a crescent-shaped scratch from which blood was just beginning to ooze. The mark appeared to be a perfect imprint of a human hand. Someone had grabbed my ankle.

I scanned the trees, looking for someone lurking nearby. I thought I saw something disappear behind a large blackberry bush, a flash of white at head height. Then it was gone. I blinked, squinting at the bush. There *was* something...

"Haley, what is it?" Eddie asked as he came around from behind me, holding the first-aid kit.

"Eddie, look at that," I said, pointing into the trees.

There was a path leading off into the woods. It was old and overgrown, its mouth nearly obscured by the blackberry bush. I wouldn't have seen it at all if I hadn't been scanning the trees carefully.

"Huh," Eddie said. He handed me some wet wipes from our first-aid kit and pulled our map out of his pack. "I don't remember there being a trail here." Eddie scanned the map, pinpointing our location on the Pinhoti. "Hold on. Someone drew it in with a pencil."

There was indeed a penciled-in trail drawn on our map. It meandered through the forest for about a mile and a half. The end of it, right outside the forest boundary, was marked with a tiny X. As I gazed at it, I heard a familiar whisper in my ear. I even felt his breath on my earlobe.

489

"Hidden gems," the old ranger's voice said. I jumped, looking around wildly for the man who sounded like he was standing right beside me. No one was there. I shuddered and glanced at Eddie, but he was still studying the map.

I rubbed the dirt off my hands with a wipe, then started on the scrapes on my knee and chin. The soap stung a little, but the pain grounded me, pulled me away from the brink of terror. I stood gingerly, testing my weight on the ankle that bore the handprint. It was sore, but nothing was broken, and I could walk just fine. Slowly, I pulled my sock up just enough to cover the handprint, but whether I was hiding it from Eddie or myself, I wasn't sure. Then I crossed the trail and poked my head around the blackberry bush, careful to avoid the thorns.

The track stretched straight into the forest for about a quarter mile before it curved away into the trees. A thin mist clung to the bushes and tree saplings that would one day erase the trail for good.

"It's really overgrown, but it still looks passable," I said.

"I wonder who marked it on our map," Eddie said, puzzled.

I turned back around to face Eddie again. "I want to see where it goes."

"What?" He peered at me over the top of the map.

"I think we should check it out," I said, grinning as hard as I could around my swollen lip.

"No," he replied, folding the map to put it away. "We're on a schedule."

"Oh, come on, Eddie, it's not like we could get lost. And it's only a couple miles long, tops."

"Haley, we have no way to tell if it's drawn to scale. And what if something happens to us out there? If one of us falls and breaks something? No one would know where to look for us."

"But think about what could be at the end of it," I insisted. *Hidden gems.* I was more stubborn than Eddie, we both knew it, but he wasn't going to make it easy for me to wear him down. "There could be a huge waterfall, or a cave that Native Americans used to camp in, or an old coal mine!"

Eddie frowned. "I don't know, we probably wouldn't find anything that cool. More than likely it's an old logging road, and all we'll find is a bunch of old stumps."

"Bet on it."

"No."

Eddie wasn't ready to give in yet, but I had piqued his curiosity. He was peering beyond the blackberry bush now, his eyes shining with interest. I sighed. I had only one play left. After that, I'd have to resort to pouting. I really didn't want to have to do that, although the effect would probably be magnified by my swollen lip.

"All right," I said. "It looks like it's just about two miles long on the map. How about we go that far, and if we haven't come to the end of the track after that, we'll turn back."

Eddie considered for a moment. "Fine, you win. Let's go."

"Sweet, that's more like it!" I scooted around the bush and started down the overgrown track without waiting for Eddie to follow.

I was elated, then, to strike out into the unknown, and pleased that Eddie hadn't put up much of a fight. Now, I wish Eddie had stuck to his guns, that he hadn't let me win.

The forest towering above this new track was different from anything Eddie and I had seen so far. The trees were broader, older, their trunks covered with thick layers of moss and lichen. Even the undergrowth was wilder — the young oak and hickory saplings were choked by vines and bushes. Many of the vines sported wicked-looking thorns and crept onto the old track, threatening to wrap around our ankles. The boughs leaned in close overhead, darkening the sky. The bright morning had turned into twilight before we'd walked more than thirty minutes.

"I think we should go back," Eddie whispered, as though he were afraid to break the silence that had closed over us like a heavy blanket. Even the birds were unusually quiet.

"We've barely gone a mile," I whispered back. "We agreed to go two miles in."

"Yeah, but this place is freaking me out. I don't want to get lost out here."

"We'll be fine as long as we stay on this path."

Eddie didn't look convinced, but he didn't complain again.

The silence weighed on us as we walked, made us tired and irritable. And it didn't help that the sky kept getting darker, even though it was still before noon. I was about to tell Eddie that we should just give up and go back when the path curved away to the left. I jogged ahead a bit, hoping I would find the end of the trail, or at least something interesting that we could show for our efforts.

As I rounded the bend, an electric tingle in the air made my hair stand on end. Eddie called my name, but his voice was muffled, as though he was shouting from the other side of a wall. I took another step forward. The electricity faded.

The trees crowded the path even closer now, and it had become so dark that I had to fish my flashlight out of my pack. I flicked it on and gasped in surprise. There was an ancient entryway straddling the path not fifty feet ahead of me. It appeared to have once borne a gate that had long since rusted off its hinges. The words: "Ullassee Gulch" were carved into an old, lichen-covered wood sign suspended above the entry. Below that, in much smaller lettering, I could just barely make out: "est. 1923."

A hand grabbed my arm and I whirled around, raising my flashlight to get a better view of my attacker. But it was just Eddie. His eyes were wild, and in the shadows thrown by my flashlight beam, his face once again took on the nightmarish, sunken appearance that I'd been greeted with at the airport. I shuddered and directed the beam away from his face.

"You disappeared!" Eddie hissed.

"What are you talking about? I just jogged ahead to see what was on the other side of the bend."

"I know, but..." Eddie looked confused. "You were running up to the curve, and then, you just kind of..."

"Rounded it?" I wanted to laugh, to make light of Eddie's concern. But between the sudden dark and Eddie's obvious fear, I was starting to feel unsettled. I swallowed hard against a lump that was forming in my throat.

"No, it was like you were just... gone. I couldn't even hear your footsteps anymore," Eddie explained.

"It must have been a trick of the light," I said, trying to settle our nerves. I swung my flashlight back toward the entry with its sign. "Look at *that*."

Eddie blinked, then rummaged for his own flashlight. He flicked it on, and the twinned shadows thrown by the dual beams seemed somehow more menacing.

"What's that?" he whispered.

"Ullassee Gulch, apparently," I said, trying to sound blasé, but my voice quavered a bit. I grinned at Eddie. "Want to check it out?"

Eddie gazed at the sign as though he were in a daze. "Yeah, all right," he said, then walked toward the entry, his steps slow and plodding. I followed behind him, unwilling to admit just how *afraid* I was, and feeling foolish for being afraid in the first place.

Just beyond the ancient entry to Ullassee Gulch, the forest opened into a wide clearing populated only by scraggly grasses and the occasional gnarled, stunted tree. The ground turned soggy, like we had crossed into a swamp, and our feet made sucking noises as we walked. I bent down to tighten my laces, afraid of losing one of my nice hiking boots to the mire. That's when I noticed something was wrong.

"Eddie, is it… darker?" I asked. The sky should have brightened considerably when the canopy parted overhead, but now it was pitch black like in the darkest hours of night.

"Uh huh," he grunted. "Look at that."

Eddie was pointing his flashlight into the gloom off to my left. The husk of an ancient cabin sneered back at us in the wan light. The building was falling to pieces, its beams covered in moss and choked by wild rosebushes. Shadows clung to the eaves and empty windows, too thick for the flashlight to banish them completely.

"Woah, creepy," I said. "I guess someone used to live out here?"

"Not just one someone," Eddie said. He panned his flashlight around the clearing, and the outlines of several dilapidated buildings emerged from the shadows. Most of the buildings were small log cabins. Nestled back against the press of trees directly opposite where we stood was a church. Its roof was partly caved in, but its steeple was still intact. The cross that had once perched atop it had broken into the shape of an arrow pointing up to the sky.

"So, this was a town?" I asked, panning my flashlight around the buildings. They seemed to be arranged around a central square that was overgrown with scrub grass.

"Probably an old mining town," Eddie said. "There used to be lots of them all over the state. But I wonder why none of the rangers told me there was one so close to the forest boundary?"

I thought back to the strange old ranger I'd seen the night before we began our hike. *Hidden gems...* Had he known this old town was out here?

"So, did the mine dry up or something, and they all left?"

"Yeah, probably... Haley, look."

Eddie had trained his flashlight on a large clump of grass growing in the center of the square. There seemed to be something reflective hidden amongst the plants.

"What's that?" I asked.

"I don't know," Eddie said. His voice was dreamy, thick, like he was talking in his sleep. Slowly, he began to walk toward the center of town.

Sudden terror gripped my chest. Every instinct I had told me to run.

"Eddie, I think we should go back," I said as I crept behind him toward the clump of grass and whatever was reflecting the beam of his flashlight. He continued walking, as though he hadn't heard me.

Eddie stopped when we drew even with the clump of grass. The plants formed a ring around what appeared to be a circular pool. It was impossible to tell how deep it was in the dark. The water was perfectly smooth, a black mirror. Pale mist clung to the water's surface, undisturbed by our approach. And this pool... it almost seemed alive. It radiated malice, filling the air around it with hateful energy that made my skin crawl. I suppressed a shudder.

Eddie switched off his flashlight. When I didn't do the same, he put his hand over my light, covering the beam. I jerked away, but he had a tight grip over the end of my flashlight. It went flying into the grass and landed with a *sploosh*. The beam flickered, then went out.

"Hey!" I shouted at Eddie as we were plunged into darkness. Again, he didn't react. He just stared down into the black pool, transfixed.

The mist was pulsing with an unearthly red glow. The light started somewhere below the surface of the black water, diffused upward through the mist, and went out. And then it appeared again. The glow pulsed over and over in a lazy rhythm. My legs trembled.

"Eddie, let's get out of here," I said, tugging at his arm. It was like trying to budge a statue. Eddie stared into the black water, the red light reflected in his eyes with every pulse.

Panicked, I whirled back toward the entrance to Ullassee Gulch. A heavy metal gate stood across the entrance, its two sides latched together with a huge iron lock. I gaped at it. We had just passed through that entry five minutes before; there hadn't been a gate there at all! Or, had there been? Maybe we went around the entry? The gate stood within its arched entryway, tauntingly solid, the evidence before my eyes making me doubt my memory.

I scanned the trees around the edge of the clearing. They seemed more crowded than before, somehow. Vines bearing wicked three-inch thorns curled around their trunks.

We were trapped.

Eddie was completely entranced by the weird red light, which had begun pulsing faster. I didn't know what to do, but I knew I had to make Eddie pay attention to me.

I screamed, as loud and as long as I could, in Eddie's ear. After several seconds, Eddie jumped and rubbed a hand over the ear I'd assaulted.

"Dammit, Haley! What'd you do that for?"

"Come on, Eddie," I said. I yanked on his arm again, pulling him away from the light, toward the first house we'd seen. At least in there we'd be away from that creepy pool. "And give me your flashlight."

"What happened to yours?" Eddie asked, stumbling along as I dragged him behind me. I didn't answer.

Once we were inside the remains of the old house, I allowed myself to relax slightly. It was enough to just be away from that red light, for now. I shrugged off my backpack, setting it down against the interior wall, and flicked Eddie's flashlight on.

The house was comprised of a single room. A rotted bedframe stood next to one wall; the mattress, which had likely been filled with straw, long since chewed to pieces by mice. A large traveler's trunk moldered next to the frame. A crumbling stone fireplace was recessed into the opposite wall. There was a table in between, which had a tarnished silver dinner set laid out on it, as though the occupant were just about to sit down to eat.

"Do you think they ate a last meal before they left?" Eddie asked, indicating the silver place settings.

"Probably," I said. I crossed to the table and picked up the fork, examining it closely. "But it seems unlikely that anyone would just leave their family silver behind. I mean, look, it's engraved and everything."

I handed the fork to Eddie, who squinted at it for a moment before replacing it next to the plate. An "A" was engraved in calligraphy on the end of the handle, accompanied by decorative scrollwork. The rest of the dinner set had matching engravings.

"Maybe they left in a hurry," Eddie said.

The hair on the back of my neck prickled. I crossed over to the trunk at the foot of the rotted bedframe, intending to have a peek inside. The lid came apart in my hands as I tried to lift it. The contents were only in somewhat better condition. Lying on top of a stack of dirty old clothes was a weathered leather-bound book. I picked it up gingerly and opened the cover. The pages were stained by time, but the writing was still legible.

"Eddie, look at this. It's a journal." The name "William 'Billy' Aldritch" was scrawled in messy handwriting across the top of the first page. Below the name were the words, "Foreman, Ullassee Gulch Mine, Coosa Coal Company."

"That must be who lived here," Eddie said. "It explains the 'A' on the silver."

"Sure, but why would someone abandon their home and all their possessions? It doesn't make a lot of sense."

Eddie shrugged. "Maybe there's something in the journal?"

I flipped through the first two pages, stopping at one dated June 1922, and began to read aloud:

"The Coosa Coal Company hired me on to head up their new mine at a place the injuns who used to live around these parts called *Ullassee*. It's true wild country, beautiful in all aspects. There are hidden gems here and there, if one knows where to look. The mine site is nestled down in a steep gulch, next to a swift, clear stream. The injuns could never tame this place; these lands are God's gift to white men.

"We pitched our tents at the base of the gulch. We may not have to dig the mine for a while yet. Coal is so abundant round these parts that we've been picking it up right off the ground. We're to start clearing land for the town tomorrow. There's a nice flat area just above the gulch that should serve nicely. The negroes we brought along appear to be nervous about the place, but I'm confident that the superior intellect and strength of my race will prevail to tame this wild country."

I cringed, but I had to admit I was intrigued. This Billy Aldritch had built Ullassee Gulch; he likely also knew what had happened to it. I glanced at Eddie before flipping ahead a few pages. He rolled his eyes but appeared to be just as curious as I was.

"July 1923. We've been plagued by difficulties erecting our homes. The ground became unbearably swampy after the first rain and hasn't dried out since. Believing it to be due to the actions of a persistent beaver, I sent a team of negroes downstream to root out the creature, but its nest must be well-hidden, for they found no sign of it. At least the church is standing proud at the edge of our square, supplicant to God in its defiance of the elements. I have decided to call our little company town Ullassee Gulch."

I flipped through several more pages, catching references to the homes being finished, the mine becoming profitable, and the miner's families arriving in town, before something interesting caught my eye.

"February 1924. A black, sticky substance rather like tar has begun seeping out of the ground in the center of town. It's formed an ankle-deep pool that never dries. The wind never even leaves so much as a ripple on its surface. And, I believe, this strange black substance is contaminating all the ground the town stands upon. Last Sunday, Reverend Carter found our baptismal font full of the stuff. At first, we thought it was the negroes pulling pranks (they were outraged when we wouldn't let them attend services with the white folks), but the Reverend says it's leaking in from the ground. He calls it a harbinger of evil and recommends that we leave town. I told him we weren't going running back to the Company bosses with our tails between our legs, and we'd just have to pray and hope that God would intervene. Personally, I think it's due to nothing more than those negroes' inability to find that damned beaver."

I almost didn't want to admit it, but I agreed with the preacher. Aldritch should have packed up and left right then. He never got the chance to later.

"June 1924. Stephen Derry's son went missing several days back. His mother was all in hysterics, but most of us were convinced he was just wandering in the woods, like all little boys do. But then we found Johnny this morning, lying face down in the odd black pool in the center of town. Dead. When we turned him over, it was the most gruesome sight. The poor boy's face had been bashed in. I doubt Stephen's wife will ever recover. The poor woman had to be carried back to their house while we moved the body.

"August 1924. Al Smith and his wife went missing a few days ago, along with Brandon Lake and several of the negroes. No bodies have been found, but Mrs. Derry keeps a close eye on the black pool. We pray the Smiths and Mr. Lake will be found alive.

"November 1924. The mine flooded yesterday. We began a new tunnel and were only a few strikes in when the same sticky black substance that seeps out from underneath the town burst from the rock like the water called forth by Moses himself. Myself and the rest of the miners barely escaped with our lives. Upon returning to the mine to survey the damage, the gruesome scene we found was enough to turn even the hardest stomachs. Floating in the black substance were human remains. Some were long dead, nothing more than skeletons, but others were fresh, and we recognized Mr. and Mrs. Smith, Brandon Lake, and the missing negroes among them. There were dozens of bodies in that black tar. The memory of the sight haunts me, both by day and when I close my eyes at night.

"My mining crew and their families are fleeing the town. Many of them didn't even stop to pack up their belongings. They just left. I've written to Coosa Coal explaining to them why operations have been terminated at the Ullassee Mine.

"I know I should waste no time in leaving town as well, but the mystery of the black pool in the central square nags at my mind. Of late, there has been a strange mist hovering over it at night that seems at times to glow the deepest red..."

"That's it," I said, closing the book. "That's where it ends, in the middle of a sentence."

I moved to toss the book back into the crumbling trunk and noticed something else lying on top of the tattered clothes. I reached in and picked it up. It was an old photograph of a group of men, their faces blackened with coal dust, standing in front of what appeared to be a mine shaft. The man in the center looked familiar. He was bald except for a tuft of white hair that sprouted above each ear.

"Oh shit," I whispered, the photo falling from my hands, forgotten. "Eddie, we need to get out of here, now."

There was no reply. I glanced over to where Eddie had been standing, but he was gone. I went to the door and peered back toward the center of town, shining Eddie's flashlight wildly around in the dark.

Eddie was walking toward the black pool.

But he wasn't alone.

Alongside him was Billy Aldritch. It had been him all along, leading us here to Ullassee Gulch. And now he was leading Eddie by the arm to the center of that black pool.

"Eddie!" I called. "Eddie, stop, please!"

Eddie didn't react, but Billy Aldritch did. He turned his head toward me, throwing a malicious grin over his shoulder. Then he put one finger to his lips, telling me to hush.

"Eddie!" I screamed.

I ran toward the pair, but I was too slow in arriving.

Eddie stopped in the center of the black pool and looked up at the sky. Aldritch stood to one side, still staring at me with that horrible grin. The mist wrapped around Eddie's ankles, then his legs, then his torso, the red light pulsing faster and faster as the mist swirled and coalesced around him. Just as I reached the edge of the pool, the mist closed above Eddie's head and he was gone.

"Eddie!" I screamed again.

Billy Aldritch—or his ghost, I'm still not sure—just stood there and laughed at me as I screamed. Then he, too, disappeared, and I was alone.

Absolute silence descended over the clearing, leaving only the frantic beating of my heart.

Then came another scream, one that made my scalp tingle.

I looked up.

Eddie was falling headfirst out of the sky toward me. I met his wild, terrified eyes with my own as he fell. He landed in the center of the black pool with a sickening crunch. I will never forget that sound for as long as I live. Eddie's blood and that black goo splattered across my face as he landed. And then he just lay there, in the ankle-deep black pool, utterly motionless.

Part of me knew he was dead, but there was some tiny spark of foolish hope that made me step into that black, sticky puddle to cradle his body in my arms. I turned him over and nearly retched. His face was battered, broken, the right side of it sunken and oozing blood, right eye swollen shut. His mouth lolled open to reveal a mess of bloodied flesh and cracked teeth.

I don't know how long I sat there with Eddie's battered head in my lap, crying. It had to have been a long time. I only opened my eyes because I felt the same electric tingle I'd felt when I turned the bend in the path and saw Ullassee Gulch for the first time.

The black pool was once again pulsing with red light, the strange mist curling and inching its way up my arms. Fear clutched at my chest. I bolted, leaving Eddie's broken body behind, and Billy Aldritch's laughter echoing in my ears.

I ran off blindly into the woods. The thorns tore at my clothes and skin, but I barely even noticed. I just ran and ran, not even knowing where I was going. Finally, I broke through the trees and found myself in the middle of a road, headlights coming toward me in the dark.

"All right, thank you, Ms. Jackson. That's quite enough, I've got what I need," the police officer said. He turned off the tape recorder and leaned back in his chair, regarding me through half-closed eyes.

"You don't believe me, do you?" I asked, fragile hope fluttering behind the words.

"No, as a matter of fact, I don't."

A lump rose in my throat; hot tears started spilling down my cheeks. "But it's all true, I swear! I can take you back there, you'll see—"

"Let me tell you what I think happened," the officer said, leaning toward me slightly. "I think, once you got out into the woods, that black boy—"

"Eddie," I interrupted. "My friend, Eddie."

The police officer just stared at me for a moment, as though making sure I was done talking. "I think that black boy started getting some funny ideas in his head about what he could get away with doing to you—sexually."

What? I couldn't believe what I was hearing. This couldn't be happening.

"Maybe he made some unwanted advances toward you. Maybe he even raped you." The police officer raised his eyebrows at me conspiratorially. "Either way, I think you found yourself in a position where you had to defend yourself from him and ended up accidentally taking his life. In order to defend your own, of course."

"Excuse me?" I said, unable to listen any longer. "I *just* told you exactly what happened, Eddie would never—"

"But," the officer continued, drowning out my protest. "I think you don't want to get anyone in trouble, so you made up this whole cockamamie ghost story. Sweetheart, you shouldn't have bothered. No one could blame you for defending yourself."

"That's not what happened," I spluttered. "This is ridiculous! I just *told* you—"

"Now," the officer spoke over me again, "I've called you an ambulance. They'll take you to the hospital and get you all checked out and feeling better, and then you can go home to California." He reached over and patted my knee with a smile. "You can put this whole thing behind you and get on with your life."

"What? No, you can't do this!" I screeched. "What about Eddie?"

The officer stood and crossed the room. "What about him?" Then he slipped through the door, locking it behind him.

I pounded my fists against the door and screamed. "You're a liar! That's not what happened! His body's still out there!" I shouted it over and over again, until my throat felt raw and swollen. Finally, exhausted, I slumped against the wall, my mind in a haze of shock, sadness, and rage. I barely remember the paramedics carrying me to the ambulance.

Nothing I could say would change what that fucking racist cop put in his police report. I don't even know his name, or what station we were at, so it's not like I could even file a complaint against him. For a long time, I thought no one could ever believe what happened in Ullassee Gulch. It was too... impossible. That's why I came to you. Because I thought you might believe me. I'm the only one who knows the truth about Ullassee Gulch; the truth about what happened to Eddie Jones. And Eddie's truth deserves to be told.

ABOUT THE AUTHOR
A.P. HAWKINS

A.P. Hawkins lives in Houston, Texas, with her husband and their cat, Stella. She spends her free time writing, reading, and caring for a collection of houseplants. She also tries to get outside now and then, and loves to go camping. You can follow her on Facebook, Twitter, and Instagram. She also writes about space pirates on Wattpad.

DISCOVER OTHER BOOKS AVAILABLE THROUGH DARKWATER SYNDICATE

The Gullwing Odyssey
By: Antonio Simon, Jr.

"The Gullwing Odyssey rests solidly on the shaking shoulders of a good laugh — and that's what sets it apart from ninety percent of fantasies on the market."

— Midwest Book Review

When an unusual assignment sends Marco overseas, he finds himself dodging pirates and a hummingbird with an appetite for human brains. Little does he know the fate of a civilization may rest upon his shoulders. In spite of himself, Marco becomes the hero he strives not to be.

It Came From The Garage
By: Stephen King, Guy N. Smith, Antonio Simon, Jr., et. al.

Shift your fear into top gear. Set your pulse racing with this collection of automotive horror that fires on all cylinders. This bad boy comes fully-optioned with fifteen tales of classic cars and motorcycles behaving badly; and the star-studded lineup is sure to provide all the nightmare fuel you can handle. You're in for a ride.

The Many Deaths Of Cyan Wraithwate
By: R. Perez de Pereda

The bad part about being immortal is that you cannot die. Cyan learns that not dying is worse than not living — the magic that made him immortal turns more of his body to lifeless iron with each passing day. Knowing time is short before he becomes just another statue in a town square, he sets off on a quest to rid himself of his cursed immortality.

Shadows And Teeth
By: Guy N. Smith, R. Perez de Pereda, Antonio Simon, Jr., et. al.

Out of the shadows and meaner than ever, volume three of this award-winning horror series packs international star power. Featuring ten brand-new stories by the legendary Guy N. Smith, Adam Millard, Nicholas Paschall, R. Perez de Pereda, and others, this collection is certain to keep you up at night. Take care as you reach into these dark places, for the things here bite, and you may withdraw a hand short of a few fingers.

Hidalgo's House Of Horrors
By: Antonio Simon, Jr.

Written in second-person perspective, this book makes you the star of your own blood-soaked horror adventure.

Baron Hidalgo's country villa has sat abandoned ever since he went missing years ago. His heirs have hired you to go there and make an accounting of any valuables you find. The last group that went in has vanished without a trace.

Just getting to the old house will prove a challenge. The local villagers are mistrusting of strangers. Murderous bandits prowl the roads at night. A daunting forest lies between you and your goal, and just what are those lights coming from the lake at night? All this, to say nothing of what you might encounter once you step through the door to Hidalgo's House of Horrors. Enter if you dare!

ABOUT DARKWATER MEDIA GROUP

Founded in 2020, Darkwater Media Group takes up the legacy of its predecessor, Darkwater Syndicate, "the publishing company with a defense contractor's name." We publish unique and exceptional literary experiences in fantasy, science fiction, horror, comedy, thrillers and specialty non-fiction. We are headquartered in Miami, Florida.

Facebook.com/DarkwaterMediaGroup

Twitter.com/Darkwater_Media

Patreon.com/DarkwaterMediaGroup

DarkwaterMediaGroup.com